There is unease in the chill winter of Cambridge in 1358. A thief is at work in the houses of the wealthy, colleges are vying with each other for funds and academic recognition, and the shrine of St Simon Stock is attracting both pilgrims and those who prey on them – charlatans peddling fake relics and dubious pardons.

When the body of one of the town's richest taverners is found in Michaelhouse it at first seems his death was accidental, but when Bartholomew views the corpse he knows it is murder. There is no shortage of suspects to investigate, from the tenants who have publicly argued with the victim to his merrily 'grieving' widow, but the trail has been blurred by someone who is using the discovery of the body to try and discredit the college.

Against a background of rising tension between the colleges and the increasing audacity of the thief, Bartholomew and Brother Michael hunt desperately for the proof that will unmask the identity of the killer and reveal the motivation of someone determined to ruin both Michaelhouse and all those connected to it . . .

Also by Susanna Gregory

The Matthew Bartholomew Series

The Thomas Chaloner Series

THE KILLER
OF PILGRIMS

The Sixteenth Chronicle of
Matthew Bartholomew

Susanna Gregory

SPHERE

First published in Great Britain in 2010 by Sphere

A CIP catalogue record for this book
is available from the British Library.

ISBN 978-1-84744-298-7

Papers used by Sphere are natural, renewable and recyclable
products sourced from well-managed forests and certified
in accordance with the rules of the Forest Stewardship Council.

Mixed Sources
Product group from well-managed
forests and other controlled sources
www.fsc.org Cert no. SGS-COC-004081
© 1996 Forest Stewardship Council

Typeset in New Baskerville by Palimpsest Book Production Limited,
Grangemouth, Stirlingshire
Printed and bound in Great Britain by Clays Ltd, St Ives plc

Sphere
An imprint of
Little, Brown Book Group
100 Victoria Embankment
London EC4Y 0DY

An Hachette UK Company
www.hachette.co.uk

www.littlebrown.co.uk

For Geoff Parks

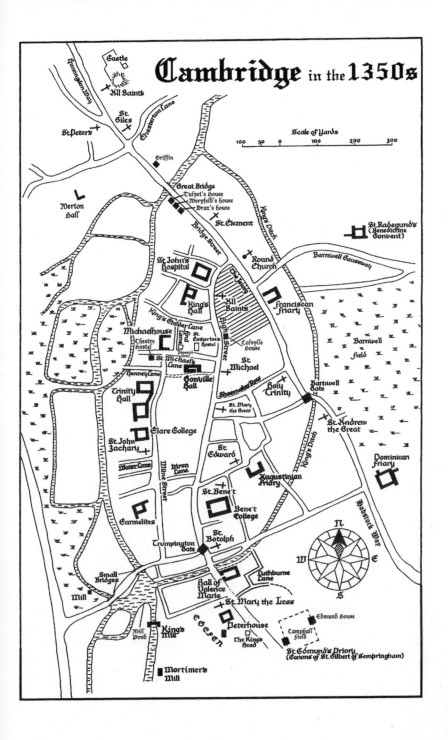

PROLOGUE

Early Spring 1350, Canterbury

At last, the Great Pestilence had relinquished its deadly grip. There had not been a new case in three months, and people were allowing themselves to hope that it had gone for good. It had left behind a terrible mark, though. Whole villages lay empty, houses were abandoned and derelict, weeds choked the fields, and every churchyard was full to overflowing with the dead.

The previous December, the Archbishop of Canterbury had written to the Bishop of London, suggesting it was time to thank God for delivering His people from the dreadful scourge. The devout had hastened to comply – it would not do to be ungracious, and provoke a second wave of the dreadful disease. Some folk, feeling prayers were not enough, had opted to go on pilgrimages, too, to make sure the Almighty truly appreciated the full extent of their gratitude.

Unfortunately, undertaking such journeys was no easy matter. The devastating sickness meant roads and bridges had been allowed to fall into disrepair, and nature had taken its toll, too – even the most important routes were now blocked by fallen trees, encroached upon by brambles, or washed away by rain and floods. In places, they had disappeared completely, leaving the traveller to wander hopelessly until some helpful local pointed him in the right direction.

Of course, not everyone on the King's highways was friendly. Bands of brigands roamed, safe in the knowledge that the forces of law and order had been seriously depleted by death. Because of this, sensible pilgrims travelled in groups, seeking safety in numbers.

The party that paused at the top of a hill to gaze at Canterbury in the distance had been lucky. The weather had been kind, the tracks easy to follow, and would-be robbers repelled without too much trouble. They were a disparate crowd, comprising clerics, soldiers, merchants and paupers, and they had stayed together only because it would have been dangerous to do otherwise. The sick man had scant respect for any of them, and longed to reach St Thomas Becket's shrine, so he could dispense with their tiresome company. He waited impatiently for them to finish their gawping and their self-serving prayers, eager to be on his way.

Canterbury itself was hectic, noisy and filthy. The sick man supposed its streets were cobbled, but they were so deeply carpeted in manure, rubbish and discarded scraps of food that it was impossible to tell. The stench was over-whelming, and made his eyes water so much that he could barely see the cathedral's soaring towers and delicate pinnacles ahead.

Once he had battled his way through the array of beggars who clustered around the door, the sick man knelt and gave thanks for his safe arrival. Then he rose and walked slowly through the massive nave. The shrine was at the far end, a cluster of columns, filigreed arches and precious stones. It, too, was encircled by a heaving mass of humanity, all clamouring pleas and demands. More candles than he had ever seen in one place were burning – offerings from grateful penitents – and their collective glow was so bright that it dazzled the eyes.

The cathedral's priests were moving through the throng, accepting gifts of money, jewellery, food and whatever else had been brought for the saint's delectation. No wonder the place was so wealthy, the sick man thought wryly, watching his travelling companions pay their tributes.

The hubbub around the tomb was far too distracting for meaningful prayer, so he wandered through the cathedral's echoing aisles, thinking to wait for a quieter moment before asking for a cure. Little stalls had been set up there, selling food, books, candles, clothing and anything else that travellers might need. The last booth was peddling pilgrim 'badges', its wares laid out in neat lines on a smart black cloth. There were crude pewter images of St Thomas that could be pinned on hats or cloaks, to tell all who saw them that their wearers had visited the shrine, and there were expensive ampoules of 'Becket water'.

'These little phials each contain a drop of the saint's blood,' declared the pardoner who owned the display. 'That means they are sacred. Relics in their own right.'

Impressed, the sick man inspected them more closely. Many were works of art, the tiny bottles enmeshed in delicate strands of gold and silver. The liquid inside was faintly pink – blood mixed with holy water.

'What are these?' he asked, pointing to a row of scallop shells.

'Tokens from the shrine of St James at Santiago de Compostela,' replied the pardoner, a handsome man with very white teeth. He grinned, sensing a sale. 'And here is a cross from Jerusalem, and a leaden image of the Virgin from Rocamadour in France.'

'But if I wore those, everyone who saw them would assume I had been to these places,' said the sick man, bemused. 'And I have not. Not yet, at least.'

The pardoner lowered his voice conspiratorially. 'These

are sacred things, so that even touching them will confer blessings on you. And if you do not need such a boon yourself, then you can give them to a loved one who does. Or you can sell them, of course.'

'Sell them?' The sick man was rather shocked.

The pardoner nodded earnestly. 'They fetch high prices, especially in this day and age, when no one knows for certain whether the plague is really gone. People buy my tokens for protection.'

'I see,' said the sick man, nodding. Then he frowned. 'Why do you have so many? Surely, their owners cannot have sold them to you? If folk have been to Jerusalem, Santiago or Rocamadour, they will want to keep these blessings for themselves.'

A distinctly furtive expression crossed the pardoner's face. 'Sometimes they need money to get home again, which I can provide. And sometimes the tokens just drop off their clothes when they hurl themselves in front of St Thomas's tomb. I usually look around at night, when the cathedral is quiet, and I am often lucky.'

The sick man stepped back when his travelling companions descended on the stall, clucking and cooing over the merchandise. Several made purchases, and he was staggered by the amount of money that exchanged hands. The pardoner was right: his *was* a lucrative business. And if the badges really were holy, then perhaps they would work miracles, too. For the first time since the onset of his disease, the sick man felt the stirrings of hope.

Surreptitiously, he looked at the scallop shell he had palmed while the pardoner had been talking. He did not feel as though he was about to be struck down for stealing it. Indeed, he had the sense that it was better off with him than with a villain who would hawk it for silver. Could it cure him? It had not eased his symptoms as far as he could

4

tell, but perhaps it would take more than one badge to combat the disease that was eating him from the inside out. He needed more – as many as he could get. Smiling to himself, he eased into the shadows and began to make his plans.

January 1358, Cambridge
There was a fringe of ice along the edge of the River Cam, and its brown, swirling waters, swollen with recent rain, looked cold and dangerous in the grey light of pre-dawn. Frost speckled the rushes in the shallows, and John Jolye wondered whether it would snow again. He hoped so. The soft white blanket that had enveloped the town the previous week had been tremendous fun, and he and his friends from the College of Trinity Hall had spent a wonderful afternoon careening down Castle Hill on planks of wood.

'Have you finished yet?' he called softly, stamping his feet in an attempt to warm them. Acting as lookout was not the most exciting of tasks, and he wished he had been allocated a more active role in the prank. It had been his idea, after all. 'I am freezing.'

'Almost.' The reply was full of suppressed laughter. 'And if this does not confound the dunces from the hostels, then I do not know what will. They will never work out how we did it!'

Jolye was not so sure about that – hostel scholars were not stupid. But he did not want to spoil his friends' sport, so he held his tongue. Besides, it had been more than a week since members of Essex Hostel had sneaked into Trinity Hall when everyone was asleep and filled it with scores of roosting chickens, and it was becoming urgent that the challenge was answered. Honour was at stake, after all – it would not do for a poverty-stricken, lowly hostel to get the better of a fine, wealthy College.

5

'Someone will come along soon!' he hissed, becoming impatient. What was taking them so long? 'It is already getting light, and this is a public footpath.'

'It is far too early for anyone else to be up,' came the scornful response. 'There! It is done! Chestre Hostel's boats are now standing stern to bow on top of each other, rising in a column that is almost the height of three men. When they try to dismantle it, the pegs we used to lock the boats together will drop unseen into the water, and they will assume we did it by balance alone.'

'They will marvel at our ability to confound the rules of nature!' crowed another. 'Well done, Jolye! This plan was a stroke of genius.'

Jolye felt a surge of pride. At fifteen, he was one of Trinity Hall's youngest students, and his cronies did not often praise him. He was about to respond with a suitably nonchalant remark when he heard voices from farther along the path. His classmates heard them, too, and began trotting towards the lane that would take them home.

Jolye started to follow, but he had not been involved in the warm work of lugging heavy boats around, and his feet were like lumps of ice. He tried to break into a run when the footsteps drew closer, but could only manage a totter. Suddenly, there was a hand in the middle of his back, and he was shoved roughly forward. He stumbled, and a second push sent him face-first into the river.

The shock of the frigid water took his breath away, and for a moment all he could do was lie there. Then his body reacted, and he found himself turning and flailing back towards the bank. It was not easy, because the current was strong, and threatened to sweep him away.

'That was a stupid thing to do!' he gasped angrily to the three dark figures that stood by the boats. His teeth chattered almost uncontrollably. 'Help me out.'

He held out his hand, expecting to be hauled to safety, but none of them moved. He blinked water from his eyes, trying see their faces. Were they hostel lads? But the hostel–College competition was only a bit of fun, and certainly not serious enough to warrant shoving rivals in icy rivers. Or were they townsmen, who hated the University and would love to see a scholar get a soaking? Unfortunately, the light was not good enough for him to tell, and they were just silent silhouettes.

'Please!' he croaked. The water was so cold it hurt. 'You have made your point. Now help me.'

He staggered forward, and had almost reached dry land when an oar touched his shoulder, and he found himself prodded backwards. He floundered, choking as his head went under. The current tugged him downstream. What were they thinking? Did they *want* him to drown? He managed to grab a rotten pier as he was washed past, and struggled towards the bank again.

'No!' he screamed, as the paddle pushed him back a second time. The river caught him, carrying him some distance before swirling him into a slack pool near the back of Michaelhouse. Again, he tried to escape the water's icy clutch, but the silhouettes were waiting and so was the oar.

'I am sorry,' he whispered pitifully. He glanced at the opposite bank, knowing he could escape his tormentors if he managed to reach it, but he had never learned to swim, and it might as well be a hundred miles away. 'Whatever I have done to offend you, I am sorry. Now please—'

The next poke propelled him into the middle of the river, where the current was strongest. Water filled his mouth and nose. He tried to call for help as he was swept under the Great Bridge, but no one heard. His head dipped under the surface and did not rise again.

CHAPTER 1

Early February 1358, Cambridge

When the yellow-headed thief reached the Griffin, a large tavern located just beyond the Great Bridge, Matthew Bartholomew knew he was going to escape. Sure enough, the fellow tore into the stables, and emerged moments later on a prancing stallion.

Bartholomew put on a last, desperate spurt of speed and made a grab for the reins, but the man kicked him away. Bartholomew fell backwards, landing heavily among the frost-hardened ruts that scarred the road. A cart bore down on him, its driver yelling for him to move, and he only just managed to roll away from its lumbering wheels. Heart pounding, he scrambled to his feet, and watched his quarry disappear along the track that led to the nearby village of Chesterton.

Bartholomew was a physician, who taught medicine at the College of Michaelhouse. Thanks to his unorthodox ideas, he was not one of the University's most respected scholars, but even so, he knew he should not have been haring after thieves at an hour when he should have been in church. It was hardly dignified.

He had been summoned before dawn by one of his patients, a fierce old lady named Emma de Colvyll. As she had been describing her symptoms to him, they had heard noises coming from her parlour – a burglar was in her house, and instinct had led Bartholomew to obey her screeched command to give chase. As he rested his hands on his knees, struggling to catch his breath, he recoiled at the notion of telling her he had failed. Despite her advanced years, she was a force to be reckoned with, and even the Sheriff – one of the bravest men in the shire – freely admitted that she terrified him.

He waited until his breathing returned to normal, then began to retrace his steps. There was always a market on Mondays, and despite the early hour, the streets were already crowded with carts bearing fish, grain, pottery, candles, wool, baskets and vegetables. There were also animals, herded in hissing, honking, lowing and bleating packs towards Butchery Row, and he ducked smartly behind a water-butt when a feisty bull decided it had no intention of being taken anywhere and made a determined bid for escape.

When he arrived at Emma's High Street mansion, he paused for a moment to admire it. It was unquestionably one of the finest buildings in Cambridge, boasting three spacious chambers on the ground floor, and a number of smaller ones above that provided sleeping quarters for her family and sizeable retinue. The window shutters were new and strong – a wise precaution, given that disagreements between town and University were frequent and often turned nasty – and there was a very sturdy front door.

Of course, Bartholomew thought acidly, Emma had other reasons for being conscious of her security. She had grown rich on the back of the plague, a ruthless opportunist who had made her fortune by buying up properties left vacant after the deaths of their owners. She had paid the grieving heirs a pittance, and was now reaping the benefits of a sellers' market.

Her ever-expanding empire had recently required her to move into the town centre so that she could better

9

monitor her myriad affairs. This had been greeted with mixed emotions by Cambridge's residents. On the one hand, she was generous to worthy causes, but on the other, most people were rather frightened of her and did not like her being in their midst.

Bartholomew was about to knock on her door when a movement farther down the street caught his eye. It was the scholars of Michaelhouse, leaving church after their morning devotions. The College's Master, Ralph de Langelee, headed the procession, and behind him were his six Fellows – they totalled seven with Bartholomew – and sixty or so students, commoners and servants.

Langelee nodded approvingly when he saw what Bartholomew was doing. Emma had offered to fund the repair of Michaelhouse's notoriously leaky roofs, although her bounty had not come without a price: in return, she wanted masses for her late husband's soul, and free medical treatment for herself. Langelee was delighted with the arrangement, but Bartholomew was not: Emma was a demanding client, and tending her meant less time for his teaching and other patients.

One of the Fellows detached himself from the line, and walked towards the physician. Brother Michael, a portly Benedictine, was a theologian and Bartholomew's closest friend. He was also the University's Senior Proctor, which meant he was in charge of maintaining law and order among Cambridge's several hundred scholars. Over the years, he had contrived to expand and enhance his authority to the point where he now ran the entire University, and its Chancellor was little more than a figure-head – someone to take the blame in times of trouble.

'Has Emma demanded yet *another* consultation?' he asked, pulling Bartholomew away from the door so they could talk. 'You spend half your life with her these days.'

10

'She summoned me before dawn,' replied Bartholomew tiredly. 'But we were interrupted by a burglar. When he ran away, she ordered me to give chase.'

'Lord!' murmured Michael, round eyed. 'It is a rash fellow who dares set thieving feet in *her* domain – she will have him hanged for certain. Did you catch him?'

'No.' Michael's words made Bartholomew glad he had not. 'And I am about to tell her so.'

Michael frowned. 'Then perhaps I should accompany you, lest she is seized by the urge to run you through. The presence of the Senior Proctor *may* serve to curtail her more murderous instincts.'

Bartholomew was not entirely sure he was joking. 'Thank you. Personally, I would rather have leaking roofs than be obliged to deal with her. It may sound feeble, but I find her rather sinister.'

'So do I. Unfortunately, Langelee drew up the contract when I was away in Clare, and by the time I returned, all was signed and settled. I was disgusted – not with him, but with the rest of you Fellows for letting him go ahead with it.'

'We did not *let* him go ahead, Brother,' objected Bartholomew. 'He just went. Ever since last autumn, when one of his scholars transpired to be corrupt, he has insisted on making all the important decisions alone. We argued against accepting Emma's charity, but he overrode us.'

'He would not have overridden me,' declared Michael, a hard, determined glint glowing in his baggy green eyes.

'No,' agreed Bartholomew. 'But we should not judge him too harshly. We lost a lot of money on reckless financial ventures last year, and this hard winter means food prices are unusually high. He is only trying to keep us solvent.'

'Then he should have found another way – I dislike the

11

fact that you are at Emma's beck and call all hours of the day and night. It is not right.' Michael grimaced as he glanced at their benefactress's handsome house. 'I suppose we had better go and break the news that you were less than successful with her thief. But I cannot face her on an empty stomach. We shall eat first.'

'I cannot return to Michaelhouse for breakfast,' said Bartholomew in alarm, not liking to think what Emma would say if he did. Meals at College could be lengthy, and she would be waiting.

'No,' agreed Michael. 'So we shall visit the Brazen George instead. That will not take long, and I do not see why *everything* we do should revolve around that wretched woman's convenience.'

They began to walk the short distance to Michael's favourite tavern. Trading had started in the Market Square and labourers were at their daily grind, so the cacophony of commerce and industry was well under way – yells, clangs and the rumble of iron-shod wheels on cobbles. The High Street thronged with people. There were scholars in the uniforms of their Colleges or hostels, merchants in fur-lined cloaks, apprentices in leather aprons or grimy tunics, and even a quartet of pilgrims heading for the Carmelite Priory. The pilgrims were identifiable by the wooden staffs they carried, and by the badges pinned on their clothes that told people which holy places they had visited

'The Carmelites are doing well these days,' remarked Michael, watching the little party pass. 'St Simon Stock's shrine attracts a lot of visitors, and is an important source of revenue for them.'

'Is it?' asked Bartholomew, not very interested. He grinned suddenly when mention of the Carmelites reminded him of another of the religious Orders. 'Have you identified the pranksters who put the ox and cart on the Gilbertines' chapel roof yet?'

'No,' replied the monk tightly. 'I have not.'

'It was a skilful trick,' Bartholomew went on, full of admiration for the perpetrators' ingenuity. 'I cannot imagine how they lifted a bull, a cart and thirty sacks of sand on to a roof of that height.'

'It was stupid,' countered Michael, whose duty it was to catch the culprits and fine them. 'Could they not have applied their wits to something less disruptive? It took me two days to assemble the winches needed to lower them all down again.'

'Do not be such a misery!' said Bartholomew, laughing. 'Besides, students playing tricks is better than students fighting. Do you have any suspects?'

'Yes,' said Michael stiffly. 'And I shall list them all for you once we are out of this biting cold.'

Bartholomew followed him inside the Brazen George. Taverns were off-limits to scholars, on the grounds that they sold strong drink and contained townsmen, a combination likely to lead to trouble. But Michael had decided that such rules did not apply to him, and, as Senior Proctor, he was in a position to do as he pleased. Given that he fined others for enjoying what taverns had to offer, it made him something of a hypocrite, but he did not care enough to change his ways.

The Brazen George was a pleasant place, and Michael was so well known to its owner that there was a room at the back reserved for his exclusive use. The chamber had real glass in its windows and overlooked a pretty courtyard. A fire blazed merrily and welcomingly in the hearth.

'I am concerned about this thief,' said Michael, lowering his substantial bulk on to a stool and stretching his booted feet towards the flames. 'If he is reckless enough to chance

13

his hand against Emma, then no one is safe. He may try his luck on the University, and invade one of the wealthy Colleges.'

'He will not choose Michaelhouse then,' said Bartholomew, standing as close to the fire as it was possible to get without setting himself alight. Even his high-speed chase had failed to dispel the chill that morning – he had woken shivering and with icy feet, and had remained frozen ever since. Because the College was going through one of its lean phases, fires in the Fellows' rooms were an unthinkable luxury – unless they could pay for one themselves, which he could not.

'No,' agreed Michael gloomily. 'We have nothing to interest a thief, more is the pity.'

'Who are your suspects for the ox and cart trick?' asked Bartholomew, to change the subject. Michaelhouse's ongoing destitution was a depressing topic for both of them.

'The Dominicans are partial to practical jokes,' Michael began. 'While Principal Kendale of Chestre Hostel is famous for his understanding of complex mechanics. They all deny it of course, presumably so they can add outwitting the Senior Proctor to their list of achievements.'

'Kendale?' asked Bartholomew in surprise. 'I doubt *he* took part in a jape. He seems too . . .'

'Surly?' suggested Michael when his friend hesitated, looking for the right word. 'Malicious?'

'Humourless,' finished Bartholomew. 'I doubt he has a sense of fun.'

When the taverner appeared, Michael ordered his 'usual' – a substantial repast that involved a lot more than he would have been given at Michaelhouse.

'Kendale *does* have a sense of fun,' he said, when they were alone again. 'Unfortunately, it is one that finds amusement in the misfortune of others. When that King's Hall student was injured in the trick involving the bull last week, he and his students laughed so hard that I was obliged to spend the rest of the day making sure they were not lynched for their heartlessness.'

'I cannot imagine what started this current wave of antipathy between Colleges and hostels,' said Bartholomew. 'I know there has always been some jealousy and resentment, but it was never this strong.'

Cambridge's eight Colleges had endowments, which meant they tended to be larger and richer than the hostels, and occupied nicer buildings – although Michaelhouse was currently an exception to the rule. They were also more permanent; hostels came and went with bewildering rapidity, and Bartholomew was never sure how many were in existence at any one time. Some Colleges were arrogant and condescending to their less fortunate colleagues, which inevitably resulted in spats, but it was unusual for the ill feeling to simmer in quite so many foundations simultaneously.

'It is Kendale's doing,' said Michael bitterly. 'He is busily fanning the flames of discord as hard as he can, for no reason other than that it amuses him to see two factions quarrel.'

'The rivalry is mostly innocent, though,' said Bartholomew, watching the landlord bring a platter of assorted meat, bread, custard and a bowl of apples. 'No one has been hurt – except the student with the bull, and that was largely his own fault.'

'It is mostly innocent *so far*,' corrected Michael. 'But I have a bad feeling it will escalate. It is a pity, because we have been strife-free for weeks now. Relations between town and University have warmed, and the last squabble I quelled was back in October. Damn Kendale for putting an end to the harmony! I really thought we might be heading towards a lasting peace this time.'

Bartholomew doubted that would ever happen. Even when the town was not at loggerheads with the *studium generale* it had not wanted within its walls in the first place, academics were a turbulent crowd. The different religious Orders were always fighting among themselves, and there were more feuds within and between foundations than he could count. The concord they had enjoyed since October was an aberration, and he had known it was only ever a matter of time before Cambridge reverted to its usual state of conflict.

'There is a rumour that Jolye was murdered by the hostels, too,' Michael went on.

Bartholomew regarded him askance. 'The boy who fell in the river after Trinity Hall did that clever balancing act with Chestre Hostel's boats? I thought you had decided that was an accident.'

'*You* told me it was an accident,' countered Michael. 'I was led by your expertise.'

In addition to teaching medicine and being a physician, Bartholomew was also the University's Corpse Examiner, which meant he was obliged to supply an official cause of death for any scholar who died, or for any townsman who breathed his last on University property.

'I said there was nothing to *suggest* foul play,' he corrected. 'No suspicious bruises or marks. However, I also said that a lack of evidence did not necessarily mean there was no crime.'

'Well, Jolye's fellow students agree with you. They have declared him a College martyr.'

Bartholomew was alarmed. 'Do you think they will retaliate with a murder of their own?'

'Not if I can help it,' said Michael grimly. 'My beadles

16

are ever vigilant, and so am I. But eat your apples, Matt. We cannot sit here all day.'

Bartholomew followed him outside, and back on to the High Street. He looked around uneasily, searching for signs of unrest. He was horrified to see some immediately: the lads of Essex Hostel were enjoying some unedifying jostling with Clare College's law students. They desisted sheepishly when they became aware that the Senior Proctor was glaring in their direction.

'You see?' asked Michael, continuing to scowl until both groups had slunk away. 'At first, the rivalry was light-hearted and harmless – amusing exercises in resourcefulness and intelligence. But then Kendale sent the crated bull to King's Hall – he denies it, of course, but I know it was him – and now the competition will turn vicious.'

'There he is,' said Bartholomew, nodding to where Chestre's Principal was yelling at one of the town's burgesses. Kendale was a large, handsome man, who wore his thick, fair hair in a braid that made him look like a Saxon pirate. By contrast, John Drax, the town's wealthiest taverner, was small, dark and unattractive. Both had lost their tempers, and their angry voices were accompanied by a lot of finger-wagging.

'Kendale leases his hostel building from Drax,' said Michael, watching intently. 'They are doubtless quarrelling about the rent. It is a pity they are not gentlemen enough to keep their disputes private, because if they carry on like that, others will join in and we shall have a brawl.'

As if he sensed Michael's disapproving gaze, Kendale grabbed Drax's arm and hustled him down an alley. Drax resisted, but Kendale was strong, and they were soon out of sight.

'Good!' said Michael, relieved. 'Why could they not have done that in the first place? But we had better visit Emma de Colvyll, or she will be wondering what has happened to you. Did you know she currently owns more than fifteen houses in the town, not to mention estates and manors all across the Fens?'

'I know she owns Edmund House, near the Gilbertine Priory,' said Bartholomew. 'The canons are eager to buy it from her, to use as a student hostel, but she refuses to sell it. I cannot imagine why she is so determined to keep it. It is not an especially attractive place.'

'She will have her reasons,' said Michael. 'And they will be concerned with profit, you can be sure of that.'

Bartholomew knocked at Emma's door, shivering as he did so; the wind was biting, and he wondered whether it might snow again. A servant answered almost immediately. The fellow was white-faced and trembling, and Bartholomew supposed he had been given a dressing-down for not being on hand when a thief had invaded his mistress's domain.

'She is waiting for you,' was all he said.

Bartholomew and Michael followed him along a short corridor and into the solar Emma used for business. It was a luxuriously appointed room, with tasteful hangings on the walls and a plethora of thick rugs. As she was wealthy enough to afford the best, her glass window panes had been fitted in such a way as to exclude draughts. A fire blazed in the hearth, and an appetising selection of nuts, sweetmeats and dried fruits sat on a table nearby. They were clearly for Emma's consumption only, and even Michael, a shameless devourer of other people's treats, was sufficiently wary of her to refrain from descending on them.

Emma's family was with her that morning. Her daughter Alice, who was sewing by the fire, was a heavy, sullen woman who rarely spoke unless it was to voice a complaint. Her husband was Thomas Heslarton, a powerfully built soldier with a bald head and missing teeth. He was a ruffian, but there was a certain charm in his quick grin and cheerful manners, and Bartholomew found him by far the most likeable member of the clan.

With such hefty parents, their daughter Odelina was not going to be a petite beauty, and nor was she. Her fashionably tight kirtle revealed an impressive cascade of bulges, and her hair was oddly two-tone, as if she had attempted to dye it and something had gone horribly wrong. She was twenty-four, and had so far rejected the suitors her family had recommended, because a fondness for romantic ballads was encouraging her to hold out for a brave and handsome knight.

But by far the most dominating presence in the room was Emma de Colvyll herself. Extreme age had wasted her arms and legs, although she still possessed a substantial girth, and she never wore any colour except black. There was something about her that always put Bartholomew in mind of a fat spider. She had beady eyes, which had a disconcerting tendency to glitter, and she had been known to reduce grown men to tears with a single word.

'You took your time,' she snapped, when Bartholomew and Michael were shown in. She thrust out a hand, all wrinkled skin and curved nails. 'Give me the box.'

'What box?' asked Bartholomew, bemused.

Emma glowered. 'The box that yellow-haired villain stole – the one I sent you to retrieve.'

'He did not have it,' said Bartholomew. 'It would have slowed him down, so he must have—'

'It was a small one,' Emma interrupted harshly. 'I imagine he tucked it inside his tunic, so it would not have slowed him down at all.'

Bartholomew raised his hands in a shrug. 'I did not see a box. Are you sure he took it?'

19

'Of course I am sure,' hissed Emma. She eyed him coldly. 'I assume from your replies that not only did you fail to recover my property, but you failed to lay hold of the scoundrel, too. How did that happen? You were only moments behind him.'

'He could run faster than me.' The reply was curt, but Bartholomew disliked being spoken to like an errant schoolboy. 'And he had a horse saddled ready in the Griffin.'

'It was unfair to send a scholar after a felon,' added Michael, also resenting her tone. 'We are forbidden to carry weapons, and Matt might have been injured had he—'

Emma sneered. 'Everyone knows he fought at Poitiers, where he was rewarded for his valour by the Prince of Wales. A mere felon could not best him, armed or otherwise.'

Bartholomew stifled a sigh. He had spent eighteen months overseas, when bad timing had put him in Poitiers when the English army had done battle with the French. He had taken up arms, but it had been his skill in treating the wounded afterwards that had merited the Prince's approbation. Unfortunately, his book-bearer Cynric, who had been with him, loved telling war stories, and the physician's modest role in the clash had been exaggerated beyond all truth.

Emma turned to Heslarton. 'That box is important to me, Thomas. Would you mind . . .'

Heslarton beamed amiably. 'Of course, Mother! I would have gone immediately, but you said Bartholomew could manage. *I* will get your property back, never fear.'

She smiled, and Bartholomew was reminded that, despite their disparate personalities, she was fond of her loutish son-in-law, a feeling that seemed wholly reciprocated. In fact, Emma and Heslarton seemed to admire each other a good deal more than either liked Alice.

'Do be careful, Thomas,' said Alice snidely, watching the exchange with barely concealed contempt. 'Cornered thieves can be very dangerous.'

Heslarton pulled an unpleasant face at her on his way out, and Odelina did the same, before going to talk to someone who was sitting by the window. Bartholomew started: he had not known anyone else was in the room, because his attention had been on Emma and her kin. The visitor was Celia Drax, the taverner's beautiful wife. She had been Bartholomew's patient until rumours began to circulate about his penchant for unorthodox medicine, when she had promptly defected to another physician. He wondered what she was doing in the Colvylls' company.

'I will pull my mother's hair out one day,' muttered Odelina sulkily. 'She has a cruel tongue.'

'Now, now,' admonished Celia mildly. 'Come and sit by me. We have our sewing to finish.'

'Thomas will catch the villain,' said Emma confidently to Bartholomew and Michael, watching the younger women huddle together over their needles. 'By this evening, I shall have that dishonest rogue locked in my cellar.'

'You must hand him to the Sheriff,' Michael reminded her. 'It is his business to deal with felons, not yours. And if, by some remote chance, the culprit is a scholar, then he comes under *my* jurisdiction. You cannot dispense justice as you see fit.'

Emma inclined her head, although it was clear she intended to dispense whatever she pleased. Bartholomew glanced around the room, taking in the gold ornaments and jewelled candlesticks, and wondered what was in the box that meant so much to her. He asked.

'Things my late husband gave me,' she replied shortly. 'Incidentally, did Michaelhouse say those masses for his soul that I paid for? When I die, I shall be furious if I arrive

21

in Heaven and find he is not there, just because your College has not kept its side of the bargain.'

Michael raised his eyebrows, amused. 'You seem very certain that you are upward bound.'

Emma regarded him askance. 'I am generous to priests and I support worthy causes – like paying to mend your College's roof. Of course I shall have a place in the Kingdom of God.'

'I think you will find it is not that straightforward,' said Michael dryly. 'You cannot buy your way into Heaven.'

'Actually, you can,' countered Emma with considerable conviction. 'And my great wealth will secure me the best spot available. Although, obviously, I will not be needing it for many years yet.'

Michael was spared from thinking of a reply because a sudden clatter of hoofs sounded in the yard outside. Emma told Alice to open the window, so she could see what was happening. It revealed Heslarton astride a magnificent black stallion. He had assembled a posse of about ten men, and his horses were far superior to any of Michaelhouse's nags. His retainers were tough, soldierly types, and Bartholomew felt a pang of sympathy for the thief.

'Do not stay out after dark, Father,' called Odelina worriedly. 'It is not safe.'

Heslarton grinned up at her, clearly relishing the opportunity for a spot of manly activity. 'Do not worry, lass. This villain will be no match for me.'

'I was thinking of other dangers,' said Odelina unhappily. 'Such as not being able to see where you are going, and the fact that it might snow.'

'You may break your neck,' added Alice sweetly. 'That would be a pity.'

'I will return by nightfall, Odelina,' promised Heslarton,

pointedly ignoring his wife, and then he and his men were gone in a frenzy of rattling hoofs and enthusiastic whoops.

'We should go, too,' whispered Michael to Bartholomew. 'The Feast of the Purification of the Blessed Virgin Mary is tomorrow, and there is a lot to do before then.'

'You mean teaching?' asked Bartholomew, thinking of the huge classes Michaelhouse's Fellows had been burdened with after the Master had enrolled twenty new students the previous year, in an effort to raise revenues.

'I mean making sure the cooks do not stint on food,' replied Michael tartly. 'I have not had a decent meal in weeks, and the Purification is one of my favourite festivals.'

Bartholomew suspected it was one of his favourites because a former Fellow had bequeathed funds to provide a post-church feast. It was not a large benefaction, however, and there were more mouths to feed than in previous years: the monk was likely to be disappointed. Still, Bartholomew thought, surveying the ample bulk with a professional eye, it would do him no harm. Michael had lost some of his lard over the previous weeks – a combination of being busy, and the College's dwindling resources – and was much healthier for it.

'Are you coming?' asked Michael, when the physician made no reply. 'We have delivered the bad news, so you are free to leave.'

'Where are *you* going, Doctor?' demanded Emma, when the scholars aimed for the door. 'Your chasing criminals on my behalf did nothing to relieve the agonies in my jaws, so we shall finish the consultation we began earlier. The monk can leave, though.'

'I cannot stay,' said Michael, determined to give the impression that he was leaving because he wanted to, not because he had been dismissed. 'I am far too busy. Good morning, madam.'

'I am going to the kitchen,' announced Odelina, when he had gone. 'The cook is making marchpanes, and you may share them, Celia. Mother may not – she needs to watch her figure.'

As Odelina was a good deal portlier than her dam, Bartholomew expected a tart rejoinder, but Alice merely rolled her eyes and followed her daughter out. It was not many moments before Bartholomew and Emma were alone.

'My torment is getting worse,' said the old lady, putting a gnarled hand to her face.

'Well, yes, it will,' said Bartholomew. 'As I have explained before, you have a rotten tooth, and the pain will persist until it is taken out.'

'But you have also informed me that the procedure will hurt.'

'It will hurt,' Bartholomew acknowledged. 'But not for very long, and then you will recover. However, if you delay, the poisons may seep into your blood. They could make you extremely ill.'

Emma shook her head firmly. 'I do not approve of this "cure" of yours. Devise another.'

Bartholomew stifled a sigh. 'There *is* no other cure, but if you do not believe me, then hire another *medicus*. Gyseburne and Meryfeld arrived in the town a few weeks ago, and they are skilled practitioners. Or there is Rougham of Gonville Hall.'

Emma grimaced. 'Rougham is a pompous ass, while Gyseburne and Meryfeld are not members of the University. Besides, you come free, in return for my generosity in mending Michaelhouse's roof, and I do not see why I should squander money needlessly. So, you had better consult a few books and invent a different treatment, because I am not letting you near me with pliers.'

24

Bartholomew tried to make her see reason. 'But it is the only—'

'Why can you not calculate my horoscope, and use it to provide me with potent herbs? I know you own such potions, because Celia Drax told me you gave her some when she was your patient.'

'Potent herbs will afford you temporary relief, but they will not solve the problem long-term.'

'I will take my chances,' said Emma brusquely. 'Besides, only barbers pull teeth, and you are a physician. It would be most improper for you to do it.'

It was something Bartholomew's colleagues were always telling him – that not only was it forbidden for scholar-physicians to practise surgery, it was demeaning, too. But Bartholomew believed patients should have access to any treatment that might help them, and as the town's only surgeon now confined himself to trimming hair, he had no choice but to perform the procedures himself.

'It is the only—' he began again.

Emma cut across him. 'Give me some of your sense-dulling potions, so I can rest for a few hours. The agony kept me awake all last night, and I am exhausted. We shall discuss the matter again later, when my wits are not befuddled by exhaustion.'

Bartholomew was tempted to refuse, in the hope that pain would bring her to her senses, but there was something in her beady-eyed glare that warned him against it. He was not usually intimidated by patients, especially ones who were less than half his size, but Emma was not like his other clients. With a resentful sigh, he did as he was told.

It was mid-morning by the time Bartholomew had finished with Emma, and he left her house with considerable relief. Cynric, his book-bearer, was waiting outside with a list of other people who needed to see him. The most urgent was Isnard the bargeman, who had cut his hand. The gash needed to be sutured, and Bartholomew wondered how his fellow physicians treated wounds, when they would not insert stitches themselves and there was no surgeon to do it for them.

As he sewed, half listening to Isnard's inconsequential chatter, he thought how fortunate he was that Master Langelee had never tried to meddle with the way he practised medicine. But would it last? He had recently learned that most of his patients were cheerfully convinced that he was a warlock, and that they believed he owed his medical successes to a pact made with the Devil. They did not care, as long as he made them better, but his colleagues objected to having a perceived sorcerer in their midst, and constantly pressed Langelee to do something about him.

He left Isnard, still pondering the matter. He heard a yell, and glanced across the river to the water meadows beyond, where a group of townsmen were playing camp-ball. Camp-ball was a rough sport, and the rivalry between teams was intense. The men stopped playing when they saw him looking, and stared back in a way that was distinctly unfriendly. He could only suppose they were practising some new manoeuvre and did not want him to report it to the opposition.

Ignoring their scowls, he entered the row of hovels opposite, to tend two old women, neither of whom he could help. Their bodies were weakened by cold and hunger, and they did not have the strength to fight the lung-rot that was consuming them. When he had finished, sorry his skills were unequal to saving their lives, he headed towards the Carmelite convent on Milne Street, where a case of chilblains awaited his attention. He had not gone far before he met someone he knew.

Griffin Welfry was a jovially friendly Dominican in his thirties, with a shock of tawny hair and a tonsure barely visible beneath it. He wore a leather glove on his left hand, and had once confided to Bartholomew that it was to conceal the disfiguring result of a childhood palsy. He was flexing the afflicted fingers as he walked along the towpath.

'No, it is not the cold affecting it,' he said in answer to Bartholomew's polite enquiry. 'It is agitation. The Prior-General of my Order has arranged for me to be appointed Seneschal – the University official who liaises with the exchequer in London.'

'Congratulations,' said Bartholomew warmly. He liked Welfry, and was pleased his considerable abilities were being recognised. 'You will make a fine Seneschal.'

'Do you think so?' asked Welfry doubtfully. 'My Prior-General told me only a few months ago that I was good for nothing except making people laugh. He intended it as an insult, but I was flattered. As far as I am concerned, humour is one of God's greatest gifts.'

Bartholomew did not need to be reminded of Welfry's love of mirth. All the Cambridge Dominicans liked practical jokes, but Welfry excelled at them, and since he had arrived a few months before, his brethren had rarely stopped smirking. Indeed, Bartholomew was fairly certain it had been Welfry who had hoisted the ox and cart on the Gilbertines' roof.

'I suppose I had better accept,' Welfry went on unenthusiastically. 'The Prior-General sent me to Cambridge to pen a great theological tract that will glorify our Order, but I do not seem able to start one. Perhaps these solemn duties will concentrate my mind.'

'Perhaps,' said Bartholomew, thinking the Prior-General was hankering after a lost cause. Welfry was incorrigibly mischievous, and the physician doubted he would ever use

27

his formidable intellect to its full potential. Indeed, he suspected it was only a matter of time before Welfry played some prank on the exchequer, simply because he was bored. The King's clerks were unlikely to appreciate it, and the University would suffer as a consequence.

'I have been told I must be solemn at all times,' said Welfry glumly. Then a grin stole across his face. 'But maybe I should regard it as a challenge – I am *sure* I can make the exchequer laugh. Incidentally, how is the King's Hall student who was gored by the bull? That was a nasty trick.'

'It was,' agreed Bartholomew. 'But he is recovering. I have been told it was the work of Chestre Hostel. What do you think?'

Welfry grimaced. 'There is insufficient evidence to say, although they did happen to be walking past when the crate was opened, which was suspicious. However, I cannot believe they intended harm. Jokes are never funny if someone is hurt when they are implemented.'

Bartholomew watched him walk away, wishing everyone shared Welfry's benign attitude.

The Carmelites, popularly known as the White Friars, had done well for themselves since their priory had been established in Cambridge the previous century. It had been founded by St Simon Stock, an early Prior-General, and from humble beginnings it had expanded until they owned a spacious site and a number of elegant buildings.

Bartholomew was admitted to their compound by a lay-brother, and escorted to the pretty cottage in which Prior Etone lived. Etone was a grim-faced man, said to spend more time with his account books than at his prayers, although Bartholomew had always found him pleasant enough. He was suffering from chilblains, a common complaint in winter, when footwear never dried and feet were rarely warm. While Bartholomew applied a poultice to the sore heels, Etone regaled him with a detailed description of the new shrine he intended to build.

'The number of pilgrims warrants the expenditure,' he explained. 'Four more arrived just this morning and they look wealthy. I am sure they will leave us a nice benefaction when they go.'

Bartholomew glanced up at him. 'Why do pilgrims come? What shrine do they visit?'

Etone regarded him askance. 'How can you ask such questions? I thought you were local!'

'I am, but—'

'It is because of what happened to St Simon Stock when he was here,' interrupted Etone indignantly. 'He had a vision: our Lady of Mount Carmel appeared to him, and presented him with the scapular all Carmelites now wear.'

A scapular was two pieces of cloth joined together and worn over the shoulders. It formed a distinctive part of the White Friars' uniform.

'I have heard the tale,' said Bartholomew defensively. 'But I thought it was a myth – that no one could prove Simon Stock even had a dream, let alone when he was in Cambridge.'

'It is most assuredly true!' cried Etone. 'And the increasing pilgrim trade proves it. Our Lady handed St Simon Stock his scapular here, in our very own priory, and I intend to exploit . . . I mean *develop* the place for the benefit of all mankind.'

'I see,' said Bartholomew. 'But just because pilgrims come does not mean it is a genuine—'

'It *is* genuine!' insisted Etone. He stood carefully, and slipped his feet into soft shoes with the backs cut away. 'Come with me, and I shall show you where it happened. You will feel its sanctity. And if you do not, it means you are Satan's spawn and God has not deigned to touch you.'

Bartholomew was not very susceptible to atmospheres, being a practical man of science, and did not want to be denounced as the Devil's offspring by an influential friar.

'Another time, Father,' he mumbled hastily. 'I still have several patients who need—'

'Even diligent physicians should never be too busy for God,' declared Etone piously. 'Come.'

Supposing he would have to prevaricate if not immediately overwhelmed by the shrine's holiness, Bartholomew followed him across the yard to a wooden hut. It was well made, and had been nicely painted, but it was still a hut.

'Is this it?' he asked uneasily, not sure he could feign suitably convincing reverence over something that looked as though it belonged at the bottom of a garden.

Without speaking, Etone pushed open the door. Inside was a tiny altar with a brass cross, two candlesticks and an ornate, jewel-studded chest, which he unlocked with a key that hung around his neck. Then he stood aside, so the physician could inspect its contents. Bartholomew did so, and saw a piece of cloth. It was old, dirty and of indeterminate colour. He studied it for a moment, then looked blankly at Etone, wondering what he was supposed to say.

'It is a piece of the scapular Our Lady presented to St Simon Stock,' averred Etone reverently, crossing himself. 'So, you see, this is not just a sacred place because of the vision that occurred here, but because we have this important relic.'

Bartholomew regarded him uncertainly, itching to ask how he had come by it: according to the legend, Simon Stock, as per the instructions given in his dream, was said to have worn the garment for the rest of his life and then had been buried in it. Etone did not look like a tomb robber.

'It is a disgrace!' came a sudden, furious shout from outside. 'We are pilgrims, and you think people would respect that.'

'It is a bad winter and the poor are desperate.' Michael's voice was soothing and calm. 'I doubt he knew what he was taking. He just saw the glint of metal, and assumed it was a brooch.'

'It was a badge from the Holy Land,' came the agitated voice. '*Not* a brooch.'

Bartholomew followed Etone outside, relieved to be spared the awkwardness of pretending that he had been touched by what he had been shown, when the reality was that he had felt nothing at all. Perhaps God did consider him a disciple of Satan, he thought uneasily, and his constant flying in the face of all that was orthodox had finally been too much. It was not a comfortable notion.

Michael was standing in the yard with the four pilgrims they had seen earlier – two men and two nuns. All looked angry.

'What is the matter?' demanded Etone, hobbling towards them. 'What has happened?'

'Brazen robbery,' declared one of the pilgrims, turning to face him. He was a thickset man with an unhealthy complexion that said he was probably ill. His hat and cloak bore more pilgrim insignia than Bartholomew had ever seen on a single person, and he imagined the fellow must have spent half his life visiting shrines, because besides the distinctive ampoules of Canterbury and St Peter's keys from Rome, at least two suggested he had been to Jerusalem, as well.

'Robbery?' repeated Etone uneasily. 'Not in my priory, Master Poynton.'

'Yes, here!' declared Poynton heatedly. 'One of my badges has been stolen. It was pinned to my saddlebag, and now it has gone.'

'I saw it happen,' added one of the nuns. 'I saw the *signaculum* snatched with my own eyes.'

'So did I,' added the second nun. 'The villain aimed straight for it, and ripped it away. He did not even look at our purses.'

'*Signacula* are extremely valuable,' snapped Poynton. 'Especially that one. It was gold – a cross from the Holy Land, no less.'

'What was it doing on your saddlebag, then?' asked Bartholomew, before he could stop himself. But it was a fair question: an item of such worth should have been treated with more care.

'Because there is no more room on my clothes,' snarled Poynton, rounding on him. 'And these items are meant to be seen, so everyone will know of the great journeys I have undertaken for the sake of my body and my soul. Who are you, anyway?'

While Bartholomew thought Poynton's body and soul must be in a very poor state indeed, if they required quite so many acts of penance, Etone introduced him. Then he indicated the pilgrims.

'Master Poynton is a merchant,' he said. 'Hugh Fen is a pardoner, while Agnes and Margaret Neel are nuns of my own Order. They were both married to the same man.'

'But not at the same time,' added one of the nuns hastily. They were both short, middle-aged and plump, and in their identical habits, were difficult to tell apart.

'A pardoner,' said Michael, regarding Fen with distaste. He detested pardoners – men who peddled indulgences and relics to the desperate. Fen, however, looked a cut above his fellows. He was a tall, handsome man with a neat

32

black beard, and if *he* had undertaken lots of pilgrimages, he did not advertise the fact by covering himself with tokens. He bowed politely to Michael, revealing fine white teeth in a smile, although he must have detected the disapproval in the monk's voice.

'He makes a fine living from it,' said Poynton. 'There is much money to be made from pilgrims.'

'I hope so,' muttered Etone. He smiled ingratiatingly at the merchant. 'Brother Michael will retrieve your cross, Master Poynton, never fear. He is our Senior Proctor, and very good at investigating crimes that occur on University property.'

'I am good,' agreed Michael immodestly. 'But I do not see how I shall solve this one. All you can tell me is that the thief wore a green tunic, but I shall need more than that if I am to succeed.'

'He dashed in from the street,' said Poynton, bristling with anger at the memory. 'It happened so fast that I only had a glimpse of him. Damned villain!'

'He had bright yellow hair,' said Fen helpfully. 'Lots of it.'

'Yellow hair?' asked Bartholomew, looking sharply at him. 'Are you sure?'

'It cannot be the same man you chased, Matt,' said Michael in a low voice. '*He* fled the town, and Heslarton is now hot on his heels. He is unlikely to have returned within a couple of hours and committed a second offence.'

'Why not?' Bartholomew whispered back. 'If Heslarton is scouring the Chesterton road, then Cambridge is as safe a place as any to hide. Here, there are crowds to disappear into.'

'I accept that,' said Michael. 'But the operative word here is *hide*. If he did return, he will be lying low, not drawing attention to himself by stealing from pilgrims.'

Bartholomew shrugged. 'If you say so. But it is an odd coincidence.'

When Prior Etone changed the subject from theft to shrines, Bartholomew took his leave, unwilling to be asked in front of quite so many devout penitents whether he had been struck by the sanctity of Simon Stock's scapular. He muttered something about patients, and continued with his rounds. He visited a student with stomach pains, then aimed for Michaelhouse, eager to spend at least some time teaching before the day ended – it was already mid-afternoon.

He was walking down St Michael's Lane, pondering a lecture he was to give on the theories of Maimonides the following day, when he became aware that his path was blocked by a wall of men. Academic thoughts flew from his mind when he recognised Principal Kendale and the scholars of Chestre Hostel.

Chestre was located not far from Michaelhouse, so the two foundations' paths often crossed. Michaelhouse's Fellows were mostly sensible, sober men, who took care to ensure the encounters were amiable, but the same could not be said for their students. Ever since Kendale's trick had seen a College man gored by a bull, they had taken to bawling insults at Chestre. There had been no physical fighting so far, but Bartholomew sensed it would not be long in coming.

That day, Chestre's scholars had ranged themselves across the alley in such a way that no one could pass. Kendale was in the middle, distinctive with his braided hair and sturdy bulk. He was a philosopher, with exciting ideas about mathematics and natural philosophy, and Bartholomew had been impressed when he had heard him in the debating chamber.

'You are in our way, Michaelhouse,' Kendale said coldly. 'You had better retrace your steps.'

Bartholomew was half tempted to do as he suggested, just to avoid a confrontation, but was aware that if the same tactic was then tried on Michaelhouse's students, there would be a fight for certain. With a stifled sigh of resignation – he did not want to bandy words with Chestre when he could be teaching – he adopted his most reasonable tone of voice.

'This is no way to behave,' he said quietly. 'Why not live peacefully, and take advantage of—'

'Peacefully?' sneered Chestre's Bible Scholar, a man named Neyll. He was a bulky, pugilistic Scot in his early twenties, with dark hair and curious black eyebrows that formed a thick, unbroken line across his forehead. There was something about him that reminded Bartholomew of an ape, and he could not imagine a fellow less suited to the task of daily scripture reading. 'You mean to lull us into a false sense of safety, so the Colleges can slit our throats while we sleep!'

'No one means you harm,' said Bartholomew, although he suspected that the bull incident might well have changed that. 'And it is—'

'*All* College scum mean us harm,' Neyll flashed back. 'But they will never best us.'

Bartholomew declined to be drawn. He smiled at Kendale and tried a different tack. 'I enjoyed your lecture the other day. Your contention that non-uniformly accelerated motion is—'

'I was wasting my breath,' said Kendale disdainfully. 'No one at the Colleges has the wits to understand my analyses. I might just have well have been speaking Greek.'

'You could have done,' retorted Bartholomew coolly. There was only so far he would allow himself to be insulted. 'Many of us would still have followed your reasoning.'

35

'Liar!' snarled Neyll, raising his fists as he stalked forward. 'I am going to give you a—'

'Hold, Chestre!' came a loud, belligerent yell.

Bartholomew glanced around and saw a group of Michaelhouse students returning from a sermon in St Bene't's Church. They outnumbered Kendale's lads by at least two to one, and Neyll's aggressive advance immediately faltered. At their head was John Valence, Bartholomew's best pupil, a freckle-faced lad with floppy fair hair.

'We were just discussing Kendale's lecture on the mean speed theorem,' said Bartholomew quickly, before there was trouble. 'But we have finished now, and it is time to go home.'

Valence did not look convinced, but began to walk towards Michaelhouse anyway, beckoning his cronies to follow. Neyll was 'accidentally' jostled as they passed, and his dark eyebrows drew down in a savage V, but he was not so reckless as to voice an objection.

'You are a warlock, Bartholomew,' hissed Kendale, as the physician turned to leave, too. 'And a heretic – not the sort of man who should be teaching in any university. I will see you ousted.'

Bartholomew ignored him, but was relieved when he reached the sanctuary afforded by Michaelhouse's sturdy gates.

'At least we know where we are again now,' said Walter, the College's surly porter, after he had opened the gate and Bartholomew had remarked sadly that the recent peace seemed to be crumbling. 'I did not like everyone being nice to each other. It did not feel right.'

'You mean you prefer to be constantly on the brink of a riot?' asked Bartholomew archly.

36

Walter nodded, unabashed. 'Of course I do. It means I can suspect everyone of evil intent, which is much more satisfying than sickly cordiality. And the trouble is only within the University anyway – the town is quite happy to sit back and watch us squabble among ourselves this time.'

He picked up his pet peacock and hugged it. It crooned and nestled against him. Bartholomew had always been surprised by the relationship between porter and bird, because both were sour tempered and inclined to be solitary.

'Incidentally, the uncanny calm in the town is Emma de Colvyll's doing,' Walter went on when Bartholomew made no reply. 'She has driven the other criminals out of business, see.'

'She is not a criminal,' said Bartholomew. 'She is a businesswoman.'

'She *is* a criminal,' asserted Walter firmly. 'She may not go around burgling and robbing, but there are other ways to deprive a man of his wealth. She is deeply wicked, and I dislike the fact that my College accepted her charity.'

He scowled into the yard. Scaffolding swathed the building where Bartholomew lived, and he was alarmed when he saw most of the roof tiles had been removed since he had gone out. If it rained – and the sky was ominously dark – the rooms beneath would be drenched. He hoped the workmen knew what they were doing.

'It will not be for long,' he said, wincing when a carelessly placed strut slithered off the roof to land with an almighty crash that reverberated around the whole College. The peacock issued one of its piercing shrieks in reply. The mason imitated it, and his workmates guffawed uproariously. None of them could be seen, because they were all on the far side of the roof – the section that overlooked the gardens at the back. 'The repairs will soon be finished.'

'The repairs *will* soon be finished,' agreed Walter, hugging his bird more tightly. 'But the debt will last for ever, and it will not be long before Emma starts demanding payment. And I do not refer to money. She will want other things.' His voice dropped meaningfully. 'Like services.'

Bartholomew frowned, puzzled. 'Yes, she has asked for services. The priests among us have agreed to say masses for her husband's soul, while Master Langelee ordered me to tend her—'

'I do not mean prayers and medicine,' interrupted Walter impatiently. 'I mean other things. She will be asking for dubious favours soon. I tell you, it is not a good idea to do business with her, even if she is making us watertight. Which I seriously doubt.'

'What do you mean?' asked Bartholomew. 'The workmen seem to be doing well enough.'

'The mason – Yffi – is careless and shoddy. Take this morning, for example. He arrived at dawn, and has been labouring ever since. Look at how much he has done.'

Bartholomew looked at the roof, trying to understand Walter's point. 'His apprentices have removed all the old tiles, and he has laid two rows of new ones. He has achieved a lot.'

'Exactly!' pounced Walter. 'A good mason would have taken twice as long. The roof will leak again as soon as he leaves, and all this chaos and upheaval will have been for nothing. *And* we shall have Emma de Colvyll after us for dark favours.'

Bartholomew left, hoping Walter was wrong, then stood for a moment, looking around him. His College comprised a handsome stone-built hall, with two accommodation wings set at right angles to it. He lived in the northern wing, the older and shabbier of the pair, where he occupied two chambers – a large one he shared with his students, and a cupboard-like space that was used for storing the accoutrements necessary for his work as a physician.

There was just enough space in the little room for a mattress, and he had taken to sleeping there following an incident involving missing potions the previous term: he felt people were less likely to help themselves to what were some very dangerous substances if he was present. The smell had been uncomfortable to begin with, but he had quickly grown used to it, and his students were pleased to have the additional space in the main chamber.

He started to walk again, but had not gone far before he was intercepted by Robert de Blaston, the carpenter. Blaston, his wife Yolande and their fourteen children were Bartholomew's patients, and he had known them for years. Blaston was a conscientious, talented craftsman, who would never be rich because he was too honest. Bartholomew was fond of him, and considered him a rare ray of integrity in a town that was mostly out for its own ends.

'I do not know about that roof,' Blaston said, shaking his head in disapproval. 'Yffi has not used enough battens, and I doubt the ones he *has* put up are thick enough to support a structure of that weight – tiles are heavy.'

Bartholomew was no builder, but could see that Blaston had a point – the wooden frame Yffi had constructed *did* appear too flimsy. 'I will speak to the Master about it.'

He aimed for the hall straight away. Blaston's concerns had made him uneasy: Emma's thriftiness, combined with the natural skimming that went along with any building project, meant corners were going to be cut. And that might prove dangerous to Michaelhouse's residents.

He passed through the door bearing the founder's coat of arms, now woefully caked in dust from the renovations, then trotted up the spiral staircase to the hall, where the day's teaching was under way. As usual, benches had been placed to face individual masters, who then held forth to classes that ranged in size from two students to ten, depending on the subject.

Normally, there was no problem with everyone being in the same room – the Fellows were used to lecturing at the same time as their colleagues, and the students were used to tuning out other lessons to attend to their own – but that day they were obliged to contend with the workmen, too. This included not only rattling pulleys, assorted crashes and hammering, but the manly banter that went along with them. Closing the window shutters would have eliminated some of the racket, but then lamps would have been needed, and fuel was far too costly to squander in such a way.

'Blaston and Walter are worried about the quality of Yffi's work,' Bartholomew murmured in Langelee's ear as he passed, *en route* to his own class. 'And so am I.'

The Master of Michaelhouse was a burly man with a barrel chest. He looked more like a wrestler than a philosopher, and was not a talented academic. He had been the Archbishop of York's henchman before deciding on an academic career, and remarks he had let slip about his duties indicated he had not been employed in any capacity the prelate would care to have made public.

'Me, too,' said Langelee worriedly. 'There do not seem to be enough battens, although Yffi told me I did not know what I was talking about when I said so. Damned impertinence! But I will tackle him again when teaching is finished.'

Bartholomew was about to leave him to his work when he noticed that one corner of the hall was empty. It was where Thelnetham, the College's Gilbertine theologian usually taught, but his students were sitting with Michael's pupils.

40

'Where is Thelnetham?' he asked. The Gilbertine was conscientious about teaching, and it was rare for him to miss a lesson.

'At his friary,' replied Langelee. 'There is a meeting to discuss the purchase of some house or other, and he wanted to be there, to voice an opinion. I envy him. I would not have minded an excuse to miss hollering my way through the afternoon, either.'

'Nor I,' agreed Suttone, a portly Carmelite, looking up from his grammar books. 'We shall all be after you for sore-throat remedies before the day is done, Matthew. I am already hoarse.'

It was not long before Bartholomew appreciated what they meant. The masons were enjoying a lewd discussion about the famously creative talents of Blaston's wife. Yolande worked as a prostitute to supplement the family income, and when Yffi began to describe some of her more innovative techniques, Bartholomew saw he was losing his class's attention – they were all staring in open-mouthed fascination towards the roof on which the builders were working.

'What does Galen say about blood that is excessively salty?' he asked loudly, indicating that Valence should answer the question.

But Valence was transfixed by Yffi's description of what Yolande could do with a handful of chestnuts and a warm cloth, and it was Rob Deynman, the dim-witted librarian, who answered. Deynman had been a medical student himself, until he had been 'promoted' in an effort to keep him from practising on an unwary public, and prided himself on what he could remember from the many years of lessons he had attended. Unfortunately, his memory was rarely equal to his enthusiasm.

'He said salty blood is white,' he replied, with one of

his bright and rather vacant grins. 'Because salt is white. And if blood is white, then it means it has turned into phlegm.'

'Lord!' muttered Bartholomew, wondering whether anything he had taught the lad had been retained in anything like its original context. 'Can anyone else tell me what—'

But he was interrupted by a furious screech from outside, which had students and masters alike rushing to the window to see what was going on. It was Agatha the laundress, the formidable matron who had inveigled herself into a position of some power among the servants. It was an unorthodox arrangement – women were not permitted inside Colleges – but neither the Master nor his Fellows were bold enough to tell her so. She was chasing a dog, which had a ham in its jaws. Cheers from the roof indicated the builders had also abandoned their work to enjoy the spectacle.

Determined to retrieve the meat, Agatha gradually corralled the animal into a corner, where it took refuge behind a large pile of tiles, all covered with an oiled sheet. Then she lunged. The dog yowled its outrage as she laid hold of its tail, although its jaws remained firmly fastened around its booty. It became entangled in the sheet in its efforts to escape. Workmen and students alike howled their laughter, although the Fellows were more restrained, knowing from personal experience what could happen if Agatha took umbrage.

'Go and help her, Bartholomew,' instructed Langelee, fighting to keep a straight face. 'Or we shall be here all day, and lessons will suffer.'

Bartholomew went to oblige, hurrying down the spiral staircase before Agatha or the dog could harm each other. When he emerged in the yard, she was hauling furiously on the sheet in an effort to locate her quarry, roughly enough that some of the tiles were falling off their stacks. Yffi was scrambling down the scaffolding, yelling angrily about the damage. Blaston and the watching apprentices were helpless with laughter.

'Stop, Agatha,' urged Bartholomew, running towards her. 'Let me help you.'

'I do not need help,' snarled Agatha, jerking the sheet so violently that several more tiles crashed to the ground. The dog's agitated yips added to the general cacophony. 'I just want to—'

With a tearing sound, the sheet came away, sending Agatha lurching backwards. The dog was catapulted free and made the most of the opportunity by racing towards the gate. But neither she nor Bartholomew noticed it. Their attention was taken by what her tugging had exposed – a man lying half buried by the tiles she had dislodged.

CHAPTER 2

'Is he dead?' demanded Langelee, hovering over Bartholomew as the physician struggled to haul the fallen tiles from the prostrate figure beneath. 'Who is it? Which of the builders?'

'It is none of us,' replied Yffi shakily. The mason was a crop-haired man with the kind of belly that indicated he was fond of ale; he was fond of camp-ball, too, which said a good deal about his belligerent character. He and his apprentices stood to one side of the pile, while Blaston was on the other. 'We are all present and correct.'

'Will someone help me?' asked Bartholomew, glancing first at the labourers, then his colleagues. The students and Agatha had been sent back inside, but the Master and his Fellows had remained.

'I am not going anywhere near a corpse,' declared Yffi vehemently. 'The miasma of death will hang about me afterwards and bring me bad luck.'

His apprentices crossed themselves, and so did Blaston. Rolling his eyes, Langelee stepped up, and began flinging away stones with a reckless abandon that made it dangerous for bystanders.

'Then who *is* under here?' he demanded, as he worked. 'It is no one from Michaelhouse, because students, Fellows and staff are all accounted for.'

'We shall be needing a bier, regardless,' said Bartholomew. 'Where is Cynric?'

'I am here,' came a quiet voice at his shoulder. He

44

jumped. His Welsh book-bearer was as soft-footed as a cat, and he had not heard him approach.

'This is your fault,' said Blaston, pointing an unsteady finger at Yffi. 'You heaped these slabs badly, and now a man lies dead.'

'There was nothing wrong with my stacking!' cried Yffi, alarmed. 'The tiles were perfectly safe until that woman got among them like a rampaging bull.'

'We should discuss this later, when we have the poor fellow out,' said Langelee, helping Bartholomew haul away the last of the heavy stones. 'Oh, Lord! That one landed square on his face. How will we identify him now?'

'I know him.'

Everyone turned to see Thelnetham standing there, freshly returned from the meeting in his priory. He was by far the best-dressed of the Fellows, even surpassing Michael, who was vain about his appearance. He was known in the University for enlivening his Gilbertine habit with a variety of costly accessories, and was flagrantly effeminate.

'Well?' demanded Langelee. 'Tell us his name.'

'It is John Drax,' replied Thelnetham quietly.

'Drax the taverner?' asked Langelee. 'How can you tell?'

All the Fellows – except Langelee, whose previous work for the Archbishop of York had inured him to grisly sights – looked away as Bartholomew began to examine the body. None were approving of or comfortable with his ability to determine causes of death, while Father William, the College's bigoted Franciscan – recently returned from exile in the Fens – had declared to the world at large the previous year that it was what made him a warlock.

'I recognise his clothes,' replied Thelnetham, pointedly turning his back on the physician. 'I have an interest in finery, as you know. Plus there is the fact that he is missing several fingers.'

45

'So he is!' exclaimed Blaston, risking a peep at the mangled remains. He looked white and sick, and Bartholomew hoped he would not faint. 'I heard he lost those working for Yffi.'

'That was not my fault, either,' declared Yffi, more alarmed than ever. 'But I compensated him handsomely even so, and he used the money to buy himself an inn that was so successful that he bought another. And then another. So, I actually did him a favour with the incident that . . .'

'He *was* rich,' agreed Langelee. 'He often gave our College benefactions. In fact, it was he who bought the beeswax candles we shall use in the Purification ceremonies tomorrow.'

'I recognise the medallion he is wearing, too,' added Thelnetham. 'He told me his wife had encouraged him to buy it. I asked, because I liked the look of it and was considering purchasing one for myself.'

'Celia!' exclaimed Langelee in dismay. 'God's blood! One of us will have to go and tell her.'

'Tell her what?' asked Michael. 'What was he doing behind Yffi's tiles in the first place?'

'He has never visited us before,' said Thelnetham. 'In the past, when he wanted to make donations, he always summoned one of us to his mansion on Bridge Street.'

'I did not see him come in,' said Walter, who had just arrived to join the onlookers. 'But I have been in the latrines – that pottage we had earlier did not agree with me.'

'You mean you left the gate unattended?' asked Clippesby. It was generally accepted that the kindly, mild-mannered Dominican was insane, mostly due to his habit of talking to animals and claiming that they answered him back. There were occasions, though, when Bartholomew thought Clippesby made more sense than the rest of the College combined.

'Only for a moment,' said Walter defensively. 'And it was an emergency.'

'So, Drax just walked in,' concluded Michael. 'I wonder why?'

'You had better ask Celia,' said Langelee. 'But be careful how you do it, Brother, because we do not want her to sue the College for his death. Yffi claims this was not his fault, but it was not ours, either, and we cannot afford to compensate her for her loss.'

'I am sure she will appreciate your sympathy, Master,' said Michael caustically. 'But you are right. Drax should have stood up and declared himself when Agatha started to tug on the sheet. Then the tiles would not have fallen on him.'

Seeing Bartholomew about to probe a wound in the corpse's stomach, Michael ordered all the labourers back to work, lest they witnessed something that would give credence to the tales regarding the physician's penchant for sorcery. He dismissed Cynric and Walter, too.

'I wonder if he left us anything in his will,' Langelee was musing. 'Given his generosity in the past, I have high hopes. I am sorry Drax is dead, but a legacy will more than console me.'

'I hope he did not,' countered Thelnetham. 'He died in our College, and we already have a questionable reputation, thanks to Bartholomew's unorthodoxy, Clippesby's madness and your previous existence as an archbishop's hireling. We do not want rumours to circulate that we kill townsmen for the contents of their wills.'

'What nonsense!' cried Langelee, stung. 'We have a fine, upstanding reputation!'

His Fellows said nothing – they knew they did not.

'Accidents happen,' Langelee went on indignantly. 'No one can blame us for what happened.'

47

'It was not an accident,' said Bartholomew, looking up at last. 'Drax was murdered.'

There was a stunned, disbelieving silence after Bartholomew had made his announcement. It was Michael who found his voice first. 'How do you know?'

Bartholomew hesitated, loath to provide too much information lest it should lead to renewed accusations of sorcery from William.

'You can tell us,' said the Franciscan gruffly, guessing the reason for Bartholomew's reluctance to speak. He was not normally sensitive, but his recent banishment had encouraged him to be a little more sympathetic to the feelings of others. 'I will not make disparaging remarks about your hideous trade, because you cannot help being a physician. Not everyone can specialise in theology.'

'You are too kind, Father,' murmured Bartholomew, aware of smirks being exchanged between Thelnetham and Ayera, the College's newest member. Neither liked the Franciscan, despising him for his weak intellect, his filthy robes and the narrow-mindedness of his opinions.

'Matt and I will take Drax to the church, and he can explain his theory to me there,' said Michael, knowing exactly why his friend was reluctant to elaborate. 'The rest of you can return to your teaching. Our students' day has been interrupted long enough.'

'No,' argued Langelee. 'He can tell us here. If Drax *has* been murdered, we need to know.'

'I disagree,' said Thelnetham, flicking imaginary dust from his immaculate habit. 'I have no desire to be regaled with ghoulish details. It was bad enough overhearing his lecture on fractured skulls the other day. It made me quite queasy, and I had to be escorted outside for air.'

'Thank God anatomy is illegal in our country,' added

48

Ayera. 'Or he would be waving entrails around to demonstrate his points.'

Usually, Bartholomew liked Ayera, a tall, intelligent geometrician who shared Langelee's fondness for outdoor pursuits and Bartholomew's own love of teaching, but there were times when the man annoyed him. One was whenever the subject of anatomy was raised – Ayera disapproved of it with a passion Bartholomew found difficult to fathom. And Thelnetham had a nasty habit of encouraging Ayera's irritating condemnation.

'There is no "waving" of organs in anatomy,' he snapped, unable to help himself. He had attended several dissections when he had visited the universities in Padua and Salerno, and had been impressed by the precision and neatness of the art. 'It is all conducted with meticulous—'

'You mean you have actually seen anatomy being performed?' interrupted Thelnetham. He crossed himself, appalled.

Bartholomew had yet to gain Thelnetham's measure, even though they had been acquainted for several months. He opened his mouth to reply, but then was not sure what to say.

'So what if he has?' asked Langelee. 'It is not illegal in foreign universities, and he has an enquiring mind. It is only natural that he should make the most of what was on offer.'

Thelnetham sniffed. 'Well, I do not want to hear about it, and I do not want to hear what he has to say about Drax, either. If you will excuse me, Master, I would rather teach. At least one of us should, because I can see from here that our students are throwing things around.'

As one, the Fellows looked towards the hall, where, sure enough, missiles were zipping past the windows. Langelee grimaced, and started to stride towards them. Immediately, there was a scraping of benches and a rattle of feet on floorboards, and Bartholomew had no doubt that by the time the Master arrived the students would be sitting, cherub-faced, in neat rows, and any sign of whatever they had been doing would have been whisked away.

'Well?' asked Michael, when Ayera, Thelnetham, Suttone and Clippesby had followed their Master's lead, and only he, Bartholomew and William remained. 'Explain.'

'There is a puncture wound in Drax's stomach.' Bartholomew lifted the dead man's tunic so they could see it. 'It would have bled profusely, yet there is very little blood where he lies. This suggests he died elsewhere, and his body was brought here later. I can also tell you that he is cold and slightly stiff around the jaws, both of which suggest he has been dead for several hours.'

'Lord!' muttered Michael, shocked. 'Are you telling me that someone toted a corpse into our College and shoved it behind the masons' supplies?'

Bartholomew nodded. 'I am not sure what to think about the culprit's choice of hiding place. Was it because he knew it might be several days before these tiles were uncovered – and Agatha's assault was just bad luck? Was he hoping to implicate the workmen? Or *are* the workmen to blame, and they had been planning to remove Drax to a more permanent resting place later?'

'I do not like that Yffi,' said William darkly. 'He has the look of a killer about him. And I know these things, because *I* am a Franciscan friar.'

'Never mind that,' said Michael impatiently, unwilling to waste time on William's odd remarks. He sighed. 'We had better have a word with these builders.'

'I suppose so,' said Bartholomew. 'Although bringing a corpse here – especially to the area given over to their supplies – was a rash thing to have done. Moreover, how

50

did the killer get it in here in the first place? Not *all* the workmen are likely to have been involved, while our students are always gazing out of the windows. How did the culprit do it without being seen?'

Michael was thoughtful. 'But our students were distracted, were they not? With vivid descriptions about the antics of Yolande de Blaston, which drew all eyes to the roof?'

'Concerning a handful of chestnuts and a damp cloth,' provided William helpfully, indicating that the students had not been the only ones absorbed in the builders' commentary.

'Do you think Yffi staged a diversion?' asked Bartholomew.

Michael sighed. 'I have no idea. But something untoward is unfolding, and I am not ready to discount anyone as a suspect until I understand what.'

The masons had not resumed their labours, but were standing in a cluster, discussing what had happened in low, excited voices. Yffi was doing most of the talking, and his apprentices leaned close to hear what he had to say on the matter. Blaston, who had no apprentices of his own, was standing nearby, regarding them with undisguised disdain.

'They think it is a joke,' he whispered, when Bartholomew and Michael approached. 'A man is dead, and all they can do is huddle together and chatter like a flock of crows.'

Bartholomew studied the masons closely but could detect no signs of unease or guilt in any of them. Of course, that meant nothing – the culprit would have to be bold and fearless, to drag a corpse around inside a well-populated College in the first place.

'I do not suppose *you* noticed anything suspicious, did you?' Michael asked Blaston hopefully.

Blaston shook his head apologetically. 'I am sorry, Brother. I was in the stable, making new frames for the window shutters.'

'All day?'

Blaston thought for a moment. 'No. Not long after dawn, I went out to buy more nails.'

'Did anyone see you?'

Blaston was alarmed by the question. 'Well, no, because the smith was away, so I took what I needed and left the money under his anvil, just like I always do. He trusts me. Why do you ask? Am *I* a suspect for this horrible crime?'

'Of course not,' said Bartholomew soothingly. 'We are just trying to gain a clear picture of who was where. Did you see anyone wandering about the College, other than scholars and staff?'

'Yes – there were several visitors,' replied Blaston, re-assured. 'Walter will give you a list.'

'Unfortunately, he has a habit of loitering in the latrines,' said Michael. 'I doubt he can help.'

'Well, then.' Blaston scratched his head. 'There was a delivery of more sand for the mortar. Those pilgrims poked their heads round the door – Prior Etone was showing them the town, and they were being nosy. Then Agatha the laundress's cousin arrived, wanting kitchen scraps.'

'He must be desperate,' muttered Michael. 'Our left-overs are left because they are inedible.'

'Folk *are* desperate, Brother,' said Blaston quietly. 'It is a terrible winter.'

Michael nodded slowly. 'Yes, it is. I hate to mention this, Blaston, but did you hear what Yffi and his lads were saying about your wife?'

Blaston nodded, and an expression of immense pride

52

suffused his face. 'Yolande is an incredible woman, and it pleases me to know folk admire her talents. I heard everything, and she will be very flattered when I repeat it to her.'

Michael's jaw dropped, but Bartholomew was not surprised. He had heard Blaston say as much on previous occasions, and knew exactly what the carpenter thought of his wife's abilities in other men's bedchambers. Before the monk could make some remark that might detract from Blaston's pleasure, Bartholomew gestured for Yffi and his apprentices to approach.

'We need to know what you saw today,' he told them.

'Nothing,' replied Yffi with a shrug. 'We have been on the roof all day, and it is difficult to see down into the yard from up there. We all went to peer over the edge when Agatha started chasing that dog, but it was the only time *I* looked down all day.'

'What about the rest of you?' asked Michael. Yffi's assistants were all undersized youths in baggy leggings and grimy tunics. 'Surely, one of you must have climbed down at some point for more supplies? Or even stood for a moment to stretch and take a breath?'

'We did come down from time to time,' acknowledged one called Peterkin. 'But we were in a hurry, so did not waste time gawking around. All I can say is that there was no body behind our tiles at dawn this morning, because I went behind there to pee. And I would have noticed.'

'Someone entered our College and hid a corpse among your supplies,' said Michael, rather accusingly. 'In broad daylight. Surely, *one* of you must have seen something to help us find out who did it?'

There were a lot of shaken heads and muttered denials. 'You cannot let your mind wander on roofs,' said Peterkin, rather sanctimoniously. 'It is asking for accidents.'

53

Michael sighed his exasperation, and tried a different tack. 'Did any of you know Drax?'

'Not really,' replied Yffi. 'We all drink in the Griffin, which he owned, but we rarely spoke.'

'I did not like him,' said Blaston unhappily. 'He knew this winter has been hard, and that decent men are struggling to make ends meet, but he still charged top prices for his wares.'

'That is true,' said Yffi, while his lads nodded agreement. 'Why do you think he bought prayers from Michaelhouse? His conscience plagued him, and he needed your masses to salve it.'

'But none of us were angry enough about it to kill him,' added Peterkin hastily.

Michael asked a few more questions but they elicited nothing useful, so he ordered them back to work. When they had gone, he stood next to the stack of tiles and squinted at the roof.

'If Yffi and his boys *were* all up there, they would *not* have been able to see down here – although we would still have been able to hear their banter. So they may be telling the truth.'

Bartholomew nodded. 'Drax was not a large man, so it would not take many moments to haul him here and deposit him. The killer could well have done it while Yffi and his apprentices were on the roof and Blaston was in the stables. Of course, he would have to hope none of our students happened to be looking out of the window at the time.'

'But it could have happened when they were transfixed by Yffi's lewd banter,' mused Michael. 'I was interested to hear that those pilgrims were nosing around at the salient time, though, especially that pardoner. You know what I think of pardoners. Perhaps Fen saw our home and decided it looked like a good repository for the body of his victim.'

'Why would he do that?' asked Bartholomew, startled by the assertion. 'If he did kill Drax, why risk capture by toting the corpse around?'

'Pardoners are an unfathomable breed,' declared Michael, never rational where they were concerned. 'Who knows what passes through their sly minds? But I shall find out when I interrogate Master Fen later. I do not want you with me, though. You are too willing to see the good in people, and he will use your weakness to his advantage.'

'As you wish,' said Bartholomew, relieved to be spared the ordeal.

Cynric had been busy while Bartholomew and Michael had been talking to the workmen, and not only had he arranged for servants to carry Drax to St Michael's Church, but he had conducted a systematic search of the College buildings, too, and was able to report that there were no signs of blood or a struggle in any of them.

'What about the grounds?' asked Michael. 'In the orchard or around the vegetable plots?'

Cynric shook his head. 'The grass would have been trampled if a murder had occurred in the wilder parts, while I would have seen blood around the bits that are more carefully tended. Drax was not killed in the College, Brother. I am sure of it.'

'So you *were* right, Matt,' said Michael. 'Drax was killed elsewhere and was dumped here. But why? The tiles will go on our roof soon, so he was not going to remain undiscovered for long. And why pick on us, anyway?'

'Could it be anything to do with the College–hostel dispute?' asked Bartholomew. 'It would represent a rather horrible turn in the rivalry, but having a murdered taverner on our property will certainly not endear us to the town. It may even encourage them to attack us.'

'I cannot believe that is the answer,' said Michael, although with more hope than conviction. 'Because it *would* represent a rather horrible turn – one that is not in keeping with carts on roofs, cunningly balanced boats, or filling halls with roosting chickens. We shall bear it in mind, but I feel certain you are wrong.' He sighed tiredly. 'You had better inspect Drax's corpse again now.'

'Why?' Bartholomew wanted to return to his teaching. 'I have already told you all I can.'

'I doubt you conducted a thorough examination with Ayera and Thelnetham snorting their disapproval behind you,' said Michael tartly. 'So you will go to St Michael's Church and do it properly. And if you refuse, I shall withhold the fee you will be paid as my Corpse Examiner.'

The threat was both unfair and unkind. As Corpse Examiner, Bartholomew was paid three pennies for every cadaver he assessed, and he needed the money badly, because prices had risen sharply since the beginning of winter. Michael knew he was struggling to buy the medicines necessary for those of his patients who could not afford their own.

'I will not be able to tell you anything else,' he grumbled, as they walked up St Michael's Lane. 'And you should think of Drax's wife. It would be dreadful if someone like Yffi got there with the news first, because I doubt he has a gentle way with words.'

'I know,' replied Michael. 'So you can paw the cadaver, while I visit the widow.'

'We saw her earlier today,' said Bartholomew, sorry for the unpleasant shock she was about to receive. 'She is a friend of Emma's granddaughter – Odelina – and was at Emma's house.'

'So she was.' Michael's eyes narrowed. 'So I had better ask whether she stayed there all morning. It would not be the first time a wife dispatched an unloved husband, after all.'

'You cannot investigate this case,' said Bartholomew, seeing the monk had the bit between his teeth. 'Drax was not a scholar, and there is nothing to indicate he died on University property, either. *Ergo*, his death falls under Dick Tulyet's jurisdiction. He is the Sheriff.'

'Dick will have far more important business to attend,' predicted Michael. 'Besides, Drax was found in my College, so I have a right to find out what happened to him.'

'Actually, Dick told me only last week that there is not much to do these days, because Emma has frightened all the petty criminals away. He spends all his time on administration, and he is bored. You may find he is less willing to relinquish the matter than you think.'

'Then we shall have to work together. However, I would rather work with you than him, and—'

'No,' said Bartholomew firmly. 'I do not have time, especially with Emma summoning me every time she feels a twinge in her jaws.'

'You cannot be that busy,' argued Michael. 'Two new physicians arrived in Cambridge a few weeks ago and relieved you of some of your patients. You should have plenty of spare time.'

'It is a bad winter, Brother. Even with Gyseburne and Meryfeld here, we can barely keep up with the demand for consultations.'

'You can find the time to help me. You must, because this concerns your College – your *home*. But here we are at the High Street, where you turn right to the church, and I turn left for the Drax mansion. I shall expect your report later.'

* * *

St Michael's was a pretty building with a low, squat tower and a huge chancel. It was a peaceful place, because its thick walls muted the din of the busy street outside, and the only sound was the coo of roosting pigeons. Bartholomew aimed for the little Stanton Chapel, named for the wealthy lawyer who had founded Michaelhouse and rebuilt the church more than thirty years before.

When he arrived, he stared at Drax for a moment, then began to remove the taverner's blood-soaked clothing. It did not take long to confirm his initial findings: that the wound in Drax's stomach would have been almost instantly fatal, while the stiff jaws indicated it had happened hours before. The location and angle of the injury made suicide unlikely.

As he replaced the clothes, he thought about Drax. He had not known him well, although he had met him when Drax had made much-needed donations to the College. The taverner had not been particularly generous, but every little helped, and Michaelhouse was grateful for his kindness. In return, the College's priests had said masses for his soul. Langelee was scrupulous about ensuring this was done, which was why people like Drax and Emma were willing to do business with him.

Bartholomew recalled seeing Drax earlier that day, quarrelling with Kendale. It had been just after dawn, and although estimating time of death was an imprecise business, he suspected the taverner had died not long afterwards. Had the argument escalated once Kendale had pulled Drax down the alley? But if so, why would Kendale dump his victim's corpse in Michaelhouse? Why not just tip it in the river, or stow it in a cart, to take to some remote spot in the Fens?

Feeling he had learned all he could, Bartholomew lifted Drax into the parish coffin – it did not seem decent to leave his tile-crushed face on display – and he was just fastening the lid when he heard footsteps. It was Celia. Odelina was with her, still crammed into her unflatteringly tight dress. She was breathless – she was not as fit as the older woman – and Celia had clearly set a rapid pace from her Bridge Street home. Behind them, struggling to keep up, was Michael.

'Where is my husband?' demanded Celia. Her imperious gaze settled on the coffin. 'You have not shoved him in there, have you?'

'Well, yes,' said Bartholomew uncomfortably. 'I am sorry. It did not—'

'No matter,' Celia interrupted briskly. 'But show me his face. It may not be John, and I do not want to invest in mourning apparel if you have the wrong man.'

'Perhaps you might inspect his hand instead,' Bartholomew suggested tactfully.

'Why?' asked Celia coldly. 'Have you performed some dark magic that has changed his appearance? Your fondness for witchery is why I am no longer your patient, if you recall.'

'Your husband's fingers,' whispered Odelina, before Bartholomew could reply. 'Robin the surgeon chopped them off after that accident with Yffi, and Doctor Bartholomew obviously thinks that identifying them will be less distressing than looking on his poor dead face.' She looked away quickly. 'This is all very horrible!'

'Oh, yes,' said Celia, relenting. 'I had forgotten his missing digits. Yffi's blood money allowed us to buy the Griffin tavern. Then we used its profits to buy more inns, so we now have seven. *And* three lovely houses, including the big one we lease to Kendale – he calls it Chestre Hostel.'

'The Griffin,' mused Bartholomew, recalling it was where

the yellow-headed man had fled after stealing Emma's box. It seemed a strange coincidence.

But Celia was becoming impatient, so he reached under the lid and extracted the pertinent limb, thinking she seemed more annoyed than distressed by her spouse's demise. Odelina was pale and shaking, but her grandmother and father were protective of her, and he doubted she had encountered many corpses. He saw her look studiously the other way as Celia bent to examine Drax's hand.

'I always thought it odd that these two women should be such great friends,' whispered Michael, as the two scholars stepped away to give them privacy. 'But then Langelee explained it to me: the beautiful Celia is the heroine in the romantic ballads that Odelina so adores.'

'Odelina does seem to worship her,' agreed Bartholomew, watching them together. 'But what does Celia gain from the association?'

'According to Langelee, a warm welcome in the house of the town's most influential businesswoman. There is a lot a resourceful, ambitious lady like Celia can learn from Emma.'

Before he could say more, Celia began to haul on the ring that still adorned one of Drax's two remaining fingers. Unfortunately, it was a tight fit, and she could not twist it free. After a few moments, during which Bartholomew was obliged to make a lunge for the coffin, to prevent it from being yanked off its trestles, she turned to him.

'Will you get it for me? You are always clamouring to hack out Emma's bad tooth, so I am sure you have a knife to hand. If not, then borrow mine.' Celia removed a slender blade from her belt. 'But hurry, if you please. I do not like this church. It is draughty and smells of dead birds.'

Bartholomew did as she asked, pointedly avoiding the

use of sharp implements. He blinked in disbelief when she immediately donned the retrieved ring, flexing her hand to admire the effect. Odelina was also dismayed by the brazen materialism, and he supposed it did not square with her image of Celia as the noble heroine.

'What happened to John?' Celia asked, turning abruptly to Michael. 'You say he was found dead in your College, but I do not understand why he should have been there in the first place.'

'Neither do we,' replied Michael, also struggling to mask his distaste. 'He was stabbed, and his body hidden behind some tiles. Unfortunately, a member of our College tugged on the sheet that covered them, causing a couple to topple—'

'You mean he was *murdered*?' demanded Celia. For the first time since entering the church, she seemed shocked. 'You must be mistaken! No one would kill John.'

'Unfortunately, it would seem someone did,' said Michael. 'But I shall find out who.'

'Lord!' breathed Celia, gazing at him. 'He always expected to die in bed at a ripe old age.'

'You discussed death with him?' asked Michael keenly.

Celia nodded. 'Sometimes, when we were bored and had nothing else to do. These winter evenings are very long, and it is easy to run out of nice things to talk about.'

'I cannot say I have ever had that problem,' said Michael. 'What exactly did—'

'I suppose I had better start making arrangements for his funeral,' interrupted Celia. 'But before I go, there are a couple more things I want from his corpse: the medallion he wore around his neck and the pilgrim brooch pinned in his hat. However, now I know he was murdered, I do not feel equal to rummaging for them myself. Would you mind obliging me, Doctor?'

'Yes, I would, actually.' Bartholomew felt as though he was being asked to rob a grave.

'Odelina,' said Celia, turning to her friend with a coaxing smile. 'You love me, do you not? Slip your hand inside the box and grab the trinkets.'

'No!' cried Odelina, appalled. 'I cannot touch a murdered man in a church! It might bring me bad luck regarding getting a husband.'

'Perhaps you should leave them where they are,' suggested Michael coolly. 'The dead are entitled to carry some personal effects to the grave, and you already have his ring.'

'I am not one for making sentimental gestures over corpses,' retorted Celia. 'Gold is gold, and it belongs with the living. Or is there another reason why Michaelhouse is unwilling to help a grieving widow? Such as that they have already removed these items for themselves?'

'Matt will retrieve them for you,' said Michael stiffly. Bartholomew started to object, but the monk overrode him. 'I will not have it said that our College steals from the dead – or from the living, for that matter. And while he is busy, you can tell me about any spats or disagreements your husband might have had.'

Celia watched Bartholomew lift the lid and begin unravelling the chain from Drax's neck. 'Well, Principal Kendale objected to the fact that John was going to raise the rent on Chestre Hostel – John hated Kendale, and hoped the increase would encourage him to leave. Then several of our customers argued with him, because he refused to give them credit for ale.'

Bartholomew dropped the salvaged necklace into Celia's eager hand. She wiped it on her sleeve then slipped it around her neck. He regarded her in astonishment. She scowled at him, and indicated that he should stop staring, and retrieve the badge.

'Why did he refuse?' asked Michael, struggling to conceal his revulsion. 'If they were regulars?'

'Because it might be weeks before the weather breaks, and they earn enough to pay us back. Or they might die of starvation in the interim. We are a business, not a charity.'

'Your husband made donations to Michaelhouse,' Bartholomew pointed out. 'That is charity.'

'Yes, but he got prayers in return. It was a commercial arrangement, although *I* shall not be buying anything from you. *I* do not deal with warlocks and fat monks who ask impudent questions.'

'I am not fat,' objected Michael. 'I have big bones. And I am not impudent, either. I am merely trying to ascertain why your husband died. But tell me about your life together. Was it happy?'

'Do not answer,' advised Odelina sharply. 'He is trying to trap you, because he thinks *you* might have murdered John and toted his corpse to Michaelhouse.'

'Do you?' asked Celia, treating the monk to a forthright stare. 'Why? John was not the most scintillating of men, but we liked each other well enough. Now, give me the badge, Doctor.'

'Here is the hat,' said Bartholomew. 'But I cannot see a pilgrim token.'

'It is pinned on the *inside*,' explained Celia. 'Because he wanted to keep it safe. It is from Walsingham, you see – the shrine where the Virgin appears from time to time.'

'Had he been on a pilgrimage, then?' asked Bartholomew, surprised. Drax had not seemed like the kind of man to absent himself from his taverns in order to undertake arduous journeys.

'No,' replied Celia. 'He bought it from a pardoner, who told him that owning it was the next best thing to going

63

on one of these expeditions himself. It will earn him less time in Purgatory.'

'If you believe that, then why do you want to take it from him?' asked Bartholomew. Talking to Celia reminded him why he had not minded when she had informed him that she was transferring her allegiance to another physician. He had always found it difficult to like her.

'Because *I* want to spend less time in Purgatory, too,' replied Celia shortly. 'So look inside the coffin, if you please. It must have fallen off.'

'Not necessarily,' said Bartholomew, examining the hat. 'There is a hole here, where something has been ripped away.'

'What are you saying?' asked Celia warily. 'That John was murdered for his pilgrim badge?'

'Was it valuable?' asked Bartholomew, not bothering to reply. She knew as well as he did that the poor were struggling to feed their families that winter. 'Made of precious metal or jewels?'

'Naturally,' replied Celia. 'We neither of us are interested in pewter. And I want it back, so when you find his killer, be sure to prise it from his murderous grasp.'

She turned and flounced away, leaving Odelina to scurry after her. Michael watched with his eyebrows raised so high that they disappeared under his thin brown fringe.

'Well!' he drawled. 'So much for the grieving widow!'

The following day was dry, but bitterly cold, and Bartholomew shivered as he trudged from patient to patient. Few had fires in their homes, and he was not surprised they were succumbing to chills and fevers. His last visit was to a cottage near the Mill Pond, where a young fisherman was suffering from a badly sprained ankle.

Bartholomew bound it up with a poultice of pine resin and wax, and advised him not to stand on it for a few days.

'Thank you,' said the fisherman, leaning back in relief. 'It really hurt. It was your Master's doing – we are on the same camp-ball team, and he is always so damned rough in practices. We ask him to save his violence for the opposing side, but he forgets himself in the heat of the moment.'

Camp-ball was Langelee's greatest passion. It was hardly a genteel pastime for the head of a Cambridge College, but it was not one he could be persuaded to give up.

'Would you have a word with him about needless fervour?' the fisherman went on. 'Of course it is too late for Friday. I shall not be able to play, which is a wicked shame.'

'Friday?' asked Bartholomew. 'Do you mean for the annual competition between the Gilbertines and the Carmelites?'

Each year, the two priories chose teams to represent them on the field – obviously, such dignified gentlemen were not going to indulge in the rough and tumble themselves – and the occasion drew enormous crowds. It was an honour to be selected to play, and Langelee had been beside himself with pride when he had been one of the lucky few.

The fisherman nodded bitterly. 'And I will not be there, thanks to your Master.'

Bartholomew returned to Michaelhouse, and taught until it was time for his students to attend a mock disputation with Thelnetham, thus leaving him free to see more patients. Before he left, he mentioned the fisherman's complaint to Langelee, who dismissed it with a careless flick of his hand, muttering something about weaklings not being welcome on *his* team anyway.

Bartholomew left the College, and tended two fevers and a case of cracked ribs. Then he went to visit Chancellor Tynkell, who was suffering from one of his periodic stomach upsets, and was just leaving when he met Michael. The monk was tired and dispirited.

'Where have you been?' he demanded irritably. 'I needed your help with Drax's murder today.'

'What have you learned?' asked Bartholomew, predicting from the monk's sour mood that he would rather talk than listen to excuses about teaching and patients.

'Nothing!' Michael spat. 'He was unpopular among his customers because he refused them credit, but that is hardly a reason to kill. And I have been told that he and Celia were not close, but we knew that already – the woman was hardly overwhelmed with distress yesterday.'

'No,' agreed Bartholomew. He glanced at Michael, and was surprised to see that a haunted expression had taken the place of his ire. 'What is wrong?'

'I have a very bad feeling about this case, and the more I think about it, the more worried I become. Drax's body was deposited in our College – our *home*. Clearly, it was a deliberate attempt to harm us, so we must unravel the mystery before the culprit does something worse.'

Bartholomew was thoughtful. 'Drax's death must be connected to the theft at the Carmelite Priory – the villain there went straight for the gold badge on Poynton's saddle, while Drax's rings and necklaces were ignored but his badge – his *hidden* badge – was snatched off hard enough to tear his hat. The thief targeted only *signacula* in both cases.'

'You may be right,' acknowledged Michael. 'But why pick on these particular two men?'

Bartholomew shrugged. 'Perhaps because they owned valuable tokens. And they may *not* be the only two victims, anyway – just the only two that you know about. Have you questioned Emma de Colvyll yet? The thief who took her box had yellow hair, and—'

'It was *not* the same man,' snapped Michael. 'As I told you yesterday, Emma's assailant will be lying low, hoping Heslarton does not catch him. He would not have returned to Cambridge and committed a very public theft and a murder.'

'I disagree. Two yellow-haired villains in one day is a curious coincidence. Too curious.'

'They are different,' reiterated Michael testily. 'And if you persist in seeing an association between two entirely separate incidents, we shall lead ourselves astray.'

'If you say so,' said Bartholomew, sure that Michael was wrong.

The monk blew out his cheeks in a sigh, and some of the tetchiness went out of him. 'It has been a wretchedly frustrating morning. I wish you had been with me – you are good at reading people, and I need all the help I can get. Incidentally, did you hear that Welfry has been appointed Seneschal? I like the man, but he is hardly a suitable candidate for a post of such gravitas.'

'Give him a chance, Brother. I think he means to do his best.'

'I do not doubt his good intentions, but he will quickly become bored with the rigours of the post, and then we shall be inundated with silly jests. And the exchequer clerks are not noted for their sense of humour. I told the Dominican Prior-General that Welfry was a poor choice, but he said it was either him or Prior Morden.'

'Morden is a decent man.'

'So you have always said, but he does not have the wits to deal with sly exchequer clerks, and they would cheat us of our due. At least Welfry is intelligent. But I should not be worrying about him yet – catching the killer-thief is much more urgent. Will you help me?'

'Later today,' promised Bartholomew. 'If I am not needed by patients.'

'Tomorrow,' countered Michael. He smiled suddenly. 'It is the Feast of the Purification of the Blessed Virgin Mary this afternoon, one of my favourite festivals. And *not* because there will be food afterwards, before you think to cast aspersions on my piety. The truth is that I like the music.'

'As long as your choir does not sing and spoil it,' murmured Bartholomew, but not loud enough for the monk to hear. The College's singers comprised a large section of the town's poor, and were famous for their lack of talent. Michael was their conductor.

'Where are you going?' the monk asked, when Bartholomew started to walk away from Michaelhouse. 'It is almost time for the noonday meal.'

'To the Carmelite Friary. John Horneby has a sore throat.'

'No!' exclaimed Michael in horror. 'Then you must cure him immediately! He is to give the Stock Extraordinary Lecture next week, and it will be one of the greatest speeches ever delivered – one that will have theological ramifications that will reverberate for decades.'

'So I have heard,' said Bartholomew flatly. Theologians were always delivering desperately important discourses, and he was a little weary of them. 'Will you be there?'

'Of course. And scholars from all over the country are flocking to hear him, so nothing – *nothing* – must prevent him from speaking. I had better come with you, to ensure he has the best possible care. The honour of our University is at stake here, Matt.'

The Carmelite Friary was busy that day. A contingent of White Friars had just arrived from London, the usual crowd of penitents milled around the shrine, and a service for the Purification was under way in the chapel. Bartholomew and Michael were just being conducted to the room where the sick theologian lay, when they were accosted by the four pilgrims.

'Have you found it?' demanded Poynton without preamble. His florid face made him look unwell, and Bartholomew wondered again whether illness had prompted his pilgrimages. 'My token from the Holy Land?'

'I am afraid not,' replied Michael. 'Although I spent the entire morning making enquiries. So has my colleague here. Can you see how he is limping? That is caused by the blisters earned from the distances he has walked on your behalf.'

Bartholomew looked at the ground, uncomfortable with the lie. He had been limping, but it was because he had fallen off a horse the previous October, and the cold weather was creating an ache in a bone that was not long healed. It had happened when he and Michael had been travelling to Clare in Suffolk, and had been ambushed by robbers. Michael had decided the incident was God's way of telling them they were not supposed to go, and had insisted on turning back. But Bartholomew liked what he had been told about the place, and intended to visit it later that year, when spring came.

'We are very grateful for your efforts,' said Fen politely.

'Good,' said Michael. 'We shall continue our labours later, despite the fact that this is a holy day and we should be at our devotions. As should you.'

'I know how to make my devotions,' snarled Poynton. 'I have been on twenty-two pilgrimages, and do not need a monk to direct me.' He looked the Benedictine up and down in disdain.

'We are on our way to the chapel now,' said Fen, laying

69

a warning hand on Poynton's shoulder. 'So we shall leave you to your business.'

'I do not like them,' said Michael, when they had gone. 'Poynton is nasty, but Fen is worse. He pretends to be reasonable, but you can see the cunning burn within him. You think I say this because I despise his wicked profession, but you are wrong. I feel, with every bone in my body, that there is something untoward about that pardoner.'

'If you say so,' said Bartholomew.

He resumed his walk to Horneby's chamber, reluctant to discuss it. Michael was always accusing pardoners of devious or criminal behaviour. Of course, he was often right – he had accumulated a lot of experience with felons as Senior Proctor, and his intuition did tend to be accurate. But Bartholomew had detected nothing odd about Fen, and thought the monk was letting his prejudices run away with him. Fen seemed perfectly amiable to him.

John Horneby did not look like a famous theologian. He was young, and his boyish appearance was accentuated by the fact that he was missing two front teeth. It was not many years since he had been an unruly novice, who preferred brawling to books, and Bartholomew was not the only one who had been amazed by his sudden and wholly unanticipated transformation into a serious scholar.

'Bartholomew,' he croaked, as the two scholars were shown into his room. There was nothing in it except a bed, a table for studying and a hook for his spare habit. The table was piled high with books, though. 'I hope you can help me, because I cannot lecture like this.'

While Bartholomew inspected the back of Horneby's throat with a lantern, Michael examined the tomes on the table. Books were enormously expensive, and the fact that Horneby had been allocated so many at one time was testament to the high esteem in which he was held by his Order.

'You have the theories of Doctor Stokes,' Michael said, picking up a manuscript. 'The Dominican. I cannot say I admire his scribblings.'

'He is dry,' agreed Horneby. 'But his thinking on the Indivisibility of the Holy Trinity is—'

'Do not speak,' advised Bartholomew. He adjusted the lantern, then turned to the lay-brother who had escorted them to the room. 'This lamp flickers horribly. Is there a better one?'

'That is the best light in the whole convent,' replied the servant. 'And I tested them all myself, because Prior Etone wants Master Horneby to be able to read at night. The honour of the Carmelites rests on the lecture he is to give, so we are all doing everything we can to ensure he is ready for it.'

'And I am sure it will be superb,' said Michael warmly, smiling at the Carmelite. 'I have heard you speak on several occasions, and I know you will do your Order and our University justice.'

The monk possessed a fine mind himself and did not often compliment people so effusively, so Bartholomew could only suppose Horneby had reached heights he had not yet appreciated. Horneby started to thank him, but stopped when he caught the physician's warning glance.

The friar's throat was red, although Bartholomew could not see well enough to tell whether there were also the yellow flecks that would be indicative of infection. He decided to assume the worst, and prescribed a particularly strong medicine to rectify the matter. Horneby sipped the potion, and nodded to say the pain was less. Bartholomew left him to rest, cautioning the lay-brother to keep him quiet, and not to let him engage in unnecessary chatter.

As Bartholomew and Michael headed for the gate, the monk pulled a disapproving face when Poynton, Fen and the nuns sailed past the queue that had formed to pay homage to Simon Stock's scapular, and pushed themselves in at the front. There were indignant glances from the other pilgrims, but no one seemed inclined to berate them for their selfishness, perhaps because Poynton and his companions were the Carmelites' honoured guests. Idly, Bartholomew wondered whether the White Friars would be quite so accommodating if the quartet were not so obviously rich.

'Do you think that scapular is genuine?' Michael asked, speaking softly so as not to be overheard and offend anyone. 'I find it hard to believe that a saint who lived almost a hundred years ago, and who died in some distant foreign city, should have left a bit of his habit in Cambridge.'

'I am not qualified to say,' replied Bartholomew. The notion that half the town considered him a warlock made him wary of voicing opinions that might be construed as heretical, even to Michael. 'Prior Etone showed it to me yesterday, though. It looked old.'

'So do I at times, but that does not make me an object to be venerated. Personally, I am uncomfortable with this particular shrine. For years, St Simon Stock's vision was said to be a legend, with no actual truth to it, but all of a sudden here we are with a holy place of pilgrimage. And it is attracting pardoners, which cannot be a good thing.'

'And thieves, if yesterday was anything to go by.'

'True,' agreed Michael. 'The shrine will draw scoundrels as well as benefactors, and Poynton will not be the last visitor to fall prey to sticky fingers.'

By the time they returned to the College, it was nearing the hour when the rite of Purification would begin, so

Bartholomew went to change into his ceremonial robes – a red hat and a scarlet gown that were worn only on special occasions. Unfortunately, both were looking decidedly shabby, but he could not afford to buy replacements when there was so much medicine to be purchased.

'Ask your sister for new ones, sir,' suggested Valence. 'She can well afford them.'

It was true enough, and Edith was always pressing gifts of food and money on her impecunious brother, but he was acutely conscious of the fact that he was rarely in a position to reciprocate. It was not a comfortable feeling, and he disliked being so often in her debt.

'She will give you whatever you want,' Valence went on when there was no reply. 'And you repay her in kind, by turning out every time one of her husband's apprentices has a scratch or a snuffle. She told me the other day that she was lucky to have you.'

'Did she?' asked Bartholomew, pleased. Edith's good opinion was important to him.

'Yes, because she does not like any of the other physicians. She says Rougham is arrogant, Gyseburne is sinister, and Meryfeld does not know what he is talking about.'

'Oh,' said Bartholomew, deflated. He jammed the hat on his head, and supposed people might not notice the state of his clothes if the light was poor – it was an overcast day.

'The feast this afternoon promises to be good,' Valence chatted on happily. 'Agatha has cooked a whole pig! We have not had a decent pile of meat in weeks!'

'No,' agreed Bartholomew. But his mind was on medicine, pondering how he had struggled to see Horneby's sore throat with the Carmelites' best lamp. 'Are you friends with Welfry the Dominican? I have seen you with him several times.'

Valence immediately became wary. 'He lives in his friary, sir. And Master Langelee prefers that we do not fraternise with men from other foundations, so we rarely meet.'

'He prefers that you do not visit taverns, either, but that does not stop you from doing it,' Bartholomew remarked tartly. 'How well do you know Welfry?'

'I may have had a drink or two in his company,' acknowledged Valence. He coloured furiously when he realised what he had just admitted. 'Not in a tavern, of course.'

'Of course. Did he tell you how he managed that trick with the flaming lights last week? The one where St Mary the Great was illuminated as if by a vast candle?'

'That was not Welfry, sir. Kendale from Chestre Hostel did that.'

Bartholomew regarded him askance. 'Are you sure? Lighting up St Mary the Great seems too innocent a stunt for him. I imagine he would have devised something more . . . deadly.'

'The Dominicans *are* notorious pranksters,' acknowledged Valence. 'And the affair at the church *is* the kind of escapade they love. But they are innocent of that particular jape.'

'You seem very sure. Can I assume you were with Welfry at the time? In a tavern?'

'We may have enjoyed an ale in the Cardinal's Cap, now you mention it,' admitted Valence reluctantly. 'He is an intelligent man, and I enjoy his company. But the Cap is not really a tavern. It is more a society, where gentlemen gather for erudite conversation.'

'Right,' said Bartholomew. There was no point in remonstrating. Valence knew the rules, and if he was willing to risk being fined by the beadles – Brother Michael's army of law-enforcers – then that was his business. The same went for Welfry, too. He considered the friar. 'I cannot

74

imagine why he took the cowl. I do not think I have ever encountered a man less suited to life in a habit.'

'Many clever men take holy orders because it is the only way they can be among books. But he is a *good* man, sir – generous to the poor, and endlessly patient with the sick.' Valence grinned. 'He does love to laugh, though. His Prior-General ordered him to Cambridge in the hope that an abundance of erudite conversation would quell his penchant for mischief, but . . .'

'But his Prior-General miscalculated.' Bartholomew smiled back. 'Some of his tricks have been very ingenious, though – such as his picture of stairs that always go up and never down, and the tiny ship inside the glass phial. That is why I assumed it was he who lit up St Mary the Great.'

'Kendale is ingenious, too – Welfry's equal in intellect, although it galls me to say so, because he is a vile brute who hates the Colleges. But why are you interested in the church incident, sir? Do you plan a similar trick yourself?'

Bartholomew laughed at the notion. 'No! I struggled to inspect a swollen throat with a flickering lamp today. If the brilliance of Kendale's illumination could be harnessed, it might be possible to devise a lantern with a steady gleam – and that would make our work much easier.'

Valence considered. 'I suppose it would. Of course, Kendale's real aim was to set Gonville Hall alight – sparks went very close to their roof, and everyone knows he waited until the wind was blowing in their direction before he ignited his display. Has Brother Michael guessed the culprit?'

'Not yet.'

Valence sniffed. 'Welfry and I inspected the church afterwards. He thinks Kendale put buckets of black sludge at strategic points, linked by burning twine, so they would all go up at more or less the same time. The sludge contained brimstone, which is why it burned so bright.'

'What else was in it?'

'Welfry said it was probably charcoal and some kind of oil. He asked Kendale for the formula, but the miserable bastard refused to tell him. The Colleges answered Kendale's challenge well, though, do you not think? Our trick showed we are just as clever as the hostels.'

'You put the ox and cart on the Gilbertines' roof. But I thought Welfry was behind that – and he is not a member of a College, so should not be attempting to best hostels.'

Valence raised his eyebrows in surprise. 'Have you not heard? The Dominicans and Carmelites are on the Colleges' side, because we are all permanent foundations with endowments. The Gilbertines decided to back the hostels, on the grounds that they are poor and they feel sorry for them.'

'I see,' said Bartholomew. 'Do the convents' priors know about this affiliation, or is it something that has been decided by novices?'

Valence smirked and declined to answer. 'It is only a bit of fun, sir. Cambridge has been dull since the University and the town have buried the hatchet. Moreover, most of the criminals have been ousted by Emma de Colvyll, so nothing ever happens now. The rivalry between the Colleges and the hostels will keep us amused until we have a real spat to occupy us.'

Bartholomew regarded him askance, amazed he should admit to holding such an attitude.

'Unfortunately, Kendale is trying to turn our harmless competition into something nasty,' Valence continued. 'He encourages hostel men to yell abuse at College members in the street, and relations between us grow more strained every day.'

Bartholomew was worried. 'Will the Colleges respond to Kendale's trick involving the crated bull?'

'Of course,' replied Valence. 'But it will not be with anything violent, careless or stupid. *We* are not savages.'

CHAPTER 3

When Bartholomew arrived at St Michael's Church, his colleagues were in the chancel, discussing last-minute details for the Purification ceremony. As he walked up the nave to join them he saw a large number of people he knew, which included some he would not have expected to have been there. Among the latter were Emma and her family. Heslarton had brought a chair for her, and was fussing around it with cushions. Odelina and her mother stood to one side, and Bartholomew was surprised to see Celia with them, looking bright and inappropriately cheerful.

'I find consolation in religion, Doctor,' she whispered, when her eyes happened to meet his. Her expression was brazenly insincere. 'As do many recent widows.'

Bartholomew inclined his head, although it had been on the tip of his tongue to retort that most had the grace to wait until after the funeral before going out with friends. As he resumed his walk, his heart sank when he realised many of the congregation were members of the Michaelhouse Choir. And they all exuded an aura of tense anticipation, which strongly indicated they were planning to make what they liked to call music.

The choir was a large body of men – and some women – who had joined because they wanted the free bread and ale that was provided after practices. What they lacked in talent, they made up for in volume, and they prided themselves on being one of the loudest phenomena in the shire, audible over a distance of two miles, if the wind was blowing in the wrong direction.

'They are not going to sing, are they?' Bartholomew asked, glancing behind him at the assembled mass.

'Yes,' replied Michael stiffly. He was protective of his ensemble, although as a talented musician himself, he was fully aware of its limitations. 'They are a choir, and singing is what choirs do.'

'They are a rabble,' countered Thelnetham. 'Here only for the free food.'

Bartholomew spoke before Michael could reply to the charge. 'There seem to be more of them than usual. Do we have enough to feed them all?'

'I will manage,' said Michael. 'Especially if you donate the three pennies you earned from inspecting Drax.'

'But I need that for medicine,' objected Bartholomew in dismay.

'Food is more important than remedies,' said Michael soberly. 'Did you hear that the price of grain has risen again? A loaf of bread now costs more than a labourer can earn in a day.'

It was a dismal state of affairs, and Bartholomew wondered how many more of the poor would starve before winter relinquished its icy hold.

'Celia Drax is here,' remarked Thelnetham, surveying the congregation critically. 'It did not take *her* long to recover from the news that her husband was murdered.'

'No,' agreed Bartholomew. 'But she said she finds consolation in religion.'

Michael snorted his disbelief. 'Yffi is here, too. Incidentally, I still think he is involved in what happened to Drax. I will interview him again tomorrow, and have the truth. I would have done it today, but the wretched man did not appear for work this morning.'

'But he has taken all the tiles off the roof!' exclaimed Thelnetham, horrified. 'If it rains, we shall have water cascading—'

'Believe me, I know,' interrupted Michael. 'My ceiling currently comprises a sheet nailed to the rafters. I almost froze to death last night. But we shall discuss this later – the rite is starting.'

Michaelhouse was good at ceremonies, because so many of its Fellows were in religious Orders. Thelnetham presided, ably assisted by Clippesby and Suttone, all attired in their best habits. Father William, in his grubby robes, was relegated to the role of crucifer, while Michael was in charge of music. Bartholomew, Langelee and Ayera were only obliged to stand in the chancel in their scarlet gowns, and watch.

Thelnetham began by blessing a large number of beeswax candles, which, Bartholomew recalled, had been donated by Drax. Then, after sprinkling them with incense, he lit them, and the choir swung into action. Bartholomew knew it was the Nunc Dimittis, because that was always chanted at this point, although it was unrecognisable as such. He exchanged an amused grin with Ayera, then struggled for a suitably reverent expression when Michael glanced in his direction.

It was difficult to remain sombre, though, when Emma and her household were open-mouthed in astonishment at the cacophony – with the exception of Heslarton, who was nodding in time to the rhythm, such as it was. As the volume grew, despite Michael's frantic arm-waving to indicate this was not what he wanted, their incredulity intensified, and Bartholomew was aware that both Langelee and Ayera were shaking with laughter next to him.

Thelnetham processed slowly down the aisle when the choir began to wail the antiphon *Adorna thalamum tuum*

Sion, followed by every Michaelhouse scholar, each carrying one of the candles. Deynman opened the door, and the procession moved into the cemetery, the scholars shielding the lights with their hands to prevent them from blowing out. The daylight was fading as the short winter afternoon drew to a close, so the candles were bright in the gloom. Similar services were being held in every other church in the town, and the beautifully harmonic voices of St Mary the Great were carried on the wind, melodic and mystical in the dying day.

Unfortunately, the Michaelhouse Choir heard them, and this was not to be borne. There were some glares of indignation, and Isnard raised his arm to indicate the matter was to be rectified. Michael tried to stop them, but to no avail: a challenge had been perceived, and it was going to be answered. The tenors launched into the Nunc Dimittis again, but the basses preferred an Ave Maria, while the higher parts flitted from piece to piece as and when the fancy took them.

Isnard's conducting grew more urgent, and the volume rose further still. The racket brought the High Street to a standstill, as carts careened into each other. Several dogs started to howl, although they could not be heard over the din, and neither could the whinnies of frightened horses.

Thelnetham stepped up the pace of the ceremony, eager to be back inside so the clamour could be brought to an end. The Fellows hurried to keep up with him, while the students at the very end of the line were obliged to break into a run. Several were helpless with laughter, and by the time Thelnetham had circumnavigated the churchyard and was heading back up the aisle, his procession was in shambles.

He blessed the image of the Holy Child that Suttone was holding, then read the canticle *Benedictus Dominus Deus*

Israel before the choir could sing that, too. But there was one more musical interlude to be performed, and scholars and congregation alike were relieved when Michael shot his singers a glance that told them they had better not join in, and chanted the *Inviolata* himself.

Bartholomew closed his eyes as the monk's rich baritone filled the church, enjoying the way it echoed around the stones. When the last notes had faded away and he opened his eyes again, it was to find the church filled with flickering gold light. Then it was plunged into darkness as the scholars blew out their candles. The ritual of Purification was over.

'I have heard worse,' said Bartholomew consolingly, as he walked home next to Michael. The High Street was still in chaos, with two broken wagons and a man wailing over the fact that his sheep had been frightened into a stampede. 'They were not as bad today as they were at Christmas.'

'They were louder, though,' said Michael. He grinned, a little wickedly. 'How many other foundations do you think we managed to disrupt this time? At Christmas, we received complaints from five, but I think we may have surpassed ourselves this afternoon.'

'It would not surprise me to learn that they disrupted the Pope in Avignon. Can you not tell them that producing that sort of din is bad for the ears? It hurt mine, and I was some distance away. I cannot imagine what it must be like to be among them.'

Michael's expression was pained. 'I do tell them, but my advice is forgotten once they are in public. You should have heard them practise the Ave Maria last week. It was beautiful – moving.'

Bartholomew seriously doubted it, but said nothing. He could hear the sounds of merriment behind him, as the singers, delighted with the impact they had made, shared the bread and ale Michael had provided. He was glad they would have at least one good meal that day, and began to look forward to the feast, aware that it was some time since he had eaten well, too.

But he was to be disappointed, because when he arrived at Michaelhouse, Cynric was waiting with a message. The singing had aggravated Emma's toothache, and she wanted him to visit immediately, to see what might be done about it.

'You will have to go,' said Langelee, overhearing. 'I appreciate that your inclination will be to ignore the summons and enjoy the feast, but you must put duty first.'

'I never ignore summonses from patients,' objected Bartholomew indignantly. 'Even when I know that patient will continue to be unwell until she agrees to have her tooth removed.'

'Well, do what you can for her,' instructed Langelee. 'I know you disapprove of me accepting her charity, but I did what had to be done, and you must make the best of it.' He turned to Michael. 'Have you found out who killed Drax yet? He was a benefactor, too, and I do not want it said that helping Michaelhouse is dangerous.'

'Not yet,' replied Michael. 'But tomorrow I shall learn from Yffi whether he created a diversion so the body could be dumped here – and if he did, I shall have the name of the killer.'

'And if he did not?' asked Langelee.

'Then I shall have another word with Celia. I sense there is a lot more to be gleaned from her.'

Despite his words to Langelee, Bartholomew *was* sorry to be leaving Michaelhouse, and resentful, too – summonses from patients meant he had missed breakfast and the noonday meal, and it was not every day his College had decent food. He hoped Michael would save him some.

'I am in agony,' Emma announced without preamble, when a chubby-faced maid had escorted him to her solar. In the dim light, her black eyes glittered unnervingly, and she looked more like a bloated, malevolent spider than ever. 'Your choir's so-called music seared right through me.'

'Me, too,' agreed Bartholomew, taking a lamp so he could inspect the inflamed mouth. The flame flickered, and once again he wished he had a source of light that did not dance about.

'Give me more of that sense-dulling potion,' she ordered. 'It makes my wits hazy, but that is a small price to pay for relief. If I keep taking it, my tooth will eventually heal itself.'

'It will not,' countered Bartholomew. 'It will ache until it is drawn.'

'You are *not* pulling it out,' Emma snapped. 'And if you do not cure me by other means, I shall withdraw my bene-faction to your College.'

'That is your prerogative.' Bartholomew wished she would, so Michaelhouse would be rid of Yffi and his shoddy work, *and* a debt owed to a woman whom everyone thought was sinister.

She glared at him, then relented. 'You must forgive me – it is pain speaking.'

Bartholomew rubbed an ointment of cloves on the inflamed area, then prescribed a tonic of poppy juice and other soothing herbs, although it was a temporary solu-tion at best.

'You should see another physician,' he said when he had finished. 'You refuse to accept my advice, so consult them – see whether they can devise a more acceptable alterna-tive.'

He knew there was none – at least, none that was sensible – but he was tired of arguing with her.

'Very well.' He glanced at her in surprise: she had always refused when he had suggested it before. She shrugged. 'I cannot stand the pain any longer, so we shall send for Rougham, Gyseburne and Meryfeld. We shall summon them now, in fact.'

'You do not need all three,' said Bartholomew, while thinking uncharitably that she did not need Meryfeld at all. The man was little more than a folk healer, who was likely to do more harm than good. 'Either Rougham or Gyseburne will be—'

'You will wait here until they arrive,' Emma went on, cutting across him. 'They may need details of my condition, which you will provide, thus relieving me of tedious probing. If you refuse, I shall tell your Master that you have failed to live up to your end of the bargain. I doubt you want to be responsible for losing your College my goodwill.'

She snapped her fingers, and the maid scampered away to do her bidding. With a sigh, Bartholomew went to sit near the fire, heartily wishing he could tell her what to do with her benefaction. He was chilled to the bone, partly from being hungry, but also because it was a bitterly cold night. He settled himself down to wait, trying to ignore his growling stomach.

It was not long before the door opened, and Heslarton marched in. His fine clothes were mud splattered, and there were even dirty splashes on his bald pate, indicating he had done some hard riding that day. He was armed to the teeth – a heavy broadsword at his waist, a long dagger in his belt, and a bow over his shoulder.

'Well, Bartholomew?' Heslarton demanded, going to rest a sympathetic hand on his mother-in-law's shoulder. 'Have you cured her? I do not like to see her in such discomfort.'

Bartholomew stood quickly, seized with the alarming notion that if he admitted failure, Heslarton might run him through. They were a strange pair – the bullying, irascible old woman and the loutish, soldierly man – and, not for the first time, Bartholomew wondered what made them so obviously fond of each other.

'We are waiting for second opinions,' explained Emma. 'Although the Doctor has given me medicine to ease my pain. That horrible choir should be deemed a hazard to health!'

'I rather enjoyed their performance,' said Heslarton, going to stretch his hands towards the fire. 'I cannot be doing with silly, warbling melodies, and that was music for *real* men.'

'I will tell Michael,' said Bartholomew. It was not often the choir earned compliments.

'Thomas has been hunting the yellow-headed thief again,' said Emma. Her unfriendly expression told Bartholomew that this would not have been necessary had he done his duty the previous day.

'But I did not catch him,' said Heslarton. 'Yesterday, we tracked him to Chesterton before he slid into the Fens. However, it seems he immediately slunk back and committed a second crime.'

'You mean the theft from the Carmelite Priory?' asked Bartholomew. 'The pilgrims said they were victims of a man with golden hair, but Brother Michael thinks it is a different culprit.'

'Then Brother Michael is wrong,' said Heslarton. 'I spoke to the pilgrims, too: their villain wore a green tunic with gold embroidery, which matched the one ours sported. So it *is* the same fellow. He was bold, coming back when he knew a hue and cry had been raised for him.'

Emma's expression hardened into something dark and

unpleasant, revealing the ruthlessness that had allowed her to grow rich by capitalising on the misfortunes of others. 'We will have him,' was all she said, but the remark made Bartholomew's blood run cold, and again he pitied the thief.

'We will,' agreed Heslarton. 'I shall retrieve your box, Mother, never fear.'

She inclined her head, and her expression softened. 'Thank you, Thomas. But do not forget that I want *him*, too. No one steals from me and lives to tell the tale. Metaphorically speaking, of course.'

Heslarton laughed. 'I will continue to scour the marshes. Of course, we all know how easy it is for folk to disappear in them.'

They exchanged a look that gave Bartholomew the distinct impression that more was meant than folk lying low. Or perhaps it was his imagination – the room was poorly lit, and he was cold and tired. Fortunately, there was a knock on the door at that point, and he was saved from further fevered imaginings by the arrival of his fellow physicians.

When the plague had arrived in Cambridge, almost a decade before, it had left the town bereft of trained healers. In the years that followed, the survivors had died, retired or moved away, until only Bartholomew and Rougham remained to serve the entire town. Alarmed that his Fellow was beginning to spend more time on medicine than on teaching, Langelee had written to his former employer, asking whether he had any spare *medici*. Obligingly, the Archbishop had supplied Gyseburne and Meryfeld, both of whom had set up shop in their new home within a month.

Their arrival was a mixed blessing. On the one hand,

they shouldered some of the burden, but on the other, they preferred patients who could pay, so that while they relieved Bartholomew of his wealthy clients, they had left him the bulk of the poor. The outcome was a shorter list of customers, but a radically reduced income. Bartholomew did not care about the money for himself, but there was no point practising medicine if his patients did not receive the potions required to make them better, and he found he could no longer afford to buy all that was needed.

He watched his colleagues being shown into Emma's solar. Meryfeld was short, plump and energetic, and was always rubbing his hands together, like a fly that had landed on meat. He smiled a lot, and his amiable charm meant he was already popular. By contrast, Gyseburne never smiled at all. He had long, grey hair, a narrow face, and Bartholomew had never seen him without a urine flask – Gyseburne was of the opinion that much could be learned from urine, and tended to demand samples regardless of the ailment he was treating.

'Where is Rougham?' demanded Emma, as the door closed behind them. 'Is he not coming?'

'He is at the Carmelite Friary,' explained Meryfeld. 'Two pilgrim nuns are tipsy, and Rougham anticipates that it will take several hours to make them sober again. He begs to be excused.'

Bartholomew strongly suspected that the nuns were an excuse, and that Rougham just had more sense than to become embroiled with Emma de Colvyll.

'We can manage without him,' said Heslarton. 'Besides, I am uncomfortable with too many men of learning about. Your Latin is a foreign language to me.'

Gyseburne raised his eyebrows. 'It is a foreign language to most people,' he drawled laconically. 'Literally. But we shall use the vernacular, if you prefer.'

'English would be better,' said Heslarton. 'But enough chatter. My mother needs your services.'

'What seems to be the trouble?' asked Meryfeld. He rubbed his hands together and beamed.

'I have toothache,' declared Emma. 'And I want a cure. You can examine me first.'

Meryfeld stepped forward obligingly. Gyseburne seemed to be waiting for Bartholomew to start a conversation in the interim, so the physician said what was on his mind.

'Did you hear about the prank where St Mary the Great was illuminated like a great candle? Well, it occurred to me that the substance used might be adapted to produce a bright and steady lamp – which would be hugely helpful for night consultations.'

Gyseburne's expression was unreadable. 'Well, yes, it would, although I imagine *you* were thinking it would aid nocturnal *surgery*. Such activities are demeaning for physicians, and you should not debase yourself, or our profession, by employing them.'

Bartholomew supposed he should not have expected anything else from a traditional man like Gyseburne. 'Actually, it was the difficulty of seeing inside mouths that prompted the idea.'

'Is that so?' said Gyseburne flatly, fixing Bartholomew with a hard, searching look. 'When a real surgeon arrives – and the Archbishop of York is trying to recruit one as I speak – will you give up these undignified activities and let him deal with the gore?'

Bartholomew glanced at Gyseburne's urine flask and wondered why one bodily fluid should be considered distasteful, while another was seen as holding all the answers. It defied all logic. Fortunately, he was spared from having to answer, because Meryfeld had finished, and it was Gyseburne's turn to examine Emma.

89

Predictably, Gyseburne requested a sample, and then stood for a long time, swirling it about in a flask, his grim face more sombre than ever. Bartholomew was not sure whether he was stumped for answers, or whether he really was able to interpret the stuff better than anyone else. Eventually, he turned and regarded Bartholomew with his dark, unfathomable eyes.

'On reflection, a bright, unwavering lamp *would* be useful, so perhaps we should conduct a few experiments. I can provide some brimstone – one of my patients is a dyer, so has plenty of it.'

Meryfeld beamed at them. 'You intend to invent a decent lamp? Splendid! May I join you?'

'You promised to speak English,' objected Heslarton, looking irritably from one to the other. 'But you are gabbling away in Latin.'

'Actually, that was French,' countered Gyseburne haughtily. 'The language of choice for those of us who have anything worth saying.'

'I do not care,' declared Emma irritably, while Heslarton frowned, trying to work out whether he had been insulted. 'Tell me your verdicts. In plain speech. You first, Meryfeld.'

'You have an excess of choler,' replied Meryfeld without hesitation. 'Which is hot and dry. To remedy this, I recommend we increase your phlegm, which is cold and wet. We shall achieve this by using herbs of Mars, such as mint and pears, which are cold in the fourth degree.'

Bartholomew regarded him uncertainly. Mint and pears were governed by Venus, and were not cold at all. Moreover, they were unlikely to have any impact on a toothache.

'Gyseburne?' asked Emma. 'What is your opinion?'

'You have a rotten tooth, madam,' replied Gyseburne. 'And the pus in your urine means poison is already seeping into your body. I recommend you have the fang removed immediately, before you fall into a deadly fever from which you will not recover.'

'I like his diagnosis best,' said Emma, pointing at Meryfeld. 'So he is hired. Bartholomew and Gyseburne are dismissed. He will make me this potion tonight, and thus begin my treatment. I shall expect to be cured by morning.'

Meryfeld blanched as it occurred to him that winning Emma as a client was not necessarily a good thing, while Bartholomew was not sure whether to be relieved that the burden of dealing with her was no longer his, or worried that she was embarking on a course of treatment that would fail.

'My medicine will not work that quickly,' gulped Meryfeld, alarmed. 'You must be patient, because it might be weeks before you notice a difference.'

'But by then you might be dead,' said Gyseburne, emptying his flask on the fire and heading for the door. 'Remove the offending tooth, madam. It is the only thing that will save your life.'

'Nonsense,' objected Meryfeld, stung. 'Hot, dry pains in the head mean that—'

He was interrupted by a howl from upstairs. It was immediately followed by thundering footsteps and a lot of shouting. Words were muffled by the thick walls, but Bartholomew understood it was something to do with Emma's portly, sharp-tongued daughter. Then the chubby-faced maid burst in.

'Alice has been murdered!' she cried. 'She is dying as I speak!'

Emma betrayed no emotion at the announcement, although the blood drained from Heslarton's face. Meryfeld, as newly appointed Household Physician, darted towards the stairs to do his duty, Heslarton hot on his heels.

Before she followed, Emma indicated that Bartholomew and Gyseburne were to go, too. Gyseburne nodded acquiescence, clearly pleased to have the chance to salve his curiosity. Bartholomew went only when Emma shot him the kind of glance that said there would be trouble if he did not.

There were several chambers on the uppermost floor, and Alice occupied the largest. She was lying on the floor, a ring of servants standing mute and shocked around her. Heslarton released a strangled cry, and rushed to her side. When Meryfeld began to ask about her birth and stars, apparently intending to deliver a diagnosis based on a horoscope, Bartholomew stepped forward and rested his hand on the pulse in her neck. It was weak and slow, and when he prised open her eyes, her pupils were unnaturally large. She was shuddering violently.

'Poison,' whispered Gyseburne in his ear, crouching next to him. 'I have seen this before.'

'In Cambridge?' asked Bartholomew uneasily.

Gyseburne shook his head. 'York. In Master Langelee's house, when he worked for the Archbishop. It was a curious case, and I never could decide whether he had fed his guests something toxic, or whether the potion was intended for him, and he had had a narrow escape.'

Bartholomew regarded him in horror. 'What are you—'

'Not now,' interrupted Gyseburne. 'Should we make Alice vomit, do you think? Or walk with her, to dissolve it in her blood? Or shall we cover her with blankets, and sweat it from her body?'

'It is too late,' said Bartholomew, feeling the pulse flutter into nothing. 'She is gone.'

'No!' declared Emma, more angry than distressed when she heard his words. 'She cannot be dead! I will not allow it!'

Meryfeld helped her to sit on the bed, and gestured for the chubby maid to bring her wine.

'What happened?' asked Heslarton in a taut, strained voice.

'Alice was sitting in here with Odelina,' replied the maid. 'She was trying to sew, but the light was poor, and she kept complaining that she could not see. I was stoking up the fire.'

'Was she eating or drinking anything?' asked Bartholomew urgently, putting out his hand to prevent Emma from sipping the brew Meryfeld had just poured her.

'Wine,' replied the maid. She pointed to the goblet Emma held. 'That wine.'

Gyseburne took it and poured it into his urine flask. 'It is as I thought,' he said, holding it up to the light, then sniffing it carefully. 'It stinks of wolfsbane – a very deadly poison.'

'Where is Odelina?' asked Bartholomew. 'Was she drinking this wine, too?'

'Odelina!' cried Heslarton, looking around in concern. 'My poor child! Where is she? Find her! Search the house!'

The servants raced to do his bidding, while Heslarton paced in tiny circles, as if he did not know what else to do. Emma stretched a hand towards him, for comfort, but he ignored it. Gyseburne leaned closer to Bartholomew.

'Perhaps Odelina fed the wolfsbane to her dam,' he suggested. 'And then fled. I have heard they were not good friends – not like she is with her father.'

There were two half-full goblets on the table, along with a jug of milk. Bartholomew could not detect the odour of wolfsbane in any of them, but Gyseburne said it was in the wine, and there was no reason to disbelieve him. Clearly, Odelina had imbibed the poison, too.

93

'I did not see her leave the room,' said the maid, frightened. 'She was here when her mother . . .'

There was only one place the missing woman could be. Bartholomew dropped to his hands and knees, and looked under the bed. Odelina was curled into a ball, beginning the strange shuddering movements that had killed her mother. He grabbed her arm and dragged her out. She was still conscious, although terrified and unable to speak. Distraught, Heslarton flung himself on her, and it took both Bartholomew and Gyseburne working together to prise him off.

Meryfeld stepped forward to hold him while they tended the stricken woman, and Bartholomew thought he would be unequal to the task, but the little physician deftly secured him in the kind of headlock employed by wrestlers. Heslarton wept and howled until his energy was spent, then dissolved into quiet sobs. Emma, meanwhile, regarded her stricken granddaughter with horror.

Hoping Gyseburne's identification of the poison was correct, Bartholomew grabbed a cup and a bowl of water, and forced Odelina to drink. She groaned and tried to push him away, but he persisted until it was all gone. Then he put his fingers in her mouth until she retched. When she was done, he repeated the process, ignoring Emma's clamouring objections at his roughness.

Gyseburne understood what he was trying to do, though. He added oil to the next cup of water, along with a few drops of something Bartholomew assumed was an emetic.

'Foxglove,' said Bartholomew urgently, when he pressed his ear to Odelina's chest and heard her heart pumping sluggishly. 'There is some in my bag.'

He administered the dose Gyseburne handed him, and was gratified to detect a more normal rhythm a few

94

moments later. Odelina began to shiver, so he wrapped her in a blanket.

'Please,' she whispered. 'I am thirsty.'

'Oh, thank God!' breathed Emma. 'It is a good sign, is it not? For her to speak coherently?'

Bartholomew nodded. 'A very good sign.'

While the maid went to fetch fresh water from the kitchen, Odelina indicated that she wanted to sit up. When she reeled, Meryfeld released Heslarton, who dashed to support her. Odelina clung to him tearfully. He tried to lift her into the bed, but the task was beyond him, so he was obliged to enlist Bartholomew's help. Once she was settled, sipping water brought from the kitchen, Bartholomew began to relax, knowing she was going to recover.

'When my mother and I were first struck down, I tried to call for help,' Odelina whispered, as Heslarton fussed about her with blankets. 'But I could not speak. I crawled under the bed because I was frightened. I heard her . . . Is she . . .'

'She is dead, child,' said Emma, patting her shoulder comfortingly. 'Even with three physicians in the house, she was beyond saving. Fortunately, they had better luck with you.'

Heslarton sat next to his daughter, holding her hand in a grip that looked tight enough to be painful, and it was left to Emma to arrange the removal of his wife's corpse from the room.

'Your quick thinking saved Odelina,' said Gyseburne in Bartholomew's ear. 'She would be dead, if you had not thought to look under the bed.'

'But it was you who identified the poison,' Bartholomew pointed out. 'I would not have made her vomit without your diagnosis.'

Gyseburne gave what was almost a smile. 'Then we make a fine team, you and I. Perhaps we should work together more often.'

Bartholomew smiled back, thinking it would be pleasant to have a colleague with whom to confer sometimes. He had avoided doing so thus far, lest it led to more accusations of heterodoxy.

'She will live?' asked Heslarton unsteadily. 'All that roughness paid off ? She will be well now?'

'We believe so,' replied Gyseburne. 'Although someone should stay with her tonight.'

'I will,' offered Meryfeld immediately. 'A physician is better than a layman. And I am the Colvyll family's *medicus* now.'

Bartholomew was only too happy to pass the responsibility to Meryfeld, sure the worst was over anyway. He turned to leave, but Odelina caught his sleeve.

'Thank you,' she whispered hoarsely. 'I shall always be grateful.'

'And so will I,' said Emma, addressing all three physicians. 'I am sorry for Alice, but I shall not hold it against you. Clearly, you were called too late.'

'We had better throw away all the wine in the house, to ensure no more of this poison lurks,' said Heslarton grimly. 'And then I shall find out who put it there.'

'It was that yellow-headed thief,' declared Emma. Her black eyes flashed with fury. 'I have been wondering why he did not make off with more of my valuables. It was because he was busy tampering with our wine, and my box was all he had time to grab before he was obliged to flee.'

'Theft and murder are two very different—' began Bartholomew uncertainly.

'It was him,' declared Emma firmly. 'Other than you, he

is the only person – outside family and staff – to have set foot in my house this month.'

'What about Celia Drax?' asked Meryfeld, somewhat out of the blue. 'She visits you a lot.'

Heslarton regarded him in surprise. 'Celia is our friend, and I doubt she knows about poisons!'

'Of course she does not,' agreed Emma. 'The culprit is that thief, and I shall not rest until he is caught. Thomas will resume the hunt as soon as Odelina no longer needs him. However, given the seriousness of the crime, we should tell Brother Michael and the Sheriff to look for the murdering scoundrel, too.'

Bartholomew offered to inform them, then took his leave, Gyseburne trailing at his heels.

'Meryfeld is mad,' said Gyseburne. 'Wild horses would not encourage *me* to physic a family like that – something will go wrong, and they will kill him for it.'

Bartholomew sincerely hoped he was wrong.

The next day dawned bright and clear. It was a glorious winter morning, where the sky was blue, the frost brittle and white on rooftops, and the sun a pale gold orb rising over the distant horizon. It was cold, though, and the wind that sliced in from the north-east was bitter. Bartholomew shivered all through mass in St Michael's Church, and then shivered as Langelee led his scholars home along St Michael's Lane. He said nothing as Michael fell into step beside him, lost in a reflection on whether he might not feel so chilled if he were not so hungry.

'I am sorry, Matt,' said Michael. 'I meant to save you some food, but by the time I remembered, it had all been eaten. There was not enough of it, you see, and we all came away half starved.'

'It does not matter,' said Bartholomew, although he

thought he might change his mind if there was nothing for breakfast.

'I can still scarcely credit what you told me last night. I know Emma and her family are unpopular, but poison is so indiscriminate – a servant might have sneaked a swig and died for it.'

'Yes, and I am glad it is the Sheriff's responsibility to investigate Alice's death, not yours.'

'On the contrary,' said Michael. 'Emma claims the yellow-headed thief tainted her wine, and Heslarton's enquiries have shown that the same yellow-headed thief stole Poynton's pilgrim badge. As I am under obligation to solve the theft, it means I am hunting Alice's killer, too.'

'I thought you were dead set against the notion that they are the same man.'

'I was, but only because petty thieves tend to be cowards. I thought the one you chased would be lurking in the Fens, thanking God for his lucky escape. But now I learn he is a murderer, it puts a different complexion on matters. Poisoners are ruthless and bold, so such a fellow may well have committed one crime, then promptly returned to the town to snatch Poynton's *signaculum*.'

'Drax was missing a *signaculum*, too,' Bartholomew reminded him. 'The one he wore in his hat.'

Michael rubbed his chin. 'Then our killer had a busy day. He burgled Emma's house and left wolfsbane, was chased by you to the Griffin Inn, slipped back into the town to stab Drax and steal his token, then rushed to the Carmelite Friary for Poynton's badge, and finally returned to Michaelhouse to arrange for Drax's body to be left behind Yffi's tiles.'

'Yes,' agreed Bartholomew. 'Although there was more time between these events than you are acknowledging. However, it does look as though all these crimes were committed by one culprit. Do not tell Emma you are looking into the matter, though. It will raise her expectations, and she does not handle disappointment very well.'

'No,' agreed Michael. 'She and Odelina both – they are too used to having their own way. I pity the man Odelina marries, because no matter how noble a fellow he is, the reality will fall short of her romantic ideals and she will grow to hate him. I am glad my habit puts *me* out of her reach.'

'You think she might have made a play for you, had you been available?' asked Bartholomew, amused as always by the monk's perception of himself as a svelte Adonis.

'Of course,' replied Michael, without the flicker of a smile. 'Women find me irresistible, as I have told you before, especially the ones with a penchant for romantic ballads. Like the heroes of their stories, I combine dashing good looks with integrity and courage.'

'I see,' said Bartholomew. Then some of Yffi's scaffolding gave an ominous creak, and he turned to more realistic matters. 'I wish Michaelhouse had not accepted charity from a woman who skates so close to the edge of the law. Moreover, I did not like Gyseburne's contention that Emma might dispatch Meryfeld if he does not cure her.'

'Meryfeld knows the risks in treating a woman with her reputation – he is not stupid. But if *I* am to meddle in her affairs, I shall need help. I know you are busy with teaching and patients, but . . .'

'I will do what I can,' promised Bartholomew. 'And I have been thinking about the yellow-headed thief, too. Emma's house is stuffed full of valuables, yet he chose to take a small box – one she claims contains sentimental keepsakes from her dead husband. But why would a thief target that? I suspect the contents of this chest are more significant than she is letting on.'

99

'Possibly,' acknowledged Michael. 'But a short while later, he stole a pilgrim badge, so maybe he is just an opportunist. Or perhaps his main objective was to leave the poison, and he snatched the box to lull her into thinking that his motive was theft, not something more sinister.'

Bartholomew supposed they would have to ask him when he was caught. He nodded to where the workmen were trooping in through Michaelhouse's front gate, Blaston in the lead, cheerful and eager as usual, and Yffi and his apprentices slouching unenthusiastically at his heels.

'You said yesterday that you thought Yffi had not been entirely honest with us about Drax. Should we interview him again now?'

'We should. And we can ask why he failed to appear for work yesterday, too.'

'Drax was cold when we found him,' mused Bartholomew. 'So I think we can safely say he was killed not long after dawn. *Ergo*, we need to know where our suspects were *then*, rather than later.'

'Yes and no, Matt. We have *two* crimes here: Drax murdered, and Drax brought to Michaelhouse. Drax may have died early, but I suspect he was dumped later – probably when Yffi was praising Yolande's talents. So *I* want to know where our suspects were on *both* occasions.'

Yffi reeked of ale. He was also unsteady on his feet and his eyes were glazed in a way that said he had spent the previous night in the tavern and was still not quite sober. Bartholomew did not like the notion of him clambering around on the roof. He had a family, and although the physician had no great liking for the fellow, he did not want a wife and children left destitute.

'Actually, we are going to lay off the roof for a while,'

said Yffi, when Bartholomew voiced his concerns. 'We plan to mend the ground-floor windows for the next few days.'

Michael's eyes narrowed. 'You mean you intend to leave the roof exposed to the elements?'

Yffi shrugged. 'It will not rain, and I feel like working on solid ground for a bit.'

'This is not a good idea,' argued Michael. 'It may be fine today, but weather can change. And I dislike that sheet billowing above my head when I am trying to sleep. What if it blows off?'

'Then one of my boys will nail it back on again.'

'He will come in the middle of the night, will he? Or am I expected to sleep under the stars until morning? Or, more likely, under scudding rain clouds?'

'That is not my problem. If you do not like the way I work, tell Emma de Colvyll.'

'Oh, I shall,' said Michael icily. 'But I am not here for a debate – I want information. Tell me what happened on Monday, when we found Drax.'

'Again?' groaned Yffi, rolling his eyes. His apprentices did the same, although Blaston was more respectful. 'How many more times must I tell you that we heard and saw nothing? If you do not believe me, then climb up the scaffolding yourself. The yard cannot be seen from the roof, so a whole army of killers could have shoved corpses behind stacks of tiles, and we would have been none the wiser.'

'It is true, Brother,' added Peterkin, seeing his master's insolence was doing nothing to help. 'I wish we *did* have some clues to share with you, but we do not.'

'What were you doing yesterday?' demanded Michael.

Yffi blinked. 'Yesterday? Why do you want to know that?'

'Because I am eager to learn why you failed to appear for work,' snapped Michael.

'We went to church for the Purification,' replied Yffi

101

with mock piety. 'And before that, we were working else-where. We have commissions other than in this place, you know.'

'Only because you fail to finish what you start,' muttered Blaston, regarding him with dislike.

Michael glared at Yffi, who took an involuntary step backwards. 'You will not disappear again until our roof is finished. Do I make myself clear? And you would do well not to annoy me, because you are in a very precarious position. A body was found among *your* supplies.'

Yffi scowled. 'It is hardly my fault that some villain decided to leave a corpse behind the tiles! If you want someone to blame, then pick on your idle porter.'

'Or Blaston,' said Peterkin slyly. '*He* was down here all alone. You have not accused him, because you have known him for years, but he is just as capable of wielding a knife as the next man.'

'I want to know where you were from dawn until the body was found,' said Michael, cutting across Blaston's indignant denials. 'All of you.'

Yffi sighed impatiently. 'We were on the roof – as your porter will confirm. One or two of my lads came down for supplies, but that only took moments, and I would have noticed prolonged absences. We all have alibis in each other.'

'I work alone,' said Blaston uncomfortably. 'But the only time I went out was to buy nails, as I told you. The smith will confirm that I left money under his anvil, though. That is an alibi.'

They began to argue, and were still sniping at each other when Michael decided there was no more to be learned from them and took his leave.

'I detected a furtiveness among the masons, Matt,' he said as he walked. 'I wonder why.'

'I have a feeling they were lounging on the roof, safe in the knowledge that they could not be seen,' replied Bartholomew. 'They do not want you to tell Emma that she is paying for them to sit about.'

'It is possible, although I have a feeling there is more to it than that. Unfortunately, our questions took us no further forward – we can neither eliminate Yffi and his lads as suspects, nor arrest them.'

'Well, we know none of them *killed* Drax, because they were here when we think he was stabbed. And Drax was not dispatched in Michaelhouse, because Cynric's search found no blood.'

'Blaston was not here during the salient time, though,' said Michael unhappily. 'He was out buying nails. Alone. Moreover, he admits to disliking the victim.'

'Yffi disliked Drax, too. Along with half the town. I will not entertain Blaston as a suspect, Brother. He cares too much for his family to risk being hanged. And he is not a killer, anyway.'

'You are probably right. But we had better not dismiss him from our enquiries until we can be absolutely certain. Do not look alarmed! Fen the pardoner is much higher on my list than Blaston, and we know *he* was nosing around here the morning of the crime.'

'Have you interviewed him yet?' asked Bartholomew. 'What did he say?'

'Nothing,' replied Michael grimly. 'Because he was out admiring churches with his two fat nuns when I called at the Carmelite Priory yesterday, and so was unavailable to me. But I shall snag him today, and see whether I can force a confession—'

He was interrupted by the arrival of Meadowman, his favourite beadle.

'You are needed at Peterhouse, Brother,' said

Meadowman apologetically. 'They are squabbling with Batayl Hostel, and it is beyond my diplomatic skills to bring about a truce. There is no violence, but some very rude words are being exchanged.'

'Then I suppose Fen will have to wait,' sighed Michael, aiming for the gate.

Bartholomew and Father William were the only Fellows present for breakfast in Michaelhouse that morning, and half the students were missing, too. It did not take them long to understand why. Agatha was running dangerously low on supplies, so the meal comprised a grey, watery pottage that had been bulked out with the addition of bean pods and something that looked suspiciously like sawdust.

'She must have got it from Blaston,' said William, poking it in distaste.

The Franciscan was not a fussy eater, and if he found fault with what was on offer, Bartholomew knew the situation was serious. Suddenly, William surged to his feet and announced to the world at large that there would be no grace that day, because not even beggars could be expected to be grateful for such slop. Then he grabbed Bartholomew's arm and steered him out of the hall, towards his own room. Bartholomew resisted, knowing from past experience that sessions in William's quarters tended to mean being berated for something he had done that the friar deemed heretical.

'Come,' said William impatiently. 'My students will be back soon and I have no intention of sharing with them. But you are a colleague. And besides, you look hungry.'

Bartholomew was both pleased and surprised when the Franciscan presented him with a large piece of bread, several slices of cold meat and a pot of cheese.

'I slipped it up my sleeve during the feast,' explained

William gleefully. Bartholomew was not keen on the notion of eating something that had spent time inside the Franciscan's revolting habit, but was hungry enough to overlook the matter. 'I had a feeling Agatha would make up for yesterday's luxury with a few days of thrift, so I decided to take precautious.'

'Thank you,' said Bartholomew, when he had eaten enough to make himself feel queasy. 'It is good of you to share. I know you do not like doing it.'

'No, I do not,' agreed William blithely. 'But you missed the feast, so it is only fair.'

Uncomfortably overloaded, Bartholomew went in search of Michael, but was told by Langelee that the monk was still trying to quell the spat between a rich College and a particularly poor hostel.

'I have a bad feeling this rivalry will erupt into something dark and violent before it burns itself out,' said the Master. 'Incidentally, we had a message to say you are needed by the Carmelites.'

Bartholomew told Valence to read Theophilus's *De urinis* to his other students, thinking Gyseburne would approve of time spent on urine. Then he walked to the White Friars' convent, where Horneby said he was feeling better but was worried that continued hoarseness would affect his delivery at the Stock Extraordinary Lecture. Prior Etone was hovering anxiously on one side of the bed, while Welfry was on the other. Bartholomew raised his eyebrows at a Dominican among the Carmelites – the Orders tended not to fraternise.

'Horneby and I are old friends,' explained Welfry, when he saw Bartholomew's surprise. 'I have been helping him prepare his lecture.'

'Welfry has a brilliant mind,' said Etone begrudgingly. 'If he were to use it sensibly, he could be Horneby's equal in the debating chamber. But he prefers practical jokes to theology, and—'

'Enough, Father!' cried Welfry. His eyes danced with wry amusement – it was hardly Etone's place to reprimand him. 'You are worse than my Prior-General!'

'Well, perhaps being Seneschal will make you more sombre,' said Etone. 'And bear in mind that if Horneby's sickness persists, *you* will be the one I nominate to read his lecture.'

'Me?' asked Welfry, suddenly alarmed. 'But I am not a Carmelite.'

'No, but you are Horneby's closest friend, and the man most familiar with his theses,' said Etone. 'Unfortunately, I do not think the rest of us are up to the task. You are though.'

'Lord!' breathed Welfry. He looked at Horneby, wide-eyed. 'You had better get well as soon as possible, then, because I am disinclined to accept this "honour".'

'When is the lecture?' asked Bartholomew, struggling to inspect Horneby's throat with the Carmelites' best lamp.

Prior Etone regarded him reproachfully. 'Next Tuesday. How can you even ask such a question, when it has been the talk of the town for weeks?'

'I have been busy,' said Bartholomew defensively, supposing it was not the time to say he would not be going. Living among so many clerics meant he was bored with theology.

'That is no excuse, Matthew,' said Etone severely. 'You cannot be—'

'Will you admonish *everyone* who crosses your path today, Father?' croaked Horneby, while Welfry started to laugh. 'Leave poor Bartholomew alone, or he may decline to come the next time we call him, and where would that leave us? Meryfeld is little more than a folk healer, while there is something about Gyseburne that I do not like at all.'

'I know what you mean,' agreed Etone. 'He is distinctly sinister. And damned furtive, too.'

'True,' added Welfry. 'I asked where he lived while he studied at Oxford – I was at Balliol, you see – but he refused to say. He would not even submit to a pleasant chat about the taverns we both might have frequented. I confess, I was mystified. But perhaps all physicians are curious creatures.' He winked at Bartholomew, to show he was teasing.

But Etone took him at his word. 'They are, and Matthew is a "curious creature", too, I am afraid to say. He skates very close to the edge of unorthodoxy.'

'He does what is necessary to help his patients,' countered Horneby. 'Patients like me. So please leave him be, and let him do what he came here for.'

Bartholomew applied a poultice to Horneby's neck, feeling that the best cure was rest and time. The inflammation was receding nicely, although he had no idea whether Horneby would be completely well by the time he was scheduled to speak. They would just have to wait and see.

Welfry went with Bartholomew when he left, and they walked across the yard together. They were momentarily distracted from their discussion of Horneby's lecture when one of the pilgrim nuns loudly announced that the shrine was dirty, and needed sweeping.

'Then I will take the holy scapular to the chapel,' said Fen. 'We do not want dust settling on it.'

He disappeared inside, and emerged moments later with the reliquary under his arm. Poynton bustled forward to help, although Fen was perfectly able to carry it by himself.

'St Simon Stock may be grateful enough to confer a few blessings on you,' Poynton declared by way of explanation. 'And I am not a man to miss out on blessings.'

The nuns heard the remark, and promptly descended on the box, too, jostling as they vied for a handhold. Under such circumstances, it took some time to tote it the short distance to the chapel.

'Perhaps we should stand back,' chuckled Welfry. 'There are more likely to be thunderbolts than blessings over *that* display of piety. Have you ever been on a pilgrimage?'

Bartholomew hesitated. He had visited several sacred sites, including Rome and Santiago de Compostela, but only because he had happened to be passing. His real purpose has been to locate the woman he loved, who had left Cambridge before he could ask her to marry him. He had scoured the civilised world, but had found no trace of her. Michael had recently taken to assuring him that Matilde was safe and well, but it had been three years since she had left, and Bartholomew was finally beginning to accept that something terrible had happened to her.

'*You* have,' he said, deftly diverting the question by pointing at the discreet *signaculum* pinned to Welfry's habit. 'Although it is not a token I recognise. It looks like a shoe.'

'It is,' said Welfry with a smile. 'From the shrine of John Schorne in North Marston, who conjured the Devil into a boot. I visited it last year, and found it just as thronged with devout pilgrims as Canterbury, Walsingham or Hereford. I wear it to serve as a reminder.'

'A reminder of what?'

'Of the narrow gap between the sacred and the profane – the acceptable and the unacceptable. As you know, I love a practical joke. Well, this boot is to make me remember that my jests must always be amusing, but never irreverent or unkind. Like the physician Hippocrates, I aim to do no harm.'

Bartholomew started to ask him about the illumination of St Mary the Great, but Welfry embarked on a comical

108

account of the Carmelites' Purification feast, when the two nuns had made a drunken play for Fen. The pardoner had fled in alarm, leaving Poynton to offer himself as a substitute. Welfry was a clever raconteur, and Bartholomew was still smiling when they parted company and he knocked on the door of the Gilbertine Priory.

'There you are,' said Prior Leccheworth, an old man with a shock of jet-black hair. It looked incongruous with his wrinkled face, and Bartholomew often wondered whether he dyed it. 'One of my canons has hurt himself playing camp-ball, and there is blood. He says it is nothing, but . . .'

'Camp-ball?' echoed Bartholomew, startled. 'Is that a suitable pastime for ordained priests?'

'He is on our team,' explained Leccheworth, He saw the physician's blank look and sighed. 'For the annual match between us and the Carmelites the day after tomorrow. We usually select ruffians from the town to represent us, but Brother Jude is a talented player, and we thought he might help us win. We have recruited your Master, too, so we are in with a good chance this year.'

'I see,' said Bartholomew, although he was still amazed to learn that a canon should be taking part in such a wild event – and that his prior was willing to let him do so.

He followed Leccheworth across the yard and out on to the huge field at the back of the convent. Sitting on the grass was the largest Gilbertine he had ever seen.

'It is a trifle,' said Brother Jude, revealing an injury that would have made most men swoon. 'A scratch. Sew it up, and let me get back to the practice.'

Bartholomew sent for water to rinse the gash, then took needle and thread and began to insert stitches. He was astonished when the big man declared the pain insignificant, because he knew it was not. It was easy work, though, because Jude sat perfectly still, and there was none of the writhing and squirming he usually had to contend with.

'It should heal neatly,' he said eventually, sitting back and inspecting his handiwork.

'Damn!' muttered Jude, disappointed. 'I was hoping for an impressive battle wound. By the way, has Prior Leccheworth asked whether you will be Official Physician for Friday's game?'

'Not yet,' said Leccheworth. He smiled at Bartholomew. 'But the rules stipulate that one must be to hand, because these occasions can turn savage.'

'I know,' said Bartholomew dryly. 'But I do not think I am the right—'

'You are the *only* suitable candidate,' declared Jude firmly. 'Meryfeld is worthless, Rougham too expensive, and Gyseburne would do nothing but ask for urine. And I do not like Gyseburne, anyway – there is something sly about the cant of his eyes.'

'Do say yes, Doctor,' said Leccheworth. 'It carries a payment of three shillings.'

'All right, then,' said Bartholomew, capitulating promptly. It would keep the poor in salves and tonics for a month.

He frowned suddenly. There was a large building at the edge of the field, which looked as though it was deserted – its ground-floor windows were boarded over and its door nailed closed – but he thought he had seen a shadow move across one of its upper rooms.

'That is Edmund House,' said Leccheworth, seeing where he was looking. 'It used to belong to our convent, but we were forced to sell it after the Great Pestilence, when we needed some ready cash. Emma de Colvyll purchased it from us.'

'I remember,' said Bartholomew. 'It looks abandoned, but I thought I saw someone inside.'

110

'Pigeons,' replied Leccheworth. 'It is a pity, because they will ruin it. We are eager to buy it back now we have funds to spare, but Emma refuses to sell.'

'Has she said why?' asked Bartholomew. The building looked stable enough, but was showing signs of decay. It made no sense to let it rot when there was a buyer to hand.

Leccheworth grimaced. 'No. And I do not understand it at all.'

'Neither do I,' said Jude. 'But there is something about her that petrifies me. I am a large, strong man with an unshakeable faith in God, but little Emma de Colvyll turns my knees to water.'

Bartholomew's last visit of the morning was to Bridge Street, to tend Sheriff Tulyet's son. Dickon was nine years old, and large for his age. He terrorised the servants, had no friends because the parents of other children declined to let him anywhere near their offspring, and even his mother was beginning to be frightened of him. Tulyet was blind to his faults, though, and Dickon was growing into an extremely nasty individual. Hoping he would emerge unscathed from what was sure to be a trying encounter, Bartholomew knocked on Tulyet's door.

'Thank God you are here, Matthew,' said Mistress Tulyet in relief. 'Dickon climbed over the wall into Celia Drax's garden, and fell on a hive of bees. He has been dreadfully stung.'

'Christ!' muttered Bartholomew, not liking the notion of extracting stings from a boy who was going to fight him every inch of the way. Then he frowned. 'But Celia Drax does not live next to you – Meryfeld does. Celia is two doors down.'

'Well, perhaps he did clamber through the property of more than one neighbour,' admitted Mistress Tulyet sheepishly. 'But you had better hurry. Dickon is not very nice when he is in pain.'

Dickon was not very nice when he was not in pain, either, but Bartholomew managed to follow her to the kitchen without saying so. The boy was standing in the middle of the room howling, while servants nervously attempted to divest him of his clothes, to see whether a bee might still be trapped. He held a sword, a gift from his doting father, and stabbed at anyone who came too close. His eyes were swollen with tears, and his face was flushed, although from temper rather than distress. There was a rumour that he had been sired by the Devil, and there were times when Bartholomew was prepared to believe the tale: he suspected this was going to be one of them.

'No!' Dickon shrieked when he saw the physician. 'Go away!'

Bartholomew was tempted to do as he suggested, and then was mildly ashamed of himself. He wondered what it was about the brat that always brought out the worst in him.

'Put down the sword,' he ordered. 'If you cooperate, this will be over in a moment.'

'No!' shouted Dickon again. 'And if you come near me, I shall run you through. I know how, because my father showed me. I am to be sent away soon to become a squire in Lord Picot's household. He is a great knight, who will make me a mighty warrior.'

'Really?' asked Bartholomew, delighted that someone else would soon have the pleasure of physicking him. 'Put down the weapon and tell me about it.'

'It is not true,' whispered Mistress Tulyet. 'We have not told him yet, but Lord Picot declines to accept him. We cannot imagine why, a fine, strong lad like him.'

Bartholomew turned to the servants. 'We will rush him. You three approach from behind, and—'

112

'No,' said the steward, backing away. 'We are not paid enough to tackle Dickon.'

Bartholomew watched in dismay as they all trooped out, Mistress Tulyet among them. He turned back to Dickon, thinking fast.

'Do you know what happens if bee stings are not removed? All your fingers drop off. You cannot be a soldier with no fingers.'

He did not usually resort to underhand tactics with patients, but Dickon was a special case. The boy regarded him silently. His eyes glistened, and Bartholomew had the uncomfortable sense that they belonged to a much older person.

'You lie,' the boy said eventually.

Bartholomew smiled. 'Then let us try an experiment. If I am lying, nothing will happen to you. But if I am telling the truth, you will be fingerless by tomorrow. What do you say?'

Dickon continued to study him. Suddenly, the sword dipped and he proffered an arm. 'Very well. You may remove it.'

'It' was the operative word, because although Dickon claimed to have catapulted himself on top of the hive, he had only been stung once. Bartholomew wondered if the hapless creatures had been too intimidated to attack. The sting was quickly extracted with a pair of tweezers, and when the operation was over, both sat back in relief.

'What were you doing in Drax's garden?' Bartholomew felt compelled to ask.

'She killed her husband,' declared Dickon with utter conviction. 'So I decided to visit her – I have never talked to a murderess before, you see.'

'What makes you think Celia Drax is a murderess?' asked Bartholomew, startled.

'Because they were always arguing – they did not love each other. But she dragged me off the hive and let me out of her front door, so I do not care what she did to him. I like her.'

'Was she stung, too?' Bartholomew supposed he had better go to see whether she needed help.

Dickon nodded. 'A lot more than me.'

Bartholomew stood, eager to be away. He was just congratulating himself on escaping without harm to either of them when Dickon snatched up the sword and lunged. Bartholomew felt a sharp pain in his side, and Dickon danced away, eyes flashing with malice.

'It hurt when you pulled out the sting, and my father said bullies are not to be tolerated,' he declared, as Bartholomew regarded him in disbelief. 'Now we are even.'

'My husband *did* say bullies are not to be tolerated,' acknowledged Mistress Tulyet, when Bartholomew reported that her son had stabbed him; fortunately, in a fit of common sense, Tulyet had filed off the weapon's point. 'But Dickon is the bully. Unfortunately, he has developed a habit of interpreting our reprimands in ways that suit him.'

Bartholomew saw the unease in her eyes and knew she was beginning to see the child for the tyrant he was, even if Tulyet remained obstinately blind. There was no more to be said, so he left and headed for Celia Drax's home, rubbing his bruised side.

As Bartholomew knocked on the door to Celia's house, it occurred to him that it would be a good opportunity to quiz her about her husband. Determined to make the most of the occasion, he followed a servant into an enormous hall-like room with polished wooden floors and painted walls. At the far end was a shelf containing books, a considerable luxury, given that they were so expensive. Celia was sitting on a bench with a pair of tweezers.

'It is good of you to come,' she said reluctantly as he perched next to her and began to remove stings from her hands and arms. 'Did Dickon tell you what happened? From an upstairs window, I saw him invade my garden, and was on my way to box his ears, when he fell on the hive. Naturally, the bees objected. I dragged him away as quickly as I could, and shoved him out of my front door. Hateful brat! But never mind him. Has Brother Michael recovered my pilgrim badge yet? Such items are valuable, and I would like it back.'

Bartholomew saw she was still wearing the gold medallion she had retrieved from her husband's corpse. It made him shudder. 'Not yet.'

When she coyly left the room to look for other stings that might require his attention, he wandered towards her little library. There was a psalter, two texts by Aristotle, and a rather lurid tome of contemporary romantic poetry, which he assumed belonged to Odelina. There was also a large, brown volume that looked rather more well thumbed than the others. He took it down, and saw it was a pharmacopoeia. He frowned. Why would a taverner and his wife own such a thing? Glancing uneasily towards the door, he leafed through it until he found the entry for wolfsbane.

The page was grimy, but so were all the others, and he could not decide whether it had been marked in any particular way. At the bottom was a section about antidotes, describing how to swallow the plant without harm. He knew the claims were false, because gulping down a dose of quicksilver was likely to bring its own set of problems, while milk would have no effect one way or the other. He turned to the entry for mandrake, and read with disbelief that no

115

one would die from taking it, if they first lined their stomachs with a paste of dried earthworms.

'Found anything interesting?' Celia's voice so close behind him made him jump.

'Not really,' he replied, turning to face her. 'Are you interested in herbs?'

'No, and I cannot read, anyway. John could, though, and he was always pawing through that book, and it made me rather nervous, to tell you the truth. Perhaps he intended to poison me, but God struck him down first.'

'God did not kill your husband,' said Bartholomew quietly. 'Do you have any idea who—'

'No,' interrupted Celia curtly. 'As I told you before, no one would want to kill John. He was not a saint, but he was not a villain, either. He was just a man, with a man's failings. He was not generous to those who patronised his taverns, but he was honest. And while he drove a hard bargain with the scholars who rent Chestre Hostel, they never had to wait long for repairs.'

'I have heard you and he quarrelled, and—'

'Of course we quarrelled: we were married! But you will not understand that, living away from the society of women. You will know nothing of the ups and downs of marital life.'

'No,' said Bartholomew sadly. 'What about his friends? You are close to Odelina, but he—'

'He was not a man for forming close relationships. You may go now. Thank you for coming.'

It was hardly a profitable interview, and Bartholomew felt as though he had squandered an opportunity as he returned to the College. When Michael arrived, he told him about the encounter, along with Dickon's claim that the couple had argued. The monk listened thoughtfully.

'You think one of their spats turned violent, and she

116

stabbed him? And then she carried him to Michaelhouse, although there is no sensible reason for her to do so, and left him behind the tiles?'

'Well, someone did,' said Bartholomew tartly. 'And she was married to Drax, and she frequents the house where Alice was poisoned.'

Michael sighed. 'True. But your suspicions are not enough to let us arrest her. We need solid evidence. So I suppose I had better visit Drax's taverns, and ask his patrons what they thought of the pair of them. If I have time, I shall ask for Fen's alibi for Drax's murder, too, although I shall be home for a little something to eat by mid-afternoon, naturally.'

'Naturally,' said Bartholomew.

CHAPTER 4

While Michael embarked on his trawl of Drax's taverns, Bartholomew dedicated himself to teaching. As a result, his pupils found themselves subjected to one of his vigorous questioning sessions, and by the time the bell rang to announce that the next meal was ready, their heads were spinning. Bartholomew was despondent, disappointed by their performance. He ignored both their indignant objections that he had quizzed them on texts they had not yet studied, and their grumbles that he had no right to push them as hard as he pushed himself.

'Emma de Colvyll sang your praises today,' said Michael, as they stood at their places at the high table, waiting for Langelee to say grace. 'You made a friend when you saved Odelina.'

'I thought you planned to spend your day in alehouses.'

'I did, but it was tedious and unprofitable, so I visited Emma instead, to see whether I could winkle out more information about this yellow-headed thief.'

'And did you?'

Michael shook his head. 'No, although I hope to God we catch him before she does – she will have him torn limb from limb and dumped in the marshes. Heslarton is conducting a thorough and sensible search, which surprises me. I thought him a brainless lout, but he is showing intelligence over this manhunt, and I am afraid he might succeed.'

'Perhaps the intelligence is Emma's,' suggested

118

Bartholomew. 'He would not be averse to taking instructions from her. They respect each other.'

'They do. Perhaps Heslarton *is* a brainless lout, then, although he is by far the most likeable member of that family. Alice was spiteful and cruel, Odelina is a spoiled brat, and Emma . . . well, the less said about Emma the better.'

'Do you have any new suspects for poisoning Alice or stabbing Drax?'

'Yes, unfortunately. There are a *lot* of people who would like to see Emma's entire household poisoned, *and* who are delighted that Drax is dead. These same folk may also be inclined to steal pilgrim badges in the hope that they will save them from Purgatory.'

'Who are they?'

'People who object to the ruthless business practices of Drax and Emma. Especially Emma – I have not met anyone yet who likes her. Then there is Edmund House. She bought it from the Gilbertines in a very sly manner, and now she flaunts the incident by letting the place fall into disrepair under their very noses. They must find it galling.'

'You think the Gilbertines are killers and thieves?'

'Hush!' Michael glanced uneasily at Thelnetham, but the canon was talking to Langelee, and had not heard. 'No, of course not, but the Gilbertines are popular in the town, because they give charity. Perhaps someone has taken offence on their behalf.'

Bartholomew supposed it was possible. 'Who else?'

'The pilgrims, especially Fen.'

'Fen cannot be the culprit, because he did not dash in from the street and grab Poynton's badge – he was standing next to Poynton at the time. Moreover, he does not have yellow hair.'

Michael ignored him. 'And do not forget that Prior Etone

119

showed him our College the morning Drax was murdered – Blaston saw them. Doubtless he thought then that Michaelhouse was a good place to dispose of a body.'

Bartholomew saw the monk was not in the mood for a logical discussion, so changed the subject. 'Did you speak to Emma about Yffi leaving holes in the roof while he fiddles with the windows?'

'I did, but she said it is not her place to interfere.' Michael looked disgusted. 'She interferes when she feels like it, and is a hypocrite. But here is Langelee at last. Good! I am famished.'

Langelee intoned grace, and indicated that the servants were to bring the food. It was uninspiring fare, and although meals at Michaelhouse were supposed to be taken in silence, it was not long before the Fellows – always the worst culprits for breaking this particular rule – began talking.

'Pea soup *again*,' grumbled Michael, digging his horn spoon into the bowl that was set for him and Clippesby to share. 'And there is no meat in it.'

'There is bread, though,' said William, taking the largest piece from the basket that was being passed around. 'If you soak it in the soup, it becomes soft enough to eat.'

Bartholomew picked listlessly at the unappealing offerings, still full from the handsome breakfast William had provided.

'I visited Celia today, too,' Michael was saying to the table in general. 'She was sorting through her husband's belongings, making piles for the poor.'

'That is laudable,' said Suttone. 'They need charity in this bitter weather. Of course, Drax only died two days ago, and it seems rather soon to be disposing of his possessions.'

'Just because she is not drowning in sorrow does not

120

mean she did not care about him,' said Langelee. 'She may just be practical. Like me. I would not wallow in grief if any of *you* were stabbed and left behind a stack of tiles.'

'Your compassion overwhelms me, Master,' said Thelnetham dryly. He turned to Michael. 'Did you know that Drax went on a pilgrimage to Walsingham? He always wore a badge under his hat. He showed it to me recently, and said he had travelled to Norfolk.'

'His wife told *me* he had bought that token to save himself the journey,' said Michael, puzzled. 'I wonder which of them was telling the truth.'

'Celia is,' said Clippesby, who was feeding soup to the piglet he held in his lap. Bartholomew was amused to note it was the only creature in the hall that was enjoying its victuals.

'How do you know?' asked Thelnetham curiously. Then he held up his hand. 'On reflection, do not tell me. It will be some lunatic tale about a bird or a hedgehog.'

Clippesby had a disturbing habit of finding quiet places and then sitting very still as he communed with nature. It meant he often witnessed events not meant for his eyes, although he tended to make people wary of accepting his testimony by claiming it came from various furred or feathered friends. Of all the Michaelhouse Fellows, Thelnetham was the one who struggled hardest to come to terms with the Dominican's idiosyncrasies.

'On the contrary,' said Clippesby mildly. 'I know because I saw Drax make the purchase myself. And if you do not believe me, then ask the King's Head geese, because they were there, too.'

'Hah!' Thelnetham grimaced. 'I knew there would be an animal involved somewhere. Ignore him, Brother. The man is moon-touched.'

'Unfortunately, none of us could see the seller,' Clippesby

went on. 'But we can tell you that the transaction took place outside the Gilbertine Priory last Friday night.'

Thelnetham started. 'Last Friday? Then *I* saw the transaction, too! *And* I saw the geese, although I did not notice you. However, I wondered what had set them a-honking. I watched Drax approach a man who gave him something. It was that burly lout – Emma's son-in-law.'

'Heslarton?' asked Michael. 'Why would he be selling pilgrim badges? And why outside a convent, when Drax's wife is a regular visitor to his home, and he could have given it to her?'

'Perhaps he did not want his fearsome mother-in-law to know what he was doing,' suggested Thelnetham. He shuddered. '*I* would certainly not enjoy having the likes of her breathing down my neck at every turn. However, I did hear Heslarton tell Drax that what he was about to purchase – which I now learn was a *signaculum* – was solid gold, and that it came with a special dispensation for pardoning all sins.'

Clippesby pulled a face. 'Personally, I do not think God is very impressed by indulgences.'

'That is heresy,' said William, who always had opinions about such matters. 'The Church has been selling indulgences for years, and it is sacrilege to say they are worthless.'

'You both misunderstand the meaning of indulgences,' snapped Thelnetham testily. 'They are not pardons, to secure the buyer's salvation, and they cannot release the soul from Purgatory.'

'Thelnetham is right,' agreed Michael. 'It is the extra-sacramental remission of the temporal punishment due, in God's justice, to a sin that has been forgiven—'

'Rubbish,' interrupted Suttone. 'Some writs of indulgence specifically state *indulgentia a culpa et a poena*, which means release from guilt and from punishment.'

122

'That is *not* what it means,' declared Thelnetham. Bartholomew felt his eyes begin to close, as they often did when his colleagues embarked on theological debates. 'Such a notion runs contrary to all the teachings of the Church. What it means is—'

'It means the rich can buy their way into Heaven,' said William. 'It is unfair, but it is not for us to question these things. And anyone who disagrees with me is a fool.'

They were still arguing about the nature of pardons and indulgences when they adjourned to the conclave – the small, comfortable room next to the hall – for a few moments of respite before the rest of the day's teaching. Thelnetham announced that he had been on a pilgrimage to Canterbury, where he had bought a *signaculum* – in this case, an ampoule containing a piece of cloth soaked in St Thomas Becket's blood. He had given it to his Mother House at Sempringham.

'But they sold it to a merchant for a lot of money,' he concluded with a grimace. 'And I learned the lesson that only idiots are generous. It probably ended up with a man like Drax – a sinner who lied about doing the pilgrimage himself. Perhaps it is divine justice that he came to such an end.'

Bartholomew looked at him sharply, thinking it was not a remark most clerics would have made. He also recalled that Thelnetham had not been teaching in the hall when the accident had occurred, although the Gilbertine had joined the Fellows in watching Drax excavated afterwards. He shook himself angrily, and wondered whether he had helped Michael solve too many crimes, because it was hardly kind to think such unpleasant thoughts about his colleagues.

'Some *signacula* are very beautiful,' mused Michael

123

wistfully. 'I have always wanted to examine one closely. Perhaps even to hold it, and admire its craftsmanship.'

'I bought you one,' said Bartholomew, suddenly remembering something he had done a long time ago, and that he had all but forgotten. 'Although I cannot recall if it was especially beautiful.'

Michael regarded him askance. 'You never did!'

'It must still be in the chest in my room. I keep meaning to unpack it, but there is never enough time. I bought it two years ago, when I was looking for . . . when I was travelling.'

Bartholomew had been going to say when he had been looking for Matilde, but was disinclined to raise a subject that was still painful for him.

'Where from, exactly?' asked Michael keenly. 'I know you went to Walsingham and Lourdes.'

'From Santiago de Compostela.'

Michael gaped at him. 'But that is one of the three holiest pilgrim sites in the world, on a par with Jerusalem and Rome! Are you saying you brought me a gift from a sacred shrine, then simply forgot to hand it over, even though you have been home for nigh on eighteen months?'

Bartholomew supposed he was, but Michael was glaring, and it did not seem prudent to say so. He flailed around for a pretext to excuse his carelessness, but nothing credible came to mind.

'Do you still have it?' asked Suttone eagerly. 'I have never seen a pilgrim token from Compostela. Did you touch it against the shrine? Wash it in holy water, and do all the other things that make these items sacred?'

Bartholomew nodded. 'And the Bishop blessed it for me.'

'I had no idea you visited Compostela,' said Ayera, eyeing

124

him curiously. 'Why have you never mentioned it? I was under the impression you spent all your time in foreign universities, watching necromancers perform anatomies on hapless corpses.'

'Not *all* my time,' muttered Bartholomew.

Langelee stood. 'Then let us find this token. Michael and Suttone are not alone in never seeing one from Compostela, although I have handled plenty from Walsingham, Canterbury and so forth.'

'And Cambridge,' added Suttone. 'Cambridge is a place of pilgrimage, too, because it is where St Simon Stock had his vision. At the Carmelite Priory.'

'You want me to look *now*?' asked Bartholomew, startled when all the Fellows followed Langelee's lead and surged to their feet. 'But I may not be able to find it, and teaching starts soon.'

'The students will not mind a delay,' predicted Langelee. 'And if they do, I will tell Deynman to read to them. That will shut them up, because his Latin is all but incomprehensible.'

'Why may you not be able to find it?' demanded Michael, ignoring the fact that the Master was hardly in a position to criticise someone else's grasp of the language, given that his own was rudimentary, to say the least.

'I *think* it is in that box, but it has been a long time since I have looked in it, and—'

'Matt!' cried Michael, dismayed. 'Are you saying you might have *lost* it?'

Bartholomew regarded him guiltily. 'Very possibly, yes.'

With the Fellows at his heels, Bartholomew led the way to his room, wondering why he had forgotten the badge until now. He had been to some trouble to acquire it – cheap *signacula* were sold by the dozen to pilgrims, but he had wanted something rather better for Michael, who was a man of discerning tastes. He had purchased the best one he could find, then ensured it spent a night on top of the shrine, paid a bishop to bless it, and dipped it in holy water from Jerusalem. And after all that, he had shoved it in a travelling box and neglected to unpack it.

Valence was sitting at the desk in the window, scribbling furiously as he struggled to complete an exercise that should have been finished the previous evening. He looked up in surprise when the Fellows crammed into the chamber. Bartholomew stood with his hands on his hips, desperately trying to remember where he had put the chest in question.

'Under the bed,' supplied Valence promptly, when Michael told him what they were doing. 'Right at the back. I have always wondered what was in it, and would have looked, but it is locked.'

'Is it?' asked Bartholomew uneasily. He had no idea where to find the key.

Valence disappeared under the bed, and emerged a few moments later with the small, leather-bound box that the physician had toted all the way through France, Spain and Italy. It was dusty, battered, and trailed cobwebs. Bartholomew set it on the bed and sat next to it. The lock was substantial, and of a better quality than he remembered. He doubted he could force it.

'I do not have the key,' he said apologetically, wincing when there was a chorus of disappointed groans and cries, the loudest of them from Michael.

'Allow me,' said Langelee, drawing his dagger. 'I did this for the Archbishop many times.'

He inserted the tip of his blade into the keyhole, and began to jiggle it. Students crowded at the window, curiosity piqued by the sight of the Master and all his Fellows in Bartholomew's room. Even Clippesby's piglet was among the throng, eyes fixed intently on Langelee's manoeuvrings.

'Hah!' exclaimed the Master, as there was a sharp click and the lock sprang open. He opened the lid and peered inside. 'Here is a very fine dagger, although it is not very sharp.'

'It is a letter-opener,' explained Bartholomew. 'I bought it for you.'

'For me?' asked Langelee. He grinned his delight. 'How thoughtful! I shall begin honing it tonight. It is a beautiful implement, but it will be lovelier still when it is sharp enough to be useful.'

Bartholomew regarded him unhappily, wishing the Master was not always so ready to revert to the soldier he had once been. It was hardly seemly in an academic.

'My *signaculum*,' prompted Michael impatiently. 'Where is it?'

It was at the bottom of the chest, wrapped in cloth. There were other gifts Bartholomew had forgotten about, too – a mother-of-pearl comb for William, a tiny painting of St Francis of Assisi for Clippesby, and a book of plague poems for Suttone. There was an embroidered purse and a silver buckle, too, intended for friends who were now dead, so he gave them to Thelnetham and Ayera. While they cooed their delight, he spotted two anatomy texts he had purchased in Salerno, and closed the lid hastily. He would look at them later, when he was alone.

'What else is in there?' asked William, running the comb through his greasy locks as he eyed the chest speculatively.

'Nothing,' mumbled Bartholomew, careful not to catch anyone's eye. He was not a good liar.

'It is exquisite, Matt,' said Michael, pushing students out of the way so he could examine his gift in the light from the window. 'Gold, too.'

'Is it?' Bartholomew knew it had been expensive, but

could not recall why. Not being very interested in such things, it had not stuck in his mind.

'It will not get you into Heaven, though, Brother,' warned Thelnetham. 'As I said in the conclave, that only happens through personal merit, not because you happen to own *signacula.*'

'I know all that,' said Michael impatiently. 'But I am never going to see Compostela myself, so this is the next best thing.'

'Actually, I believe it *might* reduce your time in Purgatory,' countered Suttone. 'Matthew made the pilgrimage, but he was clearly thinking of you when he did it, so your badge is important. You are wrong, Thelnetham: owning or buying such items *can* help one's immortal soul.'

'Drax thought the same,' said Bartholomew, speaking before they could argue. He knew from experience that debates among theologians could go on for a very long time, and was eager to return to his teaching. 'He believed the Walsingham *signaculum*, bought from Heslarton, would help his soul. Why else would he have worn it in his hat?'

William pointed at Michael's token with his comb. 'Do you know how much that is worth? A fortune! Not only is it precious metal and exquisitely made, but it has all the right blessings on it, too. Men will pay dearly for that.'

'Really?' asked Langelee keenly. 'How much?'

'It is not for sale,' said Michael firmly. 'Not even for Michaelhouse's roof.'

'My Carmelite brethren sell pilgrim tokens, here in Cambridge,' said Suttone idly, his attention more on his new book than the discussion. 'Our shrine does not attract vast numbers, like the ones in Hereford, Walsingham or Canterbury, but we make a tidy profit, even so.'

'Do they hawk bits of St Simon Stock's relic?' asked Langelee. 'I have heard that folk who die wearing a

Carmelite scapular go straight to Heaven, but a scrap of the original will surely set one at God's right hand.'

'We would never sell that,' declared Suttone, looking up in horror. Then he reconsidered. 'Well, we might, I suppose, if the price was right.'

'White Friars are *not* going to get to Heaven before Franciscans,' declared William hotly. 'And I do not know what the Blessed Virgin thought she was doing when she gave that scapular to Simon Stock. She should have appeared to a Grey Friar instead, because *we* would not be charging a fortune for folk to see the spot where this delivery occurred.'

'Yes, you would,' countered Suttone. 'It is an excellent opportunity for raising much-needed revenue, and the Franciscans would have seized it with alacrity. Look at how much money they are making from Walsingham – more than we will see in a hundred years!'

'That is different,' said William stiffly, although he did not deign to explain why.

'I think I had better make a pilgrimage to the Carmelite Priory,' said Langelee. 'I did one or two dubious favours for the Archbishop of York, you see, and I would not like to think of them held against me on Judgment Day.'

Clippesby regarded him reproachfully. 'If you want forgiveness for past sins, Master, you must be truly penitent. Walking to Milne Street is not enough.'

'It is, according to Suttone,' replied Langelee cheerfully. 'And it suits me to believe him.'

Bartholomew had intended to spend what remained of the day teaching, but Michael had other ideas. Ignoring the physician's objections, he commandeered his help to search the area around Michaelhouse, to find the place where Drax had been stabbed. Unfortunately, St Michael's Lane was home to several hostels, all of which owned a number of disused or infrequently visited sheds, and the task proved to be harder than he had anticipated.

'We are wasting our time,' said Bartholomew, after a while. 'This is hopeless.'

'We *must* persist,' said Michael. 'It stands to reason that Drax was killed nearby – he was not very big, but corpses are heavy, even so. Moreover, a killer would not risk toting one too far.'

'I cannot imagine why a killer would tote one at all,' grumbled Bartholomew, poking half-heartedly around Physwick Hostel's old dairy with a stick. The place was filled, for some unaccountable reason, with broken barrels. 'Unless . . .'

'Unless what?' asked Michael, glancing up.

'We saw Kendale arguing with Drax. And Kendale's hostel is near Michaelhouse. It would not be difficult to carry a corpse to our College from Chestre. Perhaps we should be looking there: not in abandoned outbuildings, but in the hostel itself.'

Michael grimaced. 'That has already occurred to me, I assure you. Unfortunately, Kendale is the kind of man to take umbrage, and I cannot risk him taking the College–hostel dispute to a new level of acrimony. I must wait until I have solid evidence before we search *his* home.'

'Does this qualify as solid evidence?' asked Bartholomew soberly. He stood back so Michael could see what he had found. 'It is blood. A lot of it.'

'You think this is our murder scene?' asked Michael, looking away quickly. The red-black, sticky puddle was an unsettling sight.

Bartholomew crouched down to look more closely, then nodded. 'The volume seems right, and you can see a smear here, where a body was moved. However, from the pooling, I suspect Drax lay dead for some time – hours, probably – before he was taken to Michaelhouse.'

'Lord!' breathed Michael. 'Then we are dealing with a very bold and ruthless individual, because most murderers do not return to tamper with their victims after they have made their escape. It shows he must have been very determined to cause trouble for Michaelhouse.'

'Which may mean Kendale *is* the culprit – he hates the Colleges.' Bartholomew frowned. 'However, Kendale is clever, and this seems rather crude to me. Perhaps the killer is a member of a College, and he dumped Drax in Michaelhouse because he wants a hostel blamed for it.'

Michael sighed. 'Damn this ridiculous dispute! It means that even finding the spot where Drax was murdered does not help us – and we have wasted hours doing it.'

'We had better talk to Physwick,' said Bartholomew. 'They are more reasonable than Chestre, so I do not think questioning them will result in a riot.'

'It might, if they are guilty of murder,' muttered Michael, trailing after him.

Physwick Hostel was a dismal place in winter. The fire that flickered in its hearth was too small to make much difference to the temperature of the hall, and all its windows leaked. It reeked of tallow candles, unwashed feet, wet wool and boiled cabbage. Its Principal was John Howes, a skinny lawyer with oily hair and bad teeth, who had ten students and three masters under his care.

'We are sorry about Drax,' he announced, before Michael could state the purpose of his visit. 'He rented our dairy to store old ale barrels from his taverns, and we need all the money we can get in these terrible times. He did not pay much, but a penny a week is a penny a week.'

'Why did he want to store old barrels?' asked Bartholomew curiously.

'He was too mean to throw them away,' explained Howes. 'He once told me he planned to reclaim the metal hoops, and sell the wood to the charcoal burners.'

'He was killed there,' said Michael baldly. 'We found his blood.'

'Did you? How horrible!' Howes shuddered. 'That means one of us will have to go out with a mop and a bucket of water, because we cannot afford to pay anyone else to do it. Unless cleaning murder scenes comes under the Corpse Examiner's remit?' he asked hopefully.

'No, it does not,' said Bartholomew shortly. 'Did any of you see or hear anything on Monday morning that may help us catch his killer?'

'Not really. We went out twice on Monday – once not long after dawn, when we attended a service in the Gilbertines' chapel, and again mid-afternoon when we were invited to see St Simon Stock's scapular. We can see the dairy from our hall here, but we do not look at it much.'

'But they would probably have noticed the comings and goings of strangers,' murmured Michael to Bartholomew, as they took their leave. 'So their testimony *has* helped.'

Bartholomew nodded. 'It tells us for certain that Drax was killed shortly after dawn, when they went out the first time. The pooled blood proves the body lay for several hours in the dairy, then was moved to Michaelhouse when they went out for the second time – probably after I started teaching, when Blaston was in the stable, and when Yffi and his boys were on the roof discussing Yolande's skills in the bedchamber.'

'A discussion that ensured all attention was drawn upwards,' said Michael. 'Away from the yard. I see we shall have to have another word with Yffi and his louts.'

132

Once outside, they began to walk towards the Carmelite Priory, to check Physwick's alibi, although both believed Howes's testimony. They had not gone far before Bartholomew was diverted to Trinity Hall, where a student was nursing a bleeding mouth. There had been a fight between that College and Cosyn's Hostel.

'It would never have degenerated into blows a week ago,' said the Master, Adam de Wickmer worriedly. 'Our relationship with Cosyn's has always involved cheeky banter, but never violence, and I am shocked that punches have been traded.'

'So am I,' said Bartholomew. 'I do not understand why previously amiable relationships have suddenly turned sour.'

'Oh, I understand that,' said Wickmer bitterly. 'The paupers in the hostels have always been jealous of our wealth, and they are probably hoping that there will be an all-out battle in which they can invade us and steal our moveable possessions.'

Bartholomew stared at him. 'I hope you are wrong.'

'So do I,' said Wickmer. 'But the hostels are suffering from the expense of a long, hard winter, and Kendale has been fanning the flames of discontent and envy. I have a bad feeling it will all end in blood and tears.'

Later that evening, Bartholomew set off to meet his medical colleagues. Meryfeld had been intrigued by the notion of devising a lamp with a constant flame, and had decided that if university-trained physicians could not invent one, then nobody could. He had sent messages asking all three of his colleagues to come to his house, so they might commence the project.

Bartholomew was the last to arrive, because his students, alarmed by their poor performance during his earlier inquisition, had tried to make amends with a plethora of questions. The delay meant he was obliged to run all the way to Bridge Street, where Meryfeld occupied the handsome stone mansion that stood between Sheriff Tulyet's home and Celia Drax's.

When he was shown into Meryfeld's luxurious solar, Bartholomew was astonished to see that Rougham of Gonville Hall had accepted the invitation, too. Rougham was a busy man, or so he told everyone, and Bartholomew was amazed that he should deign to spare the time to experiment with colleagues. He was an unattractive fellow, arrogant and overbearing, and although he no longer cried heresy every time Bartholomew voiced an opinion, the two would never be friends.

'Meryfeld's proposition sounded intriguing,' he explained, when he saw Bartholomew's reaction to his presence. 'I struggled to read my astrological charts last night, and may have made an error when I calculated the Mayor's horoscope. A bright lamp would be very useful.'

'It is not so much the lamp as the fuel,' said Bartholomew. 'We need a mixture that will burn steadily – one that does not require too many exotic ingredients or the cost will be prohibitive.'

'Not for me,' said Rougham smugly. 'I make a respectable living from medicine, and so do Gyseburne and Meryfeld. You are the only one who lets the poor dictate his income.'

'I plan to devote more time to the poor in future,' announced Gyseburne. He shrugged when the others stared at him. 'It will be good for my soul, and God will take it into account when I die.'

'Yes – dealing with the indigent is a lot safer than doing a pilgrimage,' said Meryfeld. His face clouded for a moment. 'I was robbed and almost killed *en route* to Canterbury.'

134

'I have been to Canterbury, too,' said Gyseburne. 'Although I had no trouble with brigands, thank the good Lord. Here is the *signaculum* I bought there. It contains real Becket water.'

He showed them a tiny bottle filled with a pinkish liquid, attached to his hat by means of a silver wire. With a flourish, Meryfeld presented his, which was almost identical, but in gold, and which he wore pinned to his cloak. Bartholomew was somewhat ashamed to realise that he had seen the badges on many previous occasions, but had never thought to question their meaning.

'I am not risking it again,' said Meryfeld with a shudder. 'Of course, there will be no need for penitential journeys if I accept a few pro bono cases from Bartholomew.'

Gyseburne gave the grimace that passed as a smile. 'I am glad, because it is unfair that he sees all the poor, while we tend the rich. We *should* share the burden.'

'Well, I do not think *I* shall oblige, if it is all the same to you,' said Rougham haughtily. 'My soul is not in need of any such disagreeable sacrifices.'

Loath to waste time listening to whose soul needed what – and afraid someone might conclude that he, who did so much charity work, might own one that was especially tainted – Bartholomew turned the conversation back to the lamp. The four *medici* spent a few moments discussing the benefits their invention would bring, then turned to the practical business of experimentation. Gyseburne had brought some brimstone, Bartholomew a bag of charcoal, Meryfeld some pitch, and Rougham provided a sticky kind of oil that he said burned well.

They opened the window when the stench became too much, then were compelled to take their research into the garden when Rougham claimed he felt sick. Bartholomew began to wonder whether they were wise to meddle with substances none of them really understood, but the venture had captured his imagination, and he was intrigued by it. He was also enjoying himself – he was beginning to like his new colleagues, while Rougham seemed less abrasive in their company.

He was about to ignite their latest concoction when he saw a movement over the wall that divided Meryfeld's house from the property next door.

'Perhaps we should do this elsewhere,' he said uneasily, realising that four physicians standing around a reeking cauldron was exactly the kind of spectacle that would attract Dickon.

'Unfortunately, that is impracticable,' said Rougham. 'If we go to Michaelhouse or Gonville Hall, we will be pestered by students. And Gyseburne has no garden.'

'But Dickon Tulyet is watching,' explained Bartholomew. 'I would not like him to copy what we are doing, and hurt himself.'

'I would,' said Meryfeld fervently. 'He lobs rotten apples at me when I walk among my trees, and his language is disgusting. When I complained, Sheriff Tulyet did not believe me.'

'The boy is not his,' said Rougham, matter-of-factly. 'It is common knowledge that the Devil sired Dickon one night, when his father was out.'

'Mistress Tulyet would not have gone along with that,' said Bartholomew, feeling compelled to defend the honour of his friend's wife, although he did not care what people thought about Dickon.

'I find it strange that Dickon is so large, but his father is so small,' said Gyseburne. 'So I am inclined to believe that there *is* something diabolical about the lad.'

'Now, now,' said Bartholomew mildly. 'He is only a child.'

'I am not so sure about that,' muttered Rougham, tossing something into the pot.

'Watch what you are doing!' cried Gyseburne, as there was a sudden flare of light. Then the flames caught the potion in the pot, and there was a dull thump.

The next thing Bartholomew knew was that he was lying on his back. At first, he thought he had turned deaf, because everything sounded as though it was underwater, but then there was a peculiar pop and it cleared. Immediately, Dickon's braying laughter played about his ears. He eased himself up on one elbow and saw his colleagues also beginning to pick themselves up.

'I do not think that was the right ratio of brimstone to pitch,' said Gyseburne in something of an understatement, as they approached the pot and peered cautiously inside it.

'No,' agreed Meryfeld. 'But the light it produced was very bright – I still cannot see properly – so we are working along the right track.'

Bartholomew started to laugh when he saw the soot that covered Rougham's face. Rougham regarded him in surprise, but then Meryfeld began to chuckle, too.

'You think this is funny?' demanded Rougham irritably. 'We might have been killed. Worse yet, our failure was witnessed by that horrible child, and the tale will be all over Cambridge tomorrow.'

'No one will believe him,' said Meryfeld, although Bartholomew suspected Rougham was right to be concerned: such a tale was likely to be popular, whether it was true or not.

'I should have paid more attention to the alchemy classes I took in Paris,' said Gyseburne. 'Because then I might have been able to prevent that unedifying little episode. Rougham is right: we *might* have been killed.'

'Did you study with Nicole Oresme?' asked Bartholomew, referring to that city's most celebrated natural philosopher. He knew Gyseburne had attended the University in Oxford, but not that he had been to Paris, too, He was pleased: it was another thing they had in common.

'I might have done,' said Gyseburne shortly. Evidently not of a mind to discuss mutual acquaintances, he indicated the sticky mess that covered the pot. 'Now what shall we do?'

'We need to reduce the amount of brimstone,' said Meryfeld. 'But not tonight. We are all tired, and weariness might be dangerous while dealing with potent substances. But we have made some headway, and I am pleased with our progress. Moreover, we have learned three important lessons.'

'Yes,' agreed Bartholomew. 'First, we definitely need to conduct these tests outside, and second, we should experiment with smaller amounts of the stuff. But what is the third?'

'That we are all as mad as March hares,' said Meryfeld with a conspiratorial grin. 'Let us hope we are not taken to Stourbridge Hospital as lunatics!'

The following day was the Feast of St Gilbert of Sempringham, and because it was Thelnetham's turn to recite the dawn offices – and St Gilbert had founded his Order – Michaelhouse found itself subjected to a much longer service than usual. Michael complained bitterly about hunger pangs, then grumbled about the quality of the food presented at breakfast. He slipped away when the meal had finished, and when Bartholomew saw him in the hall a little later he was wiping crumbs from his mouth with the back of his hand.

Bartholomew was about to remark on it to Suttone, when

he saw the Carmelite doing the same thing. In fact, he thought, looking around, all his colleagues seemed to have fortified themselves from supplies in their rooms, and he was the only one destined to be hungry all morning. He was about to feel sorry for himself when Thelnetham pressed something into his hand.

'Seedcake,' he whispered. 'Made by a certain young baker I like. Eat it quickly. Teaching is due to start in a few moments, and I cannot pontificate when you have that half-starved look about you.'

Somewhat startled that a self-absorbed man like Thelnetham should deign to notice a colleague's discomfort, Bartholomew did as he was told. The cake was cloyingly sweet, and he felt slightly sick when he had finished it. There was also a curious flavour that he could not quite place, and that was not entirely pleasant. He wondered, ungraciously, whether it was past its best, and that was why Thelnetham was willing to share.

Unusually, there were no summonses from patients that morning, and as Michael was busy briefing the new Seneschal – and so unable to pursue his investigation into the killer-thief – Bartholomew was able to teach uninterrupted until noon. Again, he put his students through their paces, although he relented somewhat when the youngest one burst into tears. When the bell rang to announce the end of the morning's teaching, he found himself suddenly dizzy, and was obliged to sit on a bench until the feeling passed.

'What is the matter?' asked Michael, back from his proctorial duties and regarding him in concern. 'You are very pale. Shall I send for Rougham?'

'Christ, no!' Bartholomew saw Michael's disapproving expression – the monk rarely cursed. 'Sorry. I must have inhaled some toxic fumes in Meryfeld's house yesterday.'

'Or perhaps Dickon poisoned the tip of his sword before he stabbed you,' suggested Thelnetham. Bartholomew jumped – he had not known the Gilbertine was there. 'Shall I fetch you some wine?'

Bartholomew stood. 'Thank you, no. Cynric is beckoning, so there will be patients to see.'

'Now?' asked Michael in dismay. 'I hoped we might make some headway with our enquiries.'

'You cannot do that, Brother,' said Cynric, overhearing as he approached. 'Part of York Hostel is ablaze, and they are claiming arson by the Colleges. Beadle Meadowman says it is nothing of the kind, but the victims will take some convincing.'

'Damn this ridiculous feud!' snapped Michael, beginning to stamp towards the door. 'Am I to have *no* time for important business?'

Bartholomew felt better once he was out in the fresh air, although there was still an unpleasant ache in his innards. He wondered what he could have eaten to unsettle them, and supposed it was the seedcake – the other Fellows might be used to rich foods, but he was not, and should have known better than to wolf down so much of it in one go.

He visited Chancellor Tynkell, and was sympathetic when the man complained of a roiling stomach, then trudged to the hovels in the north of the town, where three old people were dying of falling sicknesses. There was nothing he could do for any of them, and he left feeling as though he had let them down. Next, he went to his sister's house on Milne Street, where one of the apprentices had caught a cold. He felt even more of a failure when he was obliged to say he could not cure that, either, and the ailment would have to run its course.

'What is wrong?' asked Edith, when he had finished.

140

'Are you despondent because Drax is to be buried this afternoon, and he was one of Michaelhouse's benefactors?'

'Lord!' muttered Bartholomew, disgusted with himself for forgetting. 'Langelee wants Thelnetham and me to attend that, to represent Michaelhouse.'

And, he recalled, Michael had asked him to observe the congregation, with a view to assessing whether Drax's killer might be in attendance. The monk had wanted to be there, too, to judge the situation for himself, but the fire at York Hostel meant he would probably miss it, so it was down to his Corpse Examiner to take advantage of the occasion.

'I am going, too,' said Edith, reaching for her cloak, a fine, warm garment of dark red. 'So we shall stand together. I cannot say I like Celia, but she may appreciate my support.'

'Do you know her well, then?' asked Bartholomew.

Edith shook her head. 'She married Drax shortly after he lost his fingers in an accident, and I suspect she was attracted by the compensation he was paid by Yffi. It is difficult to admire such a woman, and I confess I have not tried very hard to befriend her.'

'I heard they argued a lot,' said Bartholomew, wondering if she would confirm Dickon's claim.

Edith laughed. 'What married couple does not? Do not look dubious, Matt! If you had wed Matilde, you would know it is true.'

Bartholomew doubted it, but wished he had been granted the chance to find out.

No one at All Saints Church seemed particularly distressed by Drax's demise, and few mourners gave more than a fleeting glance at the coffin as they greeted each other cheerfully and loudly. Bartholomew was under the distinct impression that the taverner would not be missed.

'I suspected you might forget so I thought I had better

141

come, too,' said Langelee to Bartholomew, arriving with Thelnetham at his heels. 'Drax was a benefactor, and it would not do for our College to be under-represented.'

'Not a very generous benefactor,' said Thelnetham, fastidiously rearranging the puce bow that prevented his hood from flying up in the wind. 'He gave us a few candles in exchange for a princely number of masses. The man certainly knew how to drive a bargain.'

'I should not have bothered to come,' said Edith unhappily. 'I detest these occasions, and Celia does not look as though she needs the comfort of acquaintances.'

Bartholomew looked to where she pointed. Celia was composed and vibrant, clearly enjoying the attention that was being lavished on her. Odelina was at her side, simpering at any man who was young and handsome, and evidently thinking that a funeral was as good a place as any to hunt a *beau idéal*. Emma was there, too, with Heslarton, so Bartholomew excused himself and went to talk to them, intending to pose a few questions on Michael's behalf.

'Have you found the yellow-headed thief yet?' he asked.

Heslarton scowled. 'No, although not from want of trying. Still, he cannot elude me for ever. Stealing my mother's box was a vile crime, but harming my daughter . . .'

'And killing Alice,' added Emma, almost as an afterthought. 'But we shall have him. Such a man cannot be allowed to walk the streets with decent, honest folk. We shall ensure he faces justice.'

'He is committing other crimes, too,' said Heslarton. 'Just last night, a man matching his description collided with Celia. When he had gone, she found her pilgrim badge missing.'

'He made her stumble, and stole it while he pretended to steady her,' explained Emma. 'My new physician has lost a token, too. Well, he told me he dropped it, but I imagine it was stolen.'

Bartholomew was about to question them further, when a rustle of cloth made him turn around. It was Celia, all smug smiles and expensive new clothes. He did not think he had ever seen her look so radiant. Heslarton apparently thought so, too, because he gazed admiringly at her.

'I have decided *not* to blame your College for its role in my husband's demise,' she said to Bartholomew. 'So you and your colleagues can leave if you like.'

'That is not why we came,' said Bartholomew, a little indignant. 'We are here to pray for Drax.'

Celia raised her eyebrows. 'Why? I doubt the Almighty will listen to the petitions of a warlock.'

'I hear you have lost a *signaculum*,' said Bartholomew, goaded into introducing a subject he suspected would annoy her. 'Did you buy it, like your husband bought his?'

He watched Heslarton, to see if he would react to this remark, but he remained impassive, and Bartholomew was not sure what to think. However, a flash of something unreadable from Emma's black eyes warned him that he was on dangerous ground.

Celia smiled slyly. 'It was a gift from an admirer. I decided to wear it on my cloak, but then some yellow-headed thief jostled me, and it was gone. Master Heslarton has promised to see him at the end of a rope for his crime.'

'*I* am recovered,' came a voice at Bartholomew's shoulder. It was Odelina, smiling in a way that was vaguely predatory. 'You saved my life, and I shall always be grateful.'

'He probably did it with sorcery,' said Celia snidely.

Suspecting denials would serve no purpose – and a little uncomfortable when Emma regarded him as if she was favourably impressed – Bartholomew returned to Edith, to begin studying the mourners for Michael. He looked around rather helplessly, not sure where to start.

The gloomy Prior Etone and gap-toothed Horneby stood near the front, but although they chanted the responses and stood with heads bowed, their expressions were distant, as though they were thinking of other things. Welfry was with them, his boot-shaped *signaculum* dwarfed by the larger badge that marked him as the University's new Seneschal.

Etone's wealthy pilgrims knelt to one side. Muttering furiously, the two nuns leaned towards each other, and Bartholomew realised with astonishment that they were competing to see who could recite the fastest psalms. Meanwhile, Fen's eyes were fixed on the high altar, and his face wore an oddly ecstatic expression. Bartholomew followed the direction of his gaze, but could see only a wooden cross and two cheap candles. Poynton yawned, apparently struggling to stay awake.

Isnard and several cronies from the Michaelhouse Choir were behind them, and Welfry had trouble controlling his laughter when they joined in some of the musical responses. But his mirth faded abruptly when Emma edged away, one hand to her jaw. He was not a man to find amusement in the discomfort of others.

The surly scholars of Chestre Hostel were near the back, jostling anyone who came too close. Their victims included Brother Jude and Prior Leccheworth of the Gilbertines. Leccheworth stumbled impressively when he was shoved, but it was Neyll who reeled away clutching a bruised arm when the manoeuvre failed to have a similar effect on the beefy Jude.

Yffi and his lads lounged in the aisle. The apprentices looked bored, obviously wishing they were somewhere else. About halfway through the ceremony, Emma beckoned Yffi towards her and began whispering. Yffi nodded frequently, and there was an expression of sly satisfaction on the old woman's face that was distinctly unsettling.

Odelina passed the time by making eyes at two knights from the castle. Celia was next to her, hands folded prayerfully. But the ritual was a protracted one, and it was not long before she began to sigh her impatience. Heslarton stared longingly at her all the while, clearly smitten.

Finally, there was a large contingent of Drax's customers, including Blaston and a number of his artisan friends. Blaston was pale and suitably sombre, but the others were more interested in discussing whether it would be ale or wine provided after the ceremony for mourners.

Bartholomew looked around unhappily. The occasion had attracted a large crowd, but virtually everyone was there because it was expected of them – or for the free refreshments afterwards – not because they felt any sadness at Drax's passing. Of course, he thought with a guilty pang, he was no different. Chagrined, he bowed his head and said his prayers, although Celia's words kept echoing in his head, and he could not help but question whether the petitions of a man thought to commune with the Devil were doing Drax any good. At last the service ended. He saw Edith home, visited two more patients, then walked back to Michaelhouse.

When he arrived, Cynric was waiting to tell him he was needed at the Dominican Priory. With a weary sigh, he made for the gate again, grateful when the Welshman fell in at his side. His spirits were oddly low that day, and he welcomed the company.

The Dominicans' convent lay outside the town, and to reach it Bartholomew exited through the Barnwell Gate and walked along the Hadstock Way. With no buildings for shelter, it was bitterly cold, and the wind sliced wickedly through his cloak. It was not raining, but the sky was overcast, and he wondered if there was snow in the air. He said as much to Cynric.

'No,' replied the book-bearer. 'It will not snow again this year.'

'You seem very sure,' remarked Bartholomew suspiciously.

Cynric nodded. 'I am sure. I dislike snow, because it makes you leave tell-tale footprints when you visit haunts you would rather no one else knew about. So I went to a witch, and enquired how much more we might expect this year. She told me none.'

'I see,' said Bartholomew, not liking to ask what sort of places Cynric frequented that he would rather were kept secret. 'You should ask for your money back, because it is snowing now.'

Cynric inspected the flecks of ice that were settling on their clothes, and sniffed dismissively. 'This is not snow, it is a flurry. There is a difference.'

Bartholomew did not see how, but they had arrived at the priory, so he knocked on the gate. It was a large complex, comprising a church, chapels, refectory, dormitory, chapter house and a range of outbuildings. Virtually all the Dominicans had died during the plague, because they had bravely ministered to the sick and dying and had become victims themselves. But their numbers had grown since, and now they numbered about forty. They were under the command of Prior Morden – no academic but a popular leader. When a lay-brother opened the door, a gale of laughter wafted out.

'I am not coming in,' said Cynric, backing away. 'Last time, they put a bucket of water over the door, so I was doused as I passed through. These Black Friars have a childish sense of humour.'

146

They did, and Bartholomew doubted the situation had improved since the arrival of the ebullient Welfry. He entered the convent cautiously, stepping over the almost invisible rope that had been placed to make visitors trip.

Prior Morden came to greet him. He had clearly been enjoying himself: there were tears of laughter in his eyes and he could hardly keep the smile from his face. He was one of the smallest men Bartholomew had ever met, although his head and limbs were in perfect proportion to the rest of his body. He wore a beautiful cloak and matching habit, and a pair of tiny leather boots.

'We had a mishap during our afternoon meal,' said Morden, leading him towards the infirmary. He began to chortle. 'I thought we should dine on something special today, you see. The winter has been exceptionally hard, and we are all tired of bread and peas.'

'How special?' asked Bartholomew warily, hoping the entire convent had not been provided with bad meat or some such thing. He did not think Morden's idea of a joke was to poison everyone, but with the Dominicans, one could never be sure.

Morden grinned. 'I added a little colouring to the pottage, so it turned blue. But that was not what caused the real trouble. It was the roof.'

'The roof,' echoed Bartholomew flatly, wondering what was coming next.

'Brother Harold arranged for part of it to come down during the meal,' explained Morden. 'Well, not the *roof* exactly, but several baskets containing leaves, scraps of parchment, feathers and other sundries – things that float. It was his intention to shower the novices, and give them a start.'

'And I suppose the baskets fell, too, and someone happened to be underneath one,' surmised Bartholomew. 'Really, Father! This is not the first time you have

147

summoned me to treat members of your community who have suffered physical harm from these jests. They are getting out of hand.'

'I will order them curtailed,' said Morden sheepishly. 'Come. Your patient is waiting.'

'Who is it?' asked Bartholomew, thinking it was testament to the wildness of the Dominicans' sense of humour that he knew most of them fairly well.

'Welfry. He was sitting with the novices today because he has been teaching them Aristotle. Oh, well, he will know better next time.'

'Let us hope there will not *be* a next time,' muttered Bartholomew.

Welfry was lying on a cot in the infirmary. His normally smiling face was pale, and feathers and leaves still adhered to his habit. They stuck to the glove on his left hand, too, while a scrap of parchment had lodged itself in the boot-shaped *signaculum* that was pinned at his shoulder.

'Ah, Matthew,' he said weakly as Morden conducted the physician to his bedside. 'I have been brained by a basket, and my head feels as though it might split asunder.'

'I understand you were the victim of a joke,' said Bartholomew, kneeling next to him and inspecting the abused pate under its mop of tawny hair.

'A joke,' growled Welfry, looking pointedly at Morden. 'Is that what you call it?'

'It was funny,' objected Morden.

'No,' corrected Welfry sternly. 'It ended in bloodshed, which means it was *not* amusing. Harold needs to make sure this kind of thing does not happen when he executes his pranks. I am proud of my intellect, and I do not want it splattered all over the refectory in the name of humour.'

'It will not happen again,' said Morden. 'He is mortified by what has happened, and I have ordered him to work in the gardens for the next month, as a punishment.'

Welfry waved a weary hand. 'It would be better if you let me have him for a month instead. He could learn a lot – including how to secure baskets to rafters.'

'It is not a good idea to encourage Harold's penchant for clownery,' said Bartholomew in alarm.

'We shall see,' said Morden. 'But what can you do to help poor Welfry? We are all delighted by his appointment as Seneschal, but he says he might have to resign if his injury is irreparable.'

'It is not irreparable,' said Bartholomew, rummaging in his bag for the poultice of elder leaves, poppy petals and oil that he used in such situations. 'He has a nasty lump, but that is all.'

'Thank God,' said Morden, crossing himself. 'I had better tell Harold, because he is beside himself with worry. Thank you, Matthew. Here is a shilling for your pains – more than we usually pay, because I know you will spend it all on medicines for the poor.'

He was gone before the physician could thank him, tiny feet clattering across the flagstones. Bartholomew turned his attention back to the poultice.

'I keep meaning to ask you about the illumination of St Mary the Great,' he said as he worked. 'Do you know how it was managed?'

'That was Kendale, not me.' Welfry smiled wanly. 'But I wish it had been! It was an incredible achievement, especially the device he called a "fuse".'

'A fuse?'

'Yes – a piece of twine smeared with some substance that made it burn at a steady and reliable rate. It allowed all his buckets of sludge to be ignited simultaneously, and was highly ingenious.'

'I see,' said Bartholomew. 'What did his sludge comprise, exactly?'

'I wish I knew. I tried to question him, but he was . . . let us say less than forthcoming.'

'You are friends with him?'

'Hardly! My Order has taken the side of the Colleges in this ridiculous spat with the hostels, so he would sooner die than forge a friendship with me. In fact, when I asked for details of his trick, all enthusiasm and admiration, he said that unless I got out of his way, he would skewer me.'

Bartholomew shook his head in disgust. 'And that is why I am sceptical of the claims that he was the instigator. It seems too harmless a prank for him.'

'It was a challenge to the Colleges,' said Welfry, mock-serious. 'There was nothing harmless about it. Besides, Valence thinks his real intention was to set Gonville Hall alight.'

'Do you believe that?'

Welfry considered the question carefully. 'No. It would be malicious beyond words, and I cannot believe a fellow scholar would stoop so low. But it is a pity Kendale is so sullen, for he possesses a formidable intellect. I would relish some mental sparring with him.'

'Are you sure you do not know the formula for his sludge?' pressed Bartholomew. 'You cannot even hazard a guess?'

'From the odour that lingered afterwards, I would say it contained brimstone and some sort of tarry pitch. But there will have been other ingredients, and I cannot begin to imagine what they were.' Welfry brightened. 'We answered the challenge by putting the ox and cart on the Gilbertines' roof. And no one was maimed, incinerated or brained while we did so.'

'The next time the hostels play a prank, it might be best

150

not to respond. Michael spent much of today trying to quell disturbances, and more tricks will only exacerbate the matter.'

'I beg to differ,' argued Welfry. 'The ox and cart served to *calm* troubled waters – it made scholars laugh instead of fight, and hostilities eased for several days. Until Kendale thought up that nasty business with the bull. Then the situation turned angry again.'

'I hope it ends soon,' said Bartholomew fervently. 'I do not want the streets running with blood.'

'Nor do I,' said Welfry. 'But I shall do all in my power to make people smile, because I honestly believe humour is the best way to defuse this horrible tension.'

'You may be right,' conceded Bartholomew. 'I suppose it is worth a try.'

Welfry's smile turned rueful. 'I know I am not much of a friar, with my love of laughter, but if I can use my wits to confine this feud to a series of harmless pranks, then perhaps God will overlook my flaws. And if not, I can always go on a pilgrimage – this time to somewhere rather more holy than the site where John Schorne conjured the Devil into a boot.'

CHAPTER 5

Bartholomew returned to Michaelhouse and taught until it was too dark to see. He took Valence and Cynric with him on his evening rounds, Valence so he might learn, and Cynric because the book-bearer was restless and wanted to be out. There were a lot of patients, and he grew steadily more despondent when he realised the list would be reduced by two-thirds if people had access to warmth and decent food. One visit took him to the Carmelite Priory, where Prior Etone wanted another report on his protégé.

'It just needs time to heal,' he said, after struggling to look down Horneby's throat with the terrible lamp. 'The worst is past, and I can tell you no more than I did the last time – that he must sip the blackcurrant syrup I prescribed, and avoid speaking as much as possible.'

'He insisted on visiting Welfry this afternoon,' said Etone disapprovingly. 'And he talked then.'

'Welfry is my friend, and I was worried when I heard he had been hurt,' croaked Horneby. 'And he did most of the talking, anyway.'

'I can well imagine,' said Etone, not entirely pleasantly. 'But I must have Horneby fit by next Tuesday, Matthew. We cannot postpone the Stock Extraordinary Lecture.'

'Why not?' whispered Horneby. 'What can it matter if it is delayed a week?'

Etone's expression was earnest. 'Because I want those pilgrims here when it takes place. If they see we are a great centre of learning, they are more likely to be generous when they leave. The pardoner, Fen, has already intimated that he admires good scholarship.'

'We should let Horneby rest,' said Bartholomew. He could see the younger man was appalled by his Prior's motives, and did not want him to begin a speech that would strain his voice. He followed Etone out of the dormitory, and was walking across the yard to rejoin Valence and Cynric when he became aware of a commotion near the shed containing St Simon Stock's relic.

'Now what?' muttered Etone irritably, beginning to stride towards it. 'The only problem with having a shrine that attracts pilgrims is that it attracts pilgrims. I know that sounds contrary, but they are volatile creatures, and there is always some problem that needs my attention.'

It was none of Bartholomew's affair, so he headed for the gate. Cynric and Valence were nowhere to be seen, but it was late, he still had patients to see, and he was disinclined to hunt for them. He was about to leave them to their own devices, when a clamour wafted across the yard.

'It was not me!' He recognised the shrill, angry tones of one of the visiting nuns. 'And I am outraged that you should accuse me of it.'

'It must have been someone from outside the priory,' came a softer, more reasoned voice. Fen, thought Bartholomew, picturing the pardoner's handsome face and calm demeanour. 'The shrine is open to all, so anyone could have come in and made off with it.'

'No!' Etone's agonised scream tore through the air.

Alarmed, Bartholomew ran towards the hut. He pushed through the door and found it full of people. Etone was on his knees, gazing at the jewelled box that held St Simon Stock's scapular, while several of his friars milled around in agitation. Cynric and Valence were near the back, watching with undisguised curiosity.

'Someone has been in the reliquary, sir,' explained Valence in a whisper. 'And used a sharp knife to make off with a bit of St Simon's scapular.'

'Accusations are being levelled,' elaborated Cynric, his dark eyes alight with interest. 'And denials are being made. At the moment that fat nun – Margaret – is being grilled, because she was in here alone for a long time, apparently.'

'I would never defile a holy relic,' Margaret cried furiously. 'I am a pilgrim, not a thief.'

'But a pilgrim *must* be the culprit, because they are the only ones who come here,' gulped Etone. His face was white with shock as he turned to his friars. 'I want a list of everyone who has been in today. I know our relic was in one piece at dawn, because I opened the chest to have a look at it.'

'But we do not keep such a list, Father,' objected one friar. He was a skeletal man named Riborowe, who was a skilled illuminator of manuscripts. 'We let people come and go as they please.'

Etone stood and opened the box with hands that shook. Then he sank to his knees again and rested his head on the altar.

'It is all here,' he whispered, relief evident in his voice. 'The thief must have been disturbed before he could complete his wicked business. He cut the cloth, but the material is thicker than it looks, and he was thwarted. Our relic is damaged, but we still have it all.'

There were thankful murmurings, and muttered remarks that the saint was watching over what was his. Etone recited a few prayers, then stood and faced the people in the room.

'But a crime has still been committed,' he said sternly. 'And I want to know who did it and how it was permitted to happen.'

154

'I saw the lock on the reliquary had been forced,' explained Riborowe. 'So I asked the four pilgrims – who spend more time here than anyone else – whether they had noticed anything amiss.'

'He accused us of being thieves,' countered Poynton angrily. His face was redder than usual, and veins swelled on his head and neck. Not for the first time, Bartholomew thought he looked ill. 'We, who are devout pilgrims, and spend our whole lives travelling from shrine to shrine!'

'I did not—' began Riborowe, shooting a guilty glance at his prior.

'You did,' interrupted Margaret venomously. 'You said I broke into the chest and applied the scissors I use for my personal beauty to ...' She waved her hand, unable to continue.

'Clearly, none of us is the culprit,' said Fen quietly, injecting a tone of reason into the discussion. 'But perhaps we – without realising it – witnessed something that may help bring the real villain to justice. So let us not argue, but tell each other what we heard and saw, so we may work together to solve this dreadful crime.'

'Very well,' said Prior Etone with a stiff nod. 'You may go first.'

'Unfortunately, I have nothing of value to report,' said Fen apologetically. 'I prayed here all morning, then left to attend the taverner's requiem. I went for a walk afterwards, and by the time I returned, Riborowe was already yelling accusations at Sister Margaret. In other words, the misdeed was committed while I was elsewhere.'

'The reliquary lock must have been broken before I came in,' declared Margaret. 'But I did not notice the damage, because my eyes are not very good in dim light.'

'What about you?' asked Etone, turning to Poynton.

'I also prayed here alone,' replied Poynton. He was still

livid, and kept his voice level with obvious difficulty. 'I find it hard to concentrate when I am surrounded by clamouring peasants, so I always wait until they have gone. But I saw nothing to help you identify the culprit.'

'Neither did I,' added the second nun. 'I tend not to notice what other penitents do – I am more concerned with praying for my own soul than with monitoring their squalid activities.'

'It was probably that yellow-headed villain again,' said Margaret bitterly. 'He has been going around stealing *signacula*, so why not set his sights on a priceless relic?'

'Did you see him here?' asked Riborowe.

'No,' replied Margaret coolly. 'But it stands to reason.'

'Not necessarily,' said Fen. 'There is a big difference between making off with badges and stealing St Simon Stock's scapular.'

'Well, one thing is clear from this unsavoury incident,' declared Poynton. 'This nasty little town is full of thieves. You should take measures against them, Father Prior.'

'We never had any trouble before you came,' muttered Riborowe, although he spoke under his breath and Etone did not hear. The pilgrims did, though, and Poynton stepped forward.

'We should go,' said Bartholomew to Valence and Cynric, loath to witness any more of the unedifying spectacle. 'This is not our concern.'

'It is Brother Michael's, though,' whispered Cynric. 'He will be obliged to investigate an attempt to deprive Cambridge's only shrine of its holy relic.'

The next patient on Bartholomew's list was Isnard, who had tripped over a cat as he had weaved his way home from the King's Head. The bargeman denied being drunk, although the strong scent of ale that pervaded his little cottage suggested he was not being entirely honest. Bartholomew felt his spirits lift as he listened to the familiar litany of excuses; there was always something reassuringly predictable about Isnard.

Yolande de Blaston was there, too. Isnard was one of her 'regulars', because he could afford what she liked to charge. Despite only having one leg – Bartholomew had been forced to amputate the other after an accident – Isnard earned a respectable living by directing barges along the river, and had even amassed enough money to purchase a couple of boats himself.

Yolande was cooking – meals were often included in the arrangement she had with Isnard; it was not the first time they had found her stirring something delicious over a pot in his hearth. Hospitably, Isnard indicated that his visitors should sit at the table and share his supper.

'Thank you,' said Valence, immediately taking a seat and pulling a horn spoon from his belt. 'College food is getting worse by the day, and I am tired of buying my own all the time.'

'Isnard and I always have a stew on a Thursday evening,' supplied Yolande conversationally. 'We work up quite an appetite during our sessions together.'

Bartholomew saw Cynric purse his lips prudishly and Valence start to snigger, so he hastened to change the subject before Yolande or Isnard noticed, suspecting neither reaction would please them.

'How is your family, Yolande?'

'Well enough, but hungry all the time. This winter is particularly hard.'

'I help her all I can,' whispered Isnard, when she went to stir her concoction. 'But fourteen children is a lot to feed. I am glad Blaston has work at Michaelhouse, because there is not much call for carpenters these days, not when people think it is more important to spend money on bread.'

Bartholomew looked at the telltale bulge around Yolande's middle, and wondered when the fifteenth child would make its appearance. While she added the finishing touches to her stew, he rubbed a soothing balm on Isnard's one remaining knee, then sat at the table while she ladled the food into bowls. The soup and the conversation of friends served to lift his spirits a little more – until Valence began to hold forth about Drax.

'In other words, the killer took the body to Michaelhouse, and dumped it there,' the student concluded indignantly. 'It was fortunate Agatha chased that dog, or it might have been *ages* before it was discovered, because Yffi has not been around much for the last few days.'

Isnard shuddered. 'Poor Drax! I liked him – he owned several lovely taverns.'

'You like everyone, Isnard,' said Yolande disapprovingly. 'But my Robert said he was not very nice. Apparently, he bought himself an expensive pilgrim badge because he knew he was going to need it when his soul was weighed. And you do not spend a fortune on indulgences unless you have a guilty conscience.'

'Or unless you think you might be about to die,' added Cynric soberly.

Bartholomew looked at him sharply. 'What do you mean by that?'

Cynric shrugged. 'Just that Drax might have known someone was going to harm him, so he bought a *signaculum* while he was still able.'

'I heard Emma buys a lot of pardons, too,' said Yolande confidentially. 'And the prayers she needs from Michaelhouse are costing her a new roof, so *she* must have a *very* guilty conscience.'

'Emma?' queried Isnard, startled. 'Never! She is a dear, sweet old lady.'

Everyone regarded him askance.

'I am talking about Emma de Colvyll here,' said Yolande. 'Who is your "dear, sweet old lady", because we are not discussing the same person.'

'We are,' said Isnard, stung. 'She has been nothing but charming to me.'

'You do business with her?' asked Bartholomew.

Isnard nodded. 'She hires my barges to transport materials through the Fens – mostly stone and wood for repairing the various properties she buys. She deals with me honestly and fairly.'

'But she has a reputation,' said Yolande darkly.

'One designed to stop people from trying to cheat her,' argued Isnard. 'She has a generous heart. Take Michaelhouse, for example. She is mending its leaking roofs out of love for her fellow man, and all she asks in return is a few masses from its priests.'

'But my Robert says she will want more in time,' said Yolande. 'And Michaelhouse hates being in her debt. Master Langelee told me so when I entertained him last week. He said her charity has caused the biggest rift between him and his Fellows since he took the Mastership. But he said he had no choice – it would have been churlish to refuse her on the basis of their dislike.'

'It would,' agreed Isnard. 'His Fellows *are* being churlish if they are suspicious of kindness. They should learn to accept that not everyone has sly motives.'

'Did you see the ox and cart on the Gilbertines' roof?' asked Bartholomew, changing the subject before there was an argument. Cynric and Valence looked ready to pitch in with their views, which were unlikely to be complimentary to Emma, and would annoy Isnard.

159

'Yes, it was very clever,' said Yolande, smiling. 'But not nearly as amazing as when the hostels lit up St Mary the Great.'

'I disagree!' cried Valence. 'The trick at the church was just the flinging together of a few flammable substances, whereas the ox and cart required real ingenuity. It took Brother Michael days to achieve what we ... what the Colleges managed in a single night. And Brother Michael is no fool.'

'I do not like that Kendale,' said Isnard sullenly. 'He called me a drunkard – him, who cannot pass a tavern without stepping inside for an ale! And all his lads are fond of a drop or two.'

'They are out a lot at night, too,' added Yolande, while Valence nodded vigorous agreement with Isnard. 'I see them when I visit my clients. Tell Brother Michael to watch them, Doctor, because I am sure they mean mischief.'

'Their home, Chestre Hostel, is haunted,' said Cynric matter-of-factly. 'It did not use to be, but those hostel men brought an evil aura with them, and now it pervades the building.'

'Cynric!' said Bartholomew sharply, aware that this was the sort of tale that might be repeated and then blown out of all proportion. He did not want the hostels to accuse the Colleges of rumour-mongering, thus providing an excuse for the full-scale war that everyone sensed was brewing.

'Actually, he is right,' said Yolande. 'There *is* something nasty about Chestre. Why do you think Drax tried to raise the rent? To get rid of them! Of course, it saw him dead for his pains.'

'You think Chestre killed Drax?' asked Bartholomew. 'Do you have any evidence to suggest—'

'I do not need evidence,' declared Yolande loftily.

160

'Because I have intuition. Kendale and his horrible students live near where Drax died and where he was dumped, and they objected to the fact that he wanted to raise the rent. Of course they are the culprits.'

'Did you hear that Celia Drax was robbed?' asked Isnard, when the physician was silent. 'She lost a pilgrim badge, which is odd, because a number of them have gone astray recently.'

Yolande nodded. 'Poynton had one filched off his saddlebag, and the Mayor told me just today that he had two pinched from the Guildhall. Then there is Meryfeld the physician – he thought his had fallen off his cloak, but in the light of these other thefts, he has reconsidered.'

Bartholomew stood. It was getting late and he was tired. He thanked Isnard for his hospitality.

'Be careful,' said the bargeman as he left. 'You may think Cambridge is safe at the moment, because we have had no serious trouble for weeks, but there is something nasty in the air. Perhaps it is the hostels itching for a fight. Or perhaps it is the thief with his penchant for pilgrim relics, which is as black a sin as any. Regardless, our town feels very dangerous to me.'

His warning sent a tingle of unease down Bartholomew's spine.

Cynric slipped away on business of his own when they reached the main road. Bartholomew was tempted to call him back, not liking the notion of him being out alone after what Isnard had said, but then he came to his senses. Cynric was a seasoned warrior, and knew how to look after himself.

'The last patient is none other than the loathsome Kendale himself,' said Valence. He gave a feeble laugh. 'I am not sure we should go, given what Isnard has just told us about him.'

161

Bartholomew recalled his last encounter with Kendale, when the Principal and his students had accosted him in St Michael's Lane and initiated a contest about who should have right of way.

'He has a cheek to think you will help him,' Valence went on when there was no reply. 'Neyll told Walter that Rougham, Gyseburne and Meryfeld have all refused to visit, and that you are his last hope. But that is no reason to tend a man like Kendale.'

'Did Neyll say what is wrong?' asked Bartholomew. He did not usually refuse to see patients, but did not relish the prospect of setting foot in a house full of men who hated members of Colleges.

'He has a crushed hand,' explained Valence. 'An accident. Neyll told me they have stopped the bleeding, but that it needs stitches and possibly set bones.'

'Then why did you not mention it sooner?' demanded Bartholomew, aghast. 'We should have gone there first. You give the impression that it is a routine call, but it is an emergency!'

'I forgot,' said Valence. He saw Bartholomew's sceptical glance. 'I *did*!'

There was no point in remonstrating. 'Tell Michael where I am. And if I do not return by—'

'I am not letting you visit Chestre alone,' declared Valence, straightening his shoulders defiantly. 'Michaelhouse students are *not* afraid of hostel men.'

Bartholomew tried to dissuade him, but Valence was adamant. He gave way, and they walked briskly down the lane to the grand house currently leased by Kendale. Valence knocked, and while they waited for a reply, Bartholomew studied the building that Cynric said was haunted.

During the day, he would have dismissed the book-bearer's notion as fancy, but at night there was something

162

vaguely unearthly about the place. It was darker than the surrounding houses, and its roof overhung rather forebodingly. In addition, its windows formed a pattern that looked like two eyes and a leering mouth. When he saw the route his thoughts had taken, Bartholomew shook his head, disgusted with himself for allowing his imagination to run so wild.

Neyll answered the door immediately, and his black eyebrows drew down into a hostile scowl when he saw Bartholomew and Valence. The physician took a step back. Was someone playing a joke, deliberately sending them into an awkward situation?

'We were beginning to think you were too frightened to come,' the Bible Scholar growled sullenly. 'Well? Are you just going to stand there, or are you coming in?'

Inside, Bartholomew was disconcerted to note that Kendale and his students had decorated Chestre's walls with the skulls of animals they had slaughtered. Some were very fearsome, with great curling horns and gaping eye sockets. He saw Valence cross himself and felt the urge to do the same. He might have done, but Neyll was watching, and he had his pride.

The house comprised a large hall on the ground floor, plus two smaller rooms for private teaching or reading. A flight of stairs led to the upper storey, and in the gloom he could see more bones adorning those walls, too; he wondered why Kendale had not settled for tapestries or murals, like everyone else. More steps led to a cellar, which a trail of muddy footprints suggested was in frequent use – probably, he thought, noting the number of telltale splashes on the walls, because it was where they stored their claret.

'At last!' exclaimed Kendale. He was sitting by the fire, and his hand was a mess of bloody cloths. All his students

163

were there, and the place reeked of wine. 'I know we hostel men are not a high priority, but I did not think you would leave me in agony for quite so long.'

'I am sorry,' said Bartholomew, genuinely contrite. 'It has been a busy evening.'

He knelt next to Kendale, and gently removed the dressings. The hand had indeed been crushed – the fingers were bruised, and there were deep cuts across the back of them.

'I slipped on some ice,' said Kendale, by means of explanation.

'This is not the sort of injury that can be sustained by falling,' remarked Bartholomew absently, inspecting it in the light of the fire.

'Are you accusing me of lying?' demanded Kendale. There was an immediate menacing murmur from his students, and two or three came angrily to their feet.

'Only if you are accusing me of being unable to distinguish between injuries caused by a tumble, and injuries caused by compression,' retorted Bartholomew tartly, declining to be intimidated.

Kendale regarded him silently for a moment, then laughed, although it was not a pleasant sound. 'All right, I did not slip. I caught it in the door.'

'It must have been quite a door,' muttered Bartholomew, not believing that tale, either.

'You are as bad as Meryfeld,' sneered Neyll. 'He is all nosy questions, too. The last time he came, he asked so many of them that we had to put a knife to his throat, to shut him up.'

Bartholomew glanced at him, to see whether he was making a joke, but the dour visage told him that the Bible Scholar was no more capable of humour than he was of flying to the moon. And if his claim was true, then it was not surprising the other *medici* had declined to answer Kendale's summons.

'Meryfeld is your physician?' Bartholomew asked. 'Then why did he not come tonight?'

'Neyll's teasing must have frightened him off,' said Kendale. 'But does it matter how my hand came to be injured? I want you to mend it, not analyse how it could have been avoided.'

'Of course it matters,' replied Bartholomew. 'Knowing how a wound was caused tells me what sort of damage might lie beneath the skin. For example, the hard edges of a door will result in different harm than if your hand was caught between two flat surfaces.'

'It was not two flat surfaces,' said Kendale, after a moment of thought. 'As I said, it was a door.'

Bartholomew was disinclined to argue. He asked for a lamp, then began to suture the larger cuts with stitches any seamstress would have been proud of. Kendale gritted his teeth, although the reek of wine on his breath indicated he should not have been feeling a great deal.

'Thank you,' said Kendale, sitting back in relief when the operation was over and the hand was wrapped in clean bandages. 'And now sit down, and have a drink.'

'It is late,' said Bartholomew. 'And I do not—'

'Drink,' ordered Neyll, slamming a goblet on the table in front of him and filling it to the brim. 'In my country, no guest leaves without refreshment. Not even members of pompous, rich Colleges. You, too, Valence. Sit, or we will be deeply offended.'

Bartholomew did not want his refusal to be used as an excuse for a spat, so with a sigh of resignation, he perched on the bench next to Valence and picked up the goblet. 'To good relations,' he said, raising it in salute. 'Between the hostels and the Colleges.'

'I do not know about that,' growled Kendale. 'I am more inclined to toast continued hostilities. It is a lot more satisfying.'

There was a cheer from the students, and the toast was repeated in a feisty roar.

Because he was tired, the wine went straight to Bartholomew's head. He finished it with difficulty, and started to stand, but Neyll grabbed his shoulder and pushed him back down again, while another student refilled the goblet. Meanwhile, Valence was already on his third cupful.

'We really must go,' said Bartholomew, trying to struggle away from Neyll's meaty hand. It was hopeless: the burly Bible Scholar was extremely strong.

'Why?' demanded Kendale. 'You cannot have more patients at this time of the night. Or are you too good to drink in our hostel?'

'Of course not,' said Bartholomew. 'But patients summon me at all hours, and—'

'Drink!' ordered Kendale, flicking his fingers at an ale-bellied lad, who brought another jug of claret to the hearth. Kendale swallowed two brimming cups in quick succession, and indicated that the student was to pour him a third.

'Easy,' advised Bartholomew. 'Too much wine is not good after the shock of a wound.'

Kendale sneered. 'I am from the north. We can drink as much as we like without it having the slightest effect on us. Why do you think we win so many battles?'

Bartholomew was not entirely sure how these two claims fitted together. 'I see,' he hedged.

'My family's history is peppered with glorious victories,' Kendale went on. His students gave another cheer, and he grinned at them. 'Indeed, we all have warrior blood running in our veins, which is why we can drink any mere College man into a state of oblivion.'

'I am sure you can,' said Bartholomew, hoping he and Valence would not be expected to meet the challenge. He changed the subject hastily. 'What percentage of brimstone to pitch did you use when you lit up St Mary the Great? You see, I would like a lamp that burns with a constant light. It would be useful for situations like these, where it is difficult to see what—'

'You could not see properly?' demanded Kendale. 'No wonder it hurt!'

'I did not mean—' began Bartholomew, realising he would have to watch what he said.

'Drink up,' interrupted Neyll. 'Or is our claret not fine enough for you?'

'It is very nice,' said Bartholomew, taking another gulp. Someone had refilled his cup again, and he wondered whether they intended to keep him there all night. 'Now, about the light—'

'No,' said Kendale firmly. 'Why should I tell you how to create something that might make you rich? I would be better inventing such a lamp myself.'

'Do it, then,' urged Bartholomew. 'It would have all manner of useful applications.'

'No,' said Kendale again. 'I have better things to do. Such as besting arrogant Colleges.'

There was yet another cheer from the students, and Kendale raised his goblet in a sloppy salute. Cups were drained and slammed down on tables, and the ale-bellied student began filling them again. Bartholomew tried to snatch his away, but his fingers were now clumsy and he was too late. He glanced at Valence and saw him glare defiantly at Neyll before downing the contents of his beaker in a single swallow. Neyll did the same, then reached for the jug.

'Stop,' ordered Bartholomew, loath to spend the rest of the night dealing with cases of excessive intoxication, especially as he was now far from sober himself. 'You have been more than generous, Principal Kendale, but it is time for us to go home.'

'Yes, give us our fee, and we will be gone,' slurred Valence. 'A shilling.'

Bartholomew winced. Payment had been a long way from his mind, and he wished it had been a long way from Valence's, too. It was not the time for issuing demands for cash.

'A shilling?' demanded the ale-paunched student. 'That is brazen robbery!'

'It is non-negotiable, Gib,' stated Valence, trying to stand and failing. He slumped into Neyll, who slopped wine on the floor. 'You should have asked for a quotation before we started if you intended to bargain with us.'

'Bartholomew is a surgeon, not a builder,' snapped Gib. 'You do not haggle with surgeons.'

'He is a physician,' declared Valence hotly. He hiccuped. 'Not a surgeon.'

'If Bartholomew were a physician, he would have prepared my horoscope and inspected my urine,' said Kendale. 'But he sutured my wounds. That is surgery. And surgeons are lowly, base creatures, so we shall pay accordingly. One penny.'

'That is outrageous!' exploded Valence, trying to stand again. 'You are cheating—'

'Enough,' snapped Bartholomew, wondering whether Chestre had intended to provoke a quarrel all along. He felt the room tip as he stood, and it was not easy to haul Valence up from the bench and keep him from falling. 'Thank you for your hospitality. Now please excuse us.'

Valence managed a malicious grin. 'The stitches will

need to be removed in a week, Kendale. Do not attempt it yourself, because you will fatally poison your blood and die.'

Neyll moved fast, and snatched Valence away from Bartholomew, to grab him by the throat. Bartholomew tried to interpose himself between them, but Gib blocked his way. Valence gagged as Neyll's fingers tightened. Bartholomew tried to dodge around Gib, but the lad pushed him hard enough to make him stagger. His medicine bag slipped off his shoulder, scattering its contents across the floor. Then Gib drew a dagger.

'Stop!'

Kendale had spoken softly, but his voice carried enough authority to make Neyll release Valence and Gib lower his weapon. Valence tottered away, hands to his neck. In the silence that followed, one of the younger students knelt and began shoving phials, pots and dressings back into Bartholomew's bag. Then he handed it to the physician, and stood back.

'There,' said Kendale smoothly. 'No harm done. But it is very late, and I am tired. Goodnight.'

Bartholomew nodded coolly, seized Valence's arm and left without another word. His heart hammered in his chest, and he expected at any moment that the Chestre students would attack them *en masse*. But no one moved, and it was with considerable relief that he stepped into the street outside.

He tried to set a brisk pace towards Michaelhouse, but his legs were like rubber and Valence was weaving all over the place. They reached the College eventually and hammered on the gate, but Walter was evidently doing his rounds, so they were obliged to wait to be let in. Bartholomew sought the support of a wall, and leaned against it, feeling the world ripple and sway unpleasantly around him.

'That was powerful wine,' slurred Valence, also aiming for the wall, but missing and slumping to the ground. There was begrudging admiration in his voice. 'I hate to say something positive about a hostel, but those Chestre boys certainly know how to handle their drink!'

'That is not necessarily a good thing,' began Bartholomew. 'The body's humours will—'

He tensed when a flicker of movement caught his eye. He tugged Valence into the shadows, afraid Kendale might have changed his mind and had given his louts permission to finish what they had started. But Kendale did not so much as glance at Michaelhouse as he padded past, his students streaming at his heels.

'I wonder where they are going,' mused Valence drunkenly, trying to stand. 'We had better follow them and see.'

Bartholomew regarded him askance. 'I do not think so!'

'But they may mean us harm,' objected Valence. Unable to walk, he began to crawl along the lane, so Bartholomew was forced to grab a handful of tunic, to stop him. 'Let me go! I must see!'

'No,' said Bartholomew firmly. 'We have had enough trouble for one night.'

The following morning was cloudy, but just as cold. There was a dusting of frost, and Michael claimed he might as well have slept outside, given that he had nothing but a sheet for a roof. Bartholomew felt he was in just as bleak a position, because Yffi had removed the window shutters from the ground-floor rooms, and the night had been windy. Bottles had jangled and parchment had rustled all night. He was usually a heavy sleeper, capable of dozing through all but the most frenetic of commotions, but the wine and the fracas at Chestre had left him unsettled, and he found himself waking every few moments.

170

'I will show Chestre what happens to ruffians who intimidate members of my College,' snarled Michael angrily, after the physician described what had happened.

'You cannot, Brother. Technically, all they did was give us wine and engage us in conversation. Besides, Kendale may well have done it to exacerbate the trouble between the hostels and the Colleges, and we should not play into his hands.'

'No,' acknowledged Michael reluctantly. 'We should not. But I will be watching him, and if he puts one foot wrong, he will learn what it means to annoy the Senior Proctor.'

Once washed and dressed, Bartholomew limped lethargically into the yard to join his colleagues for their morning devotions. The leg he had broken falling off his horse the previous year ached from the cold, and the wine had left him with a nasty headache. Langelee regarded him in alarm.

'You cannot be ill!' he cried. 'Not when you are supposed to be Official Physician for the camp-ball this afternoon. Prior Leccheworth said he would not let the game go ahead unless there was a qualified *medicus* on hand, to deal with mishaps.'

'I disapprove of camp-ball,' said Suttone, who was in an awkward position: should he support his Order or his Master? 'Why could the Gilbertines not sponsor a lecture instead?'

'Because they know what people like,' explained Langelee impatiently. 'Which do you think will be more popular among the masses – a lecture or an exciting game, full of blood and savagery?'

'Christ!' muttered Bartholomew.

'And hundreds of people will be there to watch,' Langelee went on, turning back to him. 'So you had better pull yourself together. Go and lie down. Use my room, if

171

you like. There is a fire burning, and the blankets are reasonably clean.'

'I am not ill,' said Bartholomew. He became aware that Thelnetham was regarding him oddly. He had been about to tell his colleagues what had happened at Chestre, but the Gilbertine's expression made him reconsider, although he was not sure why. 'Just tired.'

'Then rest,' ordered Langelee. 'If you are not fighting fit by this afternoon I shall be very disappointed. And you do not want me disappointed, believe me.'

'You had better do as he says,' murmured Michael, while Bartholomew tried to decide whether he had just been threatened with violence. 'And afterwards, Valence can read to your class while you come with me to see Celia Drax. I know we have spoken to her already, but I am sure there is more to be learned from her.'

Bartholomew decided to take Langelee at his word, and exchange a chilly hour in church for a pleasant interlude reading by the fire. He heard the procession leave a few moments later, and was already engrossed in Galen's *Tegni*, when the door opened and Thelnetham walked in.

'Are you sure you are not ill?' the Gilbertine asked. 'You are paler than usual.'

For some reason, Bartholomew felt uneasy with Thelnetham in the room. The canon was older and smaller than he, and represented no kind of physical threat, but there was something about his manner that morning which was unsettling. His eyes seemed oddly bright, and his smile brittle.

'Too much wine last night,' explained Bartholomew, supposing he might as well be honest.

'I see,' said Thelnetham, his expression unreadable. 'But I am forgetting the purpose of my visit. Agatha is outside, and wants to know if she can bring you some broth. She

172

is reluctant to enter our rooms uninvited, as you know.'

Agatha always did exactly as she pleased, and it was Thelnetham who made a fuss about her going where she was not supposed to be. Bartholomew could only suppose the Gilbertine had intercepted her, and ordered her to wait. He could not imagine she would be pleased, and knew he had to make amends fast – Agatha was vengeful, and her grudges lasted a long time.

'I will come,' he said, starting to stand. But Thelnetham waved him back down.

'It is unseemly to entertain women in our quarters, but I will overlook the matter today, as you are unwell. I shall tell her she may enter, just this once.'

Within moments, Agatha's bulk filled the door, all sturdy hips and swinging skirts. Bartholomew was relieved when he saw Thelnetham had not accompanied her.

'Here,' she said, handing Bartholomew a steaming bowl. 'You cannot be ill for the camp-ball, because I am looking forward to it. And do not say Leccheworth can appoint another Official Physician, for none of the others will sew wounds.'

Bartholomew sipped the broth, and was surprised to find it was good, proving that decent victuals could be produced in Michaelhouse on occasion. While he drank, Agatha regaled him with opinions. She covered a wide range of topics, including the stolen pilgrim regalia, the University's excitement over the Stock Extraordinary Lecture, Emma's ruthless greed in acquiring property, and Seneschal Welfry's skill in practical jokes.

'He has become the Colleges' champion,' she declared. 'But unfortunately, he is so determined that no one will be hurt during his pranks that he lets himself be limited. Kendale, on the other hand, does not care about safety. And if a College member is injured, he is delighted.'

Bartholomew suspected she was right. Her next subject was Celia Drax, and the new widow's unseemly behaviour since her husband's death.

'She is out all the time, enjoying herself. Of course, it was all timed perfectly.'

'What was?' Bartholomew asked, bemused.

'The two deaths – Celia's husband and Heslarton's wife. They are free to be together now.'

'They are lovers?' asked Bartholomew, startled. But then he recalled how Heslarton had looked at Celia during Drax's funeral, and supposed Agatha might be right.

'Of course they are,' declared Agatha. 'And everyone in the town knows it. Except you, it would seem. And Drax and Alice were murdered on successive days, so it is obvious what happened – Heslarton and Celia plotted together to get rid of them.'

'It could be coincidence,' said Bartholomew. Or could it? What about the pharmacopoeia he had found in Celia's house, which listed wolfsbane as a herb that could kill? But would they *really* put poison in wine Heslarton's beloved daughter might drink? And why would either want Drax's body left in Michaelhouse?

'Drax had a book,' Bartholomew began tentatively. 'One that listed herbs and their uses . . .'

Agatha folded her arms, and a look of immense satisfaction settled on her heavy features. 'Well, there you are, then. Drax could not read, but Celia can.'

'Celia told me it was the other way around: Drax was literate, but she is not.'

Agatha's eyes narrowed. 'Then you had better find out why she lied to you.'

Although Agatha's broth had soothed Bartholomew's headache and settled his stomach, her gossip and theories

174

had left him acutely uneasy. When Michael arrived, he repeated what she had said. The monk listened carefully, rubbing his jowls.

'It *is* possible that Celia and Heslarton dispatched their spouses. And it would certainly make for a tidy solution. Unfortunately, a pharmacopoeia and an alleged affair do not represent evidence – we need more than that to charge them. Moreover, we know the killer has a penchant for pilgrim badges, but Celia and Heslarton are wealthy – they can buy such items, and have no need to steal.'

'*Emma* is wealthy,' argued Bartholomew. 'But Heslarton may not have disposable income of his own. Meanwhile, Celia is the kind of woman who removes valuables from corpses.'

'True,' acknowledged Michael. 'However – and I am reluctant to mention this, because you will be angry – they are not my only suspects for Drax's murder. I am not ready to exclude Blaston from our enquiries yet. He had the motive *and* the opportunity.'

'Blaston is not a killer,' said Bartholomew tiredly. 'You know he is not, and we will be wasting our time if we pursue him.'

'You are almost certainly right,' agreed Michael. 'But the cold application of logic means he must remain a suspect until he can be properly eliminated. Of course, we should not forget what we saw with our own eyes – namely Drax quarrelling with Kendale not long before he died. Kendale had motive and opportunity, too.'

Bartholomew supposed he did, and Chestre's lads were certainly belligerent enough to dispatch a landlord who was threatening to raise their rent. 'I do not feel equal to tackling them today.'

'We could not, even if you did. We do not have

175

sufficient evidence, and they will make trouble if we level accusations without it – trouble we cannot afford.'

'That has never stopped you before.'

'Kendale will whip the hostels into a frenzy of indignation if I do not have a watertight case, and I do not want to see the Colleges in flames.' Michael grinned suddenly. 'Incidentally, your students told Langelee that you have been overtaxing yourself in the classroom, and he has ordered me to keep you away from the hall today, lest you find yourself unable to manage the camp-ball later.'

'The sly devils!' exclaimed Bartholomew, half angry and half amused by their effrontery. 'They have not enjoyed being grilled these past few days, and see it as a way to earn a respite. It is not me they are protecting, but themselves.'

Michael laughed. 'Well, I am grateful to them, because I need your help this morning.'

They left the College and walked up St Michael's Lane, then turned left along the High Street, aiming for Celia's house. They had not gone far before they met Dick Tulyet.

The man who represented the King's peace in the county was slightly built with a youthful face that encouraged criminals to underestimate him. None ever did it again, and the people of Cambridge knew they were lucky to have such a dedicated officer to serve them. Tulyet had worked well with Michael in the past, and there were none of the territorial tussles that usually occurred between two ill-defined jurisdictions. That day, however, he was scowling, and did not return the scholars' friendly greetings.

'I did not provoke Dickon into stabbing me,' said Bartholomew, immediately defensive.

'I know.' Tulyet's expression softened when Dickon was mentioned, and Bartholomew was amazed, yet again, that he should be so astute when dealing with criminals, but so blind towards his hellion son. 'And he says he is sorry for attacking you.'

Bartholomew doubted the boy had said any such thing.

'You should not have given him a sword,' admonished Michael. 'Matt might have been killed.'

'The hero of Poitiers?' asked Tulyet dryly. 'I doubt it! But that is not what is vexing me today. I am peeved with *you*, Brother. Drax was a townsman. *Ergo*, as you always say, his murder is mine to investigate. But you have been exploring the case without consulting me.'

'You can work together from now on, then,' said Bartholomew, thinking his students were going to be in for a shock when he returned. 'Michael is on his way to speak to Celia.'

'Not so fast,' said Tulyet, grabbing his sleeve as he turned to leave. 'I have a bone to pick with you, too. But first, I will hear why the good Brother has been trampling all over my authority.'

'You have never objected to me trampling before,' said Michael, stung. 'Besides, it is likely that Drax's killer is the same villain who has been stealing pilgrim badges, *and* who poisoned Alice. But we can collaborate now if you like. I am more than happy to share all I have discovered.'

Tulyet sighed, mollified by Michael's conciliatory tone. 'Very well. I am sorry I barked at you. I would hate you to resign, because I doubt another senior proctor would be so reasonable.'

'There is no danger of that,' said Michael comfortably. 'I like running the University, and will only give it up when I am made a bishop or an abbot. Of course, it is only a matter of time before the offers roll in, but I shall be selective about what I accept.'

'I see,' said Tulyet, looking closely at the monk to see whether he was jesting. He frowned, evidently unable to tell, although Bartholomew knew Michael was perfectly serious.

'I know why you want this case,' the monk went on. 'You are used to criminals running riot and the University causing trouble. But all the felons have been driven away by Emma, and the University is more interested in squabbling with itself than the town at the moment. You are bored, and yearn for something that will stretch your wits.'

'On the contrary, I have mountains of administration to occupy me,' said Tulyet indignantly. 'Running a shire this size is not easy, you know.' Then he glanced at Michael's arched eyebrows and shot him a reluctant grin. 'All right, you have me – I *am* tired of sitting in an office, and Drax's death *does* represent an interesting diversion. We shall do as you suggest, and work together.'

'Then you can buy me an ale in the Brazen George while I brief you,' said Michael comfortably. 'It will help lubricate my memory, and ensure I do not leave anything out.'

'Felons want ale when they provide me with information, too,' said Tulyet, amused. 'But you had better make it worth my while. Times are hard, even for sheriffs, and ale has become expensive. Life would be a good deal simpler if I accepted some of the bribes that come my way. At least, that is what Dickon tells me.'

'Refuse them,' advised Bartholomew, thinking Dickon was not a good source for wise counsel. 'You will find life is a lot more complex once you start breaking the law.'

Michael ordered a platter of assorted meat as well as ale in the Brazen George, on the grounds that he thought more clearly when his attention was not diverted by his growling stomach.

'Tell me what you have learned,' ordered Tulyet, once the landlord had served the victuals and had left them in peace. He already looked more cheerful, and his expression was positively eager as he leaned across the table to be sure he missed nothing.

'Drax was stabbed early on Monday morning,' obliged Michael, as he began to eat.

'But he was not taken to Michaelhouse until mid-afternoon,' said Bartholomew. 'We know, because of Physwick's testimony, and the blood in their dairy, where he died.'

'My first suspects were Yffi and his apprentices,' Michael went on. 'But they were on the roof all day, with the exception of the occasional foray downwards for supplies. One *may* have dashed out to kill Drax. However, I do not believe any of them brought his body to our College.'

'Do you not?' asked Tulyet doubtfully. 'Why?'

'Because toting corpses around necessitates some degree of caution – waiting for a point when the lane was empty, watching for possible witnesses, and so on. It would have taken time, and the others would have noticed a more prolonged absence.'

'So they might,' agreed Tulyet. 'But why would they betray one of their own to you?'

'I doubt they would,' said Michael. 'But they are not clever, and I would have caught them out by now. However, I remain unhappy with their role in the affair – it is odd that they saw nothing suspicious, while their lewd discussion almost certainly provided the diversion the killer needed to enter Michaelhouse – and I plan to interrogate them again today.'

'I will do it,' said Tulyet keenly. 'In the castle. It is astonishing how a spell inside my walls can loosen tongues. Leave Yffi and his apprentices to me.'

'Very well, but please do not keep them long. It looks like rain, and my room is currently without a roof.'

179

'I cannot imagine why your College accepted free repairs from Emma de Colvyll,' said Tulyet disapprovingly. 'There is something about her that I distrust intensely. Moreover, I do not like the way she earns her money – by taking advantage of the grief-stricken and the desperate.'

'I agree,' said Michael soberly. 'Unfortunately, Langelee does not.'

'What about Blaston as the culprit?' asked Tulyet, turning his mind back to murder. 'He is a decent, hard-working man, but he has been very vocal about the high price of ale in Drax's taverns.'

'He left the College for nails, so has no alibi for the murder,' replied Michael, before Bartholomew could stop him. 'He is no killer, but I am keeping an open mind anyway.'

'And I shall do the same,' said Tulyet. 'Do you have any other suspects?'

'Fen the pardoner,' replied Michael immediately. 'He was seen – by Blaston – poking his head around our College gates not long before Drax's corpse was so callously left there.'

'Poynton and the two nuns also looked inside Michaelhouse,' Bartholomew pointed out. 'So did Prior Etone. But none of them – including Fen – has a motive for killing Drax.'

'I can make a few enquiries about them,' offered Tulyet, when Michael glared at Bartholomew. 'I know the pilgrims stayed at one of Drax's inns – the Griffin – the night before they arrived at the Carmelite Friary, and Poynton in particular seems easily provoked. Are these your only suspects, or are there more?'

'Chestre Hostel argued with Drax about an increase in rent,' replied Michael. 'And there was a quarrel between them on the morning of the murder. Chestre is not far from Michaelhouse – they may have dumped the body there as some bizarre form of attack on the Colleges.'

'They might,' agreed Tulyet. 'But I shall leave Chestre to you. Kendale is extremely devious, and I doubt a mere secular will catch him out in lies or contradictions. But be careful. I detect something dangerous about him – he is not a man to cross lightly.'

Bartholomew regarded Tulyet uneasily, not liking the notion that Kendale had unsettled a hard, practical, coura-geous man like the Sheriff. Michael did not seem to share his concerns, though, and went on to outline the case against the last of his suspects: Celia and Heslarton. Tulyet looked thoughtful when informed of the rumour that they were enjoying an amour.

'That is an interesting hypothesis, but can you be sure that Alice was the intended victim?'

'What do you mean?' asked Bartholomew.

'Emma is unpopular in the town, and Heslarton is her henchman. Perhaps the poison struck the wrong victims.'

Michael nodded slowly. 'Emma is more than unpopular – she is feared and hated.'

Tulyet agreed. 'She is involved in a number of unpleasant disputes, but the worst is the one with the Gilbertine Priory over Edmund House. She bought it for a pittance, when they were in desperate need of ready cash, but she leaves it empty and rotting, despite the fact that they have offered to pay well above the odds to have it back.'

'Do you know why she has taken such a stance?' asked Michael.

Tulyet shook his head. 'I asked her, but she fobbed me off with some tale about Heslarton being fond of the place.'

'Are you suggesting a Gilbertine might be our cul-prit?' asked Bartholomew unhappily. Two canons came immediately to mind: the enigmatic Thelnetham, who had been behaving oddly of late, and Brother Jude, who was enough of a ruffian to enjoy camp-ball.

'I am suggesting nothing, just telling you what I know of Emma's dealings.' Tulyet turned to Michael. 'Now what about these pilgrim badges? I understand you believe the thief and the killer is one and the same?'

'The first crime was against Poynton in the Carmelite Friary,' obliged Michael. 'But since then, the villain has also targeted the Mayor, Meryfeld, a wealthy burgess named Frevill, two Franciscans and Drax.'

'I heard he picked on Celia, too,' said Tulyet. 'And if that is the case, she cannot be the killer – not if the culprit is also our thief.'

'We only have her word that it happened,' said Michael. 'And in my experience, criminals lie.'

'You can add Welfry to your list of victims, too,' said Tulyet. 'He has not made a formal complaint, but Prior Morden mentioned it. Apparently, it was a badge of which he was very fond.'

'John Schorne's boot?' asked Bartholomew. Its loss would be a blow to Welfry, and the pity was that the thief would probably throw it away once he realised it was from an unofficial shrine and thus was essentially worthless.

'What have you learned, Dick?' asked Michael. 'So far, we have provided more information than we have been given.'

'That is because you have been more successful than me,' replied Tulyet gloomily. 'I questioned Emma's entire household about the theft of her box *and* the poisoning, but learned nothing. They are terrified of her, so prising information from them was like drawing teeth.'

'How *is* Emma's tooth?' asked Bartholomew. 'I do not suppose you noticed?'

Tulyet regarded him askance. 'I cannot say I did, no.'

'You mentioned a bone to pick with Matt?' said Michael. 'What was it?'

Tulyet's scowl returned, and Bartholomew wished Michael had not reminded him of it. 'I shall have to show you. Come with me.'

Exchanging bemused glances, Bartholomew and Michael followed the Sheriff along the High Street to the Guildhall. Scholars were normally barred from it, because it was where town matters were discussed, and the University was not welcome. Bartholomew had only ever been inside it once, when he was a boy and his brother-in-law had taken him. It was a fine place, unashamedly brazen about the fact that a lot of money had been spent on it. That day, its front entrance was ringed with spectators, and Tulyet was forced to shoulder his way through them to reach it.

But when he opened the door and ushered Bartholomew and Michael inside, it was not the extravagance of the interior furnishings that caught their eye – it was the massive war machine that sat in it. The device was a trebuchet, which was used for hurling missiles at the walls of enemy fortresses, and it usually stood in the castle grounds. Its mighty throwing arm grazed the ceiling of the lofty chamber, while its wheels only just fitted between the tiers of benches that were permanently affixed to the walls. Bartholomew glanced at the average-sized door through which they had just walked, then back to the contraption.

'How in God's name did you get that in here?'

'You tell me,' said Tulyet coolly.

Bartholomew frowned. 'I suppose you must have dismantled it, then reassembled the pieces once they were all inside. But why would you do such a thing?'

'I assure you, *I* did not,' said Tulyet stiffly. 'And do not play the innocent with me, Matt. This prank is not amusing.'

Bartholomew disagreed, and was all admiration for whoever had devised it. Then he turned to the Sheriff and saw he was being regarded in a way that was not at all friendly. He felt his jaw drop. 'Surely, you cannot think *I*—'

'I know you did,' interrupted Tulyet. 'You must have dropped your bag at some point, because we found two medicine phials with your writing on them, plus one of the implements you use for surgery. And do not tell me you are too busy for such tricks, because Dickon saw you blowing up pots in Meryfeld's garden. That suggests you have plenty of free hours for mischief.'

Bartholomew saw Michael begin to snigger. 'I *did* drop my bag,' he admitted. 'But it happened in Chestre Hostel, not here.'

He considered the events of the previous night. Kendale's injury had *not* been caused by a door, but might well have occurred while a trebuchet was being dismantled. Kendale and his lads must have stolen the war machine from the castle, returned home to await treatment for Kendale's damaged hand, then gone to reassemble the device when they were sure the Guildhall would be empty. Bartholomew had seen them set off with his own eyes, from outside Michaelhouse.

'Kendale is the culprit?' asked Michael, amusement fading when Bartholomew explained what he thought had probably happened. 'Am I to assume this is a challenge to the Colleges, then? That we must brace ourselves for more mischief in retaliation?'

'I do not care about scholars' spats,' said Tulyet resentfully. 'But I *do* care about my Guildhall. How am I supposed to hold meetings with this monstrosity in here?'

'Kendale pulled it to pieces and rebuilt it within the

space of a few hours,' said Bartholomew. 'And he has probably never touched a device like this before. Surely your soldiers, who are familiar with its workings, can reverse the process? Or are you telling me that scholars—'

'No,' declared Tulyet, grimly determined. 'Your University will not best the town. Not in this matter and not in any other, either.'

CHAPTER 6

Michael scowled as they left the Guildhall, annoyed that he should have to deal with student pranks when he was busy with more important matters. But he began to smirk when Bartholomew described the experiment he had conducted with his fellow physicians in Meryfeld's garden. And he laughed aloud when he heard how they had all been knocked off their feet, an unrestrained guffaw that was infectious and had people who heard it smiling in their turn.

'I wish I had been there,' he declared, when he had his mirth under control. 'Not standing by the pot, obviously, but with Dickon, spying over the wall.'

'The tale will be all over the town soon,' said Bartholomew gloomily. 'And it will do nothing to convince people that I do not dabble in sorcery.'

'But you *were* dabbling in sorcery,' Michael pointed out, beginning to laugh again. 'Or alchemy at least, which is much the same thing. And you corrupted your colleagues into doing likewise. What is wrong with just buying a decent lamp?'

'Because there is no such thing. At least, not one that projects a steady light for delicate procedures such as . . .'

'Such as surgery,' finished Michael, when Bartholomew faltered. 'Well, if you do not want this story to be blown out of all proportion, I recommend you keep your motives to yourself. And next time you experiment, make sure Dickon is out.'

186

When they reached Celia's house, a maid informed them that her mistress had gone riding, and was not expected back until the afternoon.

'Riding?' asked Michael in distaste. 'Is that any kind of activity for a recent widow?'

The maid refused to meet his eyes. 'Come back later,' she said, closing the door.

'Celia's behaviour is reckless,' said Michael, turning to leave. 'She might as well wear a placard around her neck, claiming she is glad her husband is dead. Does it mean she *did* have a hand in his murder, as we have speculated?'

'Or does it mean she is innocent?' asked Bartholomew. 'If she were guilty, surely she would have put on a convincing show of grief, just to make sure people do *not* suspect her of foul play?'

'The Lord only knows,' sighed Michael, as they retraced their steps down Bridge Street. 'I thought I would enjoy working on this case – an opportunity to tax my wits. But the hostel–College spat means I cannot give it my full attention. Did I tell you I spent half the night on patrol?'

'Doing what?'

'Ensuring York Hostel did not incinerate a College in revenge for the blaze that destroyed their stable yesterday. The fire was almost certainly an accident, but York brays it was an act of arson. It is all very annoying.'

'There is Gyseburne,' said Bartholomew, nodding to where his grim-faced colleague was striding towards them, long, grey hair flying. 'Why is he glaring at me?'

'Is it true, Bartholomew?' Gyseburne asked without preamble. 'You stole a great war machine from the castle and used some form of sorcery to spirit it through the Guildhall's door?'

Bartholomew groaned, and it was Michael who answered.

187

'A student prank, but there was no magic involved, just simple ingenuity. There was no Matt involved, either.'

'Are you sure?' Gyseburne asked. 'Because I heard he dropped various identifiable belongings.'

'That was part of the deception,' interrupted Michael. 'No doubt Chestre Hostel thinks it highly amusing to have a senior member of a College blamed for their mischief.'

Gyseburne made an expression that might have been a smile. 'I suppose it is the sort of thing students might do. I was one once, and masterminded all manner of hilarious tricks.'

'Did you?' asked Bartholomew, trying to imagine the dour Gyseburne as a young and carefree prankster. The image would not come.

'I do not like Chestre Hostel,' Gyseburne confided. 'They summoned me last night, but I refused to oblige. It goes against the grain to ignore pleas for help, especially from men who can pay, but they unnerve me, so I decided to have nothing to do with them.'

Bartholomew wished he had done the same. But Gyseburne was right: it was a physician's duty to help those in need, and he had sworn sacred oaths to say he would always do so.

'I heard about the jape in the Dominican Priory too,' said Gyseburne, ranging off on another matter. 'But Seneschal Welfry is better now, and came to inspect the Guildhall first thing this morning. He professed himself very impressed by your . . . by the trick.'

'Oh no!' moaned Michael. 'He is going to devise some other prank to answer the challenge.'

'He might, but his motive will be fun, not malice,' said Gyseburne. 'Like me, he is a God-fearing, peaceful man who has been on a pilgrimage, although his was only to some shrine where the Devil was trapped in a shoe. Mine was to Canterbury. I walked all the way, and felt I had done a great thing when the towers of the cathedral came into sight. I was unwell at the time, and the journey went a long way to curing me.'

'Yet you do not wear a badge to proclaim what you have done,' observed Michael.

Gyseburne's expression was pained. 'You have touched on a sore point, Brother, because it has been stolen from me. I am distressed, because it was a pretty thing, and cost me a fortune.'

'Did you see the thief?' asked Michael eagerly. 'Or have any idea who he might be?'

'He broke into my house when I was asleep. I have been racking my brains to think of suspects, and while I do not like to cast aspersions . . .'

'Who?' demanded Michael, when Gyseburne faltered.

Gyseburne looked away when he spoke, uncomfortable telling tales. 'Well, Alice Heslarton remarked on it, and pointed it out to her family. Then those horrible Chestre men asked if it was authentic, and so did Yffi the builder. Horneby and Etone of the Carmelites eyed it covetously, and so, I am sorry to say, did Michaelhouse's Thelnetham. And then there was Seneschal Welfry . . .'

'None of them have yellow hair,' said Bartholomew. 'And the thief was—'

'Have you ever heard of wigs?' asked Gyseburne acidly. 'The presence or absence of yellow hair means nothing, as far as I am concerned.'

Michael watched him go, his expression perturbed. 'He has a point about the wig. However, I think we can cross Etone, Horneby, Welfry and Thelnetham off his list.'

'Can we?' Michael's startled glance made Bartholomew feel treacherous, but he pressed on anyway. 'I do not know

Thelnetham well, despite us living in the same College for six months.'

Michael started to object, but then looked thoughtful. 'I have not gained his measure, either, and he has been behaving very oddly of late. But even so, I do not see him as a relic-thief.'

'Perhaps not,' said Bartholomew, although he remained unconvinced.

'Do you think Gyseburne is telling the truth about his pilgrimage?' asked Michael, after a short and rather uncomfortable silence. 'I mean, do you think he actually went?'

Bartholomew regarded him in surprise. 'Of course he went! Why would he lie about that?'

'To make us think him a pious man.' Michael shot a furtive glance behind him before Bartholomew could counter the accusation. 'Come this way, Matt. We are going to Michaelhouse to interview Yffi and his cronies.'

'Dick said he was going to do that.'

'I know, but I would sooner ask my own questions. Hurry up! We do not want him to catch us.'

With grave misgivings about going against the wishes of the Sheriff, Bartholomew followed him home. But when they arrived, it was to find Walter standing in the street, howling a litany of vile curses. It took a moment for Bartholomew to see the reason for his curious behaviour, but when he did, he stared in astonishment. Michaelhouse's front gates were missing.

'I went to the latrines, and when I came back they were gone,' wailed Walter, addressing a furious Master. All the Fellows and a large number of students had gathered, and were standing in the yard.

'It is not your fault,' said Clippesby, resting a calming hand on his shoulder. 'But if you did not see anything suspicious, then what about your peacock? He would have been here, even if you—'

'We do not have time for this nonsense,' snapped Thelnetham, pushing the Dominican roughly out of the way. 'Let me question Walter.'

'Hey!' objected Bartholomew angrily, seeing Clippesby stagger. 'There is no need for that.'

Thelnetham rounded on him with such vigour that he took a step back. 'Do not tell me what to do, you damned heretic! Your College is under attack, and this is no time to pander to lunatics.'

William interposed his unsavoury bulk between them. 'Do not call Matthew a heretic,' he snarled. '*I* am the only one allowed to do that, and only then because he knows I do not mean it.'

Bartholomew knew nothing of the sort. 'Stealing our gates must be one of these practical jokes,' he said to Langelee. 'It is not as clever as assembling a trebuchet in the Guildhall, but it still took ingenuity and planning. They are heavy, and it would not have been easy to spirit them away in broad daylight with no one seeing.'

'*Did* they do it with no one seeing?' asked Langelee, looking around at his assembled scholars. 'Did any of you notice anything that might be construed as suspicious?'

'It was Chestre,' said Valence resentfully. 'They live nearby, and must have waited until Walter was in the latrines and the rest of us were listening to Master Thelnetham's lecture on whores.'

'On what?' blurted Bartholomew, thinking he must have misheard.

'On prostitutes in the Bible,' elaborated Langelee. 'It was very interesting and had us transfixed.'

'It did,' agreed Clippesby ruefully. 'Even I was fascinated, and I keep *my* vows of chastity.'

191

The less said on that subject the better, given that he tended to be in a minority, even among those Fellows who were in holy orders, and Michael stepped forward hastily.

'I doubt Kendale did this,' he said, seeing some of the students were keen to march on Chestre and demand answers with their fists. 'Not so soon after manhandling that trebuchet all around town. We must look elsewhere for the culprits.'

'I will help you find them,' said William grimly, and there was an immediate clamour of identical offers from everyone else.

Michael raised an imperious hand. 'I can manage alone, thank you. And none of you will attempt your own investigations. Do I make myself clear? You may cause Michaelhouse irreparable harm if you go about making wild accusations, and we do not want other parts of our home disappearing.'

He glared until he had reluctant nods from the students, then turned to the Fellows. William was apt to be bloody-minded in such situations, but this time it was Thelnetham causing trouble.

'I shall do as I feel fit,' the Gilbertine declared. 'This is an outrage, and—'

'You will do as the Senior Proctor suggests,' said Langelee in a voice that held considerable menace. 'I may not possess the authority to dismiss Fellows, but there are other ways of making nuisances disappear.'

Bartholomew listened to the exchange nervously, not exactly sure what Langelee was saying but acutely aware that Thelnetham would be wise to do as he was told. Without a word, the Gilbertine stalked away, habit billowing behind him. Langelee watched him go, then turned to Michael.

'Get the gates back, Brother,' he ordered. 'We are vulnerable without them.'

'Where are the builders?' asked Michael. 'Can they not run us up a temporary pair?'

'Yffi and his boys failed to arrive again this morning,' supplied William. 'Blaston is here, making new window shutters, but I doubt he can produce gates on his own. At least, not quickly.'

'Yffi is missing yet another day of work?' demanded Michael. He gestured up at the sky. 'But it looks like rain, and we have no roof!'

Langelee grimaced. 'If it is not one thing it is another with this place. And what ails Thelnetham? He has always been prickly, but he has never indulged in open rebellion before.'

'He is probably worried about the camp-ball this afternoon,' said William. 'His Order's honour is at stake, and I happen to know he takes that sort of thing very seriously.'

'He should,' said Langelee. He flexed the bulging muscles in his arm, and grinned rather diabolically. 'But he need not fear. I shall ensure the Gilbertines emerge victorious.'

'Never mind that,' said Michael irritably. 'What are we going to do about the fact that we have no roof, and that great grey clouds are gathering?'

'I saw Yffi earlier, carrying a lot of equipment to the Carmelite Friary,' said Langelee. 'I was going to find out what thinks he is doing the moment Thelnetham finished pontificating on harlots.'

'I do not want my students learning about harlots, not even the ones in the Bible,' said Bartholomew, starting to walk across the yard. 'They are supposed to be studying medicine.'

Langelee darted after him, swinging him around by the arm to peer into his face. He was very strong, and Bartholomew staggered.

'You are still too pale for my liking, and I do not want you teaching until after the camp-ball,' the Master decreed in the kind of voice that said objections would be futile. 'Stroll about the town with Michael if you will, but do not exhaust yourself with students. Besides, Thelnetham is a priest, so they are not going to hear anything too outrageous.'

Bartholomew was not so sure about that, given the rapt attention the Gilbertine seemed to have engendered in his audience. But he could see Langelee meant what he said, and so with great reluctance, he followed the monk across the yard to talk to Blaston about the gates.

The carpenter was in a world of his own as he assembled his shutters, working with deft, confident movements. He jumped when he became aware of Bartholomew and Michael beside him.

'I was concentrating,' he said sheepishly. 'The wood Emma bought is warped, so I need to think about which piece goes where, or you will end up with gaps. And we do not want those.'

'I wish it was *you* working on the roof,' said Michael fervently. 'Could you not run up a ladder and nail a few tiles down? Yffi does not seem very interested in doing it.'

Blaston laughed. 'Tiling is a skilled task, Brother, and I will not undertake anything I cannot do well. Of course, I could probably do a better job than Yffi – I have no respect for his workmanship.'

'You are not the only one,' muttered Michael. 'Did *you* see anyone tampering with our gates?'

'Unfortunately not,' said Blaston ruefully. 'Or I would have stopped them. But my work absorbs me, as you have just seen, and I notice very little once I start.'

'When we spoke before, you mentioned your unhappiness with the high prices Drax charged for ale. Will you tell me exactly what—'

Blaston's eyes opened wide with alarm. 'You think I killed him because his ale was too expensive! But I was here, in Michaelhouse, when he was murdered.'

'Actually, you were not,' countered Michael. 'Drax died when you told us you left to buy nails.'

'The smith will tell you I went to his forge and left him money,' objected Blaston. '*Ask* him.'

'I have, and he did. I am not accusing you, Blaston. I am merely pointing out a fact – namely that no one can vouch for you at the time of Drax's death.'

'Then what about Yffi?' demanded Blaston angrily. '*His* alibi is those vile lads, who would think nothing of lying to protect him – or rather, to protect their jobs. Moreover, *he* disliked Drax's high prices, too, and was always complaining about them. Ask *him* these questions, not me!'

Bartholomew was dismayed to see tears glitter as Blaston turned back to his work. He grabbed Michael's arm and tugged him away, determined that the carpenter should be distressed no further.

'You hurt his feelings with your "facts", Brother,' he said reproachfully, when they were out of earshot. 'We both know he is innocent, so why torment him?'

Michael glared. 'Because it would be remiss not to explore *all* the lines of enquiry available to us. Blaston probably is innocent, but you think so because he is a friend and you like him, whereas I would rather eliminate him with solid evidence. Dick Tulyet will not be sentimental about what he learns, and neither should we.'

Bartholomew supposed he had a point, although he did not feel like admitting it. 'Where are you going next?'

'It is time I put my needs first, and my investigations second. I am going to ask Yffi why he has left us with no roof. Are you coming, or are you afraid I might say something to offend him, too?'

With a sigh, Bartholomew followed him through Michaelhouse's gateless entrance.

The Carmelite Priory was a good deal calmer than it had been during the kerfuffle over the attempt to snatch St Simon Stock's scapular. The shrine was busy, as usual, but it was now being guarded by two sturdy lay-brothers. Bartholomew and Michael arrived just as the visiting pilgrims emerged from it. The physician was surprised to see Horneby and Welfry with them.

'You should be resting,' he told the Carmelite.

Horneby smiled. 'I woke this morning feeling much better, although, as you can hear, I am still hoarse. Then Welfry said St Simon Stock might be willing to ensure I have a strong voice for the lecture I am to give in his honour, so we went to pray in his shrine.'

Welfry crossed himself. 'I hope he listened, and will be inclined to oblige. I am looking forward to Horneby's address – the University is dull during term time, when everyone is too busy teaching to propound new theories, and I need something to enliven my life.'

'I do not suppose you enlivened it by stealing my College's gates, did you?' asked Michael coolly. 'Someone spirited them away this morning.'

Welfry looked startled, then laughed when Michael explained what had happened. The monk was unimpressed by his reaction.

'I would not have thought the Seneschal would delight in silly ventures,' he said icily.

'Then you do not know him very well,' muttered Horneby.

'I am all admiration for the hostels' ingenuity today,'

declared Welfry, still smiling. 'Taking the gates is not as clever as the trebuchet business, but—'

'How do you know it was a hostel that stole them?' Michael pounced.

'Oh, come, Brother!' exclaimed Welfry. 'Of course it was a hostel. Who else would pick on a College? I shall have to think of an answering trick to—'

'No,' ordered Michael sharply. 'This ridiculous rivalry has gone far enough. We shall have a war on our hands if it continues, and none of us want a bit of foolery to end in bloodshed.'

Welfry sobered immediately. 'Of course not, Brother. Forgive me. It must be because . . .' He trailed off, and his hand went to the place where the little boot had been pinned. A hole in the material showed where it had been ripped away.

'I heard you lost your *signaculum*,' said Bartholomew. 'I am sorry.'

'So am I,' said Welfry, genuinely downcast. 'I know Dominicans are not supposed to own personal property, but that badge represented . . . It was my reminder that . . .'

'It helped him keep his sense of fun in check,' explained Horneby. 'He thinks laughter makes him a poor friar, although I cannot say I agree. There is nothing wrong with making people smile, and if more men were like Welfry, Cambridge would be a happier place.'

Welfry blushed, clearly uncomfortable with his friend's approbation. He turned awkward and tongue-tied, uncharacteristically at a loss for words.

'I had better do all I can to retrieve it, then,' said Michael. 'In the meantime, concentrate on your duties as Seneschal. That should keep you away from the temptations posed by practical jokes.'

'Come, Welfry,' said Horneby, taking his friend's arm. 'I have prepared the next part of my lecture and I would like you to read it. That should keep you out of mischief for a while.'

Keenly interested, Welfry allowed himself to be led away. Michael watched them go.

'There is something odd about their friendship,' he said. 'Welfry possesses an excellent mind, but he is too frivolous to put it to good purpose, so why does Horneby waste time with him?'

'Horneby is not wasting his time,' said Bartholomew. 'Welfry has helped him a great deal with his sermon – probably more than Horneby will ever admit.'

But Michael was not listening. He had fixed glaring eyes on Prior Etone, who was standing by the shrine with Yffi. He marched towards them, ignoring the greetings of Poynton and Fen as he stalked past. Not wanting to cause offence, Bartholomew hastened to wish the pilgrims good day.

'Has Michael located the villain who stole my badge yet?' demanded Poynton. His face was more flushed than usual, and his eyes had a yellow cast, both signs of poor health.

'If he had, he would have told you,' retorted Fen sharply, and it seemed that even his equable temper was being tested by Poynton's constant belligerence.

'I understand you stayed in the Griffin when you first arrived in the town,' said Bartholomew, also sufficiently irritated by Poynton's manner to go on the offensive. He did not share Michael's suspicions about Fen as a suspect for the killer-thief, but Poynton was another matter entirely: he might well have lied about his badge being stolen, and the crimes did seem to have started the day he arrived. 'It was owned by John Drax, who was subsequently murdered. Did you meet him?'

'Yes – and we disliked him profoundly,' Poynton declared. 'I am not surprised God saw fit to end his miserable life. His ale was expensive, and he denied his regular patrons credit.'

Fen smiled at the physician. 'Speaking of wine, Thelnetham was here earlier, and he mentioned that you partook too heavily of it last night. Are you recovered? You are very pale.'

'*Thelnetham* told you that?' demanded Poynton, while Bartholomew wondered two things: why Fen should change the subject so abruptly, and why Thelnetham should have been discussing him with strangers. 'But he is a Gilbertine, and you should not fraternise with them – we are to play them at camp-ball this afternoon, so they are the enemy.'

'Poynton has been invited to join the Carmelites' team,' explained Fen, when the merchant had stamped furiously away. 'Apparently, he is good at it, although I do not believe it is a pastime worthy of a pilgrim. But now you must excuse me, too, because I have not finished my prayers.'

Bartholomew wanted to pursue the matter of Drax but Fen either did not hear or chose to ignore the question he began to ask. Thwarted, the physician walked towards Michael, who was engaged in a head-to-head confrontation with Prior Etone and Yffi.

'—cannot rip the roof off my home,' the monk was shouting, 'then disappear on another job.'

'But this is far more important than your roof, Brother,' snapped Etone. 'Yffi is to build us a proper shrine. The incident yesterday told us that we need something more secure, and we were delighted when he said he could begin work immediately.'

'I am sure you were!' yelled Michael. 'But that is not the point. He has been engaged to repair Michaelhouse,

199

and he cannot leave us with no windows and no roof while he makes you a temple.'

Yffi sighed heavily. 'All right. I will go to Michaelhouse, and my apprentices will stay here. Then everyone will be happy. And do not say that is unacceptable, Brother, because the work on your roof has reached the point where only a master mason can make headway anyway. My lads would have been standing around doing nothing, regardless.'

Michael was clearly unconvinced, but Yffi grabbed a sack of tools and stalked towards the gate, indicating with a wave of his hand that his apprentices were to begin measuring out the new site. Etone immediately went to pester them with unwanted advice and directions.

'Yffi has left his apprentices unattended, Brother,' remarked Bartholomew, to stall the impending diatribe. 'It is an opportunity to speak to them without a master prompting their replies.'

A determined gleam came into Michael's eyes. 'So it is! And we need not worry about objections from Etone that we are distracting them, because Poynton and Fen have just dragged him off somewhere – probably to complain about impertinent questions from you. You did ask some, I hope?'

'None that elicited helpful answers.'

'It was as Yffi told you,' said Peterkin, when the monk ordered them to repeat their story. 'We could not see the yard. It was dangerous upon that roof, and we were concentrating on our work.'

'You were discussing Yolande de Blaston,' countered Michael. 'That was not concentrating.'

The lad flushed. 'We can talk about her and do our jobs at the same time. But how could we see anything down in the yard when we were lounging around the back of the . . .' He faltered.

'Lounging?' pounced Michael.

Peterkin tried to retract his words, but it was too late. The slip allowed Michael to launch into one of his aggressive interrogations, and he soon learned that Yffi and his lads had been idling out of sight when Drax's body had been hidden.

'The first we knew about it was when Agatha started fooling around with that dog,' said Peterkin, speaking reluctantly and sulkily. 'We all looked down at the yard then.'

'Who initiated that discussion about Yolande?' demanded Michael. 'Yffi?'

A sly grin stole across Peterkin's face. 'Yes, because it amused him when all you scholars started listening to us. We could not see the yard, but we could see into your hall, and we saw we had your undivided attention. And half of you are priests, too! You should know better.'

'Yes,' said Michael bitterly. 'We should, because it was your lewd banter that let a killer deposit a corpse in our College. You are not innocent in this affair, and I intend to see you pay for it.'

He turned on his heel and strode away, leaving the grin fading from Peterkin's face, and his cronies exchanging anxious glances.

Langelee invited Bartholomew to dine with him when the physician returned to Michaelhouse, plying him with fresh bread, roasted meat, sweetmeats and a very small goblet of wine.

'If you are still thirsty, you can have some small ale,' said Langelee, snatching the cup away before Bartholomew had taken more than a token sip. 'You cannot be drunk for this afternoon.'

'I will not be drunk,' said Bartholomew testily, indicating that the Master should return it to him. It was good wine.

'Not on a thimbleful of claret. Are you nervous?'

'A little,' admitted Langelee. 'It is the biggest camp-ball game of the season.'

'Well, just be careful,' said Bartholomew, finishing the wine and standing to leave. 'We do not want anything to happen to you.'

'Nothing will happen to me,' declared Langelee, following him across the yard. 'But the opposition had better watch themselves. The Carmelites have recruited two of the louts from Chestre Hostel, and if *they* try anything sly, they will be sorry.'

'There is no evidence that it was Chestre who stole the gates,' warned Bartholomew, afraid Langelee might decide to punish the outrage on the field. 'It may have been someone else.'

'Of course it was them,' said Langelee bitterly. 'They have always hated us.'

Bartholomew looked uncomfortably at the yawning gap in the College's defences as they passed through it. It was disconcerting, and he felt acutely vulnerable, despite the student-guards on patrol.

'Do you know how the two Orders came to challenge each other to an annual camp-ball game in the first place?' he asked, as they walked up St Michael's Lane.

'After the plague, life was bleak, so the Gilbertines decided to cheer everyone up. They settled on sponsoring a bout of camp-ball because it is popular with townsfolk, as well as scholars. The Carmelites thought it a wonderful idea, and offered to fund the opposing team.'

'And it always takes place on the day after the Feast of St Gilbert of Sempringham?'

'Yes,' said Langelee. 'Because he founded the Gilbertine Order, and the canons are always in the mood for a bit of celebration around this time of year.'

When they arrived, Langelee led the way to the large expanse of land behind the priory buildings, where the event was due to take place. Some games used the whole town as a playing field, but the canons were aware that this could prove dangerous to innocent bystanders, so, in the interests of safety, they had opted to confine the action to a limited area.

The players had assembled in two knots, about thirty men in each. One group wore white sashes, to indicate they were fighting for the Carmelites, while the other had donned black for the Gilbertines. Langelee abandoned Bartholomew and raced towards the latter, tying a strip of dark material around his waist as he did so.

Spectators were also gathering, forming a thick rim around the edge of the field. Although he had certainly been aware of the game being played in recent years, something had always happened to prevent him from attending them – emergencies with patients, or duties in Michaelhouse – so it was the first time he had ever been to one, and he was astonished by the number of people who had abandoned work to enjoy themselves there. He estimated there were at least a thousand of them. Many were townsmen, and he was surprised when he saw his sister and her husband standing to one side, waving small white flags. He had not known they favoured the Carmelites over the Gilbertines, and wondered why.

Unfortunately, the game had also attracted the kind of students who were enjoying the hostel–College dispute. The feisty lads from Essex Hostel were there, and Michael and his beadles were struggling to keep them apart from the boys of Gonville Hall. Meanwhile, noisy contingents from Maud's, Batayl and York hostels were standing provocatively close to equally belligerent representatives from Peterhouse and the Hall of Valence Marie.

Emma de Colvyll and her household were also present, and had secured themselves a pleasantly sheltered spot under some trees. Emma, clad in a black cloak and perched on a high stool, looked more like a spider than ever, and Bartholomew noticed that she was being given a very wide berth by the other spectators. Odelina and Celia sat on either side of her, while their retainers stood in a row behind. They all carried white banners, and when Leccheworth happened to stroll past, Bartholomew idly asked what he had done to turn Emma against his Order.

'There are two reasons why she dislikes us,' explained the Prior, running a hand through his curiously raven locks. 'First, because Heslarton is playing for the Carmelites, and second, because of Edmund House.' He pointed to the abandoned property at the far end of the field. 'I told you the last time you were here how we were forced to sell it to her during the Death.'

'You said you were unsure why she will not sell it back to you now.'

Leccheworth nodded. 'And I remain unsure. I can only surmise she is doing it to show everyone that she does as she pleases, and does not care who she offends or annoys.'

He took Bartholomew to meet the teams. Among the Gilbertines' champions was Yffi, who studiously avoided Bartholomew's eye, knowing he should not be playing camp-ball when he was supposed to be working on Michaelhouse's roof. The giant Brother Jude stood next to him, fierce and unsmiling. Langelee was near the ale-bellied Gib and the scowling Neyll from Chestre, and Bartholomew experienced a twinge of unease when he caught Neyll glaring at the Master. Would they use the game to harm him? But there was no time to warn Langelee, because Leccheworth was pulling him away to greet the opposition.

The Carmelites had recruited Poynton, Heslarton and a

number of loutish lads from Essex, Cosyn's and St Thomas's hostels. They exuded a sense of grim purpose, although Heslarton hopped from foot to foot to indicate his delight at the prospect of some serious rough and tumble. His bald head gleamed pinkly, and his roguish smile revealed a number of missing teeth. Bartholomew took the opportunity to ask a few questions when he found himself next to the man and no one else appeared to be listening.

'I understand you sold Drax a pilgrim badge,' he began. 'Why was—'

'I did not!' exclaimed Heslarton, regarding him belligerently. 'I am a businessman, not a priest, and holy objects can be dangerous in the wrong hands. I leave such items well alone.'

Bartholomew frowned. Was he telling the truth? He recalled that it was Thelnetham who had identified the seller; Clippesby had been unable to do so. Could the Gilbertine have been mistaken? He was spared from thinking of a reply, because Poynton bustled forward, shoving roughly past Heslarton, whose eyebrows went up at the needless jostling.

'Your friend the monk is worthless – it has been four days since my badge was stolen.' Poynton drew himself up to his full height. 'But I have taken matters into my own hands. By representing St Simon Stock's Order in this game, I shall win his approbation, and he will deliver the badge back to me by divine means. He told me as much in a dream.'

'St Simon Stock appeared to you?' asked Bartholomew, supposing it was only ever a matter of time before pilgrims began claiming miracles and visions. For many, visiting a shrine was an intensely moving experience, and he knew that alone was enough to affect impressionable minds.

Poynton waved his hand. 'Well, it was more of a nightmare, to be honest – one I had just a few moments ago,

205

as I was lying down to summon my strength for the game – but I woke certain he applauds my decision to play. My fellow pilgrims agree with my interpretation, and are here to cheer me on.'

He gestured to where the two nuns stood shivering together, looking very much as though they wished they were somewhere else. Fen was with them, his expression distant and distracted. They stood with a massive contingent of White Friars that included Horneby, whose neck was swathed in scarves to protect it from the cold. Welfry was next to him. He yelled something to the Carmelite team, and they responded with a rousing cheer. Horneby started to add something else, but Welfry rounded on him quickly, warning him to save his voice.

'Are you sure you should be playing today?' asked Bartholomew, turning back to Poynton. 'The game is practised very roughly in Cambridge, and your health is not—'

'My health is none of your concern,' snapped Poynton furiously. 'How dare you infer that I might have a disease! I am as hale and hearty as the next man.'

He turned abruptly and stalked away. Bartholomew was familiar with patients refusing to accept the seriousness of their condition, but even the most stubborn ones tended not to use camp-ball games to challenge what their bodies were trying to tell them. But it was none of his affair, and he turned his attention to the spectators who lined the field.

The townsmen among them were exchanging friendly banter, while the Carmelites and Gilbertines appeared to be on friendly terms. On the surface, all seemed amiable, but he was acutely aware of undercurrents. Scholars were coagulating in identifiable factions, while all was not entirely peaceful on the field, either. Neyll and Gib were scowling at Langelee, who was berating a resentful Yffi for abandoning his work on the roof. Meanwhile, Poynton had

206

jostled Heslarton a second time, earning himself a black glare.

With a sense of foreboding, Bartholomew wondered how many of them would walk away unscathed when the game was over.

There was nothing to do until the contest started, so Bartholomew went to stand with his colleagues from Michaelhouse. He was unsettled to note that Kendale had taken up station not far away, and was regarding them in a manner that was distinctly hostile.

'Where is Suttone?' he asked worriedly, aware that one of their number was missing.

'Headache,' explained Michael. 'I do not blame him. He is a Carmelite, but the Master of his College is playing for the Gilbertines. Deciding which team to support would not have been easy.'

'I disagree,' said Thelnetham coldly. 'It should be *very* easy: his first loyalty should be to his Order – the organisation in which he took his sacred vows. Mine certainly is.'

'Heslarton,' said Bartholomew, before the others could take issue with him. 'Are you sure it was he you saw selling Drax the pilgrim badge? Only I have just asked him and he denies it.'

'Of course he denies it,' snapped Thelnetham. 'He is frightened of his evil mother-in-law, and will not want her to know what he has been doing in his spare time.'

'He is not frightened of her,' said Bartholomew. 'On the contrary, they are fond of each other.'

'I am sure they are,' said Thelnetham curtly. 'But that does not mean he is not also terrified.'

He stalked away towards his brethren. Bartholomew watched him go, thinking, not for the first time, that he was not sure what to make of Thelnetham. But it was no time to ponder the Gilbertine, and he was more immediately concerned with the camp-ball game.

'A lot of people who do not like each other are here today,' he remarked to Michael.

'I know,' replied Michael. 'And Essex, York, Batayl and Maud's are using the occasion to encourage other hostels to join their campaign against the Colleges. But my beadles are watching, so there should be no trouble – among the onlookers, at least. The field is another matter, but you are here to set bones and mend wounds.'

Bartholomew turned as Gyseburne, Meryfeld and Rougham approached. All three wore rich cloaks and thick tunics, and he felt poor and shabby by comparison, reminded that everyone except him seemed able to make a princely living from medicine.

'We came to congratulate you on your appointment as Official Physician,' said Gyseburne. 'It is a lucrative post, because not only does it carry a remuneration of three shillings, but the injured – and they will be myriad – will need follow-up consultations later.'

Bartholomew regarded him in dismay, wondering how he was going to fit them all in. Seeing his alarm, a triumphant expression flashed across Rougham's face.

'We will help,' he offered smoothly, speaking as if the idea had just occurred to him. 'Most players can afford to pay for post-game horoscopes, so we do not anticipate problems with taking some of them off your hands. As a personal favour, of course.'

'It will be no bother,' added Meryfeld, rubbing his hands together, although Gyseburne would not meet Bartholomew's eyes. 'We are all happy to help a busy colleague.'

'Thank you,' said Bartholomew, supposing they intended

to leave him the ones with no money – and he could not refuse their 'kindness', because he simply did not have time for new patients. He turned back to his Michaelhouse friends, feeling that at least *they* were not trying to cheat him.

'It is to be savage-camp,' said Langelee gleefully, coming to join them. 'This will be fun!'

'What is savage-camp?' asked Ayera warily.

'It means we can kick the ball, which is known as "kicking camp", but we keep our boots on, which makes it savage,' explained Langelee. 'Leccheworth and Etone wanted us to remove our footwear, but I persuaded them that it is too cold.' He grinned. 'This is my favourite form of the game!'

Bartholomew was alarmed. It was not unknown for men to die playing savage-camp. He wondered what the two priors thought they were doing by agreeing to such a measure. He started to object, but Michael, who was watching the spectators, narrowed his eyes suddenly.

'What is *he* doing?'

Everyone looked to where he pointed, and saw Fen with his arms around the two pilgrim nuns. The women appeared to be enjoying themselves, although most of Fen's attention was on Kendale, who was talking to him.

'They complained about the cold,' explained Clippesby. For some reason known only to himself, he had brought two chickens with him, both fitted with tiny leather halters to keep them from wandering away. They scratched the grass around his feet. 'So he is trying to warm them up.'

'And I am the Pope,' said Michael. 'What is he *really* doing? Seducing two women of God?'

'It is more likely to be the other way around,' said Langelee. 'They asked *him* to warm *them*. I have met them on several occasions, and they made no secret of the fact that they want to bed me.'

'Really, Master!' exclaimed William, expressing the astonishment of all the Fellows at this bald announcement. 'The things you say!'

'I only speak the truth,' shrugged Langelee.

But Michael was more interested in the pardoner. 'Kendale and Fen are prime suspects in the killer-thief case. What are they saying to each other? Can anyone read lips?'

'Would you like my hens to ease forward and listen?' offered Clippesby. 'They are good at—'

'No,' said Michael. 'Stay away from them, Clippesby. I do not want you hurt.'

'Fen will not hurt anyone,' objected Clippesby, startled. 'He is a good man!'

'Pardoners are, by definition, evil, ruthless and unscrupulous, and they prey on the vulnerable and weak,' declared Michael uncompromisingly. 'It does not surprise me at all to see this one engage in sly exchanges with a man who is exacerbating the hostel–College dispute.'

'Kendale *is* aggravating the trouble,' agreed William soberly. 'The hostels have always been jealous of the Colleges, but they have never taken against us *en masse* before. He will have our streets running with blood before too long.'

Bartholomew had a bad feeling William might be right.

The Gilbertines' field afforded scant protection from the wind that sliced in from the north, and the pilgrim nuns were not the only ones who were cold. Everywhere, people began stamping their feet and flapping their arms in an effort to keep warm. Unfortunately, there was some technical problem with the pitch, and the game was delayed

210

until it could be resolved. Langelee tried to explain what was happening, but none of his Fellows understood what he was talking about.

'Tell Horneby this is no place for a man with a bad throat,' begged Welfry, coming to grab Bartholomew's arm while they waited. His face was taut with concern. 'We do not want a relapse.'

Bartholomew agreed, and followed him to where the Carmelites were huddled together in a futile attempt to stave off the chill.

'Tell me how you came to lose your *signaculum*,' he said as they walked. 'Michael is looking into similar thefts, you see.'

'I heard,' said Welfry. 'But I doubt my testimony will help – it all happened so fast. I was returning from visiting Horneby when a yellow-headed man shoved me against a wall and demanded that I hand it over. I am ashamed to say I did as he ordered without demur. I was a rank coward!'

'You did the right thing – no bauble is worth your life. Could you tell whether he wore a wig?'

Welfry frowned. 'It did not *look* like a wig, but as I said, it all happened very fast.'

'Then can you describe him?'

'Not really – average weight and height, rough voice, very strong hands. However, I can say he was wholly unfamiliar to me, and I have a good memory for faces. He is no one I have met before.'

'Who, then? A visiting pilgrim?'

'It is possible, although I would not have thought so. Such folk come to beg forgiveness, not to compound their sins by committing new ones.'

'Is your hand paining you today?' asked Bartholomew. 'You keep rubbing it.'

'You are observant.' Welfry flexed his gloved hand as he

211

smiled. 'I chafe it without thinking when the weather is cold, lest it freeze without my noticing – I no longer have any feeling in it, you see. It happened once before, and thawing it afterwards was excruciating.'

'There are poultices that may help with that. I could make you some.'

'Would you?' asked Welfry hopefully. 'I would be grateful, but we had better leave it until you are not so busy.' He smiled again. 'My motives are selfish, of course. If you have more time, you might be inclined to linger and discuss natural philosophy with me. But here is Horneby, and his health is rather more pressing than mine at the moment.'

'He is right,' said Bartholomew, when Horneby heard the last part of Welfry's remark and groaned. 'Windy fields in the middle of winter are *not* good places for men with sore throats.'

'I no longer have a sore throat,' objected Horneby. 'Besides, I want to see the game.'

'You do?' asked Bartholomew uncertainly. 'Why? It promises to be bloody.'

Horneby grinned mischievously. 'The unruly youth who caused you so much trouble in the past is not quite gone yet. I still enjoy a bit of a skirmish.'

It was an odd thing for a friar to admit, and Bartholomew was starting to tell him this, when there was a shout to say that the problem with the pitch had been resolved, and the game could begin. Priors Etone and Leccheworth summoned both teams to the centre of the field and, as an official, Bartholomew was ordered to go, too. So was Michael, who had been chosen for the role of 'Indifferent Man' – the neutral person who would toss the ball into the air and start the game. The ball was an inflated pig's bladder, which someone had painted to look like a severed head. The

212

artist had been uncannily accurate, even down to the red paint around the base, to represent blood.

'You are not supposed to be armed,' objected Bartholomew, eyeing with dismay the arsenal most players carried: knives, sharp sticks, pieces of chain, and lumps of metal that allowed the holder to pack more of a punch.

'But weapons are part of the game,' declared Langelee, who was one of the most heavily laden.

'I am not wasting my day tending wounds that can be avoided,' stated Bartholomew firmly. 'So you can all disarm, or I am going home.'

'You will have to do as he asks, because you cannot play without a physician,' said Prior Leccheworth, while Etone nodded agreement. Both seemed pleased by Bartholomew's ultimatum. 'It is against the rules.'

'Damn you for a killjoy, Bartholomew,' muttered Langelee, as he began to do as he was told. Resentfully, the other players did likewise, and soon there was a huge pile of armaments at the physician's feet. Most dashed away to take their places before they could be searched for more, and Bartholomew was sure they had not given up everything they had secreted about them. Unfortunately, he was equally sure that there was not much more he could do about it.

'Prior Etone and I are obliged to remind you of the rules,' announced Leccheworth eventually to the participants. 'Not that there are many. Well, two and an optional one, to be precise.'

'First, each team has two goals,' continued Etone. 'The object of the game is to pass the ball into your own goals, and to prevent the opposition from getting the ball into theirs.'

'Second, there will be no biting,' continued Leccheworth. 'And third, if you would not mind, no swearing, either. This is a convent, and I do not want my novices hearing anything uncouth.'

'Right you are then, Father,' said Langelee amiably. 'We shall take our positions, and the game will be under way as soon as the ball leaves the hand of the Indifferent Man, who is Michael this year. In the meantime, I advise you and Bartholomew to leave the field with all possible speed.'

'What do you mean?' demanded Michael uneasily. 'You told me all the Indifferent Man has to do is throw the ball in the air, and walk back to the side.'

'*Running* to the side would be safer,' said Neyll with a nasty grin. 'As fast as you can.'

The teams lined up about ten yards distant from each other. As soon as Bartholomew and the priors left, the competitors issued a great roar that seemed to make the ground tremble. The Indifferent Man hurled the ball into the air, and all the players immediately began to converge on it. Bartholomew started back in alarm when he saw Michael was going to be crushed under the onslaught, but Etone stopped him. The two sides met with a crash that reminded the physician painfully of the Battle of Poitiers.

'Michael does not look very "indifferent" now,' chortled Leccheworth, as the monk disappeared in a mêlée of flailing arms and legs. 'I have never seen a man look so frightened!'

Bartholomew tried to free himself, to go to his friend's aid, but Etone held tight. Then Michael appeared, clawing his way free of the frenzy. He made a determined dash for safety, but Neyll emerged from the scrimmage and stuck out a sly foot. Unfortunately for the Bible Scholar, once Michael's bulk was on the move, it was not easily stopped, and it was Neyll who went sprawling.

It did not take Bartholomew long to decide that camp-ball was not very interesting as a spectator sport. All that could be seen most of the time was a pile of heaving bodies, and he rarely knew where the ball was. He suspected the same was true for the players, and that they had forgotten their goals in the general enjoyment of punching, kicking and slapping each other.

His skills were needed almost immediately. First, Brother Jude was knocked senseless, then Gib hobbled from the field, howling in agony.

'What is wrong?' shouted Bartholomew, struggling to make himself heard over the Chestre man's screeches. There was nothing obviously amiss, and he was not sure what he was expected to do.

'My leg is broken, of course!' bellowed Gib. 'Call yourself a physician?'

'It is not broken,' countered Bartholomew. 'It is not even bruised.'

'It is snapped in two!' Gib was making such a fuss that more people were watching him than the game. 'And you are only pretending there is nothing wrong because you made yourself sick on our wine last night. It is vengeance!'

Bartholomew was about to deny the charge, when the action on the field came to a sudden stop. He glanced across to see some players milling around aimlessly, while the others had formed a massive heap. They untangled themselves slowly, but the one at the very bottom of the pile lay still. Neyll shouted that he was holding up the action, and prodded the inert figure with his foot. Before the Scot could do any damage, Bartholomew abandoned Gib and ran towards them.

Before he was halfway there, he could see it was Poynton, identifiable by his fine clothes, now sadly stained with mud. He reached the victim and dropped to his knees. But there was nothing he could do to help, because Poynton was dead.

*   *   *

Although fatalities were not uncommon in camp-ball, it was the first time Bartholomew had had to deal with one, and he found it an unsettling experience. He called for a stretcher, and escorted the body from the field. He expected the game to end there and then, and was startled when there was a call for the return of the Indifferent Man so it could begin afresh.

'But a player is dead,' he objected, shocked.

'And the Indifferent Man intends to investigate the matter,' added Michael.

'Of course,' said Langelee impatiently. 'Do not let us interfere. Father William, how would you like the honour of being indifferent, given that Michael declines? You can run fast, I believe.'

'This is hardly seemly, Prior Leccheworth,' declared Michael, watching in horror as William trotted out on to the field to oblige. 'It is—'

'I dare not stop it,' whispered Leccheworth, his face white against his black hair. 'There is nothing in the rules – such as they are – that says a game must be aborted in the event of a death. And people have been looking forward to this match for weeks. There would be a riot!'

'He is right,' agreed Etone. 'There must be upwards of a thousand people here, including the kind of apprentices and students who react badly to disappointment. It will be better for everyone if we let the game continue. But it is a shame the casualty is Poynton: corpses do not make benefactions.'

His fellow Carmelites had a rather more compassionate attitude to the pilgrim's demise, and they and Welfry were already on their knees, intoning prayers for the dead. They were joined by most of the Gilbertines, although Thelnetham was not among them. He was nowhere to be seen, and Bartholomew wondered where he had gone.

Michael wanted Bartholomew to examine Poynton's body before it was taken away, but the physician had the living to tend. Within moments, he was obliged to bandage a cut in Heslarton's arm, and apply a poultice to Neyll's knee. Kendale came to stand next to his fallen Bible Scholar, gripping his shoulder encouragingly. Gib, on the other hand, had recovered from his 'broken' leg and had rejoined the game, throwing punches with unrestrained enthusiasm.

'Treat Neyll gently, physician,' ordered Kendale, his breath hot on Bartholomew's ear. 'Chestre will not countenance any roughness. And you need not bother to tend my injured hand again, because Meryfeld has offered to do it.'

Neyll grinned malevolently. 'I told him I would burn down his house if he refused, and he was not sure whether I was in jest or not. He agreed, just to be on the safe side.'

Bartholomew ignored them both, too busy to bandy words. When Michael saw Kendale looming over his friend in a manner he deemed threatening, he hurried over.

'Step away, Kendale,' he ordered. 'And incidentally, I expect our gates to be returned by this evening. If you do not oblige, I will see Chestre closed down, and your pupils sent home.'

'Will you indeed?' drawled Kendale. 'Well, unfortunately for you, you have no evidence that we are the culprits, and you cannot suppress a hostel on a suspicion. If you even attempt it, I shall inform the King – I have kin at court, so you can be sure my threat is not an idle one. Besides, we are innocent.'

'Then who *is* responsible?' demanded Michael.

Kendale shrugged. 'I imagine a brash College like Michaelhouse has all manner of enemies, and Chestre is not the only hostel that would like to see it cut down to size.'

Michael glared at him, then turned on Neyll. 'What can you tell me about Poynton's death? You were on the field, so what did you see?'

A spiteful expression suffused the Bible Scholar's face. 'I saw Master Langelee paying rather close attention to Poynton before the mishap. Perhaps you should question *him*. I, however, was nowhere near the pilgrim when he died.'

'Neyll is lying,' said Bartholomew, after Kendale had helped his student limp away. 'He *was* near Poynton, because he was one of those extricated from the pile. I saw Yffi help him up.'

'Why should he lie?' asked Michael worriedly. 'Did he crush Poynton deliberately and is trying to ensure we do not prosecute him? Of course, malicious intent would be difficult to prove, given the level of violence on the field today.'

'Difficult to disprove, too,' Bartholomew pointed out. 'But Neyll was right about one thing: Langelee *was* by Poynton during the fatal skirmish. If we accuse Chestre, they will almost certainly respond with similar claims about our Master.'

'And anyone who knows Langelee will be aware of his penchant for savagery,' concluded Michael. 'Damn them! They will use Langelee's wild reputation to protect themselves.'

CHAPTER 7

It felt like an age until a bell rang to announce the game was over. The uninjured players – down to about ten per team – left the field slapping each other's shoulders in manly bonhomie. Langelee, smeared in blood, though none of it was his own, came to greet his colleagues with a beaming grin.

'By God, I enjoyed that,' he declared. 'I am sorry about Poynton, though. Was his neck broken or was he crushed? I have known both to happen before, which is why I am careful never to end up on the bottom of those piles.'

'You *enjoyed* it?' cried Thelnetham in disbelief. 'But our team lost! You only managed three goals, whereas the Carmelites scored ten. It was what is known in military terms as a rout.'

'Rubbish!' cried Langelee. 'We were the better players. Goals are not everything, you know.'

'I think you will find they are,' countered Thelnetham. He brushed himself down fussily, and Bartholomew wondered again where he had been earlier, when his brethren had been praying over Poynton's corpse. 'At least, they are if you are trying to win.'

'Were there goals?' asked William. 'I did not see any. And to be honest, I would not have known who had won, either, if Prior Leccheworth had not announced the result. As far as I could tell, it was just a lot of skirmishing. Indeed, I am not even sure the ball was involved in the last part. It seemed to be lying forgotten at the edge of the field.'

'Did any of you see what happened to Poynton?' Michael asked.

'He caught the ball, and went down under a wave of men,' replied Thelnetham promptly. 'The first four to reach him were Master Langelee, Yffi, Neyll and Heslarton.'

'Heslarton?' asked William. 'But he was on Poynton's side! Why should *he* join the scrum?'

'One forgets these niceties in the heat of the moment,' explained Langelee. 'But do not ask *me* about it, Brother. There were so many scrimmages today that I cannot recall one from another.'

Michael walked to where Yffi was standing with his apprentices, being commiserated because his team had lost.

'At least we killed one of the bastards,' Yffi was saying viciously. 'And I am not sure I believe Prior Etone's claim that his team got ten goals, because *I* did not see any of them. Of course, I did not see the three we had, either . . .'

'You were among the first to reach Poynton when he caught the ball,' said Michael, launching immediately into an interrogation. 'Tell me what happened.'

Yffi scratched his head with a rough, callused hand. 'Langelee, Neyll and I raced to get it back. So did Heslarton, although *he* was on Poynton's side, and was supposed to be protecting him. But it is difficult to remember who is who on these occasions, so you should not hold it against him.'

'Right,' said Michael, thus indicating he would think what he pleased.

'Then others hurled themselves on the pile, and I suppose Poynton could not breathe under the weight of the bodies,' continued Yffi. 'It would not be the first time, nor will it be the last.'

While Bartholomew treated a staggering array of gashes, grazes and bruises, assisted none too ably by Rougham, Meryfeld and Gyseburne, Michael continued to ask questions. Everyone's story – players and spectators alike – was the same: Poynton had died because the human body was not designed to be trapped under so much weight.

When the monk had satisfied himself that there was no more to be learned from witnesses, he turned his attention to the body, only to find that Welfry and Horneby had organised a bier, and were already carrying it to the Carmelite Priory. He hurried after them, arriving just as they were setting the corpse before the altar. Fen and the two nuns were with them, and when they had finished, the pardoner stepped forward and gently laid a badge on Poynton's chest.

'That is a Holy Land cross,' said Horneby softly, eyeing it in awe. 'From Jerusalem.'

'It was his favourite,' said Fen in a broken voice. 'We have been travelling together for years, and I shall miss him terribly. I shall undertake to return his belongings to his family myself, especially his *signacula*. It is what he would have wanted.'

'Would he?' asked Horneby. 'You do not think he might prefer to leave one or two of the valuable ones here? He was talking about helping us rebuild our shrine, and I speak not because I want his money, but because we must ensure that we follow his wishes.'

'Right,' murmured Fen flatly. 'But we should let his kin decide how to honour him.'

Michael narrowed his eyes. 'As a pardoner, you sell pilgrim tokens, do you not?'

Fen regarded him coolly. 'On occasion, but I assure you, that is not the reason I want to assume possession of Poynton's. My motives are honourable.'

221

'Of course they are,' said Welfry soothingly, speaking before Michael could respond. 'But this is not the place to discuss such matters. Will you join me in a prayer for his soul?'

Without appearing insensitive, no one had any choice but to agree, so Michael, Horneby, Fen and the nuns knelt while Welfry began to intone several lengthy petitions. It was cold in the chapel, and the three surviving pilgrims were openly relieved when at last he finished. They took their leave quickly, and Michael watched them go with narrowed eyes.

'They are chilled to the bone, Brother,' said Horneby, seeing what he was thinking. 'It has been a long afternoon, and the wind was biting. I understand why they are eager to find a fire.'

Welfry agreed. 'They are running to warm themselves, not to paw through Poynton's things.'

My poor friend!' said Horneby, regarding the Dominican sheepishly. 'You came today because I promised you some fun, to make up for the distress of losing your *signaculum*, but I suspect you feel you have been most shamelessly misled.'

Welfry nodded unhappily. 'Watching men punch and kick each other is not my idea of entertainment, and I am sorry for Poynton. There was nothing to laugh about this afternoon.'

'Then let us remedy that,' said Horneby. 'Father William has given me a theological tract to read – one he penned himself. I warrant there will be something in that to bring a smile to your face.'

Welfry did not look convinced, but allowed himself to be led away, leaving Michael alone with Poynton. The monk stared down at the arrogant, unattractive face for a long time, grateful the death was an accident, and not something else he would have to investigate. Eventually, Bartholomew arrived, looking for him.

'You had better examine Poynton,' Michael said tiredly. 'The Gilbertine Priory counts as University land, because some of its canons are scholars. His death comes under our jurisdiction.'

'Now?' asked Bartholomew unenthusiastically. 'I am cold, wet and tired.'

'So am I,' snapped Michael. 'But I will need a cause of death for my records, and I would like the matter concluded today. Then I can concentrate on catching the killer-thief and preventing the Colleges and hostels from tearing each other apart.'

With a sigh of resignation, Bartholomew obliged, but soon forgot his discomfort when he discovered what lay beneath the fine garments. He had suspected Poynton was ill, but he was appalled to learn the extent to which disease had ravaged its victim. He regarded the pilgrim with compassion, feeling it went some way to explaining why Poynton had been so irascible. It also explained why he had devoted so much time to pilgrimage – and why he had been so distressed when his *signaculum* had been stolen. Doubtless he knew he was living on borrowed time and would soon need any blessings such items might confer on their owners.

'Well?' Michael asked, impatient to be gone. 'Which was it? Crushing or a broken neck?'

'Neither,' replied Bartholomew, tearing his thoughts away from Poynton's sickness to more practical matters. 'He died from a knife in the heart.'

There was silence in the Carmelite chapel after Bartholomew made his announcement. In the distance, Welfry was laughing, his voice a merry chime above

223

Horneby's deeper chuckle. Etone and some of his friars were chanting a mass in the shrine, and a cockerel crowed in the yard.

'I have spoken to dozens of witnesses who tell me otherwise,' said Michael eventually.

'I cannot help that, Brother. The fact is that his neck is not broken, and there is no significant damage to his chest – other than the fact that someone has shoved a knife through it. He was also mortally sick, although that has no bearing on his demise.'

'Murder?' asked Michael in disbelief. 'In front of a thousand spectators and sixty players?'

Bartholomew shrugged. 'Or accident. The competitors were ordered to disarm before the game, but most managed to keep hold of at least one weapon. Then, during that colossal scrum, a blade may have slipped from its hiding place and into Poynton without its owner knowing anything about it.'

'But it is equally possible that he may have been killed on purpose?'

Bartholomew nodded. 'But Poynton's body cannot tell us which.'

Michael grimaced. 'I do not believe in coincidences, and it seems suspicious to me that *he* should be the one to die – a victim of the *signaculum*-snatcher. Or an alleged victim, at least.'

'He was on your list of suspects as the killer-thief,' recalled Bartholomew. 'On the grounds that he poked his head around our College gates the morning Drax was dumped there.'

'Along with Fen and those two horrible nuns.' Michael sighed, and closed his eyes wearily. 'Damn! The Carmelites will be outraged when they learn a potential benefactor has been unlawfully slain, and may blame the Gilbertines

– Yffi, Neyll and Langelee, all members of the Gilbertines' side, were the first to jump on Poynton, after all. There will be trouble for certain.'

'Heslarton jumped on him, too, and *he* was playing for the Carmelites. But to be honest, I do not think anyone cared who was on whose team. The whole thing was just an excuse for a brawl.'

Michael's anxieties intensified. 'The Carmelites have always sided with the Colleges, while the Gilbertines prefer the hostels. Etone and Leccheworth – both sensible men – usually intervene if the rivalry turns sour, but if rabble-rousers like Kendale learn what happened to Poynton, the ill feeling between the two convents may escalate beyond their control.'

'Then we had better keep the matter to ourselves until we understand exactly what happened. If we ever do – this will be not be an easy nut to crack. Incidentally, I heard Trinity Hall discussing Jolye again today.'

'Jolye?' asked Michael. 'The lad who drowned after playing the prank with the balanced boats?'

'Yes. You recorded it as an accident, but Trinity Hall is now braying that he was murdered by a hostel. I told them there was no evidence to suggest such a thing, but you know how these rumours take on a life of their own, especially when fuelled by unscrupulous men.'

'Men like Kendale,' sighed Michael. 'So who killed Poynton, do you think?'

Bartholomew considered carefully before replying. 'Just before the fatal scrimmage, Gib claimed to have broken his leg. He made a terrible fuss, although there was nothing wrong with him, and within a few moments he was back on the field.'

'What are you saying? That he created a distraction, to allow an accomplice to commit murder?'

225

Bartholomew shrugged. 'Neyll was one of the four who first hurled themselves on Poynton. However, although a lot of people watched Gib's curious antics, not everyone did – so if it *was* a diversion, it was not a very effective one. I am not sure what to think, Brother. Perhaps Gib is just one of those players who enjoys making a scene over a scratch.'

Michael looked tired. 'But regardless, we have another suspicious death to investigate?'

'If it *was* suspicious. Accidents are not uncommon in camp-ball.'

'Perhaps that is what someone hopes we will think. But the Senior Proctor will not be manipulated. If Poynton was murdered, I shall find out.'

They left the chapel just as the three pilgrims were emerging from the refectory, one nun still chewing vigorously. Clearly, Poynton's death had not deprived the visitors of their appetites. The trio began to hurry towards the guest house, where smoke billowing from a chimney said a fire had been lit within. Michael muttered to Bartholomew that he had not yet had the chance to interrogate them properly, and intercepted them.

'Were any of you watching the camp-ball when Poynton died?' he asked, after some strained pleasantries had been exchanged. 'Or were you more intent on talking to devious characters like Kendale?'

'Is Kendale devious?' asked Fen in surprise. 'He is a scholar, so I assumed he was decent.'

Bartholomew looked hard at him, wondering if he was being facetious, but found he could not tell. Michael's eyes narrowed, though.

'What were you discussing?' he demanded.

'That is none of your business,' replied Fen sharply. Then he rubbed his face with a hand that shook. 'Forgive me. It is shock speaking – as I said, Poynton and I have travelled together for a long time, and his death has distressed me. Kendale asked whether I could locate Bradwardine's *Tractatus de continuo* for him. I deal in books occasionally, you see.'

'It is true,' said the nun called Agnes. Or was it Margaret? She pulled a disagreeable face. 'The conversation went on for some time, and we were ignored.'

Michael changed the subject abruptly. 'What did you see when Poynton died?'

Margaret smiled coyly. 'Very little, because we were huddled inside Master Fen's cloak.'

'When he was in it, too,' simpered Agnes. 'It meant our vision was limited.'

Fen cleared his throat uncomfortably. 'Most of *my* attention was on Kendale, but I did happen to glance at the field during the fatal skirmish. Unfortunately, all I saw was a flurry of arms and legs. I wish I could help you, but I cannot. And now I shall bid you good evening.'

He bowed politely, and walked towards the guest house. The two nuns scurried after him, trying to catch up so they could cling to his arms. Michael watched them go, hands on hips.

'Fen is a liar,' he declared. 'Moreover, he intends to deflower those silly ladies, if he has not done so already. I could see the lust shining in his eyes.'

'I disagree,' said Bartholomew. 'He is not interested in them, and the gleam you saw was tears of grief. He was fond of Poynton, and is genuinely distressed by his death.'

'Rubbish! You are too easily swayed by a pleasant face and courtly manners.'

'And you are too easily influenced by a man's profession,' countered Bartholomew. 'Not all pardoners cheat their customers, and Fen is a pilgrim. Pilgrims generally avoid committing crimes while they are conducting major acts of penitence.'

'How do you know Fen is a genuine pilgrim? Perhaps his real intention was to befriend Poynton and lay hold of his *signacula* the moment this disease claimed his life.'

'I do not believe it. And Fen can have nothing to do with Poynton's death, because he was on the sidelines when Poynton was stabbed.'

'Killers can be bought,' argued Michael. 'And for a small fraction of what Fen stands to earn from selling Poynton's *signacula*. He is implicated in this death, Matt. I am sure of it.'

Their debate was cut short by the arrival of Cynric. He was mud-smeared, and Bartholomew suspected he had been enjoying a celebratory ale with the camp-ball players in the King's Head.

'Oh, no!' exclaimed Michael, putting out his hand suddenly. 'Rain! My room will be awash!'

'It will,' agreed Cynric. 'Because the sheet over your ceiling will not repel anything more than a shower, and I suspect we are in for a good downpour tonight.' He turned to Bartholomew. 'But I came to tell you that Emma de Colvyll has summoned you, boy.'

'She is no longer my patient,' said Bartholomew, glad to be able to refuse her. 'Meryfeld—'

'The messenger said Meryfeld needs a second opinion. *He* wants you to go, too.'

Bartholomew had no desire to visit Emma. He was chilled through from an afternoon of kneeling in frost-encrusted grass to tend wounds, and he was still fragile from Chestre's hospitality the night before. He felt like going home, to sit by the conclave fire and enjoy the comforting, familiar conversation of his colleagues.

'You had better go – your conscience will plague you all

night if you do not,' said Michael. 'And while you are there, see if you can learn two things. First, the status of Heslarton's enquiry into the yellow-headed thief. And second, whether it was Heslarton's knife that killed Poynton.'

'How am I supposed to do that?' objected Bartholomew, not very happy about probing such delicate matters when the sinister Emma was likely to be present.

'I am sure you will find a way,' said Michael.

They parted company on the High Street. Bartholomew knocked on Emma's door, which was opened by the chubby-faced maid. She conducted him to the solar where her mistress spent most of her time. Emma was sitting by the hearth, black eyes glittering in the firelight. Celia Drax, elegant and laconic, was sewing in the window, while Heslarton sat opposite her, honing his sword. Their knees were touching, and Bartholomew recalled Agatha's contention that they were lovers. There was no sign of Meryfeld.

'Did you enjoy the camp-ball, Doctor?' asked Heslarton, looking up from his whetting to grin. He seemed to have fewer teeth than when Bartholomew had last seen him. 'Everyone says my two goals were the best of the day.'

'I am sure they were,' said Bartholomew. 'Where is Meryfeld?'

'It was entertaining to see that pilgrim die,' declared Emma, ignoring his question. 'There is nothing like a death to liven up a game.'

Bartholomew had heard her make insensitive remarks before, but never one that was quite so brazenly callous. 'Did you see what happened to him?' he asked, struggling to mask his distaste.

Emma nodded smugly. 'He caught the ball and went down under a wall of men. How did he die, Doctor? Was it crushing or a broken neck? Thomas and I have a small wager on it, you see, and I would like the matter resolved tonight, so I can gloat over him when he is proven wrong.'

'I forgot he was on my side, and ran to grab the ball,' said Heslarton, either uncaring of or oblivious to Bartholomew's grimace of distaste at Emma's confession. 'By the time I realised my mistake, Langelee, Yffi and Neyll were looming, and then everything happened very fast. There was a huge scrum, and it took ages to unravel it. Unfortunately, Poynton was at the bottom. Some players are heavy, so my money is on crushing.'

'No – necks are easily broken,' countered Emma. Bartholomew did not like to imagine how she knew. She flicked imperious fingers at him. 'Well? Who is right?'

'It is not something I am free to discuss,' he replied coolly. 'You are neither his friends nor his next of kin.'

'Give him some wine,' suggested Celia. 'It may loosen his tongue.'

'No, thank you,' said Bartholomew, recalling what had happened to Alice and Odelina.

'It is quite safe,' said Emma, seeming to read his mind. 'The servants threw away all the old stock, and everything is tasted before it comes to us now.'

'Tasted by whom?' asked Bartholomew uneasily.

Emma smiled slyly. 'Rats. Thomas keeps a ready supply of them in the cellar. And that yellow-headed thief will join them there when he is caught.'

Bartholomew stared at her, taking in the beady eyes and thin lips, devoid of humour and kindness, and was hard pressed to suppress a shudder. She appeared especially malevolent that evening, because her head was swathed in a curious back turban and it, combined with her round body and short, thin limbs, served to make her look more like a predatory insect than ever.

'You are still hunting him, then?' he forced himself to ask, although instinct urged him to race away as fast as his legs would carry him, and have nothing to do with her or her household.

'Of course,' said Heslarton. 'He murdered my wife, hurt my daughter, and made off with my mother-in-law's most treasured possessions. *And* he jostled Celia and stole her badge.'

'You *think* the thief is the poisoner,' said Bartholomew, aiming to make him think twice before doing anything rash. 'You do not *know* it, not for certain.'

'Of course it was him,' countered Celia. 'He was the only stranger to enter this house that day. Other than you, of course – the physician who dabbles in sorcery.'

'I have no objection to sorcery,' said Emma, before Bartholomew could defend himself. 'I employ it myself on occasion, and find it very useful. But Doctor Bartholomew did not contaminate the wine, Celia. I was with him the whole time he was here, and I would have noticed.'

'I suppose you would,' said Celia, rather ambiguously.

'Where is Meryfeld?' Bartholomew asked again, this time more firmly. He had better things to do than stand around and be insulted by Celia. 'The messenger said he needed a second opinion.'

'He does,' said Emma. 'He just does not know it yet. He calculated my horoscope, you see, but I am not very happy with it. I want you to make me another.'

Bartholomew regarded her with dislike, supposing the servant had been told to lie about Meryfeld's complicity. He was annoyed by the deception, and determined not to oblige her.

'You do not want a horoscope from me,' he said frostily. 'I make mistakes.'

'You will not make mistakes in mine,' said Emma, in the

231

kind of voice that implied there would be trouble if he did. 'No, do not edge towards the door, man! I want another one done, because Meryfeld's said I had to go on a pilgrimage in order to get well. And I am not going anywhere.'

'I cannot interfere,' said Bartholomew curtly. 'You are Meryfeld's patient now, and I do not poach my colleagues' clients.'

'Why not? They poach from you,' interjected Celia slyly. 'They have stolen nearly all your rich customers, leaving you with just the poor ones. Here is your chance to pay them back.'

'No,' said Bartholomew firmly. 'And a pilgrimage will not cure you, Mistress Emma. Your tooth will continue to ache until it is pulled out.'

Emma shook her head in disbelief. 'You earned my regard by saving Odelina – and I do not bestow my good opinion on many people. So why do you not strive to keep it? Most people would *love* to be in your position.'

Bartholomew was not sure how to reply, but rescue came in the form of Heslarton, who had tired of the discussion and suddenly stood up. Bartholomew tensed, anticipating violence, but the burly henchman merely indicated the stairs with a flick of his bald head.

'Odelina took a chill this afternoon, and is asking for you. If you will not help my mother or settle our wager, then perhaps you will see to her instead. I will take you to her.'

'Meryfeld will—' began Bartholomew.

'She does not want Meryfeld,' said Heslarton. 'She dislikes the way he keeps rubbing his filthy hands together, and I confess I see her point. The man gives *me* the shivers!'

Bartholomew did not want to visit Odelina, but decided a consultation was likely to be quicker than the argument that was going to arise from a refusal. It would not take him a moment to deal with a chill, after all. He followed Heslarton up the stairs to a fine chamber on the upper floor, where Odelina was reclining on a bed, clad in a tight, cream-coloured gown that put him in mind of a grub.

'There you are, Doctor,' she cooed, when her father had gone. 'I thought you were not coming. Have you brought me a gift?'

'A gift?' asked Bartholomew, bemused.

'That is the custom, is it not, when visiting the sick? To take a little something to make them feel better? A piece of jewellery, perhaps. Or some dried fruit.'

'It is not the custom for physicians,' remarked Bartholomew. 'It would hardly be practical!'

Odelina's smile faded. 'But surely, I am different from your other patients?'

While he struggled for a tactful response, Bartholomew's eye fell on a book. It was one his sister had made him read to her many years before, and concerned a heroine with a tragic disease who was miraculously cured by a gift from a suitor. He glanced at Odelina's clothes and posture, and was suddenly certain that she saw herself as the protagonist. With a sigh of irritation – she was surely too old for such games? – he resolved not to go along with the charade.

'I am not well,' she said feebly. Then her voice strengthened. 'But I might feel better if you were to give me a talisman. You saved my life, thus forging a unique bond between us.'

'It is not unique,' stated Bartholomew firmly. 'All my patients are—'

'I was almost at Heaven's gates when you snatched me back,' countered Odelina. 'And that makes me special to you. I cannot imagine you rescue many patients from impending death?'

'Well, no,' admitted Bartholomew, cornered. 'Not many. But—'

'Well, then.' Odelina beamed, and she held out a plump hand. 'Give me something of yours. Anything will do. A thread from your tabard, a scrap of your cloak.'

'How about a remedy to make you sleep? I can tell your maid how to make it.'

Her face fell. 'You are cruel! You know I do not want one of those!'

'I know nothing of the kind,' snapped Bartholomew. 'And I cannot start yanking my clothes apart for threads and scraps, anyway. They are old, and likely to fall off.'

The expression on her face made him wonder whether she found this notion as disagreeable as he thought she should have done.

'Sing to me, then,' she ordered. 'I have heard that music helps the sick become well again, so it will be like dispensing medicine.'

'I rarely sing.' Bartholomew had had enough of her. 'And loud noises are dangerous after catching chills at camp-ball games. So are long visits from physicians. Sleep now. Goodnight.'

Bartholomew returned to Michaelhouse as fast as he could, hurrying through the wet streets and grateful to be away from Emma's stronghold. He stepped through the great gap where the gates had hung, nodding to the student-guards, and walked across the yard to his room. He found Valence there, working on yet another exercise that should have been completed the previous day.

'There has been quite a commotion here tonight, sir,' the student said, seeing where his teacher was looking and hastening to distract him. 'Rain seeped through the sheet in Brother Michael's room, and it is no longer habitable. And look at our walls!'

Bartholomew was dismayed to see rivulets coursing down them. His students were going to be in for a damp and miserable night. The medicines room, where he slept himself, was equally dismal, with water pooling on the floor and oozing through the ceiling.

'Brother Michael and his theologians have been moved to the servants' quarters,' Valence went on. 'And the servants are relegated to the kitchen. Fortunately, none of them objected.'

Bartholomew was sure they had not, because the kitchen was by far the warmest room in the College, and he would not have minded sleeping there himself.

'I will organise a watch,' said Valence. He saw his master's blank look. 'To protect your supplies. Neither this chamber nor the storeroom have window shutters any more, and our front gates have gone. In other words, anyone can slip into the College and help himself. The guards are doing their best, but . . .'

'There is not much to steal, Valence. I cannot recall a time when I have been so low on remedies.'

'All the more reason to defend what is left, then,' said Valence practically.

Bartholomew thanked him and went to the hall, where he learned that supper had been served, eaten and cleared away. Fortunately, Suttone had provided cakes and wine in the conclave for the Fellows, to celebrate his Order's victory over the Gilbertines. Bartholomew glanced uneasily at Thelnetham, not sure he would take kindly to what was effectively gloating, but the canon was sitting impassively by the fire, and it was impossible to gauge what he was thinking.

Not surprisingly, Langelee was holding forth about the

game, delighting in the opportunity to analyse every move and skirmish. Clippesby was listening, although Ayera's eyes were glazed. William and Suttone were discussing a theological text together, and Michael was out.

'Essex Hostel had a lot of dead rats delivered to it this evening,' Ayera explained, when Bartholomew asked where the monk had gone. 'So he is trying to prevent Essex from marching on Trinity Hall and tossing the lot back through their windows.'

Bartholomew sat at the table, and helped himself to a Lombard slice. It was sweet, rich and cloying. He poured some wine to help it down, but when he raised the cup to his lips he found he could not bring himself to swallow anything else, so he set it back on the table untouched. Langelee abandoned his monologue, and came to sit next to him, lowering his voice so the others would not hear.

'Michael told me – in confidence – that Poynton was stabbed, and wanted my opinion as to how it might have happened. I have been pondering the matter. Obviously, some players must have kept their weapons after you ordered us to disarm.'

'I know they did,' said Bartholomew dryly. 'And you were one of them.'

Langelee grinned sheepishly. 'Well, I did not want to be at a disadvantage. I knew damn well that Heslarton had a dagger, while Neyll and Gib are louts, who would never play camp-ball without a blade. Then Brother Jude is fond of knives, and so is Yffi.'

The list continued for some time, and Bartholomew saw his efforts to make the game safer had been a sham. He might have eliminated the more obvious weapons, but every competitor had still been armed to the teeth.

'So what have you concluded from all this?' he asked. 'Who killed Poynton?'

'It must have been one of the three men who reached him first,' replied Langelee. 'Because he was directly beneath them and they acted as a shield, separating him from the second wave of players. *Ergo*, your suspects are Heslarton, Yffi and Neyll.'

'Neyll claims you are the culprit,' said Bartholomew, feeling Langelee's analysis told him nothing he had not already found out for himself. 'Probably because you belong to a College.'

Langelee waved a dismissive hand. 'He is always trying to cause trouble between us and the hostels, but the dispute is ridiculous, and I refuse to let Michaelhouse become embroiled.'

'Good,' said Bartholomew. 'So which of these three do you think is the killer?'

'Heslarton,' replied Langelee, without hesitation. 'It is not always easy to remember who is on one's own team, but Poynton was distinctive. I would not have forgotten a fellow like him, and I cannot imagine Heslarton would have done, either.'

Bartholomew was thoughtful. Langelee knew a great deal about camp-ball, so his opinion was worth considering. But why should Heslarton kill an ailing pilgrim? Was it for his remaining *signacula*? Or, rather more sinisterly, had Heslarton uncovered evidence to suggest Poynton was somehow involved with the yellow-headed thief?

'Speaking of Heslarton, I visited his home earlier,' said Langelee, when Bartholomew made no reply. 'I went to beg Emma's help – to see whether she would order Yffi back to work on our roof. Odelina was there, and she made some remarks.' He winked and touched the side of his nose.

'What kind of remarks?' Bartholomew had no idea what the gesture was supposed to convey.

'Ones that say she has developed a hankering for you,' replied Langelee, a little impatiently. 'So I am afraid you will have to bed her.'

Bartholomew blinked. 'I am sorry?'

'Yes, I imagine you will be, because she is an unattractive lass. But it cannot be helped.'

Bartholomew gaped at him. 'You want me to lie with our benefactress's granddaughter?'

Langelee nodded, as if such a discussion between Master and Fellow were the most natural thing in the world. 'It will almost certainly result in more gifts, because Emma dotes on her. In other words, if Odelina asks Emma to build us a new accommodation wing, I am sure she will oblige. I know it will be unpleasant for you, but you can always keep your eyes closed.'

'Christ!' muttered Bartholomew, feeling rather weak at the knees.

Langelee slapped a manly arm around his shoulders. 'Come to my chambers later and I shall give you advice on how to go about it.'

'I do not need advice. I know how to manage these matters myself. But—'

Langelee's next slap was hard enough to hurt, and he guffawed conspiratorially. 'Good! Then do your duty, and we shall say no more about it.'

'I am not doing it,' said Bartholomew firmly. 'Not with Odelina. She is a patient, for God's sake.'

'Even better. No one will raise any eyebrows when you visit her. Do not be a fool, Bartholomew. We need the generosity of people like Emma de Colvyll, and the occasional frolic with Odelina might make all the difference. Would you really condemn us, your friends, to live in poverty, just because you cannot bring yourself to pleasure a young woman?'

'Emma is far too shrewd a businesswoman to be influenced by Odelina. Besides, you may have misread the situation. She might object to her granddaughter's seduction, and withdraw her support altogether – perhaps demanding a refund from us into the bargain.'

Langelee was thoughtful. 'True. Perhaps I had better make a few discreet enquiries before you undertake this mission. You are right: it would not do to get it wrong.'

When Langelee wandered away to resume his commentary on the game to Clippesby and Ayera, Bartholomew worked on his lectures for the following day. One by one, the other Fellows retired to their beds, until he was the only one remaining. He laboured on a little while longer, but the lantern's dim light and oily fumes were giving him a headache. With a sigh, he closed his books and left the conclave, to walk slowly across the yard. He jumped violently when a shadow stepped out of a doorway to accost him.

'Easy!' said Thelnetham, starting in his turn. 'It is only me.'

'What are you doing?' demanded Bartholomew, more curtly than he had intended. He glanced at the missing gates and wished the pranksters had thought of another way to express their cleverness, because he did not feel safe as long as they were gone.

'I live here, if you recall,' replied Thelnetham acidly. 'Beyond this porch is the entrance to my room. I was taking a little fresh air before retiring to it.'

'Oh,' said Bartholomew. He could not have said why, but he did not believe Thelnetham, and was under the distinct impression that he had been lurking. 'What do you want?'

'To do a colleague a good turn, actually.' Thelnetham sounded offended. 'Your students have begged beds

239

elsewhere, because rain has invaded your quarters, and I wondered whether you might like a mattress on my floor. We are cramped, but we can manage one more.'

'Thank you,' said Bartholomew, relenting. 'It is kind, but the medicine room will suffice.'

'That is awash, too,' said Thelnetham. 'It will be like sleeping at sea.'

Bartholomew walked to the little chamber and saw with dismay that Thelnetham was right. He was tempted to accept his colleague's offer, but something stopped him. He smiled awkwardly.

'I appreciate your kindness, but I am almost certain to be called out by . . . by Emma tonight, so I doubt I will be sleeping much anyway.' He looked away, never comfortable with fabrication, but better a lie than offending a man who was probably only trying to be neighbourly.

Thelnetham sighed. 'As you please. Does Emma's tooth still pain her? She is a fool not to listen to your advice. Of course, the procedure will be painful, so her reluctance to let you loose on her jaws is understandable. Heslarton once had a molar drawn by a surgeon in Huntingdon, and he said pieces of bone were dropping out in bloody gobbets for weeks afterwards.'

No wonder Emma was wary, Bartholomew thought. 'How do you know this?'

Thelnetham shrugged. 'He must have mentioned it when I went to their house with Langelee to seal our arrangement about the roof. I saved you some cakes, by the way. You were late, and I did not think it fair that you should be left with the boring ones.'

He passed Bartholomew a parcel wrapped in cloth and started to walk away. As he did so, Bartholomew heard an odd sound from the roof. He glanced up, then hurled himself backwards when something began to drop. A chaos

240

of ropes and planks crashed to the ground, right where he had been standing. His heart thudded at the narrow escape.

'The rain must have dislodged it,' said Thelnetham, coming to peer at the mess. 'It is a good thing you have fast reactions.'

Bartholomew could not see his face, because the night was too dark. He frowned, watching the Gilbertine stride away, then shook himself. He was tired and it had been a long day – his imagination was running riot. He located the cakes he had dropped, and entered his storeroom.

His mind was too active for sleep, so he lit a lamp and began to work on his treatise on fevers – intended to be a basic guide for students, but now an unwieldy collection of observations, notes and opinions – and ate a cake while he wrote. It was good, so he had a second, and then a third. He was reaching for the fourth when there was a sharp pain in his stomach. He gripped it for a moment, then dived for a bucket when he knew he was going to be sick.

Afterwards, he did not feel like working. He lay in his damp bed, feeling his innards churn, and listened to the rain dripping through the ceiling.

It was a miserable night. Bartholomew's stomach pains subsided in the small hours, but the wind gusting through the shutterless windows made an awful racket among his bottles and jars, and no matter where he lay, the rain seemed to find him. At one point, he went to the hall in search of a dry berth, but the door had been locked in response to the missing gates. He returned to his own room, eventually falling asleep shortly before the bell rang to call everyone to morning prayers. He dozed through it, and was difficult to rouse when Michael noticed he was missing and came to find him.

241

'Were you called out last night?' asked the monk sympathetically, as Bartholomew crawled off the mattress and splashed water on his face from the bowl Cynric left for him each night – not that he needed a bowl, given the amount of rain that was available on the floor. 'You look exhausted.'

'I should have accepted Thelnetham's offer of a dry bed,' said Bartholomew ruefully. 'I kept dreaming I was sailing down the river on a leaking boat. And about Jolye.'

Michael picked up one of the Lombard slices from the table; miraculously, they had remained dry. 'The rumour is spreading that he was murdered by the hostels. Trinity Hall claims that was why they sent rats to Essex – in revenge for his unlawful death.'

'If Jolye was killed, then the culprits are more likely to be at Chestre – it was their boats that were being tampered with when he drowned. Perhaps they caught him and pushed him in.'

'Perhaps, but we will never prove it,' said Michael bitterly. 'There were no witnesses, and you found nothing on the body to allow me to make a case.'

They were silent for a while, Michael thinking about the youngster's death while he stared at the Lombard slice he held, and Bartholomew hunting around for dry clothes.

'I was out late last night,' the monk said eventually. 'Although I have nothing to show for it. After putting down the rat trouble, I interviewed camp-ball players in the King's Head, but still cannot decide whether Poynton's death was murder or accident. Then I was told that a yellow-headed stranger was drinking in the Griffin, so I went there.'

'And what did you find?'

'That he has a twisted foot – you would have caught him had *he* snatched Emma's box and hared off up the High

Street. He is not our man.' Michael raised the cake to his mouth.

'Do not eat that, Brother. They made me sick last night.'

'Because you are unused to their richness,' said Michael, taking a substantial bite. He gagged, and immediately spat it out. 'Or more likely, because they were made with rancid butter. Nasty!'

'Thelnetham gave them to me.'

'He does not like you very much,' said Michael, wiping his lips with a silken cloth. 'I think he is jealous. He is a controversial thinker, which brings its share of fame and recognition. But you are our resident heretic, and you over-shadow him.'

Bartholomew was still too befuddled with sleep to tell him his theory was nonsense. He finished dressing, then walked across the yard to where their colleagues were gathering for church. It was raining again, and William was complaining about a patch of mould growing on his ceiling.

'At least you have one,' said Michael caustically. 'I do not, while Matt spent half the night floating about on his mattress.'

'Yffi will make good on the roof today, or he will answer to me,' growled Langelee.

He spun on his heel and led his scholars up the lane, leaving the slower of them to scramble to catch up with him. Bartholomew did not mind the Master's rapid pace – it was cold and wet, and the brisk walk served to warm him a little. But even so, he shivered all through mass.

Teaching finished at noon on Saturdays, but, unimpressed by his students' performance, Bartholomew ordered them to attend a lecture Rougham was giving on Philaretus's *De pulsibus*. They objected vociferously at the loss of a free afternoon, and he was obliged to send Cynric with them, to make sure they did not abscond.

'You are driving them too hard,' remarked Michael, watching them leave, a sullen, resentful gaggle that dragged its heels and shot malicious glances at its teacher.

'They will fail their disputations if they do not work. They are not learning as fast as they should.'

'They are not learning as fast as you would like,' corrected Michael. 'But at least your tyranny is keeping them away from the hostel–College trouble. They are lively lads, far more so than students in the other disciplines, and would certainly have joined in, had they had time. Thank God you have seen that they do not. Will you come to Chestre with me?'

Bartholomew blinked at the abrupt question. 'I thought you had decided not to tackle them until you had more evidence.'

Michael grimaced. 'That was about the murders, the pilgrim badge thefts and our missing gates. But they are material witnesses to what happened to Poynton, so they cannot object to questions about him. And if the occasion arises, perhaps I shall see what a little subtle probing on other matters brings to light. Besides, I am low on clues, so it is time to rattle a few nerves.'

Bartholomew followed him over the road to Chestre Hostel. The rain had darkened its plaster to the point where it was almost black, and a strategically placed window shutter made the 'face' on the front of the building appear to be leering. Even Michael looked a little unsettled when he rapped on the door and it evinced an eerily booming echo that rumbled along the corridor within.

'We have already told you all we know,' said Kendale irritably, when the Senior Proctor and his Corpse Examiner were shown into the hall. 'And I am busy.'

He was teaching, and from the complex explanations chalked on the wall, Bartholomew could see he was deep into the mean speed theorem. He was sorry Kendale was unfriendly, because he would have liked to listen. However, he could see by the bored, bemused faces that Chestre's students did not feel the same way.

'But not too busy to offer a little hospitality,' said Neyll, exchanging a sly grin with Gib and lifting a jug. Bartholomew felt sick at the thought of it: it was far too early in the day for wine.

'It is the Feast Day of St Dorothea,' declared Michael, raising an imperious hand to stop the Bible Scholar from pouring. 'And we always abstain from strong drink then, to honour her. We cannot accept your generous offer, I am afraid.'

Neyll opened his mouth to argue, but could apparently think of nothing to say, and closed it again. Bartholomew hoped the monk had not lied, for the excuse was something that could be checked.

'Then state your business, so I can return to my lecture,' ordered Kendale arrogantly. 'Is it to ask yet more tediously bumbling questions about Poynton, like you did yesterday?'

'Yes,' replied Michael, equally haughty. 'I want to know why Gib sobbed like a girl over his bruised leg, thus allowing Neyll to murder a pilgrim on the camp-ball field.'

Even Bartholomew was taken aback by this assertion, and the students were livid. They flew to their feet, and for a moment the hall was a cacophony of clamouring voices.

'That is not my idea of subtle probing, Brother,' murmured Bartholomew, as Michael held up an authoritative hand for silence. It was ignored, and it was Kendale who restored calm.

'Sit,' he ordered his scholars. They did so immediately, and he turned to the monk. 'I assure you there was no

245

collusion between Neyll and Gib. And Neyll was only one of a score of men who inadvertently crushed Poynton, anyway. Clearly, the man owned a feeble constitution and should not have been playing such a rough game.'

Bartholomew watched Neyll and Gib intently, but their faces were blank, and he could read nothing in them. Nor could he tell whether Kendale had had an inkling that his violent students might have committed a crime. Neither could Michael, apparently, because he changed the subject.

'This business of our gates,' he began, and Bartholomew saw Kendale's hubris had nettled him into saying more than he had intended. 'It was neither amusing nor clever.'

'I quite agree,' said Kendale. 'Which is why we are not guilty. We would never demean ourselves with such a paltry trick. It is hardly in the same class as illuminating St Mary the Great!'

'Your "fuses",' began Bartholomew, still hoping to learn something useful from that escapade. 'No one can work out how you—'

'True,' interrupted Michael, cutting across him and concentrating on Kendale. 'Stealing gates *is* an asinine prank, so I know *you* are innocent. However, your students—'

'My lads had nothing to do with it,' interrupted Kendale firmly. 'And I suggest you look to a College for your culprit. They are the unimaginative ones, not we.'

'It was Seneschal Welfry,' declared Neyll, grinning. '*He* did it, so the hostels would be blamed. He had better not try anything like it on us, or I will slit his . . . I will not be pleased.'

'There you are, Brother,' said Kendale smugly. 'Speak to Welfry – that fool in a Dominican habit, who takes it upon himself to answer the hostels' challenges. Incidentally, the townfolk were disappointed by yesterday's camp-ball.

246

They said it was boring. So, I have decided to sponsor another game on Tuesday. It will be between the hostels and the Colleges, and any scholar will be welcome to join in.'

Bartholomew was appalled, knowing exactly what would happen if a lot of young men were given free rein to punch other young men from foundations they did not like.

'You cannot,' said Michael, also trying to mask his shock. 'It will be the same day as the Stock Extraordinary Lecture. You will never recruit enough players.'

But he would, of course, because camp-ball was far more interesting to students than a theological debate, and Kendale knew it. He smiled languorously.

'I am sure we shall rustle up sufficient support. And afterwards we shall provide free wine and ale, for players and spectators alike.'

If the game itself did not lead to a fight, then Chestre's powerful beverages would certainly do the trick. Bartholomew gaped at him, horrified that he should even contemplate such an irresponsible act.

'I refuse you permission,' said Michael coldly. 'You cannot hold such an event without the consent of the Senior Proctor, and that will not be forthcoming.'

Kendale held a piece of parchment aloft, and Bartholomew did not think he had ever seen a more maliciously gloating expression. 'I do not need your consent, because I have gone over your head. Chancellor Tynkell has given me what I need, and he is head of the University, is he not?'

'Only in theory,' replied Michael icily. 'Tynkell's writ will be annulled within the hour.'

'It will not,' predicted Kendale. He smiled again. 'I have powerful friends in the King's court, and Tynkell is a lot more concerned about offending them than you.'

'The game will be fun,' said Neyll insolently, delighted by the monk's growing alarm. 'A chance for the hostels to demonstrate their superiority over the fat, greedy Colleges. It will be a great spectacle – for scholars and townsfolk alike.'

'A bloody spectacle,' muttered Michael. 'Lord! There will be deaths galore.'

'You cannot do it,' blurted Bartholomew. 'Please reconsider, Kendale! Surely, your conscience tells you that this is wrong?'

'I am sponsoring a game and drinks for my fellow men,' said Kendale, while his students sniggered. 'That makes me a philanthropist. What can possibly trouble my conscience about that?'

'I will not allow this to happen,' warned Michael.

'You can try to stop me,' said Kendale softly. 'But you will not succeed.'

Michael was so angry as he stormed out of Chestre that he did not hear the jeering laughter that followed. White-faced, he stamped towards the High Street, and those who saw the expression on his face gave him a wide berth. Even Emma, who was walking with Heslarton and Odelina, closed her mouth and the remark she had been planning to make went unspoken. Odelina smiled coquettishly at Bartholomew, and reached out to snare his arm as he passed.

'I am better,' she said in a low, sultry voice. 'You were right: a good night's sleep banished my fever and rendered me hale and hearty again. I owe you a great deal.'

'You owe me nothing,' said Bartholomew shortly, aware that Heslarton was listening, and loath for the man to think his daughter might need protecting from predatory medics. Heslarton wore the broadsword he had been honing the previous night, and it looked sharp and deadly.

'No, we do not,' agreed Emma. Her malignant face creased into what he supposed was a smile. 'But we are appreciative anyway. I might do you a favour one day, if it is convenient to me.'

Bartholomew was not sure what to make of such an enigmatic offer, but he had more pressing matters to concern him at that moment, and he pushed Emma and her family from his mind as he ran to catch up with Michael. Seeing that the red fury burned as hotly as ever, he put a calming hand on the monk's shoulder. Michael shrugged it off.

'Who does Tynkell think he is?' he raged.

'The Chancellor?' suggested Bartholomew. 'Kendale is right: he *is* supposed to be in charge.'

'He has never been in charge,' snarled Michael. 'Not even in the beginning. It has always been me, so how dare he issue writs without my permission!'

There was no reasoning with him, so Bartholomew followed him to St Mary the Great, where the Chancellor's office comprised a chamber that was considerably less grand than the Senior Proctor's. They arrived to find Tynkell laid low with stomach pains, something from which he often suffered, due to a peculiar aversion to hygiene. The room stank, and Bartholomew itched to put his sleeve over his mouth. The wrath drained out of Michael when he saw Tynkell looking so pitiful.

'Why did you sign Kendale's writ?' he asked tiredly, slumping on to a bench.

'Because he came with his loutish students and frightened the life out of me,' replied Tynkell, nervously defensive. 'And then he showed me letters from his kinsmen, who are close to the King, and said they would be displeased if I refused him.'

'So?' asked Michael. 'Who cares about what they think?'

'I do, and so do you. They might persuade the King to

249

favour our sister University at Oxford, and then where would we be?'

'We may not *have* a University if this game takes place,' Michael pointed out. He reached for pen and inkpot. 'You will issue a declaration withdrawing permission. You have the perfect excuse, in that it is on the same day as the Stock Extraordinary Lecture. You can claim the conflict slipped your mind. No one will hold it against you.'

'It is too late,' said Tynkell miserably. 'Kendale has already made his intentions public, and people are looking forward to the free drinks. If we cancel now, the town will see us as a spoiler of fun, and we shall have a riot anyway.'

'But the Carmelites will be livid,' cried Michael. 'The lecture is an important event for them, and they will not want a large chunk of their audience enticed away by sport.'

'The kind of lad who likes camp-ball is unlikely to be interested in theology,' began Tynkell, but Michael overrode him, blasting on as though he had not spoken.

'Worse, they may assume the Gilbertines are responsible, because they lost the last game, and we shall have a feud between the two Orders into the bargain.'

'There will be no trouble if the event is properly policed,' argued Tynkell, although with scant conviction. 'We shall provide plenty of beadles and all the players will be searched, to ensure they have no weapons.'

'You will have to search the spectators, too,' said Bartholomew. 'I imagine there will be as much fighting off the field as on it, especially if Kendale aggravates the situation with rumours about martyrs – or worse, with another dangerous joke, like the crated bull.'

There was a polite knock on the door, and Horneby entered, wearing an enormous woollen scarf to protect his throat.

'I am sorry, Horneby,' said Michael, before he could

250

speak. 'I would not have interfered with your sermon for the world, and—'

'It is all right,' said Horneby, holding up his hand to stop him. 'Prior Etone is outraged, but I do not want trouble. So I have come to suggest a solution.'

'You have?' asked Michael hopefully. 'Then let us hear it.'

'If my sore throat returns, I cannot give my address – it will be postponed regardless of whether or not there is a camp-ball game. No one can take offence at that.'

'But you are better,' said Bartholomew. 'The swelling is gone.'

Horneby smiled. 'Then you are going to have to tell a small lie, Bartholomew. You must inform anyone who asks that I need another day to recover. I shall keep my end of the bargain by staying in my room. I do not mind – it will give me more time to prepare.'

'That would work,' said Michael, nodding. 'The vicious scrimmage between hostels and the Colleges will still continue, but at least we will not have to worry about warlike Carmelite novices starting a fight because they feel they have been slighted. It is a good idea, and very gracious of you, Horneby.'

'Actually, it was Welfry's idea,' the friar admitted, 'He abhors bloodshed.'

'Perhaps he will not make such a bad Seneschal, after all,' said Michael approvingly.

CHAPTER 8

'My efforts to prevent the hostels going to war with the Colleges are interfering with my hunt for the killer-thief,' said Michael the following day, as he and Bartholomew walked home from the church after dawn prayers. It was Sunday, which meant the ceremonies had lasted longer than usual.

Bartholomew yawned. It had been another dismal night, with the wind whipping through the missing window and water continuing to ooze through the missing roof despite Langelee's declarations that there would be trouble if they were not mended. As a result, he had slept badly again, and his wits were still sluggish.

'That is unfortunate,' he said, 'because Drax's murder should not be too difficult to solve, when you think about it. A corpse was brought to our College in broad daylight, so *someone* must have noticed it being toted around. It is almost certainly just a case of locating a witness.'

'You are right,' said Michael, after a moment of serious reflection. 'We will talk to Blaston.'

'No,' said Bartholomew immediately. 'Not Blaston. Leave him alone.'

'I shall not accuse him of anything, but he was closer to where Drax was left than anyone else. There may be a detail he forgot to mention that will allow us to solve this case. Will he be at home, do you think?'

'No,' repeated Bartholomew, sure the monk would not confine himself to innocuous questions, and Blaston was

252

a friend. 'Please, Brother. You hurt his feelings the last time we spoke.'

'I said nothing that was not true, and it is our duty to explore the matter fully – to clear his name of any suspicion, if nothing else.'

'Very well,' said Bartholomew reluctantly. 'But take care not to offend him, or you may find yourself with leaking windows in revenge. And it would serve you right.'

'Do not jest about leaks,' said Michael, following him towards the High Street, where Blaston owned a house that was far too small for his enormous family. 'You can stay with your sister, should life at Michaelhouse become unbearable, but I have nowhere else to go.'

'You have plenty of refuges,' said Bartholomew, wondering why he had not thought of Edith the previous night. 'Your Benedictine brethren at Ely House are always pleased to see you, and you have friends in other Colleges.'

'And let people know Michaelhouse is below par?' sniffed Michael. 'That would be disloyal.'

'There *is* Edith,' said Bartholomew, when he saw his sister walking towards them with her husband. 'She was at the camp-ball game yesterday, but I was too busy to talk to her.'

'I was not – she is an observant lady, and I hoped she might be able to tell me who killed Poynton. Unfortunately, she could not. She is carrying a parcel. I wonder if there is any food in it.' The monk surged forward. 'Edith! What a pleasant surprise! Is that a pie in your—'

'It is for Matt,' said Edith, jerking the package away from his questing fingers.

'We are worried about him,' explained Stanmore. 'He is always thin and pale these days – a combination of too much teaching, too many patients, and the slop your College claims is food.'

253

'There is nothing wrong with me,' said Bartholomew tiredly, wishing they would not fuss so.

'You will take this pie, and eat it all yourself,' instructed Edith, pressing it into his hand. 'No sharing with greedy Benedictines. Do you promise? And there is something else, too. You know Oswald and I went on a pilgrimage to Walsingham last year?'

'To see what the Blessed Virgin could do about the fact that your son seduced the Earl of Suffolk's daughter,' said Bartholomew, wondering what was coming next.

Edith's expression hardened. 'She was the one who did the seducing, but that is beside the point. Which is that my badge has been stolen. I only left my cloak – the nice dark red one – unattended for an instant, but when I turned around, it had gone. And the token was gone with it.'

'We believe the culprit is a scholar,' Stanmore went on. 'That is why we were coming to see you. At first, in the interests of town–University relations, we decided to over-look the matter, but then we heard that others have fallen victim to his light fingers, so we thought we had better mention it.'

Michael blanched. 'I sincerely hope you are wrong! What led you to this conclusion?'

'Because the theft took place in the Gilbertines' chapel,' explained Edith. 'The only townsfolk present, other than us, were Emma, Gyseburne and Meryfeld. None of them are likely to steal a cloak, so the thief *had* to have been a member of the University – a student or a cleric.'

'We said nothing to Prior Leccheworth, of course,' added Stanmore. 'We did not want to offend him by denouncing one of his guests as a scoundrel. But it was distressing to fall victim to a crime that took place on holy ground – a betrayal of trust.'

'Can you remember who else was there?' asked Michael unhappily.

'Yes,' replied Edith. 'All the Gilbertines and all the Carmelites, the scholars from Chestre . . . although I cannot imagine why *they* were invited, because they are a surly crowd.'

'They were included because the Gilbertines have taken the hostels' side in the University's latest quarrel,' explained Stanmore. 'And Chestre is very vocal against the Colleges.'

'Those four pilgrims were present, too,' Edith went on. She frowned. 'Of course, *they* are not members of the University, so perhaps we are wrong to accuse a scholar of the crime . . .'

'You mean Fen?' pounced Michael eagerly. 'The pardoner?'

Edith nodded. 'And finally, Thelnetham had invited Ayera. And that was all – there was no one else. But the most important fact is yet to come. Tell them, Oswald.'

'We saw a man with yellow hair,' announced Stanmore. 'We thought nothing of it at the time, but then we heard the description of the villain who robbed Emma, the Mayor, Welfry, Celia Drax, Poynton and God knows who else.'

'It was definitely a wig,' added Edith. 'And we suspect one of the guests shoved it on his head to disguise himself while he stole my badge. He may have pilfered other things, too, then reverted to his normal appearance to shake hands and smile at his hosts as he left with his ill-gotten gains.'

Michael groaned. 'A scholar stealing *signacula* and murdering townsfolk! We shall have a riot for certain, and the University is already in turmoil with the hostels at the Colleges' throats.'

'We shall say nothing, Brother,' said Stanmore quietly.

255

'You see, we have just been to visit Emma, and we do not want to be responsible for *her* making war on scholars for stealing her box.'

'We did not want to go,' added Edith. 'But she summoned us, and we did not dare refuse.'

'Really?' asked Michael, still dazed from what he had been told. 'Why?'

'Because she is powerful,' explained Stanmore. 'I am happy to ignore the orders of others I find objectionable, but there is something about her that makes me want to stay on her good side.'

'Actually, I meant why did she summon you,' said Michael. 'You do not need to justify your reluctance to annoy her, because I feel the same way.'

'She wanted to talk to us about Matt,' said Edith. 'Because he saved her granddaughter from poison, and she was eager for his family to know his efforts were appreciated.'

'I did very little,' said Bartholomew, startled. 'Gyseburne and Meryfeld were there, and—'

'And stood by while you did all the work,' interrupted Stanmore. 'We had the tale from her own lips. But this is bad news! It is risky to offend her, but it is equally risky to earn her affection. She intends to dismiss Meryfeld and rehire you, because she thinks you are more likely to cure her.'

'The only way that will happen is if a tooth is removed,' said Bartholomew.

'Do not extract her fangs!' cried Stanmore in horror. 'First, tooth-pulling is the domain of surgeons, and you should not perform such lowly tasks. And second, if anything goes wrong, I doubt she will be very forgiving.'

'But it *must* come out,' said Bartholomew, tired of explaining the obvious. 'It is rotting, which means it will release bad vapours into her blood. I have seen such cases turn fatal.'

Stanmore glanced behind him, to ensure he could not be overheard, then lowered his voice. 'Would that be such a terrible thing? The woman is evil – I feel it with every bone in my body. Perhaps you *should* let nature take its course.'

The Blaston home was a chaos of noise when Bartholomew and Michael arrived. At least four children were crying, several were enjoying a game that involved slamming pots against a table, and the rest were engaged in a furious argument about whose turn it was to go for water. It was colder inside the house than out, and there was no evidence that a fire would be lit for dinner. One child was sobbing more from distress than demands for attention, so Bartholomew picked it up.

'There is something wrong with him,' said Yolande, watching. Her usually hard face was tender. 'He will not stop grizzling.'

'He is hungry,' said Bartholomew, noting the bloated belly and overly large eyes.

'Poor mite,' murmured Michael, not liking the sound of that.

'But he vomits up the stew I feed him,' said Yolande in frustration. 'He will not keep it down.'

'Because he needs milk sops,' explained Bartholomew. 'Valence will bring him some later.'

'We do not accept charity,' said Blaston stiffly.

'It is not charity,' countered Bartholomew shortly. 'It is medicine.'

Blaston sat at the table and put his head in his hands. Yolande went to stand next to him, resting her hand on his shoulder. Suddenly, the older children stopped arguing, the middle ones ended their assault on the table, and the babies ceased bawling. The silence was eerie.

'I do not know how we will survive,' said the carpenter brokenly. 'Summer is a long way off still, and work is scarce.'

'Not for me,' said Yolande comfortingly. 'I can get plenty of new clients. Do not fret, Rob. Doctor Rougham is giving me an extra shilling tonight, and Alfred earned three pence by running errands for Master Walkot at King's Hall yesterday.'

'And I will pay you for information,' added Michael. 'I need you to think really carefully about what happened when Drax died. You said you were in the stable, but did not see anything.'

'Not again, Brother!' whispered Blaston, fixing him with haunted eyes. 'How many more times must I tell you that it had nothing to do with me?'

'We know,' said Bartholomew soothingly. A rather dangerous expression was creeping across Yolande's face; she would not stand by quietly while her husband was harassed. 'But you are our best hope for a clue as to the killer's identity. You were closer to where Drax was dumped than anyone else.'

Blaston scrubbed at his cheeks. 'The business has plagued my thoughts ever since, and I have replayed it again and again in my mind.'

'And?' prompted Michael, when the carpenter hesitated.

'And I may be wrong, but I *think* I heard Drax being dragged into the College.'

Michael laid several coins on the table, although the information was hardly worth them. 'I knew you would remember something.'

'There is more. I am fairly sure I heard footsteps, too. Two sets. In other words, *two* men came, carrying Drax between them. They could have left him out in plain sight, but instead they hid him behind the tiles and made sure he was under that sheet. I think they did it to confuse you.'

'Explain,' ordered Michael.

Blaston raised his hands in a shrug. 'To make you appreciate that someone cunning is behind the affair. Not some spur-of-the moment killer, who struck out blindly, but someone with an agenda.'

Michael nodded wearily. 'You are almost certainly right.'

'I thought at first that Yffi did it, because they were his tiles. I assumed he had intended to keep the corpse hidden until he could find somewhere more permanent for it – a plan thwarted by Agatha and the dog. But then I heard Drax was killed in Physwick's dairy, and my theory made no sense – the dairy is a much better place for storing bodies. So I reconsidered. The villain must be from the hostels, and he left a corpse in Michaelhouse because it was the nearest available College.'

'Speaking of Yffi, why is no work being done on our roof today?' asked Michael. He had already reasoned as much himself, and did not need to hear Blaston's speculations on the matter. 'I know it is Sunday, but we were awash again last night, and this is an emergency.'

'I wish I could finish the work for you,' said Blaston tiredly. 'But I am a carpenter, not a mason.'

'I shall have another word with Emma,' said Michael. 'She will encourage him back to work.'

'I doubt it. It is she who is paying for St Simon Stock's new shrine, and I imagine she thinks completing that will earn her more favour with God than mending your roof.'

'I did not know that,' said Michael grimly. 'Thank you.'

It was raining again when Bartholomew and Michael left Blaston. The monk went to petition Emma, while Bartholomew returned to the College and gave the last of his money to Valence, to buy milk and bread for Yolande's baby – Edith's pie had 'accidentally' been left behind for the others. Then he went to his room where Edith, knowing her brother well enough to predict what would happen, had arranged for a replacement pie to be sitting on his desk. He could not have eaten it to save his life: the plight of the Blaston family had sickened him. He sank down on a chest, put his head in his hands, and was still sitting so when Michael returned. The monk went straight to the parcel and unwrapped it.

'Beef!' he exclaimed in pleasure. 'And Lombard slices, too. They are my favourites, so clearly she packed them for me.'

'Actually, she told me not to share them with greedy Benedictines.'

'Well, there you are then,' said Michael with a shrug. 'I am not greedy, so she cannot have been referring to me. Eat something, Matt, and I shall join you. It will eliminate the nasty taste in my mouth, after begging Emma to order Yffi back to work and hearing her say she will not interfere.'

'I do not want any.'

'Starving yourself will not help the Blaston brats. Eat this, or I shall tell Edith you gave it to your students. And then there will be trouble.'

Bartholomew had a feeling he might do it, so took the proffered slice. It was good, although he barely tasted it, and at one point he gagged.

'Perhaps I should go on a pilgrimage,' said the monk, watching him. 'And ask for an early end to winter. What do you think?'

'That the University would be in flames by the time its Senior Proctor returned.'

Michael selected the largest of the Lombard slices and inserted it into his mouth. 'In that case, perhaps I had better stay,' he said, enunciating with difficulty. 'I shall content myself by catching this killer-thief instead. Perhaps that will suffice to see my sins forgiven.'

'What sins?' asked Bartholomew.

Michael waved an airy hand, took another cake and aimed for the door. 'Come with me to see Walter. Like Blaston, he may have remembered something else now he has had a chance to reflect.'

They found Walter and his peacock sharing a piece of bread, the porter soaking each crumb in wine before feeding it to the bird. The creature's eyes were glazed, and it was unsteady on its feet.

'Drax,' stated Michael without preamble. 'I know you were in the latrines when the body was brought here, but did anything else happen that was unusual that morning?'

Walter scowled, ever surly. 'I already told you, no.'

'Yes,' said Michael, struggling for patience. 'But please think again. Was there anything different – anything at all, no matter how small or insignificant it may seem?'

'Well, we had sightseers,' said Walter disapprovingly. 'Prior Etone brought the pilgrims to stand at our gate and gawp around – he has always admired the Colleges, which is why he sides with us against the hostels. Then Kendale and his louts tried to do the same, but I saw them off.'

'Kendale?' cried Michael, shocked. 'Why did you not mention this before?'

'Because I chased them away the instant they arrived. They had no time for mischief – I saw to that.' Then Walter looked thoughtful. 'Although I suppose they *could* have brought Drax's body here a bit later, when I was in the latrines.'

Michael closed his eyes and whispered something, presumably a prayer for fortitude. Then he opened them again and looked at Bartholomew. 'This is enough to allow us to tackle Chestre at last, although it will not be pleasant.'

'No,' agreed Bartholomew unenthusiastically. The peacock

issued a noise he had never heard from a bird before, and pecked at the porter's sleeve to indicate it was time for more wine-dipped bread. 'Should you be feeding him that?'

Walter frowned, puzzled. 'Of course I should. He loves claret.'

'I am sure he does, but I doubt it is good for him.'

'You mean I may be doing him harm?' asked Walter, alarmed.

Bartholomew nodded, so Walter dunked the bread in water instead. The bird ignored it, and looked pointedly at the wine jug. Clearly, the creature was well on the way to becoming a sot.

'Feed him seed,' suggested Bartholomew, taking pity on the horrified porter. 'Or worms.'

'He does not eat worms!' cried Walter indignantly. 'He is cultured!'

Shaking his head in disgust, both at Walter's peculiar perception of his pet and his withholding of information that would have been helpful days ago, Michael aimed for the gateless doorway. He was almost bowled from his feet when Cynric raced into the yard. He was red faced and breathless.

'They have found him,' he gasped. 'The yellow-headed villain.'

'Found him where?' asked Bartholomew.

'Dead,' panted Cynric. 'Come and see.'

The rain had stopped when Bartholomew and Michael ran towards the High Street, hot on Cynric's heels. Because it was Sunday, the streets were quiet, and most pedestrians were scholars, going to and from their Sabbath devotions. There were friars and monks in habits of brown, grey, black and white, and students in the uniforms of their foundations. There were rather more of them than usual, and

Bartholomew noticed for the first time that those who had allied themselves with the hostels had donned some item that was red, while Colleges and their supporters favoured blue. He regarded them unhappily as he trotted past, dismayed to note that places previously neutral had now declared an affiliation. The trouble was spreading fast.

'Jolye was murdered by the hostels,' he heard the lads of Peterhouse telling the scholars of Bene't College. 'He is a martyr to our cause, and the crime *must* be avenged.'

'He fell in the river and drowned,' countered Michael sharply, skidding to a standstill. 'It was a tragic accident. Do not abuse his memory by making his death something it was not.'

The Peterhouse students nodded dutifully as they backed away, but the members of Bene't looked thoughtful, and Bartholomew knew the damage had been done.

'This damned rivalry has taken on a life of its own, Matt,' muttered Michael worriedly. 'It is gathering momentum, and it is only a matter of time before it erupts into killing and bloodshed.'

Cynric led them to the Great Bridge, a grand name for the rickety structure that spanned the River Cam. It comprised a single stone arch, with timber rails to prevent people falling over the sides, and was always on the verge of collapse. Every so often, a tax was levied to fund its repair, but the town worthies were corrupt, and the money was invariably siphoned off to other causes.

That day, a crowd had gathered on it. They included Yffi and his apprentices, who were laughing and joking with drinking cronies from the Griffin.

'You!' exclaimed Michael, stopping dead in his tracks. 'You are meant to be mending our roof.'

'It is Sunday,' replied Yffi piously. 'We do not despoil the Sabbath by labouring.'

'You were labouring this morning,' called Isnard the bargeman, who could always be found among spectators, no matter what had attracted them. 'You were in the Carmelite Priory, building their shrine. I saw you.'

'I was not *building* anything,' asserted Yffi stiffly. 'I was surveying the site.'

'You were hammering and sawing,' countered Isnard.

'Lies!' snarled Yffi, bunching his fists.

Michael stepped forward to prevent a spat, but Bartholomew was more interested in what Cynric was trying to show them. He followed the book-bearer through the throng, knelt down and peered over the edge of the bridge. A rope had been tied to one of the stanchions to form a noose, and a man with yellow hair was dangling from the end of it. It was a fairly long rope, and the man's legs were in the water, causing the body to sway as the river washed past.

Michael joined him, then turned to address the crowd. 'Who found him?'

'I did.' It was Meryfeld, stepping forward importantly and rubbing his grimy hands together. 'My windows overlook the bridge, and I saw him when I happened to glance out. He was invisible to anyone walking across it, and might have dangled there for days, had I not been vigilant.'

'Was he there yesterday?' asked Michael.

'Of course not,' replied Meryfeld tartly. 'Or I would have raised the alarm then.'

While Michael continued to question the crowd, Bartholomew grabbed the rope and began to haul. Meryfeld helped, and they soon had the body up on the bridge. The long yellow hair was plastered across the corpse's face, but when Bartholomew pushed it away, he noticed two things: that the victim was Gib from Chestre Hostel, and that he was wearing a wig.

264

'I am sorry you have to see a patient like this,' he said sympathetically, aware that his colleague was looking away in distaste. 'Hangings are never pleasant.'

Meryfeld raised his eyebrows in surprise, then peered more closely at the corpse. 'Why, it is Gib! I would never have recognised him! I wonder what drove him to take his own life.'

'What makes you think it was suicide?' asked Bartholomew, taken aback.

Meryfeld shrugged. 'It is obvious. First, his hands are not tied, as they would have been, had it been murder. Second, none of the Chestre lads like Cambridge, so they tend to be gloomy all the time. Third, he used a long rope, to ensure he could not climb back up again, should he change his mind. And last, he is not the first tortured soul to fling himself off this bridge.'

Bartholomew sat back on his heels. 'However, first, not all killers tie their victims' hands, so that proves nothing. Second, it is a big step from gloom to self-murder. Third, he could not have climbed up a *short* rope, had he had second thoughts, so its length is irrelevant. And last, there *have* been suicides on the bridge, but most have thrown themselves in the water.'

'So what are you saying?' demanded Michael, over-hearing. 'That he was murdered?'

Bartholomew pointed to Gib's ragged fingernails. 'He certainly put up a fight.'

'That happened when he clawed at the rope,' argued Meryfeld. 'Even when men are determined to die, they still rebel against the pain of a constricted neck. It is only natural.'

'But there is a bruise on his head and his arm is broken,' said Bartholomew. 'He was involved in some sort of tussle before he died.'

265

'He damaged his arm as he threw himself off the parapet,' countered Meryfeld doggedly. 'While the mark on his head occurred when we dragged him up.'

'It is difficult to bruise a corpse,' said Bartholomew. 'Their blood vessels do not rupture . . .'

He stopped speaking when he became aware that the crowd was listening, and most were regarding him rather oddly. So was Meryfeld. He stifled a sigh, and wished he did not have to watch his words whenever he drew on something he had learned from cadavers.

'I suppose you were taught this in Padua,' said Meryfeld distastefully. 'During a dissection.'

'I have never dissected anyone,' objected Bartholomew, although he could tell by the crowd's reaction that it was more interesting to think that he had. 'But my work as Corpse Examiner means I know what happens to a person after death, and they do not bruise. Only living tissues bruise.'

There was a murmur of revulsion at this revelation, and Michael rested his hand on his friend's shoulder. 'Do not say anything else,' he whispered. 'You are digging yourself a deeper pit.'

'But they believe I am a—'

'Sharing grisly details about the dead will not help your case. But never mind this now. We need to take Gib somewhere private, so you can inspect him without an audience. I want the answers to two questions. First, is this really the yellow-headed killer-thief? And second, are we now obliged to look for his murderer?'

St Clement's was the closest church, so Michael made arrangements for Gib to be carried there. While he did so, Bartholomew talked to the bridge's guards, who were unrepentant about the fact that someone had been hanged on the structure they were meant to be watching. All he learned was that Gib had probably died between midnight and five o'clock, which was when they liked to sleep.

'Assuming this *is* murder, who are our suspects?' asked Michael, speaking softly, so as not to be overheard as they followed the grim procession off the bridge and back towards the town.

'Heslarton is the obvious choice,' replied Bartholomew. 'He has been hunting the killer-thief since last Monday, and has vowed revenge on the man who not only invaded his mother-in-law's home, but probably poisoned his wife and daughter, too.'

'Poison that harmed Alice and Odelina, but that may have been intended for him or Emma.' Michael was silent for a moment, thinking. Then he said, '*Was* it Gib you chased out of their house?'

Bartholomew closed his eyes as he replayed the memory. 'The hair looks the same – a wild, yellow shock that tumbled about his shoulders. I did not see his face, not even when I grabbed the reins of his horse and he kicked me away. The thief was the same height as Gib . . .'

'But?' asked Michael, sensing a caveat.

Bartholomew's eyes snapped open when he stumbled over a pile of manure. 'But anyone can don a wig. And anyone can tie one on a corpse, too.'

Michael regarded him thoughtfully. 'In other words, someone may have fastened this hair on Gib to make us – and Heslarton – stop pursuing the real villain?'

'It is possible. However, we should not forget what Edith and Oswald told us – that all the Chestre lads were in the Gilbertines' chapel the day her *signaculum* was stolen. Perhaps Gib *did* put on a yellow wig and make off with her cloak.'

Michael nodded slowly. 'True. But let us assume for a

moment that you *are* right, and Gib *is* innocent. If we do, then Heslarton cannot be a suspect – he would not have tied a yellow wig on a corpse to stop himself searching for the real culprit! So who is left on our list?'

'All the Chestre men are fiery: there may have been a falling out among them. Then there are the killer-thief's myriad victims – Celia Drax, Emma, Welfry, Gyseburne, Meryfeld, the Mayor, Burgess Frevill, at least two Franciscans, several merchants, Poynton . . . but he is dead.' There was Edith, too, but Bartholomew saw no reason to include her name.

'Fen is not dead, though,' said Michael, eyes gleaming. 'And pardoners are a murderous breed. It is possible that Fen killed Gib for stealing something he intended to inherit from Poynton. Meanwhile, I am not sure what to make of Meryfeld and his insistence that this was suicide.'

Nor was Bartholomew. 'Gib did not seem depressed at the camp-ball game—'

'Look!' hissed Michael, pointing down the street. 'Speak of the Devil, and he will appear, because there is Fen, and his salacious nuns with him. We shall order them to inspect Gib and tell us whether it is the man who stole Poynton's *signaculum*. Remove the wig, Matt. Quickly!'

'Why?'

'Because it is distinctive, and if I wore it, they would say *I* was the culprit. Cover his head with his hood, and let us see whether they can make the identification on face and physique alone.'

It was a good idea, and Bartholomew hastened to do as he was bidden.

'Yffi has just told us what happened,' said Fen as he approached. 'Have you found Poynton's stolen *signaculum* on this villain's person?'

'We have not examined the body yet,' said Michael coolly.

'Earthly baubles are not my first consideration when discovering a corpse.'

'This was not an earthly bauble,' snapped the fat little nun called Agnes, although Fen flushed at the monk's implied criticism. 'It was a valuable token from the Holy Land. Let me see him, Brother. I want to look on his treacherous face.'

'Certainly,' said Michael, gesturing to the corpse with a courtly sweep of his hand. Bartholomew hid the wig behind his back. 'Look all you like.'

'That is him,' Agnes declared immediately. 'I would know that evil visage anywhere.'

'You are wrong,' countered Margaret. 'His hair is different.'

'There *is* something familiar about him,' mused Fen. 'But I am uncertain . . .'

'Put the wig back, Matt,' ordered Michael. 'Let us see what difference that makes.'

'Yes!' exclaimed Margaret, when the headpiece was in place. 'That is him!'

'Actually, now I think it is not,' countered Agnes. 'I have changed my mind.'

Fen stared at the body for a long time. 'I am sorry,' he said eventually. 'I still cannot be sure.'

Michael watched them walk away. 'We can dismiss the nuns' testimony as nonsense – they do not seem entirely rational to me. But Fen is another matter. He knows something, yet declines to share it. He probably wants to assess the pitfalls and advantages to himself before—'

'Stop,' interrupted Bartholomew. 'Wild claims will not help us solve this case. We need to review the evidence logically, not invent theories based on personal prejudice.'

'I noticed you did not find it easy to remove the wig,' said Michael, changing the subject rather than admit

Bartholomew was right. 'It was tied on very securely.'

Bartholomew nodded. 'Very. I suppose it was either because Gib thought he might have to run, and he did not want it to fall off and reveal his true identity. Or because someone else wanted to make sure it remained in place for the whole town to see.'

Michael sighed his exasperation. 'So even a simple thing like the tying of the wig cannot yield an unambiguous clue!'

'Then let us consider the murders for a moment,' said Bartholomew. 'Assuming Gib *is* the killer-thief, I understand why he left poison in Emma's house – she and her family are universally unpopular. And his reason for killing Drax is obvious, too – Drax was going to raise Chestre's rent, and Kendale quarrelled with him about it.'

'Blaston heard two sets of footsteps when the body was dumped, suggesting Gib had an accomplice. It must have been Kendale, whom Walter saw peering through our gates earlier that day. Chestre hates the Colleges, so they left the corpse at Michaelhouse – the nearest one to the dairy where the murder was committed – in the hope that it would see us in trouble with the town.'

'It all fits very nicely,' said Bartholomew. 'Yet . . .'

'Yet what?'

'Yet I have the distinct feeling that we are being pointed in a way some devious mind wants us to go. And the notion that anyone can tie a wig on a corpse bothers me.'

'What are you saying? That Gib is *not* the culprit?'

'I have no idea whether he is our villain or not,' said Bartholomew tiredly. 'Perhaps I am looking for overly complex solutions, and we should simply accept what seems obvious.'

'No,' said Michael. 'Because I have an odd feeling about

this case, too. And I have learned not to ignore my instincts. Or yours.'

St Clement's Church was a spacious, airy building, and its vicar, William Heyford, was famous for preaching colourful sermons that attracted enormous crowds of people. Bartholomew had attended one once, but had found it sensational and lacking in logic.

'I most certainly shall *not* house a corpse in my chancel,' Heyford declared indignantly, when Michael told him what he wanted. 'I am holding a mass in an hour, and I do not want the congregation to stay away because the place is stuffed with cadavers.'

'One body hardly equates to a stuffing,' Michael objected.

'I do not care: he cannot stay. Besides, I recognise him – he is one of those obnoxious lads from Chestre Hostel. He and his cronies have made a lot of enemies among the Colleges, and his presence here may encourage them to come and do something unspeakable.'

'Our students are not in the habit of doing unspeakable things to the dead,' protested Michael.

'Your Corpse Examiner is, though,' countered Heyford. 'And I am not having it, not in *my* church. It is a holy place, and I do not permit the mauling of mortal remains.'

'If you let Gib lie here, I will arrange for you to do the funeral,' cajoled Michael. 'You will be well paid.'

'All right, then,' agreed Heyford, capitulating with a speed that had even Michael blinking in astonishment. 'You should have said that money was involved.'

'Matt will see him settled,' said Michael, indicating that Bartholomew should follow the bier-bearers inside the church.

Bartholomew rolled his eyes, knowing the monk wanted

him to examine Gib while he kept Heyford busy outside. It was sordid, and if he was caught it would make him appear even more sinister than ever. But he could not argue when Heyford was there, so he did as he was told, muttering something vague about making sure Gib was decently laid out.

He did not have much time, so as soon as the pall-bearers had gone, he began his work. There was a single ligature mark around Gib's neck, and no indication that he might have been throttled before he went over the bridge. His arms bore several signs of violence, including the break Bartholomew had noticed earlier. There were also five distinct bruises, where it appeared he had been restrained by someone with powerful fingers. And there was a sizeable lump on his head.

Bartholomew considered his findings carefully. They told him that Gib had been grabbed with some vigour, and that he had fought back. A blow to his head had subdued him at some point. Then a rope had been tied around his neck and he had been tipped over the bridge. Unfortunately for Gib, the drop had not broken his neck, and the cause of death was strangulation. There was no longer any question in the physician's mind: Gib *had* been unlawfully killed. He put all to rights, and left.

Outside, Heyford regarded him suspiciously. 'You took a long time.'

Bartholomew brandished the wig. 'It took me a while to undo the knots.'

He could not look the priest in the eye, and was acutely aware that he probably looked very furtive. Silently, he cursed Michael for putting him in a position where lies were required.

Heyford continued to look doubtful. 'They did not look that firmly tied to me. And why not cut them with one of the many knives you carry for surgery?'

272

'Evidence,' supplied Michael, when the physician had no answer. 'Small details like knots are important, and may be the clue that leads us to the killer.'

'Killer?' asked Heyford, very quick on the uptake. 'You mean he was murdered?'

'Yes,' said Bartholomew, when Michael raised questioning eyebrows. 'I am sure of it.'

'We had better inform Chestre,' said Michael unhappily. 'Thank you for your help, Heyford.'

'You are welcome,' replied Heyford. 'But I shall hold you to your promise: I want this funeral.'

'Well?' asked Michael, when the venal vicar had been left behind, and he and Bartholomew were walking towards the town's centre. 'What did you learn?'

'That Gib did not go easily. He was a large man, and strong, so I imagine he was dispatched by more than one assailant.'

'And what about the wig? Did he tie it on himself? Or did someone else do it for him?'

'I could not tell, Brother. I am sorry.'

Michael looked worried. 'We had better hurry – it will not take long for word to reach Chestre, and we cannot have them taking matters into their own hands. They may wreak revenge on some hapless scholar from a College.'

'Take some beadles with you,' advised Bartholomew.

'Take some beadles with *us*,' corrected Michael. 'Kendale is extremely clever – he may know exactly why his student was murdered, but may be disinclined to say. I need you to watch him, to assess whether he is telling the truth. And then we shall compare notes.'

Bartholomew dragged his feet as he and Michael walked down Bridge Street. Regardless of whether Kendale and his students had had a hand in what had happened to Gib, they would make a fuss, and he was tired and dispirited, not in the mood for confrontation. Worse yet, they might decide to honour Gib's memory with more of their claret, and he felt his stomach roil at the notion of swallowing anything so potent.

'There is Welfry,' he said, pointing as they passed St John's Hospital. 'What is he doing?'

Michael glared at the Dominican. 'Crouching behind water butts is hardly seemly behaviour for a Seneschal. Did I tell you that he has already written to the exchequer, requesting tax exemptions for those of our students who are apes? It made for hilarious reading, as it happens, but you do not jest with the King's clerks. He will get us suppressed!'

'I am hiding from Odelina,' explained Welfry, when they approached. A pained expression crossed his face. 'She has taken to stalking me of late.'

'Has she?' asked Bartholomew, daring to hope it might signal the end of her pursuit of him.

'She said I remind her of a character in some ballad. It is my hand, apparently – her hero had a withered limb, but a lady kissed it and it grew well again. Odelina has offered to kiss mine.'

'Perhaps you should let her,' said Michael, amused. 'There is nothing wrong with being cured.'

Welfry was shocked. 'I am a friar, Brother! Besides, the reward for this cure is to marry her. And that would be too high a price, even if I were not wed to the Church.'

'Here she comes,' said Michael. 'But you need not worry, because she seems to have transferred her affections to Valence. God help him.'

'That means nothing,' said Welfry gloomily, watching Valence effect a hasty escape. 'She is quite capable of entertaining a fancy for more than one gentleman at the same time. Please go away. You will attract her attention, and—'

'It is too late,' said Michael. 'She is almost here. Stand up, man, or she will wonder what you are up to. You are our Seneschal, and kneeling behind barrels is hardly dignified.'

Odelina had donned a kirtle with a tight bodice of scarlet. It was identical to one Celia Drax owned, and Bartholomew could only suppose she wore it to emulate the woman she so admired. Unfortunately, it was not a style that suited Odelina's paunch and generous hips.

'Well!' Odelina exclaimed. Her eyes gleamed, and Bartholomew was reminded unpleasantly of her grandmother. 'Two handsome gentlemen in one place.'

'Two?' asked Michael, puzzled. 'Which of this pair do you consider unattractive, then, because there are three of us here.'

'I am expected at the Dominican Friary,' said Welfry, beginning to edge away.

Odelina snagged his arm. 'Surely, you can spare a few moments to converse with a pretty lady?'

'You *are* a pretty lady, mistress,' said Welfry, gently disengaging his wrist. 'And one day, you will find a fine husband, who will make you very happy. I shall pray for it to happen soon.'

'I *do* like him,' said Odelina, watching the Dominican scuttle away. 'And I am sure I could cure his withered hand, if only he would let me kiss it. Love is a powerful thing, you see, and can overcome all manner of obstacles. It is how you saved me from death, Doctor.'

'Actually, what saved you was vomiting,' said Bartholomew. 'It purged—'

'No, no, no!' cried Odelina in distaste. 'That was not it at all. I told you: we share something special, because you

275

snatched me from the grave. But where are you going? To visit my grandmother, and give her a better horoscope than the one Meryfeld has devised?'

'Actually, we are going to Chestre Hostel, to inform them that one of their students is dead,' said Bartholomew, supposing Emma's household would also have to be told the news. 'He was wearing a yellow wig, but we cannot say for certain yet whether—'

'You have the villain who poisoned me and my mother?' whispered Odelina, crossing herself. Her face was suddenly pale. 'Thank God! Who is he? What was his name?'

'Gib,' replied Michael. 'But we have many questions to ask before we can say for certain that he is the culprit. And we *must* be sure, before we besmirch his name.'

Odelina swallowed hard, seeming young and rather vulnerable. 'Gib is the one with the big ale-belly, is he not? There was a time when my grandmother considered funding a scholarship at Chestre, and Principal Kendale used Gib as a messenger. She decided to pay for the repairs to your roof instead, in the end, but Gib certainly knew his way around our house.'

'Well,' said Michael, watching her hurry away to inform her grandmother and father of what had happened. 'The noose around Chestre tightens further still.'

As it happened, Bartholomew and Michael did not need to visit Chestre, because they met Kendale and his students emerging from the Round Church. They all carried wax tablets, indicating they had been attending a lecture there, although most of the tablets were clean – few had taken notes.

'What do you want now?' demanded Kendale, when Michael put out a hand to stop them. His calculating eyes immediately took in the beadles, along with the fact that they were heavily armed. 'We have indulged in no pranks today, so do not accuse us of it. I have been pontificating on the Aristotelian pre-concept of the mean speed theorem, and all my lads were in attendance.'

'We have some sad news,' said Michael. 'Perhaps we might return to Chestre and—'

'No,' said Kendale frostily. 'You are not welcome there.'

'I see,' said Michael, cool in his turn. 'Did you say *all* your students attended this lecture?'

'Yes, and they are keen to discuss it with me. At home. Good afternoon, Brother.'

'Wait,' ordered Michael, as Kendale started to move away. 'I have come about Gib.'

'He is the most eager of them all,' snapped Kendale. 'So if you will excuse us now—'

'He is dead,' interrupted Michael. 'I am sorry to break the news in so brutal a fashion, but you left me no choice. Now, let us go to Chestre, so we can consider the matter quietly.'

Kendale's face was impossible to read, although it was certainly several shades paler. 'He is not dead,' he said after a moment. 'He is . . .'

'He is where?' asked Michael when he faltered. 'Not here with the other students, certainly.'

'He must have slipped away for a moment,' said Kendale. 'A call of nature.'

'That is right,' said Neyll, equally pallid. 'None of us noticed, because we were all entranced by Aristotle's mean theory about speed concepts . . . or whatever Principal Kendale was talking about.'

'When did you last see Gib?' asked Bartholomew, eager to ask his questions and leave. He did not feel easy among the Chestre men; not even with armed beadles at his back.

'I told you,' said Kendale. 'He must have slipped away for a moment. To a latrine.'

'That is untrue,' said Bartholomew quietly. 'He has been dead for hours. I doubt any of you have seen him since five o'clock this morning.'

'How do you know that?' demanded Neyll, dark eyes flashing. 'Have you anatomised him?'

'Of course not,' said Bartholomew, aware of several hands dropping to daggers. The beadles tensed, too. 'But the soldiers on the bridge relax their guard between midnight and five, and it seems likely that was when Gib died.'

Kendale's expression was still inscrutable. 'I suppose I have not seen him today, now you mention it. But he was a quiet soul, and I often overlooked his presence. What happened to him?'

'Is it true that Emma de Colvyll considered funding a scholarship at Chestre?' asked Michael, unwilling to answer questions until he had been provided with answers he could trust. 'And Gib acted as your messenger for a while?'

'Yes, but she elected to mend your roof instead,' said Neyll unpleasantly. 'We bear her no grudge, if that is what you are thinking. In fact, we were relieved she decided to post her charity elsewhere, because we were never comfortable about the notion of being in her debt.'

'That is true,' agreed Kendale. 'Indeed, we would not be in Michaelhouse's shoes for a kingdom. You will be repaying her "kindness" for years to come.'

Bartholomew had a very bad feeling he might be right.

'So when *did* you last see Gib?' asked Michael. 'And please be honest. I will find the truth eventually, and lies will just waste everyone's time.'

Neyll shot him a nasty look. 'He went out last night. He has a whore, you see, and often stays with her, so we thought nothing of it.'

278

'Who is the whore?' asked Bartholomew. She would have to be questioned.

'Helia, who lives in the Jewry,' replied Neyll. 'She is my whore, too, and we see her on alternate evenings. Now Gib is gone, I shall have her all the time.'

Bartholomew stared at him. Had *he* dispatched his class-mate? Spats over women were not uncommon in a town where willing partners were few and far between. Of course, it would have to be a very heady passion that led to murder.

'Did any of you quarrel with him?' asked Michael, also studying the students' reactions intently.

Kendale gave his sly smile. 'Why would we do that? He lived in our hostel, so we were all the best of friends. It is the Colleges with whom we have arguments.'

'So you love each other, and Chestre is a haven of peace and tranquillity?' asked Michael acidly.

Kendale inclined his head. 'Yes. And if Gib has been murdered – as your questions lead me to surmise – then you must look to a College for the villain. They are the ones who mean us harm.'

'Any particular College?' asked Michael.

Kendale met his gaze evenly. 'The louts at Michaelhouse do not like us.'

'Speaking of Michaelhouse,' said the monk, declining to be baited, 'I have been told that you spied on us on Monday morning.'

'Yes, I did,' replied Kendale glibly. 'Your porter saw me, did he? I thought he might. I was looking for Gib.'

'Why did you expect him to be in Michaelhouse?' asked Bartholomew suspiciously.

'Because he was missing, and I was afraid someone there might have kidnapped him. And I was right to be concerned: less than a week later, he is unlawfully slain.'

Kendale was clever, thought Bartholomew, regarding

279

him with dislike. It was cunning to claim Gib as his reason for sticking his head around Michaelhouse's gate on the morning Drax had died, because Gib was not in a position to confirm or deny the tale.

'I do not believe you,' said Michael.

Neyll drew his dagger, a great, wicked-looking thing that had been honed to a savage point. 'You accuse my Principal of lying?'

Kendale raised his bandaged hand to stop him. 'Then ask your porter *precisely* what he saw,' he said to Michael. 'If he is an honest man, he will say I looked briefly around your yard and left. No more and no less. And I have explained exactly why I did it.'

'Then did you see anything suspicious?' asked Michael, although his expression remained sceptical. 'The reason I ask is because Drax's body was dumped there not long after.'

'No,' said Kendale blithely. 'I did not see Drax, his killer or anyone else.'

'You quarrelled with Drax not long before his murder,' said Michael. 'I saw you myself. Why?'

'Because he wanted to raise our rent,' replied Kendale. He laughed suddenly, a humourless, bitter sound. 'And do you know why? Because he claimed evil spirits inhabit the place with us, and so should pay their share. Have you ever heard anything more ridiculous?'

Bartholomew found himself uncertain whether the 'ridiculous' referred to the notion of evil spirits in the building, or the fact that Drax had expected them to pay for their lodgings.

'May we inspect Gib's room?' he asked, supposing that if Gib really were the yellow-headed thief, then the proof would be in the place where he kept his other belongings.

'No,' said Neyll immediately. 'You may not.'

'I agree,' said Kendale. 'It would be most improper. His goods will be parcelled up and returned to his family, without suspicious fingers pawing through them.'

'What are you afraid we might find?' asked Michael keenly.

'We are afraid of nothing,' snapped Kendale. 'And all you will find are spare clothes, a psalter, a few rings and a handsome saddle, which we all covet. But I deny you access, so you will just have to take my word for it.'

'You say you love each other, but you do not seem overly distressed by Gib's demise,' remarked Michael, turning his thoughtful stare from Kendale to Neyll, and then around at the others. 'Why is that? Could it be there is trouble in paradise?'

'We are men,' replied Kendale coldly. 'We do not shame ourselves by weeping. We do not shame ourselves by talking to impertinent College men, either.' He turned to his scholars. 'Come.'

'I could not read them at all,' said Bartholomew, watching them slouch away. 'Their evasive answers may have been intended to throw you off the scent of their guilt, but might equally well have been to confound you, because you belong to a College.'

'Our news about Gib did not surprise them in the slightest, though – I believe they already knew. So the question is, did they know because someone ran to tell them, or because they are his killers?'

'We spent time at St Clement's, and with Welfry and Odelina,' Bartholomew pointed out. 'So the tale may well have preceded us. And despite Kendale's claims of manliness, Neyll *had* been crying – his eyes were inflamed. Of course, they could have been tears of rage.'

'And Kendale's hands were shaking,' added Michael. 'They were upset, all right, although they did an admirable

281

task of masking it. Of course, we have no way of telling whether it was guilty fear or innocent distress.'

'What about the other matter? Kendale's explanation for spying on Michaelhouse on Monday?'

The monk grimaced. 'It was a pack of lies – of course he did not expect to see Gib there.'

'So we learned nothing at all?'

'It is all grist for the mill,' said Michael, although he did not look convinced by his own optimism. 'And now we must tackle Heslarton.'

CHAPTER 9

Bartholomew and Michael were silent as they continued to walk along the High Street, each pondering the questions they had failed to answer. There were too many, and Bartholomew did not think he had ever been involved in an investigation that was so full of people he could not read.

The streets were still busy, and he was alarmed by the proliferation of students who had taken to wearing blue or red. Heltisle, the haughty Master of Bene't, waylaid Michael to complain about it.

'We were managing to stay aloof from the dispute, but then Kendale announced his camp-ball game, and now our lads feel compelled to take a stand. I cannot imagine what possessed you to give him permission to hold such an event, Brother. It was hardly sensible.'

'I did everything I could to stop it,' countered Michael irritably. 'But some things are beyond even the power of the Senior Proctor.'

'Then let us hope that keeping the peace on Tuesday is not one of them,' said Heltisle acidly.

They were delayed yet again when Michael was obliged to quell a quarrel between Ovyng Hostel and the Hall of Valence Marie – another two foundations that had only recently entered the feud. It was confined to a lot of undignified shoving, but Essex Hostel was not far away, and so was King's Hall – two places that loved a skirmish – and Bartholomew suspected they would have joined in, had the spat been allowed to continue.

It was late afternoon by the time he and Michael eventually arrived at Emma's house, and the family was dining. Celia Drax was sitting next to Heslarton, neat, clean and elegant. She picked delicately at a chicken leg, stopping frequently to dab her lips with a piece of embroidered linen. By contrast, Heslarton tore at his hunk of beef with his few remaining teeth; grease glistened on his face and ran down his brawny forearms. Odelina, still clad in her tight red kirtle, ate like her father: not for her the dainty appetites of the ladies in the ballads.

Emma, meanwhile, all fat black body and shiny eyes, appeared slightly feverish. Her plate was full, but she only picked at what she had taken, and when she did raise a morsel to her lips, it was to chew with obvious discomfort.

With cool aplomb, Michael perched on a bench and reached for the breadbasket. Odelina and the servants gaped their astonishment at his audacity, although Heslarton gave him an amiable, oily-handed wave of welcome. Emma merely gave a curt nod to say Bartholomew should join them, too.

'Yes, come and sit *here*.' Odelina patted the space next to her. 'It is me you have come to see.'

'Is it?' asked Heslarton, regarding her in surprise. 'How do you know?'

'A woman can tell these things,' purred Odelina.

She stood and stalked towards the physician. He took several steps away, but the room was crowded, and there was nowhere to go, so it was comparatively easy for her to grab his hand. He tried to disengage it, but Odelina's fingers tightened and he could not free himself without a tussle – and he did not want to use force while a protective father was watching.

'You are thin,' said Odelina, pinching his arm as a

284

butcher might test the quality of meat. 'Sit with me, and I shall cut you a selection of the fattiest bits of meat.'

'We cannot stay,' said Bartholomew, shooting Michael a desperate glance. But the monk was more interested in the food than the plight of his friend. 'We are very busy.'

'Then I am doubly flattered that you are here,' crooned Odelina. 'Come upstairs, so we can talk without being overheard.'

'Talk about what?' asked Bartholomew in alarm.

'Yes, what?' demanded Heslarton, a little aggressively.

'My health,' said Odelina, giving Heslarton the kind of look all fathers knew to distrust. 'I do not want to air personal information in public, but he needs my secrets to calculate a horoscope.'

She began to haul on Bartholomew's sleeve. He resisted, and there was a ripping sound as stitches parted company.

'Was that you or me?' asked Odelina, inspecting her gown in concern.

'It had better be him,' muttered Heslarton darkly.

'He is a warlock, Odelina,' said Celia, watching her friend's antics with aloof amusement. 'You should be wary of making him uncomfortable, lest he disappears in a puff of toxic smoke.'

It was enough to make Odelina loosen her grip, enabling Bartholomew to slither free. Celia came to her feet when the younger woman began to advance again, making a gesture to Heslarton to say she had the situation under control. She intercepted Odelina and led her to a corner, where they began whispering, hands shielding their mouths. They looked like a pair of silly adolescents, thought Bartholomew, watching in disgust.

'My daughter will be a wealthy woman one day,' said Heslarton, giving the physician a hard look. 'Many men

285

pay court to her, but I shall not let her go to anyone who is not worthy.'

'And a poverty-bound scholar is not his idea of a good match,' said Emma with a smirk that was impossible to interpret. 'I see his point. I have other ambitions for my only grandchild, too.'

'Why are you here?' Heslarton asked. 'To tell us about Gib, or to ask after my mother's teeth?'

'Meryfeld tells me his remedy is working, but I am still in agony,' said Emma, before either scholar could reply. 'I have reached a decision, though. He has until Wednesday, and if I am not better by then, *you* may remove my tooth, Doctor. Meanwhile, you can give me some of that strong medicine.'

'Actually, I cannot,' said Bartholomew, uncharacteristically pleased to be able to refuse her. 'It may react badly with whatever Meryfeld has prescribed.'

Heslarton stood suddenly, one greasy hand resting on the hilt of his sword, and for a brief moment Bartholomew thought he was going to take the tonic by force.

But Heslarton merely smiled at Emma. 'We must listen to him, mother. We do not want you made worse.'

'The real purpose of our visit is to discuss Gib,' said Michael, unwisely giving the impression that he did not much care about the state of Emma's well-being. 'Who *may* be your yellow-headed thief.'

'He is.' Emma smiled at his surprise, a rather nasty expression with more glittering of the eyes than usual. 'I went to view his mortal remains when Odelina gave us the news. Gib *was* the villain.'

'You knew him,' said Bartholomew. 'He brought messages from Chestre when you were thinking of sponsoring a scholarship. So why did you not recognise him when he stole your box?'

286

'*I* do not associate with mere students,' said Emma in disdain. 'He delivered his missives to my servants, and I never met him in person. However, the boy in St Clement's *was* the villain who invaded my home. He was missing his yellow hair, but his great paunch is distinctive.'

Bartholomew did not recall an ale-belly as he had chased the culprit up the High Street, and again found he was not sure what to believe about Gib. Or about Emma, for that matter.

'We live in a wicked world,' she went on softly. 'I thought your University would be gracious to me, after I spent so much money on your College. But now I learn it was a *scholar* who broke into my home and left poison for my beloved granddaughter.'

'We are sorry,' said Bartholomew, wondering why she had not asked the obvious question: whether her box was in the dead man's possession. The omission was suspicious, to say the least.

'*You* do not need to apologise to me,' she said, reaching out to pat his cheek. It was all he could do not to cringe away. 'It is not *your* fault students are such devious creatures.'

Bartholomew was ready to leave after Emma had identified Gib – Celia had disappeared, muttering something about going to organise a feast to celebrate her late husband's life, which meant Odelina was on the loose again – but Michael still had questions.

'Did you hunt the killer-thief again today?' he asked Heslarton, while Bartholomew backed around the table and took refuge behind Emma's chair. Odelina started to follow, but sank down on the bench at a warning glare from her grandmother.

'No,' replied Heslarton. 'He is dead, so there was no

287

need for me to scour the marshes. Of course, now I learn the villain was in the town all the time, safely inside a hostel.'

Bartholomew pounced on the inconsistency. 'You could not have known he was dead until the body was found, which was mid-morning. And if you had intended to "scour the marshes", you would have been gone long before then, to take advantage of the daylight.'

Heslarton shot to his feet a second time, and Bartholomew saw, belatedly, that he should have put the question more succinctly. 'My horse was lame. Not that it is your affair.'

'Do you only have one nag, then?' asked Michael innocently. 'I assumed you would have lots.'

Heslarton glared. 'I only have one trained for riding in bogs. The others are too expensive to risk in such perilous terrain.'

'Gib was killed between midnight and five o'clock,' said Bartholomew. He struggled to be more tactful this time. 'We want to exclude as many people from our enquiries as possible, so would you mind telling us where you were?'

'Surely, you cannot suspect *me*?' growled Heslarton dangerously. Emma's eyes narrowed.

Bartholomew raised his hands defensively. 'It is a question we are asking all the killer-thief's victims. Even my sister,' he added, when the reassurance did not seem to allay Heslarton's irritation.

'I was here,' said Heslarton shortly. He scowled, daring them to pursue the matter. Bartholomew did not think he had ever heard a more brazen lie. But help came from an unexpected quarter.

'Tell the truth, Thomas,' ordered Emma briskly. 'Someone may have seen you out and about, and that may lead Brother Michael and Doctor Bartholomew to

288

draw erroneous conclusions – ones that may work to our detriment.'

Heslarton gazed at her. 'But it is none of their business!'

'It is,' countered Emma. 'They are trying to solve a nasty crime, and they will not succeed if people mislead them. Tell them what they want to know. It is for the best.'

'No!' said Heslarton. He would not meet the eyes of anyone in the room.

'It is all right,' said Odelina suddenly. She looked at Bartholomew. 'My father is reluctant to speak because he does not want to hurt me. But the truth is that he spent the night with Celia.'

'It is not what you think,' blurted Heslarton. He licked dry lips, and his eyes were distinctly furtive. 'It was her first night alone in the house without Drax – she has been staying here since his death – and she was nervous. We read a psalter all night.'

'Your wife is barely cold,' said Michael with monkish disapproval. 'Drax, too.'

'Nothing untoward . . .' blustered Heslarton. Emma was regarding him with wry amusement, indicating the affair was no news to her. 'She was lonely and unsettled. I did the Christian thing.'

'Celia lives by the Great Bridge,' said Michael pointedly. 'Where Gib died.'

'I stayed in her house all night,' said Heslarton firmly. 'And she can verify it, although I would rather you did not ask her. I do not want her reputation sullied.'

'We can be discreet,' said Michael.

'I am sure you can,' said Emma. 'But there is no need to pursue the matter further. Thomas has shared his secret with you, and that should be enough to satisfy your curiosity.'

'Has your box been returned?' asked Bartholomew,

deciding to come at the matter from a different angle. 'Or is it—'

Emma's expression was distinctly unfriendly. 'I do not object to you questioning Thomas, or even toying with the affections of my foolish granddaughter, but that question was an insult to me. It implies I had something to do with the death of this thief – that I arranged his demise, and removed my property from his person. And that is plain rude.'

'Far from it,' countered Michael hastily. 'He was actually going to ask whether you want us to look for it when we search Gib's home.'

Emma nodded slowly. 'My apologies, Doctor. And yes, my box is still missing.'

'It will have been opened and ransacked by now,' said Michael. 'Will you give us a precise description of its contents, so we can identify any individual pieces? You declined to do so before, but if you want them back, we must have some idea of what to look for.'

Emma was silent for a moment. 'Letters of affection from my husband, a lock of his hair, and three pewter pilgrim badges from the shrine of St Thomas Cantilupe of Hereford.'

'Is that all?' asked Michael, disappointed. 'I thought it held something valuable.'

'These *are* valuable,' said Emma, turning her black eyes on him. 'They are worth more than gold to me. If you find them, I shall reward you handsomely. I will even order Yffi to finish your College roof before building the Carmelites' shrine.'

Bartholomew left Emma's lair confused and uncertain. 'We learned nothing,' he said in disgust. 'Well, we confirmed that Heslarton and Celia are lovers, but that is about all.

And the camp-ball game is the day after tomorrow – we are running out of time if we are to present a culprit for these crimes in the hope that it will defuse any trouble.'

Michael nodded although the anxious expression on his face said he was not sure whether having a culprit would help the situation. 'So we shall have to speak to Celia, to see whether Heslarton was telling the truth about his whereabouts. We had better hurry, though, because time is passing, and I have a bad feeling I shall be needed to quell more hostel–College squabbles tonight.'

'But Celia lies,' said Bartholomew morosely. 'So even if she does corroborate Heslarton's tale, I am not sure we should believe her. And, before you say it, my antipathy towards her has *nothing* to do with the fact that she likes to tell everyone that I am a warlock.'

'Perish the thought. But I wonder what an elegant, attractive lady sees in an ignorant lout like Heslarton.'

'Perhaps he has hidden depths. And he is infinitely preferable to the rest of his family. But more to the point, why does Celia want the company of a sinister hag like Emma, or whisper and giggle with the brainless Odelina? I have not forgotten the pharmacopoeia in her house, either.'

Michael nodded. 'You believe Celia poisoned Alice, because her own spouse was dead, and Alice stood in the way of her relationship with Heslarton. It is possible, I suppose. But does that mean she killed Drax and has been stealing pilgrim badges, too?'

Bartholomew shrugged. 'Well, we know she and Drax were not a happy couple, and she illustrated her penchant for *signacula* when she ordered us to strip his body. But then what? Did she and Heslarton kill Gib, and tie a yellow wig on him to make you think the case is closed?'

'It would make sense. However, I have seen Heslarton's

amorous glances, and it sounds as though last night was the first time they have been alone together since Drax died. Would he really have gone out a-killing when he could have been doing something rather more enjoyable?'

'He might, if she told him that murdering Gib was the price of her favours. However, the two of them may be innocent, and we should not let our suspicions blind us to our other solutions.'

Michael nodded agreement. 'Incidentally, Kendale asked the Gilbertines if he can use their field for his camp-ball game. I told Prior Leccheworth to refuse, but Thelnetham argued against me.'

Bartholomew looked at him sharply. 'Thelnetham? What business is it of his?'

'He said cancelling the game would cause ill feeling in the town, because Kendale has promised free ale and wine afterwards. He is afraid the resulting disappointment will be turned against the Gilbertines. He has a point, of course.'

'So, we can expect trouble no matter what Leccheworth decides,' said Bartholomew heavily. 'It will be between the Colleges and hostels if the match goes ahead, and it will be between the University and town if it does not. Kendale has a lot to answer for.'

'He has managed the situation with diabolical skill,' agreed Michael. 'He masquerades as the open-handed philanthropist, while I am the villain who wants to deprive the town of fun and free refreshments.'

'How will he pay for it? Ale and wine in that sort of quantity will be expensive. Or do you think he intends to hawk a few stolen *signacula* to cover his costs?'

'He might.' Michael closed his eyes in sudden despair. 'I do not see how we will ever get to the bottom of this case, Matt! I am at my wits' end!'

'You mean some murdering, thieving scoundrel has bested the Senior Proctor?'

Gradually, resolve suffused Michael's chubby features. 'No. Not yet, at least. But we need evidence if we are to make progress, and the situation is now so desperate that we must do whatever it takes to acquire some.'

'How will we do that?'

'You will slip into Chestre Hostel tonight, and ascertain why Kendal and Neyll were so determined that we should not examine Gib's belongings.'

Bartholomew gaped at him. 'What?'

'You have done it before, so do not look so appalled. It has to be you – I will not fit through their tiny windows. And I cannot send a beadle on such a sensitive mission.'

'No, but you can send Cynric.'

Michael smiled his relief. 'Cynric, yes! Why did I not think of that?'

Bartholomew shrugged. 'Corpse Examiners are useful in more ways than one.'

Before Bartholomew and Michael could reach Celia's house, the monk was called to mediate in a dispute between Peterhouse and Maud's Hostel – a silly argument regarding a horse that he learned Kendale had engineered – while the physician received a summons from a patient. The patient was an elderly man whose death was not unexpected, but the physician hated standing among distraught relatives while a loved one slipped away, and was in a bleak frame of mind as he walked home to Michaelhouse. Dusk had faded to night and the streets were cold, foggy and damp.

He went to his room, and stared at the puddles that covered the floor. His students had cleared everything out, except the desks, which were covered in oiled sheets. They had done the same with his medicine store, although the two locked chests that contained his most potent remedies had been left, and so had the mattress on which he slept. He slumped wearily on to one of the boxes, his thoughts full of the old man he had been unable to save.

'There you are,' said Michael, coming in a few moments later. He glanced around. 'My quarters look just as bad, although at least you still have a ceiling.'

'For the moment,' said Bartholomew, wondering how long it would take Michael's floorboards to rot from damp and exposure, and come crashing down on top of him.

'I had just resolved that ridiculous spat between Peterhouse and Maud's, when there was yet more trouble,' Michael went on. 'And this time blood was spilled – three scholars from Bene't were injured when stones were lobbed by Maud's. It was over the rumour that Jolye was murdered by the hostels.'

'There is a similar tale that says Gib was dispatched by the Colleges. I heard it as I was coming home. They are calling him the Martyr of the Hostels.'

Michael gazed at him in horror. 'No! That will make the situation infinitely worse – and it is already dire! I was expecting everything to come to a head on Tuesday at the camp-ball game, but perhaps it will explode sooner.'

They were silent for a moment, each reflecting on the events that had plunged the University into so much unnecessary disorder.

'I heard about your patient,' said Michael eventually. 'And I am sorry: he was a good man. So, because I anticipated that you might not be in the mood for tackling Celia straight away, I arranged something nicer first: an invitation to dine with Dick Tulyet. It will cheer you up, and we can question Celia afterwards.'

'I am not visiting the Tulyet house,' said Bartholomew firmly. 'Dickon might stab me again.'

'It will be in the Brazen George, and Dickon will not be there, thank the good Lord. Dick wants a report on our findings, and has information to give us in return.'

A short while later, they were ensconced in the cosy comfort of the tavern, being presented with roasted chicken, salted beef, a dish of boiled vegetables and a basket of bread. Tulyet paid the landlord, who left with a bow, closing the door behind him. Bartholomew was not hungry, and picked listlessly at the meat Michael shoved towards him.

'What is wrong?' asked Tulyet, watching him. 'You have barely spoken since you arrived.'

'Like me, he is despondent because every time we think we have solved the case, something happens to make us question whether we are looking in the right direction,' said Michael before Bartholomew could reply for himself. 'I cannot recall ever feeling so frustrated.'

'Unfortunately, we do not have time to chase around in circles,' said Tulyet worriedly. 'There are rumours that the killer-thief is a scholar – and the town is incensed at the notion. We must apprehend him before Kendale's damned camp-ball game, or your warring hostels and Colleges will be the least of our worries.'

Michael outlined what more had been learned since the last time they had spoken, and it was clear from Tulyet's face that he was disappointed by their progress.

'You are wrong to think Heslarton and Celia might have killed Drax,' he said. 'My wife told me yesterday that they have been frolicking for years, and were content with the situation as it was – neither had any desire to murder the other's spouse. Dickon knew about their relationship, too. He said Heslarton often visited Celia while Drax was out.'

'I do not suppose he noticed Heslarton paying her court last night, did he?' asked Michael hopefully. 'Heslarton claims he was with Celia when Gib was killed, but I am unconvinced.'

'I will ask,' said Tulyet. 'And now I shall tell you my news. Yffi's apprentices are in something of a state, because he went out this morning and failed to return.'

'He was among the crowd when Gib's body was retrieved,' said Bartholomew. 'I saw him.'

Tulyet nodded. 'Afterwards, he told them to keep working on the Carmelites' shrine until he returned at noon. But he did not return at noon, and was still missing when I left to come here.'

'What do you mean by missing?' asked Michael. 'Do you think he has fled the town?'

'No, I think something has happened to him. His lads say he never leaves them unsupervised for more than an hour or two, and they are genuinely concerned. Moreover, I think it odd that this should have happened so quickly after the discovery of Gib's corpse.'

Bartholomew was bemused. 'Are you saying Yffi killed Gib, and has been dispatched in his turn?'

Tulyet shrugged. 'The thought has crossed my mind, certainly.'

Michael was thoughtful. 'Kendale and his students were suspiciously calm about Gib's death. Perhaps it was because they knew that justice had already been served.'

'They are an unruly crowd,' agreed Tulyet. 'My soldiers say they are always creeping about at night. Meanwhile, you saw them arguing with Drax not long before *he* was killed, and they are refusing to let you search their hostel. It all adds up to something very suspicious.'

They talked a while longer, then Tulyet stood to leave, saying he was going to spend a pleasant evening in the company of his son, although Bartholomew wondered how he thought he was going to do both. They walked to Bridge Street together, where the two scholars aimed for Celia's home and Tulyet for the golden, welcoming lights of his comfortable mansion.

'I will not have Dickon much longer,' said Tulyet with a sad sigh. 'It is almost time for him to begin his knightly training – assuming I can find someone good enough to take him. I half hope I fail, because I shall miss him terribly when he goes. Everyone will. He is such a good-natured boy.'

'I am tempted to consult a witch about Dick,' said Michael, as he rapped on Celia's door. 'Someone must have put a spell on him, because his opinion of that little hellion is not normal. Of course, if Celia is right, I could ask you to do it, and save myself some money.'

'Do not jest about such matters, Brother,' said Bartholomew wearily. 'It is not funny.'

'It is very late for callers,' said Celia, opening her door a crack, and making it clear that the scholars were not to be permitted inside. 'What do you want?'

'To talk to you,' said Michael. Like Bartholomew, he had noticed a shadow in the room beyond: she was not alone. 'May we come in? It is cold out here.'

'I am not letting a warlock in my house after sunset,' said Celia. 'It would be asking for trouble.'

'Let them in, Celia,' came a girlish voice from behind her. Bartholomew's heart sank when he recognised it as Odelina's. 'We do not want the poor Doctor to catch a chill.'

'Or the poor Senior Proctor,' added Michael, shoving past Celia to step inside. She staggered.

There was a fire burning in the hearth, and two goblets

stood on the table. So did two sets of sewing, and if Heslarton had been there, they had been very quick to eliminate the evidence.

'We shall not take much of your time,' said Bartholomew, ducking behind Michael as Odelina surged towards him. 'We want to know what you did last night.'

Celia raised her eyebrows. 'Why, Doctor! Is that any sort of question to ask a lady, when you have been told she entertained her lover? Do you want details of our intimate activities, then?'

'But my father said you spent a romantic but chaste night looking at a psalter,' objected Odelina, regarding her friend uncertainly. 'Him on one side of the hearth, and you on the other. He said he would not do anything . . . *improper* until a decent amount of time had passed.'

'Of course,' said Celia, eyeing her pityingly. She smiled at Bartholomew. 'So there you are. We spent the night with a book. However, I would appreciate a little discretion. People talk, and I do not want a reputation.'

'It is a little late for that,' said Michael bluntly. 'You have been seen with Heslarton on previous occasions, too, especially ones when Drax happened to be away on business.'

Celia's pretty face creased into something ugly. 'Dickon! He is always spying, and you are friends with his father. I should have left the little beast to the bees.'

'So are you saying you read here all last night?' asked Michael, treating her to a searching look. 'Neither of you left the house for any reason?'

'Why should we?' said Celia shortly. 'There is much here to occupy us. And now, if that is all . . .'

'This is an impressive library,' said Michael, ignoring her dismissal and indicating the collection of books with a flabby hand. 'Are they all yours?'

'I have been through this with the warlock,' replied Celia irritably. 'They belonged to my husband. He could read, I cannot.'

'Then how did you peruse this book with Heslarton?' pounced Bartholomew, recalling that Agatha had claimed it was the other way around. 'He cannot read, either – he has already told me he has no Latin. Surely, it would be tedious for you *both* to stare at words neither of you understand?'

'That particular tome is very prettily illustrated,' replied Celia icily. 'It was prepared in the Carmelites' scriptorium, and—'

Whatever else she had been about to say was lost, because there was another knock on the door. The two women exchanged an uneasy glance, and Bartholomew wondered if they were afraid it was Heslarton, come to pay suit to his woman, and that he might contradict the tales they had told. But it was Cynric, who always seemed to know where his master was.

'You are needed urgently at Trinity Hall,' he said without preamble. 'And then at the Swan tavern in Milne Street, where there has been a fight and there are wounds that need stitching.'

Bartholomew shrugged apologetically at Michael and took his leave.

Bartholomew walked briskly towards Trinity Hall, where two scholars had been injured by flying glass when rocks had been tossed through their chapel windows. The stones were believed to have been thrown by a contingent from Batayl Hostel.

'They want to murder us,' said the one of the wounded resentfully. 'In revenge for Gib.'

'There is nothing to suggest that Gib was killed because

299

he belonged to a hostel,' said Bartholomew firmly. 'This madness must stop.'

'That is what we said, but Batayl would not listen,' said another student bitterly. 'But they will not get away with it – we *will* have our revenge.'

Bartholomew tried to reason with them, but could tell his words were falling on deaf ears. He left feeling anxious and unsettled, and his peace of mind was not much helped when he reached the Swan tavern, which stood opposite the Carmelite Friary. Apparently, a gang of youths wearing hoods and red ribbons had stormed the place, and engaged in a vicious fist fight with several lads from Bene't and Clare colleges. Townsmen had joined the mêlée, and the invaders had fled when they saw they were outnumbered.

People were milling about in the street, as they always did after an incident, and voices were raised in excitement. A dog barked furiously on the other side of the road, and as Bartholomew glanced across at it, he saw the friary gate was ajar. He was surprised, because it was usually kept locked after dark. As no one at the Swan seemed to need him urgently – the remaining combatants were more interested in quarrelling with each other than in securing his services – he walked towards the convent, Cynric at his heels.

'There!' hissed the book-bearer urgently, peering through the gate and stabbing his finger into the darkened yard. 'I see three shadows lurking.'

'They are heading for the shrine,' said Bartholomew.

'Thieves,' said Cynric grimly. 'After St Simon Stock's scapular again, I imagine. What shall we do? Catch them ourselves, or sound the alarm?'

'Sound the alarm. Ring the bell by the chapel, while I make sure they do not escape.'

He crept forward. There was a lamp in the shrine, kept burning as a symbolic presence of the saint. He pushed

300

the door open further, but it issued a tearing creak. By the altar, there was a brief exclamation of alarm, and the light was promptly doused. Without it, the building was pitch black.

Then the bell began to clang. Whoever was in the shrine bolted and, either by design or accident, Bartholomew was bowled from his feet. Then he was struck a second time as two more people hurtled past. He grabbed the hem of a flying cloak, but it was moving too fast and he did not have it for long. Then there were running footsteps and the yard was full of flickering lanterns as friars, lay-brothers, visitors and servants poured out of the buildings to see what was going on.

'What happened?' cried Prior Etone, leaping over the prostrate physician to dash into the hut.

'Thieves,' explained Cynric tersely.

'No!' wailed Etone as he reached the altar. 'The scapular! It has gone!'

'Are you sure?' asked Fen. The pardoner's face was white, and he was breathless. The two nuns stood behind him, their clothing awry.

'Of course I am sure!' shrieked Etone. 'Look for yourself. The reliquary is empty.'

There was immediate consternation, and the convent's residents began to hunt wildly and randomly around the yard. Etone dropped to his knees, and began to sob.

'Even without the scapular, this is a holy place,' said Fen comfortingly. 'Pilgrims will still come.'

'But not so many,' wept Etone. 'And probably not such wealthy ones, either.'

'Brother Michael wanted me to burgle Chestre tonight,' whispered Cynric in Bartholomew's ear. 'But I think we had better see what can be done to find this relic instead. I do not like the notion of such a holy thing in the hands of felons – the saint may be angry with us for failing to protect it.'

He and Bartholomew organised a systematic search of the convent's buildings and grounds that lasted well into the night, but it was to no avail. Thieves and scapular had gone.

The following morning was so dark with rain clouds that Walter misread the hour candle, and was late sounding the bell. But even with the extra hour in bed, Bartholomew was still tired. As he struggled to prise himself away from his straw mattress, he wondered when it was that he had last enjoyed a good, uninterrupted night's sleep.

The previous evening, Langelee had decided that the physician and his students should sleep in the hall while their own quarters were uninhabitable. It had sounded like a good idea, and Bartholomew was grateful to have somewhere dry to lie down when he had finished hunting for St Simon's Stock's relic. But rain thundered on the roof like a drum roll, and he discovered that Thelnetham and Clippesby were in the habit of using the library at night. Their reading lamps kept him awake, and so did the College cat, which insisted on trampling over him.

Michael also slept poorly – Tulyet's fears about renewed hostilities with the town had unsettled him. Feeling there was not a moment to lose, he rose long before dawn, and discussed the brewing troubles with his beadles. Then he visited the Carmelite Priory. The friars were still distraught, particularly Etone. They clamoured at him, urging and pleading with him to get their treasure back before the villain chopped it into pieces and sold them off.

'It must be the killer-thief,' he said unhappily to Bartholomew, as Langelee led the scholars back to Michaelhouse after morning mass. 'At least, I hope so –

I do not have the resources to hunt another audacious felon.'

'If so, then it is the first time he has worked with accomplices,' said Bartholomew. 'Perhaps it *was* Kendale and a couple of his pupils.'

'Unfortunately, it might be anyone,' said Michael bitterly. 'No one can give me a decent description. Not even you, who had actual physical contact.'

'I am sorry, Brother. It was very dark, and they were no more than shadows.'

'Incidentally, Fen said they might not have succeeded, had you tried harder to catch them.'

'He said as much last night, although he went quiet when I said the same applied to him. He arrived very quickly after the alarm was raised, and so did the nuns. None of them looked as though they had been sleeping.'

'They spun me a tale about praying together in the chapel.' Michael regarded his friend strangely for a moment, and then looked away. 'I have something terrible to confess.'

Bartholomew regarded him in alarm. 'Why? What have you done?'

'Lost the *signaculum* you gave me. I was vain enough to wear it in my hat this morning, but the pin must have been faulty. By the time I returned, it had gone.'

Bartholomew heaved a sigh of relief. 'Is that all? I was afraid it was something dreadful.'

'It is something dreadful!' cried Michael, agitated. 'Not only was it a gift from a man who rarely gives his friends anything other than medicine and impractical advice about diets, it was something I really wanted. It was a beautiful thing, and I feel bereft.'

'Are you sure it is lost? A lot of people have had theirs stolen.'

Michael's expression hardened. 'Fen! *He* must have taken it when I was at the Carmelite Friary! Or do you see the likes of Etone and Horneby as *signaculum* thieves?'

'I would hope not,' said Bartholomew noncommittally.

Michael was thoughtful. 'Of course, I bumped into Meryfeld and Gyseburne on my way home, too. Gyseburne reached out to brush a cobweb from my head, but I am sure I would have noticed him removing my badge. No – it was Fen.'

Bartholomew was not sure what to think, so said nothing.

'He will never be able to sell it here,' said Michael, still worrying at the matter, 'because my beadles are circulating its description. Of course, it serves me right for wearing it in the first place – I have not been on a pilgrimage, and it was sheer vanity.'

'That does not seem to stop anyone else from doing it.'

Michael sighed, then became practical. 'Come with me to see the Carmelites. The theft of the scapular is serious and urgent, and we must do all we can to retrieve it.'

'Before breakfast?' asked Bartholomew in surprise. Michael hated missing meals.

The monk nodded, and his expression was sombre. 'As I said, it is serious and urgent. The camp-ball game is tomorrow, and time is running out far too fast.'

Michael set a brisk pace to the convent, where friars stood in huddled groups and there was an atmosphere of shocked grief, as though someone had died. Etone was so distraught that Bartholomew was obliged to prepare him a tonic, to soothe him.

'Find it, Brother,' the Prior whispered brokenly. 'Please find it.'

Michael muttered some reassurances, patted his hand, and left him to Bartholomew's care. The physician did not leave until Etone slept, at which point one of his novices came to sit with him. When Bartholomew walked into the yard, he found Michael talking to Horneby, Fen and the two nuns. The women were rosy cheeked and seemed well rested, although Fen was wan.

'I shall assume the role of Prior until Etone has recovered,' Horneby was saying. 'God knows, I am no administrator, but no one else is willing to step into the breach, and we cannot be leaderless at such a time.'

'Well, you need not worry about accommodating us much longer,' said Fen kindly. 'We intend to leave soon – Poynton's family must be informed of his death as quickly as possible.'

They all looked around as the gate was opened, and Seneschal Welfry stepped inside. The Dominican saw Horneby, and ran towards him, his face a mask of shock.

'I am *so* sorry! When Prior Morton told me what had happened, I thought it was his idea of a joke. I would have come last night had I known – I could have helped search for these vile scoundrels.'

'It would have made no difference,' said Horneby sadly. 'We hunted all night and found no trace of them – and we had Cynric. If *he* could not catch them, then no one could.'

'Cynric is the physician's man,' said one of the fat nuns unpleasantly. Bartholomew thought she was Agnes. 'Perhaps he did not try as hard as he might have done.'

'What do you mean by that?' demanded Michael, hands on hips.

'What was he doing here in the first place?' Agnes snarled. 'It was late, dark and wet. Yet he was lurking around the shrine, unaccompanied by Carmelites. It is suspicious, to say the least!'

'It is not,' said Horneby quietly. 'He and Bartholomew

305

saw the gate ajar and came to investigate. And thank God they did, or we would not have known the scapular was missing until this morning. Besides, they did their best to tackle the invaders.'

'*Did* they?' sneered the other nun – Margaret. 'Are you sure about that?'

'Ladies!' said Welfry sharply. 'You would be wise to keep such nasty insinuations to yourself. There is no room for them here.'

'You are right,' said Fen softly. 'My fellow pilgrims speak out of turn. Please accept our apologies, Doctor. It has been a long night, and we are all tired.'

'Yes, you *should* beg his forgiveness,' said Horneby firmly. 'Bartholomew did all he could to prevent the thieves from escaping. I saw him knocked to the ground myself.'

'Then why did *you* not give chase?' demanded Margaret. 'If you were that close?'

'I am unwell,' said Horneby stiffly. 'Confined to my room, and—'

'I know you have postponed the Stock Extraordinary Lecture,' said Agnes, regarding him doubtfully. 'But you do not look unwell to me.'

'He *is* ill,' said Welfry, indignant on his friend's behalf. 'He should not be out of bed now, as a matter of fact, but he has rallied because of this crisis. Please do not rail at him. And do not rail at Matthew, either. He is the last man in Cambridge to steal relics.'

'I am not so sure about that,' said Agnes snidely. 'There are rumours that he dabbles in sorcery, and sacred objects are very useful when performing dark rites.'

'So we are told,' added Margaret hastily.

'You overstep the mark, sisters,' said Welfry coldly. 'And although successful physicians attract this sort of specula-

306

tion from half-wits, I am appalled to hear it from you. You should know better.'

'Matt said the front gate was open,' mused Michael, when the nuns seemed unable to think of a reply to the rebuke, and only shuffled their feet. 'Yet the thieves did not leave that way. Why?'

'Probably because they were afraid of being seen by the patrons of the Swan tavern opposite,' supplied Fen. 'The bell was ringing at that point, and everyone would have been looking over.'

'Or because they were already home,' whispered Michael to Bartholomew. 'In other words, Fen and his two fat nuns had no need to tear out of the convent, because they intended to spend the night in its comfortable guest hall. And now we hear they will soon be leaving.'

There was no more to be learned from the White Friars, so Bartholomew and Michael left them to their grieving and walked towards the High Street. Alice was going to be buried that day, and the monk was so desperate for clues regarding her death that he had already said he wanted both of them to mingle with the mourners, to see what might be gleaned from questions and eavesdropping.

'Fen and his nuns are scoundrels,' Michael growled as they walked. 'I wager *they* stole the scapular, then tried to have you blamed for the crime, to shift attention from themselves.'

'It is possible, I suppose,' acknowledged Bartholomew. 'Still, assuming the killer-thief – with helpmeets – did steal the scapular last night, at least we can say that Gib was not the culprit. You cannot have a better alibi than being dead. In other words, someone probably *did* tie the yellow wig on him in order to mislead us.'

'Our other suspects remain the same, though,' said

Michael grimly. 'Fen and his nuns at the top of the list, followed by the devious scholars of Chestre, Yffi—'

'But not Blaston,' warned Bartholomew. 'He would never tamper with holy relics. And neither would my medical colleagues, before you think to include them in your inventory.'

Michael sighed. 'Welfry did you a favour today. A tale that the town's favourite warlock stole the scapular would have spread like wildfire, but he managed to knock it on the head. He was forceful but polite. Perhaps he will not be as disastrous a Seneschal as I initially feared.'

The churchyard of St Mary the Great was already filling with mourners, most from the town, but some scholars among them. Bartholomew went to stand with Edith and Stanmore, who confided that Alice had had a nasty habit of accusing traders of giving her the wrong change. Then Blaston told him she had been critical of craftsmen and had reduced several to tears. Finally, Isnard claimed she had drunk more wine than the rest of the Colvyll clan put together.

Bartholomew regarded the bargeman thoughtfully. Was this significant? Did it mean the poisoner's target *had* been Alice, and wine had been chosen because she was the one most likely to imbibe it? Eager to learn more, he started to ask questions about Emma, but the flow of information stopped abruptly. People were far too frightened to gossip about the old lady.

'But why?' asked Bartholomew of his sister. 'She is not so terrifying.'

'She most certainly *is*,' averred Edith. 'I cannot recall ever meeting a more evil individual. Do you know what Cynric told me? Not to stand too close when we go inside the church, lest the saints object to her wicked presence and make her explode into pieces.'

'Lord!' muttered Bartholomew, struggling not to laugh. 'Cynric has a vivid imagination.'

Edith did not share his amusement, and turned to another subject. 'Fen gave Heslarton a *signaculum* from Rome to put in Alice's coffin. It was a kind thing to do.'

Michael overheard, and came to join them. 'I have just looked at it. It is made of tin, although I am sure he has plenty of gold ones. Heslarton should have held out for something better.'

'That would have been ungracious,' said Edith reproachfully. 'And Heslarton may be a ruffian, but he has some manners. But Celia is announcing something. What is she saying?'

'That everyone is invited to a celebration this evening,' explained Michael. 'In her house. It is primarily to honour her husband, but she plans to drink toasts to Alice, too.'

'Does she mean it?' asked Bartholomew, looking around. 'There are a lot of people here.'

'She means it,' said Edith. 'She is very wealthy now Drax is dead.'

Odelina was among the crowd, wearing another of her unflatteringly tight gowns. Welfry ducked hastily behind Prior Morden when she made a beeline in his direction. But despite his determination not to be mauled, his words to her were kind, and it was clear he was doing his best not to hurt her feelings. When she saw she was going to have no success with him, she aimed for Bartholomew.

'I would rather you stayed away from her, Matt,' murmured Stanmore. 'She is looking for a husband, and I do not want my family associated with Emma's. It will be bad for trade.'

'You need have no worries on that score,' said Bartholomew firmly.

'I bought my mother three general pardons,' Odelina

announced as she approached. 'I do not believe they will shorten her stay in Purgatory, but my father does, and I like to make him happy.'

'You are fond of him,' said Edith. Bartholomew winced when he saw the puzzled expression on her face, indicating she could not imagine why.

'Oh, yes,' said Odelina, nodding fervently. 'He is the gentlest, sweetest man in the world. And if he wants pardons for my mother's soul, then pardons he shall have.'

'She might do better with your prayers,' said Michael piously. 'Genuine ones.'

But Odelina was not very interested in talking to him. She fixed her gaze on Bartholomew. 'I knew you would come today,' she simpered. 'For me.'

'You should go to your grandmother,' he said, unwilling to waste time repelling her when he should be concentrating on catching a killer. 'She looks unwell.'

'Her tooth is paining her,' explained Odelina. 'It is a pity, because she was looking forward to today. She loves funerals.'

'Oh.' Bartholomew blinked. 'Ask Meryfeld to tend her. He is standing by the church door.'

Reluctantly, Odelina went to do as she was told. The moment she had gone, Thelnetham joined them. Unusually, his habit was plain, and bore none of the flagrant accessories he normally sported.

'Your medical students are hatching a plot to disrupt this afternoon's lectures,' he said, pursing his lips. 'They plan to infest the hall with rats – and no hall, no teaching.'

Bartholomew groaned. 'If it is not one problem, it is another.'

'Go,' said Thelnetham. 'I will help Michael eavesdrop on the mourners. I want these thefts and murders solved as much as the next man.'

It was an odd offer, but Bartholomew nodded his thanks and strode quickly to Michaelhouse, where he arrived just in time to see Valence lifting a large rodent from a box. The student dropped it when his master marched into the hall, and it made an immediate bid for escape, heading unerringly for the spiral staircase that led to the yard. Bartholomew folded his arms and raised his eyebrows.

'It was to test a remedy,' said Valence defensively. 'A new one we have devised to . . . to reverse the course of miscarriage in women.'

'That is not possible,' said Bartholomew. 'And even if it were, you would not prove your case by testing it on that particular rat – it was male. But as you are all here, we may as well start work early. It will give me more time to test you on what you have learned afterwards.'

He saw alarmed looks being exchanged, and grinned to himself, thinking it served the rascals right. He threw himself into the exercise with all the energy at his command, and by mid-afternoon – and he stopped only because Langelee told him the bell had rung a long time before and the servants were still waiting to serve dinner – he felt as though progress had been made.

'Christ's blood!' muttered Valence, watching him head for the high table to join the rest of the Fellows. 'I have never been worked so hard in my life! Perhaps we should all forget about being physicians, and become lawyers, instead.'

CHAPTER 10

Because his students' performance had been better than he had expected, Bartholomew gave them the rest of the afternoon off, an announcement that was greeted with a spontaneous cheer. He had been going to suggest they spent the time reading Theophilus's *De urinis*, but their reaction made him wonder whether Michael was right, and he had been pushing them too hard. But there was a desperate need for qualified physicians, and he felt it was his duty to train as many as he could.

He was still thinking about teaching when Michael approached. The monk was dressed in his best habit, and his lank brown hair had been carefully brushed around his tonsure. He had shaved, too, so his plump face was pink and clean, although his expression was anxious.

'We are going to Celia Drax's celebration,' he announced. 'All our suspects are likely to be there, and we *must* catch this killer-thief before the camp-ball game.'

Bartholomew nodded. 'And if we can make enough fuss about our success, it may even distract the hostels and Colleges from fighting, too.'

'Quite,' agreed Michael. 'It is *imperative* we uncover some clues this evening. So change that torn tabard, don a clean shirt and let us be off. Incidentally, did your students tell you that the Colleges have replied to the trebuchet incident? Or are they too frightened of you to indulge in idle chatter these days?'

Bartholomew did not like to admit that he had not given them the chance. 'I hope it was nothing to worsen the trouble,' he said nervously. 'Cynric told me that Gib and Jolye, now official martyrs for hostels and Colleges respectively, are being used as figureheads to rally support. It is becoming increasingly difficult for the peaceful scholars to remain neutral.'

'The trick is very clever, and has Welfry's hand all over it – amusing without being vicious or dangerous. I could have kissed him when members of both factions stood together to laugh.'

'What did he do?'

'I am not sure how, but he built a mountain of eggs and set Agatha in a large throne on top of them. Both laundress and chair are extremely heavy, and I cannot imagine how the whole thing does not collapse. But not one egg is so much as cracked.'

Bartholomew regarded him uneasily; only lunatics crossed Agatha. 'Does she mind?'

'She is having the time of her life. People are flocking to admire the spectacle – and admire her, too. I wish you could see it, but your duty lies at Celia Drax's home, which represents a vital opportunity to see what can be learned about these thefts and murders.'

'Does that mean you had no luck at Alice's funeral?' asked Bartholomew unhappily.

Michael winced. 'None at all. It was a waste of time – and time is something we do not have. By this hour tomorrow, the camp-ball game will be over, and who knows what might be left?'

Worriedly, Bartholomew trailed after him to Celia's house. When they arrived, it was to find every room packed with guests. An impromptu band of musicians had gathered and was belting out popular tunes, although

313

the thudding beat of the drum drowned out the other instruments. People were dancing, too, in a heaving, gyrating mass. Whoops, cries, cheers and laughter abounded, and there was a rank smell of spilled wine and sweaty bodies.

'Lord!' muttered Bartholomew. 'I have not been to one of these since I was a student.'

Michael looked around with narrowed eyes. 'We shall start by having a word with Fen and his nuns. They are by the window, talking to Prior Leccheworth.'

They started to ease their way through the jigging dancers, but were intercepted by Celia, resplendent in yet another new gown.

'All manner of vermin accepted my invitation, I see,' she said unpleasantly, yelling to make herself heard over the racket. 'Whores, impoverished students, warlocks, venal monks—'

'Is this any way to honour your husband?' demanded Michael, gesturing around him in distaste. 'He is barely cold in his grave.'

'It is what is called a wake,' bawled Celia. 'A celebration of his life. If you do not like it, leave.'

She turned and flounced away before Michael could respond. Bartholomew was tempted to do as she suggested, because he was not in the mood for rowdy parties, but the desperate hope that they might learn something to avert a crisis the following day kept him there.

'Tell Leccheworth he is wrong, Brother,' Fen cried, as the scholars approached. Tears of distress glistened in his eyes. 'He keeps saying St Simon Stock's holy scapular is a fake.'

'Really?' asked Michael, regarding the Gilbertine with raised eyebrows. 'Why?'

'Because Etone showed it to me once,' explained

Leccheworth, rather defiantly. 'And it was too grubby to be sacred. In fact, it was nasty, and I was loath to touch the thing.'

'It is a hundred years old,' argued Fen, stricken. 'Of course it is grubby! But I do not care what you think, because I know a blessed relic when I see one.' He pointedly turned his back on the Prior, and addressed Michael. 'What have you learned about the scoundrels who took it?'

'That they are familiar with the Carmelite Friary and its grounds,' replied the monk, watching him intently. Bartholomew did the same with the nuns. 'A pilgrim, perhaps.'

'Very possibly,' said Fen, nodding earnestly, and if he thought Michael's suggestion held an accusation, he gave no sign that he had taken it personally. 'The shrine attracts many people, and hundreds must have paid homage there. I wish you success in your endeavours.'

He bowed, and walked away, hotly pursued by the nuns.

'He is too sly to let anything slip,' said Michael. 'Damn! I am at a loss as how to trap him.'

'Kendale and his students are better suspects, anyway,' said Bartholomew. 'Edith's testimony told us that the culprit is probably a scholar.'

He pointed to where the Chestre men were enjoying themselves with several women he knew to be prostitutes, or Frail Sisters, as they preferred to be called. Celia had not been exaggerating when she had remarked on the range of people who had elected to accept her hospitality.

'I will speak to them,' determined Michael. 'While you watch from a distance. *They* will not trip themselves up with words, either, so see what you can deduce from their demeanour.'

315

It was resorting to desperate measures, as far as Bartholomew was concerned, but he went to stand with Horneby and Welfry, using them as cover, lest the Chestre lads should happen to glance over and guess what he was doing. Both friars were sipping watered ale, and did not look comfortable amid the lively, noisy throng.

'You should not be here,' he said to Horneby. 'You are supposed to be pretending to be ill so that no one will take offence over the cancelled Stock Extraordinary Lecture.'

'The loss of our relic has put paid to that plan – as Acting Prior, I am obliged to be visible.' Horneby shrugged. 'But we can use the theft as an excuse to postpone, so it does not really matter.'

'I feel like a virgin in a brothel,' said Welfry unhappily, while Bartholomew watched the Chestre lads grow angry over something Michael had said. 'But Drax was generous to both our priories, so it is our duty to be here. Of course, we did not expect the occasion to be quite so . . . so *spirited*.'

'I heard about your trick with the eggs,' said Bartholomew. Kendale's expression had turned taunting, and the physician could see Michael struggling to keep his temper. 'How did you do it?'

Welfry was delighted to be asked. 'Well, eggs have a certain internal strength, despite their outward fragility, so it is just a case of placing them so that they—'

'My throat hurts from shouting to make myself heard,' interrupted Horneby. Neyll was clenching his fists, and Bartholomew braced himself, ready to run to Michael's rescue if one of them flew. 'And I do not think this occasion is any place for priests. Your description of virgins in brothels is truer than you thought, Welfry, because I know for a fact that Helia over there is a whore. We had better leave.'

316

'Have you made any more loud bangs?'

Both friars and Bartholomew turned to see Dickon standing behind them, grinning.

'What is this?' asked Horneby, startled. 'Loud bangs?'

'An accident while trying to create a lamp with a clean and steady glow,' explained Bartholomew, turning his attention back to the Chestre men. 'I had the idea from Kendale's trick at St Mary the Great.'

Welfry nodded keenly. 'You asked me about the formula, and I have been thinking about it. He would have required a sticky substance to rub on his "fuses", but the solution in his buckets must have been much more fluid. Have you tried mixing different kinds of oil with the pitch?'

'The stuff you made was very sticky, Doctor,' supplied Dickon. 'I climbed over Meryfeld's wall later, and had a look at it. I tried to blow it up again, but my tinderbox would not work.'

'Dickon, you must *never* tamper with such things,' said Welfry, alarmed. 'They can be extremely dangerous, and you may hurt someone.'

'So what?' asked Dickon airily. 'Life is full of dangers, and everyone must take his chances.'

'Heavens!' breathed Welfry, when the child had gone. 'That was an eerily sinister philosophy coming from the mouth of someone so young. I doubt he learned *that* from his parents.'

'He might, if his father is the Devil,' muttered Horneby. 'But this house is definitely no place for friars if *he* is here. I am going home.'

'That was a waste of time,' said Michael angrily, arriving a few moments later. The Chestre men were already back with their ladies, carousing noisily. 'We exchanged yet more threats and ultimatums, and I learned nothing. What about you? Did you see any nervous or guilty glances?'

317

Bartholomew shook his head. 'But the prostitute called Helia is over there. Neyll claimed Gib was with her the night he died, so I am going to ask her whether it is true.'

'Yes, I service Chestre,' said Helia. She was a small, pretty woman with a pert figure and dyed red hair. 'Mostly Neyll and Gib, although Kendale comes, too, on occasion.'

'Do they ever quarrel about the arrangement?'

'Almost certainly, I would think – they are a feisty crowd. However, I can tell you one thing: I am not entertaining that Neyll again. The University should send him home – he is a pig.'

'Why is that?'

'He is a killer. Do you remember that student who drowned a month ago – Jolye? Well, it was Neyll who pushed him in the river, and would not let him out again. And I doubt Jolye was his first victim, either. You should be careful around him – the Frail Sisters do not want to lose you.'

'Can you prove Neyll killed Jolye?'

Helia wrinkled her nose. 'Well, no one *saw* it happen, but Gib told Belle, who told the University's stationer, who told his cousin, who told me. So it is absolutely true.'

'When did you last see Gib?' asked Bartholomew, suspecting there was unlikely to be much accuracy in a tale that had been passed along by quite so many gossiping tongues.

Helia was thoughtful. 'Well, we had a bit of a spat, so I did not see him this week. The *last* time we met would have been more than seven days ago. He visited me from late on Sunday night, until he left for lectures at prime on Monday.'

'Are you sure?' asked Bartholomew urgently. If Helia was right, then Gib could not have been the yellow-headed man he himself had chased from Emma's house.

'Absolutely sure. On Monday mornings, I look after Yolande's children while she visits the Mayor. It is a long-standing arrangement, and I went there the moment Gib left me. I saw him go inside his hostel, ready for his morning lessons.'

'And you did not see him after that?'

Helia shook her head. 'But he sent me a message saying he intended to honour me with his presence on Saturday night. He never arrived.'

Probably because he had been murdered *en route*, thought Bartholomew, watching as Helia left to dance with Isnard. How the bargeman managed his wild skipping with only one leg was beyond Bartholomew, and seemed to defy the laws of physics.

As Michael was with Yffi's apprentices, he went to sit with his fellow physicians until the monk had finished, surprised that the staid Rougham had deigned to attend such a riotous event. The man was a killjoy, and disliked seeing people having fun.

Rougham grinned, and raised his goblet in a happy salute. He was not usually friendly, and it did not take Bartholomew long to realise the man was drunk. So was Meryfeld, while Gyseburne was well on the way to joining them: Meryfeld's hand-rubbing was approaching frenzied proportions, while Gyseburne was on the brink of cracking a genuine smile. Gyseburne offered Bartholomew a sip of wine from the goblet he was holding. It was remarkably good, and Bartholomew thought it a pity that it was being wasted on people who were too inebriated to appreciate it.

'I am glad you are here,' slurred Rougham. 'Now we are all four physicians together, and that does not happen often. We are all too busy.'

'We should talk about medicine, then,' declared Gyseburne. 'Because we are *medici*.'

319

The others agreed with the kind of exaggerated gravity often affected by the intoxicated. Bartholomew glanced at Michael, and hoped he would not be long – he did not like discussing medicine with Rougham when he was sober, and it would be worse when the man was drunk.

'What did you give to Emma, to soothe her inflamed gums?' Gyseburne asked Meryfeld.

Meryfeld tapped the side of his nose. 'That is a secret.'

'We should not have secrets from each other,' said Rougham admonishingly. 'We should share our knowledge, for the greater good of the profession. Except sorcery. I am not interested in learning diabolical cures, Bartholomew, so you can keep those to yourself.'

'I do not know any,' said Bartholomew indignantly. 'My medicines are based on herbs that—'

'I am not telling you my cure for sore gums,' hiccuped Meryfeld. 'My poultice of lettuce and rosemary is— Damn! Now look what you made me do! It was a secret!'

'Her condition warrants a more potent remedy than that,' warned Bartholomew, concerned. 'It will not heal her, and the delay in extracting the tooth may cost her life.'

'He is right,' said Gyseburne. 'It should have come out days ago. Personally, I am surprised she is still alive, because I have seen how quickly these things can poison the blood.'

'Medicine is too contentious a subject for an occasion like this,' said Meryfeld sulkily. 'So let us debate something else instead. I have been thinking about our lamp, and I have devised a way to refine it. I think we used too much charcoal and not enough pitch. The reason for this is that pitch burns at a lower temperature than brimstone, and so will be more steady.'

'Does it?' asked Bartholomew, intrigued. 'How do you know that?'

'He does not know,' said Gyseburne. 'He is guessing. But it is worth a try. Shall we do it now?'

'No!' exclaimed Bartholomew, thinking they were likely to blow themselves up.

'Yes,' countered Meryfeld, struggling to stand. 'We shall go while the notion is fresh in our heads, and I do not live far away. Next door, in fact. Which is quite close, I believe.'

'Excellent!' slurred Rougham. 'Then let us grab the pig by the horns, and begin.'

With mounting alarm, Bartholomew saw he would have to go with them, because it would be too dangerous to leave them unsupervised. He shrugged apologetically at Michael as he left, muttering that protecting three-quarters of Cambridge's medical fraternity was just as valuable a way to spend their precious time as demanding answers from uncooperative suspects.

Rougham, Meryfeld and Gyseburne linked arms as they left Celia's house. They tried to include Bartholomew, but he did not like the notion of four physicians in a line, weaving their way along a public highway, even if only for a short distance, and lagged behind. When they reached Meryfeld's home, no one was able to fit the key in the lock. They dropped it so many times that it became a joke, and even the sour Rougham was convulsed in paroxysms of laughter.

'It is not a good idea to play with dangerous materials when you are drunk,' said Bartholomew, snatching the key and opening the door himself. 'You might do yourselves some serious harm.'

'*I* am not drunk,' declared Gyseburne indignantly, toppling inside. 'Really, Bartholomew! What a horrid thing to say! I am as sober as the Queen of Sheba.'

'And I am not drunk, either,' added Meryfeld, making for his pantry and grabbing a selection of bowls and phials. Rougham helped, making seemingly random choices from the compounds on offer. 'A tad tipsy, perhaps. But a long way from being drunk. Now, where is the oil?'

'You should do this in the garden,' said Bartholomew, rescuing the oil when Meryfeld whipped it around vigorously, threatening to slop some in the hearth, where a fire was burning.

'I will bring a lamp – it is dark outside,' said Gyseburne, tripping as he took one from a shelf. 'Lord! You must get your flagstones levelled, Meryfeld. They are a hazard.'

Bartholomew followed them to the garden, stopping to collect two pails of water *en route*, then selected a spot where they would not be seen by prying eyes from next door. He fetched the wooden table they had used the last time, and his colleagues began to toss their ingredients down on it. He read the labels with growing alarm.

'This is not sensible,' he said, when Rougham contributed a large pot of lye, some wool fat and a bottle of distilled rock oil. 'These are volatile substances, and—'

'Nonsense,' declared Meryfeld. 'We are educated men and know exactly what we are doing.'

'Actually, I have no idea what we are doing,' said Rougham with an uncharacteristic giggle. He picked up a pot of saltpetre. 'But intuition tells me a dose of *this* might produce some interesting results.'

'That is far too big a bowl,' objected Bartholomew, when he saw the size of the receptacle Gyseburne had brought for mixing. It was large enough to accommodate a fully grown sheep. 'I thought we had decided to experiment with smaller—'

'Do not be tedious,' said Meryfeld, elbowing him out of the way and emptying something red into the cauldron.

'If we use piffling amounts, the reactions will be too minute to assess.'

Bartholomew watched uneasily as the others began to add their own favourites to the concoction. They were all speaking much too loudly, embarking on a lively debate about the efficacy of tying dead pigeons around a patient's feet to combat fevers.

'I never use them myself,' declared Rougham. 'Pigeons belong in a pie, not wrapped around the soles, in my humble opinion.' He sounded anything but humble.

'They may have fleas,' added Gyseburne with a shudder. 'And I have enough of my own.'

'Well, I enjoy great success with pigeons,' declared Meryfeld. 'And with surgeons, too. I tie their eyes around a patient's neck as a remedy against sore throats.'

'No wonder surgeons are loath to ply their trade in Cambridge,' mused Gyseburne gravely.

'He means sturgeons,' said Bartholomew, heartily wishing he had stayed at Celia's house. Gyseburne shot him a blank look. 'Fish.'

'I dislike eels,' said Rougham, off on a tangent of his own. 'My Gonville Hall colleagues assure me they are more akin to worms than fish, but I am not so sure. They are all slippery and vile.'

'Are they?' asked Gyseburne. 'I have always found your Gonville colleagues quite pleasant.'

'Now there is a question,' said Meryfeld, ladling pitch into the bowl. He missed, and some oozed down the outside. 'Are eels fish or worms? We should debate that some time.'

'We are debating it now,' Gyseburne pointed out.

'Stop!' cried Bartholomew, horrified when he saw the quantity of saltpetre Rougham planned to use. 'That is far too much, and it will—'

'Take as much as you want, Rougham,' countered

Meryfeld. 'We are all rich, and can afford expensive ingre-dients in the name of science. Well, *you* are not wealthy, Bartholomew, but you could be, if you were to dispense with your poor patients.'

'Yes, but then they would come to us,' Rougham pointed out. 'And I do not want them. I like things the way they are, with him taking the dross and me compiling horo-scopes for the affluent.'

'Well, that is honest,' said Bartholomew, taken aback by the baldness of the remark. 'But the poor often have more interesting ailments. Just last week, one had a sickness that looked like leprosy, but I managed to cure it with a decoc-tion of—'

'You have a remedy for leprosy?' asked Meryfeld eagerly. 'Now we *shall* be rich.'

'He said it *looked* like leprosy,' corrected Gyseburne. He staggered, and the rock oil in the bottle he was holding glugged into the bowl. 'That means it was actually some-thing else. Perhaps we should name it after him. It will bring him the fame he will never have from being affluent.'

'What a dreadful notion,' said Rougham, shuddering in distaste. 'Who wants to be remembered for a disease? I would rather have a stained-glass window in my College chapel. Then people will see my handsome face for centuries to come.'

'Not if it is smashed by rioting students,' said Gyseburne. 'The glass, I mean. What is in this jug, Rougham? I cannot read the label. Oh, well. In it goes. Stir it around a bit, Meryfeld.'

'I would not mind this light being named after me,' said Meryfeld, giving the concoction a prod.

'The Meryfeld Lamp,' mused Rougham. Then he shook his head. 'No – it sounds like a tavern.'

'The ingredients are mixed now,' said Gyseburne,

peering into the cauldron. 'What shall we do next? Shove some in a lantern and see what happens?'

'Good idea,' said Meryfeld, making a lunge for the torch.

Bartholomew reached it first. 'We will take a small amount of your potion, and touch a flame to it. But we are wasting our time, because even if it works, you did not keep a record of the ingredients you used so we will never be able to replicate the result.'

'You are too cautious,' said Meryfeld disdainfully. 'And timidity in science is not a virtue. We shall set the lot alight, and see what happens.'

He snatched the lamp from Bartholomew and tossed it into the bowl.

Bartholomew hurled himself backwards, and managed to pull Gyseburne with him, while Rougham had been bending over to retrieve a bottle he had dropped. There was muffled boom, and for a moment the dusky garden was lit up as bright as a summer day. Meryfeld shrieked as flames shot towards him, so Bartholomew scrambled to his feet and dashed a bucket of water over him before he could ignite, leaving him coughing and spluttering.

'That was dazzling,' said Gyseburne, in something of an understatement as he picked himself up. 'And it was steady, too, but it did not last very long. Perhaps there was too much pitch.'

'Are you all right?' asked Bartholomew, peering at Meryfeld in concern. Flames licked across the table, and their light showed Meryfeld's round face to be bright pink, like a bad case of sunburn.

'The smell!' exclaimed Rougham, waving a hand in front of his face. 'It is awful!'

'Do not inhale it,' warned Bartholomew. 'I imagine it is poisonous.'

'What in God's name is going on?' It was Dick Tulyet, who had scrambled over the wall that divided his home from Meryfeld's. Dickon was with him, eyes alight at the prospect of mischief. 'We heard a lot of drunken revelry, followed by a huge bang and screams.'

'I told you they were doing something bad,' said Dickon smugly. 'I saw them leave Celia's—'

'What have you done to that table?' demanded Tulyet, watching Bartholomew struggle to smother the flames that still danced across it. Nothing was working. Water hissed and had no effect, his cloak simply ignited, and the flames even burned through the handfuls of soil he piled over them. 'What devilry have you invented?'

'Not devilry,' said Bartholomew, uncomfortably aware of how it must look. 'Simple alchemy. I suspect these flames will burn as long as there is air to feed them. So we must deprive them of it.'

'But you *have* deprived them of it,' Tulyet pointed out. 'You have heaped a great stack of earth on them, and they are still going strong. I can see the smoke.'

'They must be drawing it through the wood. They will burn out eventually.'

'You cannot leave them,' cried Tulyet, appalled. 'They might grow hungry for more fuel, and incinerate the whole town.'

'We can bury the tabletop,' suggested Bartholomew. 'That should make it safe.'

'I will fetch a spade,' offered Gyseburne, sheepish in the face of Tulyet's growing horror. 'The Sheriff is right: there is something of Satan in these flames.'

While they waited for him to come back, Tulyet poked the bench with a stick. Some of the substance adhered to it, and it burst into flames. He hurled it from him in revulsion.

326

'Dig,' he ordered, when Gyseburne returned. 'And let us make an end of this mischief.'

Gyseburne made an enthusiastic but ineffectual assault on the ground and, unwilling to be there all night, Bartholomew took the shovel from him. It was hard going, because the soil was clayey.

'I liked the bit where Doctor Bartholomew threw the pail of water in Meryfeld's face,' said Dickon gleefully, watching him work. 'Can I have a go? He is still pink.'

'Put that bucket down,' ordered Tulyet sharply. He turned back to the table. 'God preserve us! The flames seem to be getting fiercer!'

'Because the pitch is heating up, I imagine,' said Bartholomew, stopping his labours to watch. 'We must have precipitated some sort of chain reaction.'

'I do not care what it is,' said Tulyet angrily. 'Just stop it.'

'This would make an incredible weapon,' mused Meryfeld, picking up the stick Tulyet had dropped and inspecting it minutely. 'Imagine if you were in a castle, being attacked. You could drop this on your enemies, and they would never be able to extinguish it. And, as an added bonus, its fumes are toxic.'

Bartholomew felt sick, appalled that a physician should suggest such a terrible thing.

'How did you make it again?' asked Dickon.

'Actually, I cannot remember,' said Meryfeld. 'And that is a pity, because I am sure the King would pay handsomely for such a device. It would be devastating in battle.'

'Quite,' said Rougham, suddenly sober. 'And we are physicians. We do not invent methods to kill people, so I recommend we dispense with the pitch next time.'

'Pitch?' asked Dickon keenly.

'Among other ingredients,' said Rougham coolly. '*Many*

other ingredients. You cannot possibly hope to replicate what we did here this evening.'

Dickon pulled a face at him, then turned to his father. 'If I make some, I could take it to school. That would teach my classmates for not wanting to sit next to me.'

'It is not a joke, Dickon,' said Bartholomew quietly. 'This compound could subject someone to a very slow and painful death.'

'Better and better,' grinned Dickon.

'I still cannot believe you allowed yourself to be involved in such a wild scheme,' said Tulyet a short while later. He and Bartholomew were in his house, sitting in the room he used as an office, and he was pouring wine for his guest. 'I hope to God your cronies will not remember the formula tomorrow, especially Meryfeld. He strikes me as rather unscrupulous.'

'They were hurling substances into the pot willy-nilly,' said Bartholomew. He was exhausted, partly from his colleagues' irresponsible antics, partly from the worry of what might unfold the following day, and partly from too many disturbed nights. 'Even if one of them does recall what he added himself, he will never know what the others put in.'

'*You* probably do, though,' said Tulyet. 'And it is a dangerous secret.'

'It is not a new invention – I have read about "wildfire" in texts from the Ancient Near East. It is said to have brought great armies to their knees.'

Tulyet regarded him balefully. 'This is deadly knowledge, and you should not share it with anyone else. *I* find it repulsive, and I am a professional soldier, used to slaughtering my enemies. Let us hope your friends will be less reckless when they are not sodden with wine. Unless . . .'

'Unless what?' asked Bartholomew, suspecting from the tone of Tulyet's voice that he was about to be told something he would rather not hear.

'Unless one of them knew exactly what he was doing. I am sorry to malign men you probably like, but Gyseburne bothers me. He claims he studied at Oxford and Paris, but the Chancellor told me there is no record of him at either, and there is something . . . unsettling about him.'

'The Chancellor must be mistaken.'

'I doubt it. And Meryfeld is as bad. I am uncomfortable with the fact that it was he who found Gib's body, and I am not sure I believe his tale about the pilgrim badge he claims to have lost. Or Gyseburne's, for that matter. I think one of *them* may be the killer-thief.'

Bartholomew regarded him coolly. 'And is Rougham on your list of suspects, too?'

'He was,' Tulyet flashed back. 'But Yolande de Blaston is his alibi for several of these crimes, and I trust her implicitly. I am not confiding my suspicions to annoy you, Matt, but to warn you to be on your guard. One of them may have been trying to kill you tonight, to hinder your investigation.'

'That is ridiculous!' All four of us were in danger from the experiment, not just me. And even if one of them *is* the culprit, why would he harm me? You and Michael are the ones on his trail.'

'And we have had our close calls, too,' said Tulyet soberly. 'Michael when a rock was lobbed during a skirmish he was trying to quell, and me when the castle portcullis fell suddenly yesterday.'

'That portcullis has been threatening to drop for years. Its chains are rusty.'

'Perhaps. However, just ask yourself whether it was lucky no one was hurt in Meryfeld's garden, or whether someone just did not anticipate your speedy reactions when you hurled yourself away from the blast.'

'You are wrong,' persisted Bartholomew doggedly. 'I know you are.'

Tulyet changed the subject. 'What more have you learned about the case? I hope your antics were a way to gain information, because you should not have been fooling around when we have a moral obligation to use every available moment to stall tomorrow's trouble.'

'I "fooled around" because I did not want three of Cambridge's four physicians to be out of action when we might need their services,' retorted Bartholomew tartly, thinking it was not the Sheriff's place to berate him. Then he relented, knowing Tulyet was apprehensive about the next day, too, and it was worry speaking. 'I have learned something new: Helia claims Neyll murdered Jolye.'

'Really?' Tulyet was interested. 'Then do you think he dispatched Gib, too? They often quarrelled over Helia – my men were called to quell fights between them at least three times.'

'It is possible. Neyll does seem to be a violent man.'

Tulyet rubbed his chin. 'Of course, that solution makes no sense. Even Neyll – no great intellect – must know that sticking a yellow wig on a colleague and shoving him off the Great Bridge is not a good idea. It basically says that Chestre Hostel is home to the killer-thief.'

'Neyll may have acted on Kendale's orders. I agree with you that Gib's murder *seems* to do Chestre no favours, but Kendale is complex and sly, and may well have devised a way to turn such a situation to his advantage. I cannot see how, but that means nothing.'

Tulyet groaned. 'Damn scholars and their love of intrigue! Has Michael arrested Neyll?'

'I imagine he will wait until after tomorrow's game. The

tension between the Colleges and hostels is too tight to do it before. Have *you* learned anything new?'

'Yes, actually. I have eliminated Celia and Heslarton as suspects for the killer-thief.'

'Really? How?'

'I have a trustworthy informant in Emma's household, and Heslarton was with him when Drax was murdered. And if Heslarton did not kill Drax, then he is innocent of the other crimes, too, given that Michael assures me we are looking for a single culprit.'

'And Celia?'

'Reliable witnesses say she was in Emma's home for the first part of the morning that Drax died, and in mine the second.' Tulyet grimaced. 'My wife saw fit to admit to me this morning that Celia came to complain about Dickon. She *claims* he has been spying on her, but of course it is nonsense.'

Bartholomew wondered why Tulyet should think so, when the Sheriff knew perfectly well that Dickon regularly spied on their other neighbours. Prudently, he kept his thoughts to himself.

'I hate to admit it, but Chestre has bested me,' said Tulyet, after a while. 'My engineers have been unable to manoeuvre that damned trebuchet out of the Guildhall, and your hostels will be laughing at me, knowing their ingenuity is greater than mine.'

Bartholomew stood. 'Would you like me to try?'

'What, now?' asked Tulyet, startled.

'Why not? It is not so late. Besides, Michael wants Cynric to break into Chestre tonight, to look for evidence that Gib's cronies are the killer-thief. I will not be able to sleep until he is safely back.'

Tulyet frowned. 'Is that a good idea? If a College servant is caught burgling a hostel . . .'

'That is what I said, but Cynric assures me that capture is not on his agenda.'

Tulyet's eyes gleamed. 'In that case, I have an excellent idea for a diversion.'

'You do?'

'The trebuchet. If you really can get it back to the castle, we shall make sure the Chestre boys know we have solved the problem they have created. They will come to watch, to see whether it is true. And while they do, Cynric can go about his business.'

Bartholomew and Tulyet met Michael on the High Street. The monk was with his beadles, prowling the town to make sure the hostels did not reply to Welfry's egg trick with something vengeful. But nothing was happening, and he was almost disappointed to report that the streets were quiet.

'They will not stay that way for long,' warned Tulyet. 'It is the calm before the storm.'

'I am at my wits' end, Dick,' said Michael worriedly. 'I can feel a catastrophe looming, but I am powerless to avert it.'

'Then let us hope Cynric finds evidence to prove the killer-thief is Kendale and his louts,' said Tulyet. 'Without its sponsor, the game will be cancelled, and it will not matter if half the town marches on Chestre and sets it ablaze, because it would have to be closed down, anyway.'

'Well, that is one way of solving the problem, I suppose,' said Michael, round eyed. 'Although I would prefer a solution that does *not* involve arson and large numbers of rioters.'

'It is better than the alternative,' said Tulyet shortly. 'Namely that we have battles on and off the playing field, as hostels and Colleges attack each other, and my town

332

joins in. And the Chestre men are certainly my first choice of suspects for the killer-thief, anyway.'

'They are not mine,' said Michael. 'I prefer Fen and his nuns. And I have not forgotten the fact that Yffi is conveniently missing, either. Or that Matt's medical colleagues are a sinister rabble, who might think a few *signacula* will make them better healers.'

'They are not—' began Bartholomew.

'Thelnetham has been acting oddly of late, too,' said Tulyet, overriding him. 'He is not the outrageously cheerful man he was a month ago, and I have come to distrust him intensely.'

'Nonsense!' declared Michael. 'Our College does not harbour killers.'

Bartholomew said nothing, but his mind ranged back to the past, when he had learned the bitter lesson that not everyone who enrolled at Michaelhouse was a good man.

They walked the rest of the way in silence. When they reached the Guildhall, Bartholomew studied the war machine for a long time, working out angles, distances and measurements in his mind. It did not take him long to understand why Tulyet's engineers had failed: the device needed to be dismantled in a specific order, or the pieces were never going to fit through the door. Tulyet soon grew impatient with him.

'How much longer are you going to stare at the damned thing?' he demanded. 'We need it disassembled now if we are to help Cynric, not next week.'

'I think I see how they did it,' said Bartholomew. 'Do you have six strong soldiers, who can help with the lifting?'

Tulyet nodded, then lowered his voice. 'But give me a few moments to make a fuss while I assemble them – we must ensure that Chestre hears what we intend to do, or

Cynric will find himself invading their domain while they are still in it.'

Bartholomew followed him outside, where a large number of people were walking home after Celia's celebration. Among them were Rougham, Gyseburne and Meryfeld, evidently having returned to the festivities after the incident in the garden. Meryfeld and Rougham were still reeling from the wine they had imbibed, but Gyseburne appeared to be sober. In fact, he seemed to have recovered so completely that Bartholomew wondered whether he had been drunk in the first place.

'The trebuchet will be gone tonight,' Tulyet was announcing in a ringing voice to a group of men from the Guild of Corpus Christi. 'Do not worry – you shall have your meeting in here tomorrow.'

A number of people stopped to listen, and Bartholomew was pleased when he saw Kendale and Neyll were among them. It would save adopting more creative measures to ensure they had heard.

'We will not convene before the game, though,' said one of the Guild. He was Burgess Frevill, a thickset, loutish fellow who was one of the killer-thief's victims. 'I am looking forward to that.'

'Are you?' asked Tulyet in distaste. 'Why? There may be violence and bloodshed.'

'Quite,' said Frevill gleefully. 'It will be great sport to see the University tear itself to pieces. And I may join in – I have heard a scholar is responsible for murdering Drax and stealing pilgrim badges – including the one I bought from the time I went to Hereford. I dislike a large number of those snivelling academics, and one might confess if I give him a taste of my fists.'

'I would not recommend taking matters into your own hands,' said Tulyet, his voice deceptively mild. 'I shall not be pleased if you make my task tomorrow any harder than it needs to be.'

Frevill backed away with his hands in the air: only fools crossed the Sheriff. But Bartholomew had a bad feeling that the burgess's words reflected the views of others, and suspected it would be a miracle if Kendale's game passed without incident. The Chestre men had heard the exchange, too, and exchanged smug grins at the notion that the Sheriff was anticipating serious trouble. Unable to look at them, Bartholomew went to speak to his medical colleagues.

'We might be wise to abandon our experiments,' he said, thinking he could at least put an end to one area of mischief. 'The Sheriff was unimpressed, and we do not want any more explosions.'

'As you wish,' said Meryfeld. He sounded pleased, and Bartholomew found himself wondering whether he planned to continue the tests on his own, so he would not be obliged to share any profits that might accrue from the invention. 'I have plenty of other business to occupy me.'

'What other business?' asked Gyseburne immediately.

'Nothing to concern you,' said Meryfeld, rubbing his hands together. 'And now I must bid you goodnight. Oh, dear! I seem to have walked rather a long way past my front door. You should not have distracted me, Gyseburne.'

'He is an odd fellow,' said Gyseburne, watching Meryfeld totter back the way he had come. 'But it is late and I am tired, so I shall bid you goodnight, too. Take care in your dealings this evening, Bartholomew. Whatever they might be.'

'That was a peculiar thing to say,' said Michael, narrowing his eyes as Gyseburne strode away, Rougham at his side.

'What did he mean by it? It sounded uncannily like a warning.'

Uneasily, Bartholomew was forced to admit that it did

He walked back inside the Guildhall, and went to work with Tulyet's engineers and a team of burly soldiers. The door was 'accidentally' left open, to encourage folk to stay and watch.

'All the Chestre men are among the crowd outside, and I am ready,' muttered Cynric in Bartholomew's ear, making him jump. He had not heard the book-bearer approach.

'Are you sure?' he asked. 'They have not left a guard? I would have done, if I were Kendale. They have attracted a lot of ill feeling.'

'It is all of their own making,' replied Cynric. He grinned. 'I am pleased to be invading them. It will serve them right for stealing our gates. Did I tell you I found them, by the way?'

Bartholomew gaped at him. 'No! Where were they?'

'Master Clippesby had a tip from a ferret, so I followed up on it and learned that Neyll and Gib were not as clever as they thought they were, because the riverfolk saw everything.'

'The riverfolk,' mused Bartholomew, thinking of the poverty-stricken men and women who inhabited the hovels by the waterside, and who never admitted to seeing or hearing anything; it was safer for them that way. They liked Cynric, though, because his sense of social justice often entailed purloining items from Michaelhouse's kitchen for distribution among those who were poorer still.

'Neyll was the ringleader,' Cynric went on. 'Kendale was not involved – it was too crude a trick for him. They hid the gates in the Carmelite Priory, under the rubble that

336

Yffi has excavated for the foundations of St Simon Stock's new shrine.'

'Why there?' asked Bartholomew. He had assumed they were at the bottom of the river and would be found in the summer when the water level dropped.

Cynric raised his hands in a shrug. 'A gate is an enormous thing, when you think about it – there are not many places you *can* hide them.'

'Did you tell Langelee?'

'Yes, as soon as I found them. They are being retrieved as I speak.'

Bartholomew was grateful that Michaelhouse would soon be secure again, but his relief did not last long. Now the time had come, he hated the notion of sending Cynric into the lair of what might be some very ruthless villains, and wished he had not suggested it. Cynric waved away his concerns, then slipped silently through the rear door, clearly relishing the opportunity to practise the kind of skills his master wished he did not have.

'Do not worry,' said Michael. 'He knows what he is doing.'

'I am sure he does,' said Bartholomew unhappily. 'But that is not the point.'

'But we *need* answers. Earlier, when you were blowing up Meryfeld's garden, Batayl Hostel marched on Bene't College, claiming they were going to avenge Gib. Gonville joined in, and the resulting altercation was the most difficult to quell yet.'

'What does that have to do with Cynric raiding Chestre?'

'The hostels cannot promote Gib as a martyr if we prove he and his cronies were involved in something untoward. In other words, without one of its figureheads, the trouble might simmer down into something manageable.'

'It will not,' said Bartholomew unhappily. 'The Colleges will still have Jolye to rally around.'

'But the hostels are unlikely to react to the challenge if their hero is discredited. Unless you have a better idea – in which case, please share it with me – this is our best chance of averting a crisis.'

It seemed to Bartholomew that Cynric was gone for an age, although they made rapid progress with the trebuchet. Once the throwing arm had been disengaged, the great machine was very quickly disassembled, and the soldiers began the laborious task of ferrying the pieces up Castle Hill. It was not long before the last section was being eased through the door, at which point the onlookers began to disperse. It was now very late, and most of the town had been asleep for hours.

'Dick! Say something to make Chestre stay,' hissed Bartholomew in alarm, seeing Kendale move towards home, students at his heels. 'Cynric is not back – they will catch him!'

'They will not fall for such a ploy,' said Michael, equally worried. 'The Sheriff is not in the habit of encouraging folk to stay out after the curfew, and Kendale will see through any attempt to make him do so. Worse, it may warn them that they should not have left in the first place, and then Cynric really will be in danger.'

'I am going there,' determined Bartholomew. Michael seized his arm. Bartholomew tried to disengage it, but the monk was a strong man, for all his lard, and the physician could no more break free from him than he could fly to the moon.

'You may do more harm than good,' snapped Michael. 'Just wait for—'

'There!' whispered Tulyet, pointing into the darkness. 'Here he comes.'

Bartholomew sagged in relief when the book-bearer

sidled into the Guildhall, his dark features alight with excitement and satisfaction. He was carrying a small chest, and Bartholomew did not think he had ever seen him look so pleased with himself.

'I have everything you want and more,' Cynric declared. 'It was hidden under Kendale's bed, which was almost the first place I looked. The man is a fool to store it in so obvious a location.'

Eagerly, Michael seized the box. It was an unattractive piece, carved – rather oddly – with illustrations of girdles, which Bartholomew assumed was a play on the Latin word for Chestre.

'I had to break the lock,' said Cynric. 'But I think you will agree it was worth it. Look inside.'

Michael obliged. It contained several letters, a *signaculum* and a packet containing powder. He shoved the box at Tulyet to hold, and began to read the letters.

'They are from Drax,' he said, scanning them quickly. 'Threatening legal action unless Chestre agrees to pay more rent. The tone is rude, confrontational and bullying, and I am not surprised Kendale took umbrage. I would have done, too.'

'This is Gyseburne's *signaculum*!' exclaimed Tulyet, snatching it up. 'He was proud of it, and once showed me how he had adapted the pin to make it stronger – he was worried about it falling off his cloak. It is his badge without question.'

'And I may be mistaken,' said Bartholomew soberly, having taken the packet and sniffed at its contents, 'but I believe this is wolfsbane.'

'The substance that dispatched Alice and almost killed Odelina?' asked Tulyet.

Bartholomew nodded.

Tulyet slapped his hand on the box. 'I knew it! Here is

ample evidence that Chestre is responsible for all the evils that have plagued our town ever since that yellow-headed villain raided Emma's home a week ago.'

Michael agreed. 'These letters explain why Chestre dispatched Drax, the wolfsbane tells us they poisoned Alice, and Gyseburne's *signaculum* tells us they are badge thieves, too. We have our answers at last. Now all we have to do is arrest them and try to think of a way to cancel the camp-ball without a riot.'

'Wait,' said Bartholomew urgently. 'I do not trust this – it is too neat. We could not have had better evidence had we put it under Kendale's bed ourselves.'

'What are you suggesting?' asked Tulyet, staring at him. 'That Cynric planted this box?'

'Now just a moment,' said Cynric, shocked and angry. 'I would never—'

'Of course not,' said Bartholomew. 'But we should take time to consider—'

'We do not *have* time,' snapped Michael. He brandished the box. 'This is all the evidence we need, and it is time to act on it. I will assemble my beadles. Are you coming, or will you go to the castle to make sure the trebuchet is not rebuilt back to front?'

'My engineers can manage now, thank you,' said Tulyet, a little stiffly. 'Do you want me to come to Chestre with you?'

Michael shook his head. 'Not unless we want the University screaming that the town was involved in raiding one of their foundations. That would precipitate trouble for certain.'

'Then send me word the moment you have a confession,' said Tulyet. He glanced up at the sky. 'I have no idea of the time, but I doubt I will be sleeping tonight. Frevill will not be the only townsman itching to bloody a few academic noses, especially once it becomes known that scholars really *are* behind all this mischief.'

'I thought catching Chestre would calm troubled waters,' said Cynric, crestfallen.

'It will – if we can present them as a rogue foundation acting without the support or blessing of the rest of the University,' said Michael. 'But it will take time for the rumours to take hold.'

'I shall help, by setting my soldiers to spread the tale now,' said Tulyet. 'They can pass it to anyone they happen to meet on their patrols.'

'I doubt they will encounter anyone of significance out and about at this hour,' said Michael.

'Then you do not know this town very well,' said Tulyet tartly. 'Excitement is running high about tomorrow, and even if folk are asleep now, they will rise early, so as not to miss anything. I anticipate Cambridge will be awake and waiting long before dawn.'

Bartholomew tried again to explain his misgivings to Michael, but the monk was too distracted to listen. He assembled his beadles, and led them and Cynric towards Chestre, issuing instructions, orders and contingency plans as he went. It was clear he expected the hostel to fight, and Bartholomew hoped this little army would be able to subdue Kendale before too much blood was spilled.

He followed them through the dark streets. It was bitterly cold, and a mist had rolled in from the Fens. It reeked of the marshes – of rotting vegetation, stagnant water and wet grass. It was a smell he had known all his life and it was as familiar as sunshine or April rain, but there was nothing comforting in it that night – it felt dangerous and wild, and so did the town. Shadows flitted, and he saw

341

Tulyet was right to say not everyone was sleeping peacefully in their beds.

'Thank God we have our gates back,' muttered Michael as they passed their College. Langelee and Ayera were setting them back in their posts. Both looked uneasy as the monk and his pack of beadles trotted past, and Langelee indicated that Ayera was to hurry. Michaelhouse was not the only foundation to be awake: lamps burned in nearby Physwick and Ovyng hostels, while Gonville Hall was positively ablaze with torches.

'Please, Brother,' said Bartholomew, trying again to voice his concerns, which mounted with every step he took. 'Something feels very wrong about Cynric's find.'

'*What* is wrong?' snapped Michael impatiently. 'It provides everything we need to arrest these villains.'

'Exactly,' pounced Bartholomew. 'And Kendale is not stupid. I seriously doubt he would keep such a neat collection of "evidence" under his bed. Cynric said it was virtually the first place he looked, and Kendale would have been more wary about where he left it.'

'This is nonsense,' said Michael with annoyance. 'Like me, you have suspected Kendale of killing Drax from the beginning, so do not look a gift horse in the mouth. Besides, I doubt he anticipated that we would burgle him, so he probably saw no reason to find a better hiding place for his box of treasures.'

Chestre loomed through the swirling fog, and Bartholomew saw several beadles cross themselves as they approached. The dampness had darkened its plaster, and the 'face' formed by its windows was lit by lanterns within. It seemed to be scowling.

'You were brave to go in there alone, Cynric,' said Beadle Meadowman, 'when everyone knows Kendale has invited a lot of evil spirits to live with him. *I* am not keen on entering, and I am with you and a dozen stalwart men. And Doctor Bartholomew, of course, who is on good terms with the Devil and will see off any demons who try to harm us.'

'Yes – we will be safe with him,' agreed Cynric comfortably, while Bartholomew supposed it was not the time to reiterate that he *had* no such understanding with Satan. He saw other beadles nod their appreciation of the protection they thought he afforded, and wondered whether he would ever slough off the sinister reputation he had acquired.

Michael hammered on Chestre's door, and every beadle crossed himself a second time when the sound boomed hollowly and eerily along the hallway within. Bartholomew was tempted to do likewise, because it was certainly unsettling, especially in his unhappy and agitated state. He leapt in alarm when there was a sudden hissing sound and something dark whipped past his face. It looked like a huge bat, all jagged wings and pointed claws, which swooped for a moment, then fluttered into the shadows on the opposite side of the lane.

'Demons!' hissed Cynric, and several beadles yelped their fright. 'Come to inspect us.'

But Bartholomew saw a flash of movement at an upper window, and heard a muted snigger. He walked to where the thing had landed.

'Parchment,' he said, picking it up. 'Cut into a sinister shape, and propelled by some kind of membrane that holds air under pressure.'

'A trick,' said Michael in disgust. 'Something that might impress children, but that has no impact on my bold beadles. It will take more than a hoax to unsettle *their* brave hearts.'

His words had the desired effect, and his men stood a

little taller. He pounded on the door again, and eventually it was opened by Neyll, who did not seem at all surprised that the Senior Proctor and a sizeable retinue should be calling at such an hour. Bartholomew suspected he was one of those who had released the parchment spectre, in the hope that it would send them scurrying for their lives.

'What do you want?' Neyll demanded coldly. 'We are all in bed.'

'With torches burning?' asked Michael archly. 'And within moments of watching the Sheriff manhandle his trebuchet back to the castle? I do not think so!'

'The Colleges had to help Tulyet in the end,' sneered Neyll, not bothering to deny the charge. 'He is stupid! But even then, it took them days to manage what the hostels achieved in hours.'

'On the contrary,' said Michael haughtily. 'Once we had been invited to participate, the problem was solved in moments, not hours. But we are not here to discuss foolery. We have come on a far more serious matter, namely murder. Stand aside and let us enter.'

When Michael, with Bartholomew, Cynric and the beadles at his heels, marched into Chestre's hall, Kendale was sitting in a comfortable chair by the hearth. All his students were with him, every one of them holding a goblet. The place reeked of wine.

'We are discussing tomorrow's camp-ball,' Kendale said. Then his eyes widened when he saw the number of beadles who were crowding into his lair. 'What in God's name—'

'There will be no game,' interrupted Michael briskly. 'Because you will be in my prison. You have committed theft and murder, and I have evidence to prove it.'

'What are you talking about?' demanded Kendale, coming quickly to his feet. 'We have not killed anyone.

344

And we have not stolen anything, either. At least, nothing of significance. My lads have just confessed to me that they were responsible for borrowing your gates, but you have them back now, and it was only a joke. You cannot arrest us for a joke.'

'We did it without his knowledge,' added Neyll defiantly. 'So you cannot detain *him*, because he had nothing to do with the escapade.'

'I am furious about it,' said Kendale. 'It was a stupid prank, one unworthy of our talents.'

'Never mind the gates,' said Michael briskly. 'I refer to evidence that says you stabbed Drax and left his corpse in Michaelhouse, that you put poison in wine that dispatched Alice Heslarton, and that you have been stealing *signacula*. You doubtless murdered Gib, too.'

Kendale was suddenly pale. 'But you cannot have evidence, Brother, because there is none to find! We are innocent of these charges. Why would we kill Gib? He was one of us.'

Michael showed him the box. 'Here are letters, poison and a stolen *signaculum*. All were found under your bed earlier tonight, so do not deny that they are yours.'

'But I *do* deny it!' cried Kendale, shocked. 'I have never seen that chest before! And do you really think I would own something so wretched? Not only is it poorly made, but I do not go in for rudimentary puns on the Latin word for Chestre. I have more taste.'

'The letters are addressed to you,' said Michael, waving them at him. 'They are from Drax, and comprise several demands for more rent.'

'But Drax never sent letters – he was illiterate. He only ever asked for more rent verbally.'

'Then what about the poison?' demanded Michael. 'There can be no excuse for *that* being here.'

'This is outrageous and ridiculous!' shouted Kendale. 'We have no reason to harm anyone in the de Colvyll household. And may I remind you, we were *not* angry about the scholarship Emma declined to fund, because we had already decided not to accept it. We did not want to be in the debt of such a family – we have our principles. Unlike some foundations, it would seem.'

'And the badge?' asked Michael, ignoring the dig. 'How do you explain that?'

'Clearly, it was left here in a clumsy attempt to implicate us in crimes we did not commit,' said Neyll hotly, saying much what Bartholomew had already reasoned. 'Someone wants us hanged.'

'Moreover, it is only one badge,' added Kendale, coming to peer at it. '*One*. And do you know why? Because the culprit was reluctant to waste more than that in his effort to frame us. If you do not believe me, then search the place. You will not find any more.'

'It is a valid point,' said Bartholomew, when Michael looked set to argue. He lowered his voice, so Kendale would not hear. 'I tried to tell you – the choice of evidence in that box is so contrived that it screams foul play. You will not find the other badges here. Kendale is telling the truth.'

Michael nodded to his beadles, who began a systematic hunt, both in the hall and in the bedchambers above. The Chestre men gritted their teeth at the indignity of it all, and Bartholomew could tell that Neyll in particular was finding it difficult to restrain himself. Sure enough, it was not long before the beadles returned empty handed.

'There is a broken window in the scullery,' said Cynric, the last to finish. 'The one with the red shutters. When did that happen?'

'We noticed it when we came back from the Guildhall,'

replied Neyll. Then understanding dawned. 'Obviously, whoever left this so-called evidence broke in that way!'

'It was not me,' muttered Cynric to Michael, speaking too softly for his victims to hear. 'I gained entry through one of the bedrooms.'

'What about the cellar?' asked Meadowman, who had been more assiduous than his colleagues, and had even checked up the chimneys and assessed the floorboards for hidden cavities. He disliked the Chestre men, and hated the notion that they might go free.

'We use it for storing old crates and wine,' said Kendale coldly. 'But please explore it. I do not want you coming back later with more nasty accusations. You will prove us innocent *now*.'

Meadowman took him at his word, so Bartholomew and Cynric went to help. Neyll and a lean, red-haired student named Ihon followed, to monitor the proceedings.

'Much as it pains me to admit it, I think you are right,' Cynric whispered to Bartholomew. 'I was so pleased when I found that box that I did not stop to consider. But Kendale is devious, and would *not* have left a chest containing those things for any burglar to find. And that broken window says I was not the only one who slipped in uninvited tonight.'

'We made a serious mistake in coming here,' said Bartholomew worriedly. 'Now Chestre will feel justified in whipping up the antagonism between hostels and Colleges with even more fervour.'

Knowing there was nothing to find did not encourage Bartholomew to poke through the contents of Chestre's dismal basement. He sat on a barrel and watched Cynric and Meadowman work, feeling weariness wash over him. He had been tired *before* he had stayed up all night fiddling with trebuchets, and wondered whether he had the energy

347

for yet another day of turmoil. Dawn could not be far off, and he doubted he would manage to snatch even a short nap that night.

Suddenly, Cynric released a yelp of shock, and backed away from the chest he had been exploring.

'It is Yffi!' he exclaimed in horror. 'And he is stone-cold dead!'

CHAPTER 11

Meadowman, Neyll and Ihon dashed forward to see what Cynric had found. Ihon jerked away in revulsion, although Neyll was made of sterner stuff, and poked Yffi with his finger. Meadowman took one look, then shot up the stairs to fetch Michael.

'I understand your plan now, College man,' snarled Neyll, regarding Bartholomew with utter loathing. 'You *planted* that ugly little box, so the Senior Proctor would come. And then you offered to search our cellars knowing exactly what would be found, because *you* put this corpse here, too. It is Michaelhouse's revenge for the gates!'

'We do not tamper with corpses, boy,' said Cynric reproachfully. 'Especially in a place like this, where demons lurk. It would be too dangerous.'

Bartholomew tried to rally his befuddled wits. 'Are you saying you did not murder Yffi?'

'Of course we did not!' snapped Ihon. 'We are the victims of a monstrous plot, and we were fools to think we could study here safely. We should leave while we can. Now.'

'But if we do – especially today, when the camp-ball is on – they will think we are guilty for sure,' said Neyll angrily. 'They will say we arranged the game as a diversion, to let us escape.'

There was a clatter of footsteps on the stairs, and Michael arrived, followed by Kendale and his students, with the beadles bringing up the rear. It was a tight squeeze in such a small chamber. Bartholomew watched the Chestre men peer into the crate one by one, only to recoil with shock, revulsion or horror when they saw what lay within. He was as sure as he could be that none of them had known what was there, not even Kendale.

'Well?' asked Michael, folding his arms. 'I think *this* warrants an explanation.'

'Michaelhouse put him here,' shouted Neyll. 'Who else could it have been?'

But Kendale shook his head. 'The Michaelhouse men are villains to a man, but I do not see them playing pranks with corpses. Even Langelee would not stoop that low.'

'Well, if not Michaelhouse, then another of our enemies,' yelled Neyll, as Bartholomew and Cynric lifted the mason from the chest and laid him on the floor. 'Emma de Colvyll—'

'Emma?' interrupted Kendale. 'But she provided us with the wine that you have been downing so merrily. *She* means us no harm.'

Bartholomew listened to the ensuing discussion while he inspected Yffi. The cause of death was obvious: the mason had been stabbed. He began to look for other clues as to what had happened – ones that would either exonerate Chestre, or prove once and for all that they were killers.

'Why should she be generous to us?' persisted Neyll, tears of impotent rage in his eyes. 'We have nothing she wants. And she does not like us, or she would have funded that scholarship.'

'Why must you always be so suspicious?' sighed Ihon. 'Some folk *are* decent, and *do* mean us well. When we first arrived, Michaelhouse tried to make friends, but your surliness drove them off. I wish we had not let it, because we might have been living in peace now if—'

'Peace?' howled Neyll, livid. 'I do not want peace with

a College! And I was right to be wary, because look where we are now – on the brink of being charged with crimes we did not commit.'

'I abhor the Colleges too,' interjected Kendale, raising his hand to quell the debate. 'And you were right to reject Michaelhouse's sly advances, Neyll. However, you are wrong about Emma, because we have something she wants very much. Namely our collection of hunting trophies.'

'Hunting trophies?' blurted Bartholomew, startled.

'She thinks they will look nice in her solar, and wants to buy them,' explained Ihon.

'So she gave us claret, in an effort to convince us to sell,' said Kendale. He turned to the rest of the students. 'Who else means us harm? And do not recite a list of the Colleges, because that will not convince the Senior Proctor. I want names and believable motives. *Think*, because our lives depend on your answers.'

'Clearly, the *real* thief is the culprit,' said Ihon, after a moment during which the cellar was totally silent. 'The man responsible for killing Drax, Alice and Gib, and stealing all those pilgrim badges. One of the missing *signacula* was in the "evidence" box, so—'

'That much is obvious,' snapped Kendale. 'But *who* is it? Why does he bear us so much malice? I heard a rumour that it is a scholar, but which of the Colleges is home to such a ruthless villain?'

While they debated, Michael crouched next to Bartholomew, eyebrows raised questioningly.

'Yffi was killed by a single wound to the chest,' the physician replied. 'The shape of the injury is indicative of a knife, rather than a dagger, but that does not help – every man, woman and child in Cambridge owns a knife.'

'Is there nothing else?' asked Michael, disappointed.

Bartholomew nodded, then pointed to several places

where Yffi's clothes were torn. There was also a deep abrasion on his stomach, where pieces of wood had embedded themselves in the skin.

'This did not bleed much,' he said. 'Which indicates it happened after he died.'

'You mean when he was stuffed in the crate?'

Bartholomew shook his head. 'You can see for yourself that there are no jagged edges on it. However, if you look closely at the wound, you will detect flecks of red. And Cynric said the broken window in Chestre's scullery was red.'

Michael stared at him. 'In other words, Yffi was killed elsewhere, and his body was brought into Chestre via a window?'

'The evidence seems to point that way. But the Chestre men would have no reason to manhandle Yffi through a window – they would use a door. *Ergo*, I think they are telling the truth. Someone *has* left a body in their domain in the hope that they will be accused of murder. It is not the first time someone has done it – Drax was left in Michaelhouse, do not forget.'

There was a sudden clatter of footsteps on the stairs, and one of Tulyet's soldiers arrived.

'Trouble, Brother,' he called. 'Bene't College is marching on Batayl. And Maud's, Ovyng and Cosyn's hostels are empty. We think they are planning a joint assault on King's Hall.'

'You see what you have done?' Michael rounded on Kendale. 'All this unrest is *your* doing – the rivalry between hostels and Colleges was never so bitter until *you* came along.'

'Oh, yes, it was,' snapped Kendale. 'Only you, being from a College, never paid heed to it. I am right to encourage the hostels to stand up for themselves. It is

352

grossly unfair that the Colleges should wallow in riches while the hostels are poor, and it is high time the inequity was removed.'

'Michaelhouse is not wealthy,' said Bartholomew quietly. 'Sometimes, there is barely enough to eat, and we have debts. Why do you think Langelee accepted Emma's charity? Because we are desperate. *We* could never afford wine and ale for the whole town after a camp-ball game.'

Kendale stared at him. 'Well, that is not how it appears.'

'We prefer people not to know,' said Michael stiffly, shooting Bartholomew an angry glance for his indiscretion. 'But enough of this. I want you to cancel the camp-ball game, and—'

'No,' said Kendale. 'I could not, even if I wanted to. The town is expecting entertainment and free refreshments, and will attack the University if we renege. And even if *they* managed to restrain themselves, the Colleges would attack the hostels for breach of promise. Calling off the game is not the way to avert trouble. Not now.'

'He is right,' said Bartholomew. 'Your best hope for peace is a short game, and enough food and drink to appease all the would-be rioters.'

'I shall see what can be done about both,' offered Kendale. 'But only if you acknowledge our innocence of these crimes. It is obvious that someone is trying to frame us.'

The soldier coughed meaningfully – there was no time to debate the matter. Reluctantly, Michael nodded, and his capitulation was greeted by a chorus of triumphant jeers from the Chestre students. The heckling continued until he was outside. The moment the door closed behind him, there was a clink of jugs on goblets and a rousing cheer: Kendale and his lads were going to celebrate their deliverance from what had initially appeared to be a hopeless situation.

Michael glowered at the building with its lopsided leer, while Bartholomew leaned against a wall and wished he had been more forceful in voicing his reservations earlier, because it was not going to be easy living with Kendale's righteous indignation.

'I hate them,' muttered Meadowman venomously. 'And I do not think they are innocent, no matter how clever they were with their logic and their explanations.'

'There you are, Doctor,' shouted Valence, flushed and breathless. 'I have been looking for you everywhere. Emma de Colvyll has fallen into a terrible fever, and you are needed to cure her.'

'She is Meryfeld's—' began Bartholomew.

'He has been dismissed,' said Valence. 'They want you, because they fear she is dying.'

Bartholomew ordered Valence back to Michaelhouse, unwilling for his student to be out when the town felt so uneasy. The lad was reluctant to be deprived of excitement, but did as he was told.

'Stay with Michael, Cynric,' said Bartholomew, aiming for the High Street. 'He will need you.'

'So might you,' argued Cynric. He glanced up at the sky, which was beginning to lighten almost imperceptibly. 'It will be dawn soon, and I do not like what the day promises.'

Neither did Bartholomew. 'We are back to the beginning as regards suspects,' he said in frustration, breath coming in short gasps as he ran. 'We have been up all night, but have gained nothing – and I doubt Kendale's measures will see the game pass off peacefully.'

'They might help,' said Cynric, although with scant conviction. 'I was certain *he* was the villain, but now I am not even sure the culprit is a scholar, as we have been led to believe these last few days.'

354

He hauled the physician into a doorway when a gaggle of lads from Ovyng Hostel appeared. Bartholomew did not think they would harm him, given that he was their physician, but he was wearing a tabard that said he was from Michaelhouse, and there was a risk they might punch first and ask for names second. Nevertheless, he fretted at the moments that ticked away as Ovyng sauntered past – moments that might mean the difference between life and death for Emma.

'The only evidence that the villain is a scholar comes from the fact that your sister's token was stolen during an event that comprised mainly members of the University,' whispered Cynric. He sensed his master's agitation and was keen to take his mind off it, lest he decided to bolt before it was safe. Bartholomew tended to be single minded when it came to his patients' welfare.

'An event at the Gilbertine Priory,' said Bartholomew, trying to concentrate on what Cynric was saying. 'But the canons' guests included all the Carmelites, the Chestre men, my medical colleagues, Ayera, Emma and the pilgrims. With that many people, it would have been easy to don a disguise and walk about unnoticed.'

'In other words, the culprit might be anyone,' said Cynric, nodding to indicate they should begin running again. 'He might even be someone we have never met – a visitor to St Simon Stock's shrine, who considers our town fair game for his villainy.'

'No, he must be a local,' argued Bartholomew. 'A stranger would have no reason to poison Emma's wine – or put Drax's body in Michaelhouse.'

When they reached Emma's house, it was mostly in darkness, in stark contrast to the other High Street homes, which were brightly lit. Some residents, anticipating trouble, had boarded up their windows and barricaded their doors, but Emma had taken no such precautions. Bartholomew wondered why, when she was by far the most unpopular person in the town, and so most likely to be targeted for mischief. Was it because she thought no one would dare? He rubbed his head, simply too tired to think about it.

'We should go around the back,' said Cynric, setting off in that direction. 'Banging on the front door will wake the entire household, and I would sooner Heslarton stayed in bed.'

'Why?' asked Bartholomew, trotting after him. 'You do not like him? He is not our killer-thief, because he has an alibi for Drax's murder – one that has satisfied the Sheriff.'

'I like him well enough,' replied Cynric. 'He is a soldier, like me – honest and uncomplicated. But he is protective of his mother-in-law, and you will find it easier to work when he is not there.'

Bartholomew was not sure he would have described Heslarton – or Cynric, for that matter – as honest and uncomplicated. He reached the back gate, and stepped through it.

He was surprised to find the yard busy, with horses saddled and a cart loaded with chests and furniture. A number of servants moved around them, although none spoke. One stumbled in the gloom, and he wondered why they did not light torches, because Emma could certainly afford them. Cynric jerked him roughly into the shadows.

'What are you doing?' Bartholomew demanded, freeing himself irritably. 'There is no need to—'

'None of Emma's family have mentioned a journey,' hissed Cynric urgently. 'So why are they loading up so softly and secretly – and in the dark? Moreover, all the servants seem to be up, so why are there no lamps lit in the house?'

356

'Perhaps they do not want to disturb Emma,' replied Bartholomew impatiently. 'Her fever—'

'No,' whispered Cynric, doggedly determined. 'It is something more. We should leave.'

'I cannot leave,' objected Bartholomew, pulling away from him and beginning to walk towards the rear of the house. 'The pus from Emma's rotting tooth has finally . . .'

He faltered when someone materialised in front of him, carrying a lantern. It was Heslarton, but what caught Bartholomew's attention was the garment he wore. The lamplight showed it to be dark red, and the last time he had seen it was on Edith, when she had donned it for Drax's funeral. Later, it had been stolen from the Gilbertines' chapel, and her *signaculum* with it.

He gazed in shock, as clues and fragments of evidence collided together to form answers at last. Heslarton stared back, then moved fast, and Bartholomew felt himself grabbed by the throat. He struggled hard, dimly aware of Cynric racing to his assistance.

But they were in a yard filled with Heslarton's retainers, and it was not many moments before they were overpowered. He opened his mouth to shout, knowing that Michael's beadles and Tulyet's soldiers were out in force – they would hear him if he yelled loudly enough – but there was a sharp, searing pain in his head, and then nothing.

When Bartholomew's senses began to return, he found himself lying on a cold stone floor with Cynric hovering anxiously over him.

'Thank God!' muttered the book-bearer shakily, as Bartholomew opened his eyes. He crossed himself, then clutched one of his amulets. 'I thought they had killed you.'

Bartholomew's vision swirled as he sat up, and he gripped his head with both hands, seized with the illogical conviction that it might split in half if he let it go. It ached viciously, and he felt sick. He explored it tentatively, and discovered a lump at the back, where it had been struck.

'Where are we?' he asked.

'Locked in Heslarton's stable,' replied Cynric. 'It is just past dawn, and I have been trying to wake you for hours.'

'Not hours,' corrected Bartholomew. 'It was already growing light when we were summoned.'

But Cynric was not interested in listening to reason. 'I told you something odd was going on here,' he said accusingly. 'You should have listened.'

'Yes,' said Bartholomew tiredly. 'I am sorry, Cynric. You were right.'

'What made you start fighting Heslarton in the first place?' asked Cynric. He sounded exasperated. 'You should have controlled yourself, because to attack a man who was surrounded by his retainers . . . well, it was reckless, boy.'

'I did not attack him.' Recollections came in blinding flashes. 'He was wearing Edith's cloak. I should have pretended not to notice, but it took me by surprise. And he knew exactly what conclusions I had drawn from it.'

'That he was the one who stole it? And if he took that, then he must be guilty of all the other crimes, too, including murder?' Cynric swallowed hard. 'So we are being held captive by a killer.'

'But he *cannot* be the villain, because he has an alibi for Drax's death.' Bartholomew's head ached more when he tried to think. 'I do not understand.'

'Oh, it is simple enough,' said Cynric bitterly. 'The villain is Emma. *She* poisoned her own daughter, and murdered Drax, Gib and Yffi. She probably told Heslarton to kill Poynton on the camp-ball field, too. *And* she is behind the theft of the pilgrim badges. She only pretended to be a victim of the yellow-headed thief, and she has been the real culprit all along.'

'She is an old lady,' objected Bartholomew. He recalled why he had been going to see her in the first place. 'With a fever.'

'She did not have a fever until today,' said Cynric. 'Besides, she is quite capable of sending others to do her dirty work. Heslarton may not have killed Drax, but she has a whole house full of retainers at her beck and call, and some of them are fearsome louts.'

Bartholomew started to object further, but the words died in his throat. Emma certainly possessed the resources to stage such an elaborate deception. She was already wealthy, but that did not mean she would overlook an opportunity to become more so, and some of the pilgrim badges were very valuable. Moreover, she was devious and ruthless enough for such a venture, sitting in her solar like some vile black spider, dispatching minions to do her bidding.

Yet that did not make sense.

'Why did she summon me, then?' he asked. 'She would not have wanted us anywhere near her, if she is this cunning mastermind.'

'I told you – she only started her fever today,' said Cynric. 'If we had gone to the front of the house, like you wanted, you would have cured her, and we would be safe at home by now. But we went to the back, where her servants are arranging for her to flee with her ill-gotten gains. This is as much my fault as yours.'

'But *why* would she be fleeing?' asked Bartholomew, wondering whether it was exhaustion or concussion that had turned his wits to mud. All he wanted was to lie down and sleep. 'No one has the slightest inkling that she is behind all this chaos, so she has no need to abandon the empire she has so painstakingly assembled.'

'Because Brother Michael is on her trail,' said Cynric with a shrug. 'He always catches his villains, and she knows it. She is leaving while she is still able.'

'You may be right,' acknowledged Bartholomew. 'On our way here, we decided the culprit had to be someone local, rather than a stranger, because there had to be reasons for poisoning Alice and dumping Drax in Michaelhouse. Emma's motive for killing Alice is obvious: they did not like each other—'

'And she dumped Drax in Michaelhouse to discredit us, so she would not have to finish paying for our roof,' finished Cynric, although Bartholomew was unconvinced by that argument.

'Moreover, a stranger would not have known there were pilgrim tokens in her stolen box – he would have opted for a jewelled candlestick or a gold goblet.' Bartholomew rubbed his head, wishing it would stop aching. 'Or is that a reason to assume she is *not* the villain? I cannot think properly . . .'

The door opened suddenly. Cynric rose to his feet fast, but the two men standing there had bows and arrows at the ready, and indicated he was to sit back down again.

'Very good,' said Heslarton, entering behind them. 'You have guessed a lot, although you are still a long way short of the whole story. I was hoping to spare you – you did save Odelina, after all – but I am afraid that is impossible now. You are simply too dangerous.'

Heslarton leaned against the wall, and regarded his captives impassively. Behind him, the two men with bows stood alert and ready, arrows nocked. Bartholomew glanced at Cynric and hoped he would not attempt anything rash, because he could tell by the way the men stood that they would not hesitate to shoot. Fortunately, Cynric knew it too, and crouched motionless to one side.

'I have no idea why you should want Kendale and his students blamed for the crimes you committed,' said Bartholomew, struggling to make sense of what was happening. 'But you will not get away with it.'

'No?' asked Heslarton softly. 'We shall see about that.'

'Why kill Yffi?' asked Bartholomew. 'What did he—'

'He tried to blackmail me,' replied Heslarton tersely. 'Over Poynton.'

'Poynton?' asked Bartholomew. Details slithered together in his mind. 'It was *your* dagger that killed him during the camp-ball game? And Yffi knew?'

'It was an accident. But Yffi said he would claim it was deliberate, unless I paid him.'

'So you stabbed him, then decided to put the body to good use – by leaving it in Chestre.'

Heslarton shrugged. 'Why not? I have never liked those swaggering louts.'

'What about us?' demanded Cynric, before Bartholomew could remark that dislike was hardly a reason to devise such a hideous plot. 'Will you have our murders blamed on Chestre, too?'

'Yes,' said Heslarton. There was no trace of the amiable rogue now; all that was left was the ruffian. His eyes did not twinkle, and his compact strength was intimidating. 'I understand they convinced Michael that they are innocent, but your bodies should make him think again.'

'It will not work,' warned Bartholomew. 'You left clues on Yffi that allowed Michael to deduce that the corpse had been dragged through a window, and you will make similar mistakes when—'

'We have another plan – one involving Edmund House,

361

which we are about to sell to the Gilbertines. And this time, there will be no misunderstandings.' Heslarton gestured to the archers. 'Clean shots, please. We do not want a mess.'

'Why are you selling it?' asked Cynric quickly, a feeble attempt to delay the inevitable.

'Because he no longer needs it to frolic in with Celia,' said Bartholomew, speaking before Heslarton could answer for himself. He recalled the shadow he had seen there when he had tended Brother Jude's gashed leg some days before; doubtless, they had been there then. 'Now Alice and Drax are dead, they do not require a secret place for their trysts. *That* is why the family have always refused to part with it before.'

Heslarton wrinkled his nose. 'As I said, you know too much.' He nodded to the bowmen.

'Wait!' Bartholomew struggled to his feet. 'Let Cynric go. He has nothing to do with this.'

'I cannot.' Heslarton sounded genuinely apologetic, and Bartholomew saw he was uneasy with the situation in which he found himself. 'He represents too great a danger. I am sorry – I would have spared you both if I could.'

'Yes, you *will* be sorry,' agreed Cynric venomously, as the bowmen took aim. 'Because Doctor Bartholomew is the only one who can save your mother-in-law from an agonising death.'

Heslarton raised his hand to prevent the archers from shooting. 'What?'

'None of the other physicians know how to cure her,' Cynric went on. 'I heard them talking about it last night. Emma will die of her fever if she is left to them.'

'She will not,' said Heslarton, although he looked uneasy. 'It is only a bad tooth, for God's sake.'

'It has been left too long, and has poisoned her blood,'

362

stated Cynric with great conviction. 'She needs a surgeon to pull it out. And Meryfeld, Rougham and Gyseburne do not perform cautery. You know this – it is why you summoned Doctor Bartholomew this morning, not them.'

Heslarton was silent for a moment, and when he did speak, it was more to himself than his captives. 'I do not see how this can be safely achieved now.'

Bartholomew frowned. It was an odd thing to say. He watched Heslarton go over to mutter to one of his men; the other kept his bow trained unwaveringly on the prisoners. The archer left after a moment, and Heslarton came back. Bartholomew could only suppose the fellow had been sent for reinforcements. Gradually, more answers drifted into his mind.

'Emma has no idea what you have done, does she?' he said challengingly. 'And you are afraid that if you take us to help her, we will tell her that her beloved son-in-law is nothing but a killer and a thief. Your curious words – "I do not see how this can be safely achieved now" – mean you do not see how we can save her without your role being exposed.'

'I have an alibi for Drax's murder,' snapped Heslarton. 'One the Sheriff himself acknowledges. And I have one for Gib's death, too, because I was with Celia. So, if I am innocent of those two crimes, then I am innocent of the pilgrim-badge thefts, too. You have nothing on me!'

Other than the fact that he was wearing Edith's stolen cloak, thought Bartholomew, trying not to stare at it.

'And your wife?' demanded Cynric. 'Can you prove you did not kill Alice, too?'

'Why should I kill her? I did not want her dead, and I certainly would not have done anything to put my daughter at risk.'

'No,' agreed Bartholomew, able to put the facts together

363

at last. 'Odelina is responsible for what happened to Alice. She loves you and Celia, but she did not care for her mother. She committed murder, so you and Celia might marry.'

Heslarton regarded him contemptuously. 'If that were the case, she would not have swallowed the poison herself. She nearly died.'

'She read the pharmacopoeia in Celia's house, which is full of silly advice. One example is that wolfsbane can be counteracted with a hefty dose of milk. She followed the instruction – I saw a jug of it next to the wine – but there is no truth in the claim, and she became ill, too.'

'You do not know what you are talking about,' snapped Heslarton. 'She would never—'

'Odelina had to drink the wine, because it would have looked suspicious if Alice had died, but she had conveniently abstained. Then, terrified because her "antidote" was not working, she crawled under the bed. She was lucky we found her.'

Heslarton shook his head in disgust. 'You should be ashamed of yourself, spinning such vile tales about an innocent young woman who thinks the world of you.'

'She killed Drax first, though,' Bartholomew went on. 'He and Celia argued a lot, and Odelina is nothing if not loyal to her friends. She decided Celia would be happier without him.'

'She is a girl,' argued Heslarton. 'Girls do not kill. Besides, she says she did *not* harm Drax, although I admit to helping her move his body to Michaelhouse after she happened across it.'

'Why there?' asked Bartholomew, sensing he was on dangerous ground by mentioning Odelina's involvement, so changing the focus of the discussion.

'Because she wanted the Chestre men blamed. And they

probably were the culprits, anyway – they *did* quarrel with him the morning he was dispatched. I did not think we would manage it unseen, but Physwick Hostel went out mid-afternoon, and Yffi unwittingly provided a perfect distraction with a ribald discussion about Yolande de Blaston.'

'You sold Drax a pilgrim badge,' said Bartholomew, deciding there was no point in protesting Chestre's innocence. 'It was—'

'He was driving Celia insane by harping on about getting one, so I obliged him, to give her some peace. We made the transaction outside the Gilbertine Priory, although I think we were seen – your cronies Clippesby and Thelnetham were both nearby that night. And I denied it when you asked because it was none of your damned business.'

'But then you wanted it back,' said Bartholomew. 'His hat was ripped—'

'How many more times must I tell you?' snarled Heslarton. 'I did *not* kill Drax, and neither did my daughter. If his badge was stolen, then it had nothing to do with us.'

'Dickon Tulyet saw you and Odelina slip out of Celia's house the night Gib was murdered,' lied Cynric, not seeming to care that there was now a dangerous light in Heslarton's eyes. Bartholomew hoped Heslarton would not kill the boy for the book-bearer's fabrications – or him and Cynric for reintroducing Odelina into the conversation. 'Did Odelina order you to murder Gib, and tie a yellow wig on him? As another nail in Chestre's coffin?'

'She did not—' began Heslarton uncomfortably.

'Obviously, she could not overpower Gib, and toss him over the Great Bridge by herself,' Cynric went on, ignoring Bartholomew's warning glance that he was pushing

Heslarton too far. 'But you were there, ready to help with the dirty work.'

Heslarton's expression was hard and cold. 'I did what was necessary to protect my daughter. Like any loving father.'

'So *she* is the yellow-headed thief,' said Cynric with bitter satisfaction. Bartholomew closed his eyes, having reasoned the same, but dismayed that Cynric should share such a conclusion with her fiercely devoted father. 'And you helped her kill Gib, so everyone would stop looking.'

'No!' declared Heslarton. 'She would never . . . she is not . . .'

'Your guilt was obvious when you failed to go out scouring the Fens for the thief the day Gib was found.' Cynric pressed on relentlessly. 'You knew there was no point, because you learned the previous night that your beloved Odelina was the culprit. You doubtless told Emma to say Gib was definitely the yellow-haired invader, too.'

'Odelina is *not* a thief,' cried Heslarton. 'She wanted Gib blamed in order to protect another . . .'

Cynric waved a dismissive hand. 'The next day, she was careful to remind everyone that Gib knew his way around your house – that he had acted as Kendale's messenger when Emma was thinking of funding a scholarship, so would know where to look for valuables. She was very clever.'

'I was right,' said Heslarton coldly. 'You know far too much. I am sorry for Emma – I would take the risk to save her if it was just me you were accusing. But I will not let you harm Odelina.'

'Do not worry, Father.' Bartholomew looked up to see Odelina standing at the door. 'Grandmother is too ill to listen to their stories now. Doctor Bartholomew can save her without the slightest risk to ourselves. And if he fails, we will kill him *and* his servant.'

* * *

366

The prisoners were shoved out of the stable and into the yard. Bartholomew was not sure he was capable of surgery – even the comparatively straightforward business of removing a tooth – because his vision was blurred, his legs were unsteady and his hands shook. It would be irresponsible of him to attempt it, and he told Odelina so.

'You will, or your book-bearer will die,' she said coldly. She leaned close to him and lowered her voice, so her father would not hear. 'And if you try to say one word to my grandmother about what you have surmised, I will kill you where you stand.'

'Odelina,' said Bartholomew softly, hoping to appeal to the dreamy girl who had harboured a fancy for him. 'You must see that what you are doing is wrong.'

Odelina pulled a disagreeable face. 'Celia told me I was stupid to see you as one of my heroes, and I should have listened. She said you cast a spell on me, to make me adore you, but you did not love me back. Well, I am wiser now. Your gentle manners will not beguile me again.'

'I accept your anger with me,' said Bartholomew. 'But Cynric—'

'You will both be released as soon as my grandmother is well,' snapped Odelina. 'So you can stop your begging. I do not want to hear it.'

'Do not trust her,' said Cynric. 'The moment you fulfil your end of the bargain, she will—'

'I will certainly kill you if you annoy me,' blazed Odelina, whipping around to glare at him. 'But Isnard has a barge leaving for France tomorrow, and I will arrange for you both to be locked in its hold. You will be released – unharmed – when it reaches the coast. By the time you return, we will be gone.'

'How do you know the schedules of Isnard's barges?'

asked Bartholomew, rubbing his aching head. He knew he was off on a tangent, but he could not help it.

'The answer to that is obvious, boy,' said Cynric, regarding Odelina with dislike. 'Bargemen are not usually wealthy, but Isnard can afford Yolande de Blaston, the town's most expensive prostitute. Obviously, he supplements his income by sending illegal cargos through the Fens.'

'What illegal cargos?' asked Bartholomew dully.

'Good-quality tiles, window frames and timber,' explained Cynric. 'Which Emma gets from places like Michaelhouse. In other words, Yffi was hired to take the decent stuff from us and replace it with rubbish. Emma's beneficence was nothing of the kind.'

'Never mind this.' Odelina made no effort to deny the accusation. 'You have a choice, Doctor. You either help my grandmother, or we kill your servant. Then, when you are released later, you will have his death on your conscience.'

Bartholomew could see the bowmen were ready to do as she threatened, so raised his hands in surrender, ignoring Cynric's grimace of disapproval. Odelina allowed herself a small grin of satisfaction, and there was a glitter in her eyes that was uncannily like her grandmother's. Bartholomew was disgusted at himself for underestimating her: with forebears like Emma and Heslarton, he should have known there would be more to her than just someone who liked romantic ballads.

'Everyone said you are clever,' she said gloatingly, as they began to walk across the yard. Cynric trailed behind with Heslarton. 'But you are not. We have outwitted you at every turn, and you are only now beginning to put the pieces together. You are a fool!'

'Yes,' agreed Bartholomew ruefully. 'But at least I know why you picked on Gib. You developed an affection for him when he was carrying messages between Kendale and Emma. But he kept a prostitute, which disappointed your idealistic visions—'

'It was sordid!' Odelina declared, grabbing Bartholomew's arm when he stumbled. She was very strong. 'But he just laughed when I challenged him about it. When he turned his back on me, I hit him over the head with a stone. I thought I had killed him.'

'So you raced to your father for help, then decided to use his corpse to your advantage. You tied a yellow wig on his head. But he was not dead, was he? He recovered, and you had a serious struggle on his hands when he fought back.'

Odelina did not reply, and they walked in silence the rest of the way to the door. Bartholomew thought about what he had learned, aware that he still did not have the whole story. The culprit *had* been clever, but he was not sure Odelina was sufficiently sly to have outwitted Michael for the best part of nine days, and he doubted Heslarton would be much help on that front. He recalled her precise words.

'You said *we* outwitted you,' he said, climbing slowly and unsteadily up the stairs towards the old lady's bedchamber. 'You and your father killed Drax, Alice, Poynton, Yffi and Gib, but neither of you were the yellow-headed man I chased. You have an accomplice. He is bold and quick, able to steal Emma's box, snatch Poynton's *signaculum* from—'

'Enough of this nonsense,' snapped Odelina curtly. 'I am tired of it.'

'Your poor father,' said Bartholomew softly. 'He knew nothing of your association with the thief until recently, did he? If he had, he would not have tried so hard to catch him. He helped you with Gib and Drax, because he loves you and did not want to see you in trouble. But he had no idea that you are in league with a felon. When did you tell him? After you made him a gift of Edith's stolen cloak?'

'I said stop!' hissed Odelina.

'Who is he?' persisted Bartholomew. 'A scholar? A townsman?'

'Someone who is better than you,' she snarled. 'And I did *not* kill Drax, by the way. I admit to dispatching my mother and Gib, but I never touched Drax. I found him dead in Physwick's dairy – I went there to give him a piece of my mind about how he was treating Celia – and I put him in Michaelhouse to . . . But no. I shall not talk about that.'

'It was your accomplice's idea,' surmised Bartholomew. 'Doubtless he also told you how to make use of Gib and Yffi's bodies. Who is he, Odelina? You cannot protect such a rogue.'

'Stop! I am not talking about it any more, so unless you want to be shot, you had better shut up.'

She clearly meant it, so Bartholomew tried to work out the fellow's identity for himself. Fen? One of his medical colleagues? Thelnetham? All were self-assured and intelligent, and might well secure the affections of a lonely, gullible woman desperate for a champion.

Or, more likely than any of them, was it Celia, who had an eye for valuable jewellery and was Odelina's good friend? And Celia was a liar, as evidenced by the fact that she had denied being able to read, claiming the books in her house belonged to her husband. But according to Kendale's testimony, Drax was illiterate. The more Bartholomew thought about it, the more he was sure he was right. Celia was the villain.

Emma had indeed taken a turn for the worse. Her face was flushed, and her eyes were bright with fever. She moaned in pain, and when Bartholomew and Cynric were shoved unceremoniously into the room, she reached out a gnarled hand towards them.

'Make me well again, Meryfeld,' she breathed. 'Or I will cast a spell on you, and God will turn His face from you for ever. It will not be the first time I have done it.'

'Perhaps she has already put one on you, boy,' Cynric whispered. 'It would explain a lot.'

Bartholomew did not want to think about it. He tried to inspect Emma's mouth, but the light was poor and his vision swam. He blinked several times, but it made no difference, and he knew it was wrong to try to treat her.

'I cannot do this,' he said, backing away, hand to his head. 'Send for Gyseburne—'

'You *will* do it,' Odelina hissed. 'Or your book-bearer will die.'

Bartholomew looked at Cynric, who was shaking his head, urging him to refuse. He blinked again, and the blurriness eased. He took the lamp, and peered inside Emma's mouth, then tapped very softly on the infected tooth with a metal probe. Emma released a howl that made his ears ring. It also had Odelina wincing and Heslarton surging forward.

'Hurt her again, and you are dead,' he snarled furiously.

'But it *will* hurt,' said Bartholomew helplessly. 'That is why she has always refused to let me do it before. And it will be worse now, because of the delay.'

Heslarton scowled, but indicated that he should continue. Servants brought hot water and bandages, then were dismissed, although one archer was ordered to stay, bow at the ready. Father and daughter held long daggers, and it was clear they would use them if an attempt was made to escape.

Bartholomew turned his attention to medicine, and

began cleaning the implements he would need. He took his time, hoping the delay would ease the throbbing in his head. Heslarton soon became impatient.

'Why are you wasting time?' he snapped. 'She is becoming worse while you dither, and you have polished those pliers at least twice. Get on with it.'

Reluctantly, Bartholomew bathed Emma's gums with a numbing potion, and asked Cynric to hold open her jaws. The book-bearer was not very happy about it, but Bartholomew had a plan of sorts. He laid a number of little knives on the cloth at the side of the bed. Cynric saw what he was expected to do, and palmed a couple when Bartholomew 'accidentally' upset a basin of water.

'Are you sure about this?' he asked, speaking so low the physician struggled to hear him. 'What happens if Emma dies during the . . .' He waved his hand, not sure how to describe it.

'She might, so be ready to act: lob the blade at the archer, then run for help. I will deal with Heslarton and Odelina.' Bartholomew turned to their captors before Cynric could point out that help for him would probably come far too late. 'You two will have to hold her down.'

'Us?' asked Heslarton uncomfortably. 'I do not want to see what you are doing, thank you. And you have your servant to assist.'

'He is not enough. This is going to be painful, and you must keep Emma still.'

With a muttered oath, Heslarton positioned himself across his mother-in-law's chest, pinioning her arms to her sides, while Odelina took her legs. Bartholomew blinked hard, then gripped the offending tooth with a pair of pliers. As hauling would leave the rotten root in the gum, it had to be twisted out gently with his left hand, while the right held back the inflamed tissue. It would not be easy, and he hoped the thing would not drop to pieces on him.

Immediately, Emma began to buck and writhe. Cynric looked away as blood welled, and Bartholomew heard him swallow, audible even over the wails of agony emanating from the patient. He wondered whether the effort of making such a racket alone would kill Emma, and then what would happen to him and Cynric? He blinked again as Emma's bleeding maw swam in and out of focus, then took a deep breath and continued, ignoring both the screams and the thrashing. Cynric was doing a good job of keeping the head still, for which he was grateful.

Unfortunately, the tooth was malformed, and refused to come out, so he took a knife and began to cut away the bone that held it. Emma's shrieks intensified, and Bartholomew experienced a great wave of dizziness as the din seared through his pounding head. But then there was a click, and the tooth was free. He watched pus well out of the resulting cavity – a lot of it – and was not surprised she had been in agony.

'Two stitches,' he said, more to himself than his reluctant assistants. 'To hold the flap over the exposed bone. Then it is done.'

Straining to see in the unsteady gleam of the lamp, he inserted first one suture, and then a second, careful to leave a gap for the wound to drain. Then he packed it with pieces of boiled cloth. Emma was silent at last, her face white and bathed in sweat.

'Now what?' asked Heslarton. His voice shook: the procedure had upset him. Odelina was made of sterner stuff, and went to sit by the window, while Cynric edged towards the door. Bartholomew could tell by the way the book-bearer stood that a knife was concealed in each hand.

'We wait,' he replied, leaning against the wall and wiping

his forehead with his sleeve. 'She needs to be monitored, to ensure the wound stops bleeding.'

'A physician,' said Cynric immediately. 'A servant cannot be entrusted with such a delicate task. You cannot send Doctor Bartholomew off to France in a barge until—'

'Can she hear us?' interrupted Odelina, touching her grandmother's face, very gently.

Bartholomew shook his head.

'Good,' said Odelina. 'Because I do not want her to know what is going to happen next.' She turned to the bowman. 'Kill them.'

The archer and Heslarton regarded Odelina askance. Cynric nodded grimly to himself, to say he had been right to distrust her, while Bartholomew sagged against the wall.

'But we made a bargain—' began Heslarton, raising his hand to stop the bowman.

'And I am breaking it,' Odelina retorted. 'If we put them on the barge and they escape, we will hang. I am not prepared to take that risk.'

'Christ, Odelina!' muttered Heslarton. 'You have grown ruthless. It must be his influence.'

'*His* influence?' asked Bartholomew, struggling to keep his words from slurring. 'Do you mean Odelina's accomplice? I thought that was Celia.'

'Celia knows nothing of this,' snapped Heslarton. 'Leave her out of it.'

'He will not thank me for leaving them alive,' said Odelina, ignoring Bartholomew and addressing her father. 'Not now he is so close to achieving all he wants.'

'And what is that?' asked Heslarton doubtfully.

On the other side of the room, Cynric was wound as tightly as a spring, waiting for the right opportunity to strike. Bartholomew tried to brace himself, knowing he

374

had to be ready to help, no matter what the cost to himself.

'At the camp-ball game today, there will be trouble,' Odelina was explaining. 'The hostels will be blamed, and afterwards, the likes of Chestre will be ousted from Cambridge for ever.'

'Your accomplice wants the hostels discredited?' Numbly, Bartholomew struggled to make sense of what she was saying. 'But why?'

'And we shall be free to enjoy the proceeds of our hard work,' Odelina continued, ignoring him again. 'We shall all go to France. But we will never rest easy if this pair are alive.'

Heslarton shook his head, as if he could not believe what he was hearing, but drew his sword just the same. He nodded to the archer, who brought his bow to bear on Cynric, while he advanced on Bartholomew. Odelina watched with eyes that glittered more savagely than her grandmother's had ever done.

Cynric sprang into action. He hurled one blade at the archer, catching him in the throat, then jammed the other in Heslarton's side. Heslarton howled in agony and fell to his knees. Cynric was a blur of motion as he raced towards Odelina and gave her a shove that sent her sprawling. Heslarton's screams alerted the servants, who immediately poured into the room, but Cynric felled two with punches, and the others, unnerved by the fierce, warlike expression on his face, turned and fled. He snatched up Heslarton's sword, and made for the door.

'Are you coming?' he demanded, when Bartholomew made no move to follow, shocked into immobility by the speed and efficiency of the assault.

In the hallway, the surviving bowman ran towards them, sword at the ready. Cynric fended him off with a series of ferocious swipes. Bartholomew lobbed a pot, although it was more by luck than design when it struck the fellow and knocked him senseless.

Then Odelina recovered, and launched herself at the physician, nails clawing wildly at his face. Her weight was more than he could handle, and he fell to the floor with her on top of him. Cynric turned to pull her off, but Bartholomew could hear more feet clattering in the yard below – the servants had summoned reinforcements, probably in the guise of the rough, soldiery men who had helped Heslarton to scour the marshes for the yellow-headed thief.

'Run, Cynric!' he urged. 'Warn Michael.'

'Not without you,' muttered Cynric grimly.

Bartholomew wanted to argue, but there was no time. He shoved Odelina away, and when she came at him again, he chopped her in the neck with the side of his hand. She fell back, stunned.

'She hit me first,' he protested, aware of Cynric's startled look. Even so, it was not in his nature to strike women, and he did not feel easy in his mind as he scrambled to his feet. Then he saw Heslarton groaning on the floor with the blade protruding from his ribs.

'Leave him,' hissed Cynric. 'I did not kill him – which is more mercy than he was going to show us.'

He grabbed a sword from the fallen bowman and shoved it into Bartholomew's hand. Then he raced towards the stairs with one of his blood-curdling battle cries. Heslarton's men had massed there, and he plunged among them like a madman, driving them back with the sheer ferocity of his charge. Bartholomew jabbed here and there, mostly ineffectually.

Step by step, they fought their way downwards, and eventually reached the door. Bartholomew hauled it open while Cynric, howling all manner of curses and incantations in

Welsh, whirled the sword around as though he were demented. Bartholomew was vaguely aware of people in the street stopping to stare as he staggered outside Emma's domain, and then he was stumbling into the arms of someone who hurried towards him. It was Michael.

Bartholomew watched Michael's beadles do battle with those members of Emma's household who had charged into the street after him. When he was sure the beadles would win, he turned to the monk, speaking quickly and urgently, acutely aware that time was of the essence.

'I have been busy, too,' said Michael, when he had finished, indicating he was to sit on the edge of a horse trough while they talked. Bartholomew sank down gratefully. His legs were like jelly, and he could not recall when he had felt more wretched. 'Although only with rioting hostels.'

'Has there been fighting?' asked Bartholomew anxiously.

'A little. There might have been more, but Welfry saved the day. Maud's, Ovyng and Cosyn's hostels were about to set fire to King's Hall, when he jumped on a wall and screeched a riddle at the top of his voice.'

'A riddle?' echoed Bartholomew blankly.

'One he claimed the hostels could never solve. Needless to say they rose to the challenge, and by the time they had calculated the answer, tempers had cooled. It was a clever ploy, and one that saved lives. I am glad he is our Seneschal. But even so, it took all my diplomatic tact and skills to encourage them to go home afterwards.'

'Will your arrest of the killer-thief be enough to quell trouble at the camp-ball game now?' asked Bartholomew worriedly. 'Especially as it is not a scholar?'

'It is impossible to say. Are you *sure* we have the right culprits this time? There is no doubt?'

377

'No. I mean, yes.'

Michael regarded him in alarm. 'Well, which is it? We cannot afford more mistakes.'

'Heslarton and Odelina are definitely involved, but they did not work alone. She is not clever enough, despite her claims to the contrary – it was *not* her idea to shove a wig on Gib and use him to confound your investigation. Likewise, I doubt she or her father would have thought of leaving Yffi in Chestre's cellar, or of taking Drax to Michaelhouse.'

'No,' agreed Michael.

'Moreover, Heslarton says he is innocent of the thefts, and I believe him. Someone else is responsible for those. I thought it was Celia, but Odelina and Heslarton referred to a man – some fellow who plans to take them to France when his plans reach fruition.'

'Who?' demanded Michael. 'Fen? I said he was a villain, and you should have listened.'

'There are other possibilities, too,' said Bartholomew. He looked away, unwilling to list them, because they included people he liked.

Michael had no such qualms. 'Meryfeld and Gyseburne, Blaston . . .'

'Not Blaston – he is not sufficiently cunning. Thelnetham is, though . . .'

'Yes, he is, but I cannot see what he would gain from having Chestre blamed for his crimes – or from having his University plunged into turmoil by stoking up anger between Colleges and hostels.'

They were interrupted by a sudden violent skirmish among the prisoners. Cynric had been right when he said he had not hurt Heslarton badly, and the man was engaged in a furious scuffle. When they saw their master's determined resistance, his henchmen renewed their own efforts

378

to escape, and it took all the beadles, Michael and Cynric to subdue them. Bartholomew tried to help, but was too unsteady and disoriented to be of much use.

'Where is Odelina?' he asked urgently, when it was over.

'Damn!' cried Michael, looking around wildly. 'Heslarton's antics were a diversion! They were to give his wretched daughter a chance to flee.'

'I imagine she has run straight to her accomplice,' said Bartholomew, alarmed. 'The one who has some terrible plan in mind for the camp-ball game.'

Michael regarded him in horror. 'The camp-ball game! I forgot to tell you – it has been brought forward, because rain is predicted later. Vast crowds are gathering, for it is due to start within the hour.'

'Arrest *all* our suspects,' urged Bartholomew, feeling desperate situations called for desperate measures. 'If they are innocent, they will forgive you when you explain yourself. And if they are guilty, you will prevent them from—'

'Brother Michael! Brother Michael!' They turned to see Meryfeld racing towards them. For the first time since Bartholomew had met him, he was not rubbing his hands together. 'Thank God I have found you! Horneby the Carmelite has just attacked me.'

'Attacked you?' echoed Michael in astonishment. 'Why would he do that?'

'He burst into my house and locked me in my cellar without so much as a word of explanation,' shouted Meryfeld, furious and indignant. 'How dare he! I order you to apprehend him.'

'Horneby,' said Bartholomew, the last pieces of the puzzle falling into place at last. '*He* is Odelina's accomplice.'

CHAPTER 12

'*Horneby* is Odelina's accomplice?' echoed Michael, gaping at Bartholomew in astonishment. 'Impossible! He is a theologian.'

'And theologians are incapable of murder?' demanded Bartholomew. 'It is a pity, because I admire him. However, he is certainly clever enough to have masterminded all this mayhem – he has one of the best minds in the University.'

'I barely recognised him when he attacked me,' said Meryfeld, looking from one to the other as he tried to understand what they were talking about. 'His face was twisted, and I am surprised he did not kill me. In fact, I think he might have done, had he not been in such a hurry.'

Michael's expression hardened, and he quickly organised his beadles into two groups: those who would march Heslarton and his henchmen to the gaol, and those who would police the camp-ball. Bartholomew used the brief respite to rest. He closed his eyes, trying to quell the agitated churning in his stomach.

The day was bitterly cold, with grey clouds scudding overhead and a brisk northerly breeze that cut straight through his clothes. Would it cut through the spectators' clothes, too, he wondered, and encourage them to leave the game and head for the warmth of home? He jumped when he became aware that someone was behind him. It was Gyseburne, and Thelnetham was with him.

'You look terrible,' said Gyseburne, peering into his face.

380

Bartholomew sincerely hoped he was not going to demand a urine sample. 'What ails you?'

'Yet another sleepless night, I expect,' said Thelnetham, before Bartholomew could reply. 'They seem to be an occupational hazard at Michaelhouse – none of us have had proper rest in days.'

'There is no reason for you to have been disturbed,' said Bartholomew, thinking Thelnetham was not a physician or a senior proctor, so should have been sleeping like a baby.

Thelnetham regarded him oddly. 'It is hard to relax when half the College has no roof and our protective gates have been missing. And I am—'

He broke off when Welfry approached at a run. The Dominican's face was pale.

'Have you seen Horneby?' he asked urgently. 'He raced out of his friary as though the Devil was on his tail earlier. Moreover, he has burned his notes for the Stock Extraordinary Lecture. It is inexplicable behaviour, and I fear he may not be completely recovered from his recent illness.'

Meryfeld explained briefly what had been done to him, but before Welfry could respond, Michael shouted that he was ready and that he needed volunteers to help him at the camp-ball game. Welfry, Thelnetham and Gyseburne were among those who rallied to his call, but Meryfeld muttered something about visiting a patient and slunk off in the opposite direction.

'What are we hoping to prevent, exactly?' asked Thelnetham, after Michael had given a short account of all that had happened, and they were marching along the High Street towards the Gilbertine Priory.

'Trouble,' replied Michael shortly. 'We do not know what form it might take, so you must all be vigilant for the unusual. All I know is that it must be stopped.'

'Had I known Cambridge was going to be this turbulent, I would never have left York,' muttered Gyseburne to himself.

'I do not believe any of this,' whispered Welfry, his amiable face grey with shock and grief. 'You are mistaken. Horneby would never do anything so terrible.'

'Yet he has,' said Michael roughly. 'The evidence is overwhelming.'

'It is circumstantial,' argued Welfry loyally. 'And he would never . . .' He trailed off uneasily.

'What?' demanded Michael.

For a moment, Bartholomew thought the Dominican would refuse to answer, but then Welfry began to speak.

'Odelina,' he said in a choked whisper. He would not look at Michael. 'He told me he thought her a fine woman. She harboured a fancy for me, you see, and I asked his advice on how best to repel her. I thought he was in jest when he said he admired her, to make me feel better . . .'

'But he was in earnest,' finished Michael. 'What else can you tell me, Welfry? And please do not hold back. I know you and Horneby are friends, but lives are at stake here. Do you have any notion of what he might be planning?'

Welfry's face was an agony of conflict. 'He has been reading a lot of books on alchemy of late, and I think his throat trouble began after an experiment with powerful substances . . .'

'We must hurry, said Michael grimly. 'Whatever he is plotting, we cannot let him succeed.'

Welfry was stunned, shaking his head as he walked. 'There will be an explanation for all this, and Horneby will be exonerated. Then we will feel terrible for thinking such dreadful things about a man whose decency and goodness are beyond question.'

While he continued in this vein to anyone who would

listen, Thelnetham fell into step beside Bartholomew, and offered a hand when the physician stumbled over an uneven cobble. He removed a phial from his pouch.

'Drink this. You will need your strength if we are to avert a catastrophe.'

'What is it?'

'A tonic for vitality that Gyseburne gave me. Go on. It will do you good.'

It was a measure of Bartholomew's debility that he took the concoction without thinking twice about it. It tasted foul, and for a moment he thought he was going to be sick. But the sensation passed, and he was left feeling no worse than he had been before.

'I was summoned to tend Dickon this morning, because you were unavailable,' said Gyseburne, striding on his other side. 'He tried to burgle Celia Drax's house, and cut his knee on the window.'

'Dickon!' exclaimed Bartholomew, as a sudden, awful thought began to take shape in his head. 'And Horneby has been reading books on alchemy! Oh, no! Surely . . .'

'What?' asked Thelnetham uneasily. 'What have you reasoned?'

'Dickon must have talked about the compound we created,' said Bartholomew, as his stomach began to churn in horror. 'The one that burns, but that cannot be extinguished.'

'Yes, he has,' agreed Gyseburne disapprovingly. 'I have heard him myself. What of it?'

'Did Meryfeld mention anything missing after Horneby had burst into his home?' demanded Bartholomew urgently.

'He said the cauldron we used to make our lamp-fuel was gone, along with some pitch, quicklime and brimstone.' Gyseburne paled when he understood what Bartholomew

383

was thinking. 'You believe Horneby intends to use that vile abomination at the camp-ball? No! It is too terrible, and he is a friar! He would never . . .'

'I think he might,' said Bartholomew soberly. Was it his imagination, or had Thelnetham's tonic given him a sudden burst of energy? Or was it simply the challenge of preventing such a terrible atrocity that filled him with strength and determination?

It was not long before they reached the camp-ball field, and Bartholomew was horrified by the size of the crowd that had gathered – it was far larger than the one for the game between the Carmelites and the Gilbertines. Those who were scholars had formed themselves into blocks, some sporting red banners that declared them members of hostels, and others carrying blue for the Colleges or convents. Red was by far the dominant colour, although it did not deter the blue from bellowing insults and abuse.

Bartholomew's heart sank further still when he saw the factions were separated by groups of the kind of townsman who enjoyed rough sport. If there was any off-the-field skirmishing, they would join in, and the trouble would escalate to the point where Tulyet's soldiers and Michael's beadles would be unable to control it. Then the peace they had enjoyed for the past few weeks would be shattered, and town and University would be back at each other's throats again.

There was an enthusiastic roar from the crowd as the teams trotted on to the field. Bartholomew was appalled when he saw how many students had elected to play. There were at least sixty on each side, and many were lads who had already been involved in the rivalry – Essex, Maud's, Batayl and Cosyn's hostels, along with King's Hall, Gonville and Valence Marie for the Colleges.

'No one from Michaelhouse, thank God,' said Michael, following the direction of his gaze. 'Although our students are among the supporters, and will join in any fight that starts.'

Bartholomew watched Kendale, smug and arrogant in his capacity of organiser, stroll on to the field after the players amid a chorus of cheers from the hostels. This was immediately countered by boos and hisses from the Colleges, and Bartholomew saw the smile slip a little.

'Mingle,' Michael ordered his beadles and volunteers, as Kendale beckoned the competitors forward and began to outline the rules. 'Look for Horneby, and listen for any fighting talk. And if you succeed in either, come to me – do not attempt to tackle it on your own. You will almost certainly fail, and then Horneby *will* have his riot.'

They hurried away to do as they were told. Bartholomew aimed for a large contingent of Carmelites, huddled in their cloaks and shivering in the cold. Their hoods were up, shielding their faces, and it occurred to him that it was the perfect place for Horneby to hide. But when he arrived, and they turned to greet him, he saw the young friar was not among them. Etone was, though, looking old, drawn and tired.

'Have you seen Horneby?' Bartholomew demanded.

As one, the Carmelites shook their heads. 'Not since dawn,' said one. 'When Prior Etone announced that he was well enough to resume his duties.'

Etone regarded the physician with a bleak expression, and Bartholomew wondered whether he would ever recover from the loss of his relic.

There was another cheer as the two teams separated and the Indifferent Man took up position. The honour had been awarded to Chancellor Tynkell, who was puffed up with pride – until he realised what the appointment entailed, at which point he began to look frightened. Panicked into resourcefulness, he effected a powerful drop-kick, which propelled the ball away from him. The players veered after it, leaving him to depart the field with his dignity intact.

Bartholomew tore his eyes away from the spectacle and looked around desperately, wondering where Horneby might be. He spotted Rougham, appointed Official Physician for the day. The Gonville *medicus* looked stately and confident in his academic robes, although his hubris faded when the first two players limped from the field with deep cuts.

'Help me, Bartholomew,' he commanded, regarding the wounds in distaste. 'Kendale said this game was not to be savage-camp, so there would be no serious injuries. I would not have accepted the commission had I known there would be blood involved.'

'Have you seen Horneby?' asked Bartholomew, ignoring the order.

'Yes – haring towards Edmund House just a few moments ago,' replied Rougham, gesturing to the derelict building on the far side of the pitch. 'But never mind him. I need your expertise, because these wounds need stitching.'

'Then stitch,' suggested Bartholomew shortly, forgetting Michael's warning about not tackling the villain alone as he began to run around the edge of the field.

Progress was not easy. Bartholomew wore no red or blue ribbon to declare his allegiance, but this attracted aggravation from both sides. He was shoved, jostled, tripped and prodded the whole way around, and each time he stumbled, he felt more of his energy leach away. It felt like an age before he reached the house and staggered around it until he found the door. He opened it gingerly, and stepped inside, immediately aware of the stale, earthy aroma of neglect. He listened intently, trying to hear where Horneby might be, but the shouts and cheers from the field drowned out any sounds the friar might be making.

The ground floor looked as though no one had been in it since the plague, with its curtains of cobwebs, crumbling plaster and mildew-encrusted walls. A flight of stairs led to the upper floor, which Bartholomew was astonished to find furnished. Grimly, he supposed Celia had declined to romp in a ruin, and had obliged Heslarton to provide her with some basic comforts.

He pushed open the first door, alert for any sign that Horneby was waiting to ambush him, but the room was empty. Heart pounding, he did the same to the second, and saw someone lying on the floor.

It was Horneby, blood seeping into his hair from a wound on the side of his head. Bewildered, Bartholomew eased him on to his back, watching his eyes flutter open as he was moved. The injury was nasty, but not life threatening. However, someone had hit him extremely hard.

'Bartholomew,' Horneby breathed. 'You have to stop him!'

'Stop who?' asked Bartholomew in confusion. 'Who did this to you?'

'The loss of life will be terrible,' Horneby went on weakly, 'and I tried to persuade him to abandon it, but he outwitted me. Odelina must be his lover.'

'His lover?' echoed Bartholomew stupidly, wishing his wits were sharper.

'Yes, although it is hard to believe he would break his vows for such a woman.' Horneby shot Bartholomew a sheepish glance. 'Being such close friends, we sometimes discussed ladies. I said Odelina was too venal for my tastes, and he agreed. He lied to me!'

'You mean Welfry?' asked Bartholomew, his mind a dazed whirl. 'But he rejected her advances. I saw it myself.'

Horneby swallowed hard. 'He did not reject them earlier today. He has captured her heart, and she is like clay in his hands. He knows enough of romantic ballads to understand what will tie her to him. How could I have been so blind?'

'Odelina is *Welfry's* accomplice? But . . .'

But it was certainly possible, Bartholomew thought, as he trailed off. Welfry was handsome and witty, and Odelina was not the sort of woman to let priestly vows stand in the way of what she wanted. Moreover, Welfry might well have been the fleet-footed thief in the yellow wig whom Bartholomew had chased along the High Street – far more likely than the heavier, slower Horneby.

'St Simon Stock's scapular,' he said, answers coming in blinding flashes. 'The three thieves I saw making off with it must have been Welfry, Heslarton and Odelina. Welfry often visits you there, so knows better than most how to escape through your grounds. Clearly, he failed with his first attempt to snatch a piece of it, so he recruited them to help him make off with the whole thing.'

'No!' cried Horneby in a strangled voice that eerily echoed Welfry's distress earlier. 'He would not have taken my priory's most valuable possession.'

'Meryfeld's cauldron,' said Bartholomew, moving to a more urgent matter. 'Did Welfry order you to lay hold of it?'

'Yes! Dickon had mentioned it to him. He told me that if I grabbed it we could prevent it from being used on innocent people. I did as he suggested, eager to help avert an outrage. But when I presented it to him, he promptly passed it to Heslarton. I suspected then that something was wrong.'

'Why did you not report it to Michael or his beadles?'

'Because Welfry is the University's Seneschal,' explained Horneby in despair. 'The man who calmed a potentially bloody situation outside King's Hall this morning. Who would believe me? I decided to follow him instead, in an affort to learn exactly what he thinks he is doing. He came here, and shortly afterwards, Odelina arrived.'

'Then what?'

'She told him you knew almost everything about their plan. He merely smiled, and said he had acquired enough *signacula* at last, although he did not say for what. Then I must have made a sound, because she came and hit me. I cannot believe any of this. Surely, I am dreaming?'

'Welfry is strong, fast and agile,' said Bartholomew. 'Capable of snatching Poynton's badge, of donning a disguise and stealing Edith's, of breaking into Gyseburne's home to take his . . .'

'Odelina is furious that he made her grandmother and Celia his victims,' said Horneby. 'But he has promised to make it up to her. He mentioned something about already giving her father a nice red cloak as compensation. Welfry! He is my *friend*!'

'Have you burned the notes for your lecture?'

Horneby regarded him askance. 'No, of course not! I have been working on them for months.'

'Then have you been reading books on alchemy, and conducting experiments?'

'No! I have not had time, not with my lecture looming, although Welfry has always been interested in such matters. But how can you ask such irrelevant questions when there is an atrocity to prevent? You must act, Bartholomew! Now, before it is too late!'

Bartholomew tried to scramble to his feet when he heard a sound behind him, but his legs were still too unsteady.

Odelina was already swinging a heavy sword towards his neck.

Bartholomew's life might have come to an end there and then, if it had not been for Horneby. The theologian reached up and hauled Bartholomew down on top of him, so Odelina's wild swipe passed harmlessly over both their heads. While she regained her balance, Bartholomew scrambled upright, and Horneby eased himself up on to one elbow, his face ashen with shock and pain. Bartholomew knew exactly how he felt.

'Welfry has deceived us all,' the Carmelite said in a low, strained voice. 'Please, Odelina. You must see this is wrong. People will die, and it will be on *your* conscience.'

'I do not have a conscience,' declared Odelina. 'At least, that is what my father always says. And if it should happen to twinge, then Welfry has enough pilgrim tokens to buy me a clean slate.'

'Put down the sword,' ordered Bartholomew, sounding a lot more confident than he felt. But he had to stop Welfry, and there was no time to fool around with Odelina. 'You are not going to escape this time, and whatever Welfry has planned is going to fail. The Sheriff, Senior Proctor and all manner of other people are working to thwart him.'

Odelina laughed unpleasantly. 'But they will not succeed, because no one knows *he* is the one they should be hunting. He will outwit them, just as he has outwitted them before. In fact, his plan is already a success, because he wanted Horneby to be seen as the villain, and that is *exactly* what folk believe.'

Bartholomew took a tentative step towards the door, but she waved the weapon menacingly. Could he disarm her? Unfortunately, he knew he was not yet strong enough to try, not even with Thelnetham's miraculous tonic coursing in his veins. She would kill him, and then she would kill Horneby, and there would be no one left to tell Michael the truth.

'He was jealous of you, Horneby,' Odelina was saying. 'Of your intellect, although I do not think wits are an especially enviable commodity. As far as I am concerned, they make men arrogant, and unwilling to appreciate pretty ladies in search of husbands.'

'Even if Welfry succeeds, it will not help you,' said Bartholomew harshly. 'Because *you* will be in prison, awaiting execution for the murder of Drax, Gib and your mother.'

'Not me,' said Odelina smugly. 'And I did *not* kill Drax, as I keep telling you. But none of it matters, because Welfry is taking me to France on Isnard's barge. I shall marry him, and we will live happily ever after.'

'He is a priest,' said Horneby quietly. 'He cannot marry.'

'He is going to retract his vows,' asserted Odelina. 'Why do you think he has been amassing so many pilgrim badges? It is to buy himself freedom from the silly promises he made to God.'

Horneby looked as though he felt sorry for her. 'He will not settle down with you, Odelina. Marriage will deprive him of everything he loves – books, learning, jokes with the novices—'

'He loves *me*,' declared Odelina stubbornly, raising the sword. 'And we *will* wed. But you will not be alive to see the happy day.'

'Think, Odelina,' urged Horneby. He struggled to his knees. 'Do you not see what he is doing? *You* will be blamed for killing Matthew and me, leaving him to walk free.'

'He will meet me by Isnard's barge,' insisted Odelina. 'He promised.'

'He will not be there,' said Horneby, compassion in his voice, while Bartholomew listened to the discussion in an agony of tension. Every moment wasted with Odelina was time for Welfry to realise his diabolical plans, and he itched to dive at her and wrest the sword from her grip. Surely it was worth the risk, to prevent something so evil? He took another step towards the door.

'He will,' insisted Odelina. She feinted at Bartholomew, causing him to flinch, but this time there was uncertainty in the manoeuvre. Perhaps he could disarm her . . .

'Let us go, so we can prevent more mayhem,' urged Horneby with quiet reason. 'I will speak for you at your trial. He has clearly lied to you, as he has to me.'

'I will never betray him,' declared Odelina. Tears began to form in her eyes. 'And I am not listening to any more of your clever words. You are only trying to confuse me.'

'Why is he so intent on causing such mischief?' asked Horneby quickly, when her fingers tightened around the hilt and the great blade began to wobble towards Bartholomew again. 'You could at least tell us that before we die.'

For a moment, Bartholomew thought she was going to attack them without answering the question, but then she began to speak.

'He does not want Kendale in Cambridge, because he has aggravated the rivalry between the hostels and Colleges. He wants him ousted, by having him blamed for all the murders and thefts. He says the University will be better off without such men in it.'

Bartholomew regarded her in disbelief. '*Kendale* has caused trouble? What about Welfry?'

'Enough talking!' she shouted suddenly. 'I should be at Isnard's barge, not chattering here with you. Say your prayers, both of you. I will try to be merciful.'

392

She advanced on Bartholomew, but she had been holding the weapon aloft too long, and her arms were fatigued. She struggled to lift it, and the fractional delay gave him just enough time to lunge forward and grab her arm. The situation had resolved, he realised with sudden clarity, exactly as Horneby had engineered it to, and explained why the friar had been to such pains to keep her talking for so long.

Unfortunately, Odelina was still strong, while the after-effects of Bartholomew's concussion had rendered him more feeble than he had appreciated. Instead of defeating her immediately, a furious tussle ensued, during which he felt himself losing ground.

When he saw what was happening, Horneby went into action again. He rolled into a ball, and this time Bartholomew grasped his plan a good deal more quickly. He shoved Odelina towards him, so she tripped over backwards, to land with a crash that drove the air from her lungs. While she fought to catch her breath, Horneby removed the rope belt from around his waist.

'Go,' he said urgently. 'I will secure her, and stay here until you send help. I am too weak to dash out and help you confront Welfry, but I can do this. Go!'

With grim resolve, Bartholomew began to stagger to where he could see Michael moving through the spectators. He was obliged to jig away sharply when the camp-ball game surged towards him, and then was slowed by the same gamut of shoves, pokes and jostles that had delayed him on his way out. He was alarmed to note that scuffles had broken out in several places, and the beadles and Tulyet's soldiers were hard pressed to quell them.

By the time he reached Michael, he was dishevelled, breathless and his legs threatened to deposit him on the ground. He gasped out his explanation, leaning on the monk's shoulder for support as he did so.

'Welfry,' said the monk heavily, dispatching two beadles to rescue Horneby. 'But why did he order Horneby to steal your brimstone concoction? What does he intend to do with it?'

'He is ingenious, as his practical jokes have shown,' said Bartholomew, fighting off another wave of dizziness. 'He will find a way.'

'Horneby must be inside the priory,' gabbled Thelnetham, dashing up to them. 'It is cold today, so our new Seneschal has persuaded Leccheworth to serve the free wine and ale in the refectory. Horneby and his diabolical substances will be in there.'

'The culprit is not Horneby,' said Michael. 'It is Welfry himself.'

Thelnetham gaped at him. 'I do not believe you! He is a lovely man, all smiles, compassion and goodness. Well, and a little malice, too, if the truth be known. His trick with the eggs made Agatha a laughing stock—'

'There is no time for chatter,' interrupted Michael. 'Come, both of you. We must stop him.'

'No,' said Bartholomew, gesturing to the field. 'There are skirmishes breaking out everywhere, and the Senior Proctor needs to be seen doing his duty *here*. It will not matter if Welfry blows up the refectory, if there is a massive bloodbath among the spectators first.'

'Then what do you suggest?' demanded Michael in agitation.

'That you stay outside, and keep the peace. Thelnetham and I will hunt for Welfry in the priory. You can come to help us as soon as you have the situation here under control.'

Michael screwed up his face, disliking the choice he was

being offered, but he knew the importance of the Senior Proctor's visible presence when scholars were of a mind to fight.

'Can you do it?' he asked, looking doubtfully at his friend. 'You will not collapse on us?'

'I will help him if he does,' said Thelnetham. 'We will stop this villain together.'

'Very well. But be careful. The University needs its Corpse Examiner.'

'And one of its most talented lawyers,' added Thelnetham dryly. 'However, remember that it is only conjecture that Welfry is inside. We may not be able to find him.'

'You must,' urged Michael. 'The game will not last much longer, and then everyone will charge towards their free drinks. You *must* apprehend him before that happens.'

'But if we cannot, you must insist that everyone disarms before entering the refectory,' said Bartholomew. 'That should cut down the potential for violence.'

'My beadles will see to it.' Michael sketched a blessing at them. 'Now, go.'

Bartholomew took considerable care as he eased through the crowd, anxious not to provide the spark that would ignite a full-blown brawl. The lads from Batayl Hostel jostled him as he passed, but he ignored them, even when one shove was hard enough to send him sprawling on to his hands and knees. Thelnetham hauled him to his feet, and dragged him on, looking neither to left nor right.

'If they do that to a Michaelhouse student, there will be a riot for certain,' he muttered. 'Langelee ordered all the Fellows to stay with them today, to keep them away from provocation, but our colleagues will not find it easy.'

'Then perhaps you had better go and help them,' said

Bartholomew, looking at the Gilbertines' buildings and experiencing a flutter of dread in his stomach. 'This is not your fight.'

'Of course it is my fight!' snapped Thelnetham. 'It is my University, is it not? And the confrontation with this deranged monster is going to take place in the refectory of my own Order! I am terrified out of my very considerable wits, but I am not leaving you to do it alone. Father William is always talking about College loyalty, so here is my chance to prove myself.'

'Why should you need to prove yourself?'

Thelnetham looked away. 'Because it was me who told Celia Drax that you were a warlock. I was being flippant, but she took it to heart, and you lost a wealthy client because of it. I have tried to make amends with small gestures of friendship, but you have been suspicious of them. So I shall have to put my life at your disposal instead.'

'Be careful, then,' said Bartholomew, supposing a guilty conscience might well explain Thelnetham's recent curious behaviour towards him.

'I am always careful,' said Thelnetham with a rueful grin. 'And I am wearing a new habit – I do not want it damaged by whatever diabolical substance you and your medical colleagues invented.'

Bartholomew pushed open the refectory door and stepped inside. It was a massive room, with great, thick rafters, dark paintings on the walls and a flagstone floor. One or two lamps had been lit, although they did little to illuminate the place: it was dim and shadowy, a combination of an overcast day and narrow windows. Long tables had been set out, and there were buckets of ale and jugs of wine on them, along with baskets of bread and cakes. There was no sign of Welfry.

'He is not here,' said Thelnetham. He sounded relieved.

'He must be,' whispered Bartholomew. 'I can smell brimstone. He must have brought it here.'

'Then *where* is he? He is not under any of the tables, and this is a single room with no pillars to hide behind, or chests in which to seek shelter.'

Bartholomew saw he was right. Perhaps Welfry had given up when Odelina had been caught, and had fled, taking his pilgrim badges with him to pay for a new life. Bartholomew sagged, feeling that the Dominican had beaten him. Then he saw a small, sticky stain on the floor.

He stepped towards it and crouched down. It was definitely the potion he had helped to create in Meryfeld's garden. Very slowly, he looked upwards, to the rafters.

'He *is* here,' he said softly to Thelnetham.

The Gilbertine peered to where he was pointing. 'Ropes and pulleys!' he exclaimed. 'Half hidden among the shadows and the darkness. But what are they for?'

'Another practical joke,' guessed Bartholomew. 'Except this one will not be amusing, and will end in death and mutilation. I believe he intends to shower the people who come for their free drinks with a burning substance that cannot be extinguished – a ruthlessly vicious variation on the trick at the Dominican Priory, which saw him brained with a basket.'

Thelnetham turned white, and crossed himself. 'Horrible! Can you see him?'

Bartholomew shook his head. 'Tell Michael what we have found, and do not let anyone come in. I will try to disarm whatever device he has constructed.'

Thelnetham pointed to a door. 'There are the stairs that lead to the roof. God forgive me, but Welfry asked me where they went the other day, and I told him. I thought he was making polite conversation, and he is such a charming fellow . . .'

397

'It is not your fault – he deceived us all. Now go.'

Bartholomew opened the door and began to climb. The steps were narrow, pitch black and very uneven, and he could not go as fast as he would have liked. It seemed an age before he reached another door, which he opened to reveal a small ledge and a dizzying drop. But there was something else, too.

In the gloom of the ancient, dusty rafters, he could see buckets attached to ropes. They were linked by twine that had been smeared with the substance he and his medical colleagues had created, and he understood immediately what was intended to happen: a flame would be touched to the twine, allowing the perpetrator time to escape while it burned. He recalled Welfry admiring the 'fuse' Kendale had invented when he had illuminated St Mary the Great: he had stolen the idea.

Bartholomew tried to pull the twine away from the pails, but it had been tacked very securely to the wood, and he could not do it – he would have to disable the receptacles themselves. But these had been positioned far along the rafters, so they would be directly over the tables below. Cautiously, he stepped off the door ledge, and took several wobbly steps along the nearest beam. Immediately, the door closed behind him.

'Keep walking,' came Welfry's voice. 'I have a knife, and I am not afraid to use it. And even if I only injure you, you will still fall to your death. Walk away from me, and do not turn back.'

Bartholomew could not have turned back, even if he had wanted to, because the beam was too narrow. With no choice but to obey, he did as Welfry ordered.

His legs trembled, and he tried not to look down, although it was difficult, because he had to watch where he was putting his feet: the rafter was uneven, and there was a very real risk of him losing his balance and falling to his death without the Seneschal's knife helping him along. Eventually, he reached the crown-post in the middle of the rafter, and grabbed it gratefully.

'Do not stop,' called Welfry. 'There is another door at the far end. Walk to it, and close it after you. The latch sticks, so you will be trapped until someone rescues you, but you will live. However, if you stop, I will be forced to kill you.'

'No,' said Bartholomew. The next section of rafter was much more uneven, and he was in no state for acrobatics. 'Lob your knife if you will, but I am not moving.'

Immediately, a blade thudded into the wood by his face, making him jump so violently that he almost lost his footing.

'Damn!' muttered Welfry. 'But I have another, so do not think of starting back.'

'This is over, Welfry.' Bartholomew sounded a lot more confident than he felt.

'Almost,' agreed Welfry. 'My work will soon be completed.'

'How could you do this?' Bartholomew eased around the post in an effort to put himself out of knife range. 'You are one of the University's most popular members – and its latest Seneschal. How could you betray it all for a future with Odelina and a handful of *signacula*?'

'I am not going anywhere with Odelina. First, Isnard's barge is unseaworthy. But second, and more importantly, you should credit me with a little integrity – I have never broken my vows of chastity.' Welfry sighed when he saw Bartholomew no longer represented a clear target. 'I said keep moving.'

'Michael knows about your crimes,' warned Bartholomew, not holding much hope of talking the Dominican into giving up, but desperate enough to try.

'You may not have killed Drax, Alice, Gib, Yffi and Poynton yourself, but you are certainly implicated. And we know it was you who stole the *signacula* and St Simon Stock's scapular.'

'Perhaps, but he will never be able to prove it. Please start walking. I do not want to hurt you.'

'He *will* prove it.' Bartholomew could see Welfry in the gloom, holding a blade in his gloved hand. He was safe from lobbed knives behind the crown-post, but as long as he was pinned down, he could not stop the Dominican from activating his pulleys. He knew he had to do something quickly, but what? 'He even knows *why* you have done these terrible things.'

Welfry gave a short, bitter laugh. 'I doubt it.'

'You hate Kendale, so you needled him with gentle tricks, knowing he would respond with vicious ones. But when that failed to see him expelled, you ordered Heslarton to leave Yffi and a box of "evidence" in his hostel, so he would be blamed for the crimes *you* and your helpmeets had committed. You ordered Drax left in Michaelhouse for the same reason.'

'Unfortunately, it was too subtle for Brother Michael. He failed to make the connection.' Welfry sounded exasperated. 'Enough of this! Start walking again, or I will—'

'He failed to make the connection because he does not allow himself to be misled by villains,' retorted Bartholomew, struggling to keep the unsteadiness from his voice. 'But why do you—'

'It started when I saw Chestre murder Jolye,' snapped Welfry. 'Shoving him in the icy river and then refusing to let him out. It was monstrous!'

'If you witnessed a murder, you should have told Michael. He represents justice, not you.'

'My word against an entire hostel, including the wily-tongued Kendale? No one would have believed me. But they will pay for their crime.'

'What happened to you, Welfry?' asked Bartholomew softly. 'What brought you to this?'

'*You* ask me such a question?' asked Welfry with a short, mirthless laugh. 'A man abandoned by God because of his heretical ideas and fondness for sorcery?'

Bartholomew winced, but pressed on. 'How could you throw in your lot with Odelina?'

'Odelina,' sighed Welfry. 'That was the worst part: enduring her attentions to secure her help. However, she dispatched Gib, Alice – and probably Drax, too, although she denies it – of her own volition. And her father was responsible for Yffi and Poynton. I had nothing to do with any of it.'

'No, but you took advantage,' countered Bartholomew, watching Welfry finger the dagger restlessly. 'Leaving corpses in Michaelhouse and Chestre, and tying a yellow wig on Gib to make everyone think the badge thief was dead. The thief was you, although Heslarton did not know it at the time.'

Welfry inclined his head. 'And neither did Odelina – both would have killed me for targeting Emma and Celia, so I kept it from them until I had her completely in my thrall. But enough chatter, Matthew! Start walking towards the door.'

The benefits of Thelnetham's tonic had finally worn off, and Bartholomew felt sick and dizzy. He knew he would fall if he moved along the beam as ordered. And how could he thwart Welfry, if he was trapped behind a door that would not open, anyway? He began speaking again, hoping the delay would allow him time to devise a plan – although nothing had come to mind so far.

'I do not understand why you stole so many pilgrim

badges. Do you intend to sell them, to make yourself a fortune?'

'No, of course not. I know why you are struggling to keep me talking, by the way. You expect Thelnetham to fetch Michael and save you. Unfortunately, Thelnetham met with an accident.'

He jabbed his thumb downwards, and Bartholomew risked a quick glance. The Gilbertine was lying on the floor: there was blood next to his head.

'So walk to the far end of the beam and go through the door,' directed Welfry. 'I am willing to spare your life, but not at the expense of spoiling my plans. Go, or I will come and stab you.'

'If you do, you may fall yourself,' said Bartholomew, not moving.

Welfry sighed. 'I have been scampering around these beams for days, and I have a good head for heights. You cannot prevent what is about to happen, so do as I say, and save yourself.'

'What is about to happen?' pressed Bartholomew, hearing the desperation in his own voice.

'In a moment, scholars and townsmen will come racing in for their free ale and wine. My little trick will swing into action, and I shall escape in the ensuing chaos. When the commotion eventually dies down, your cries for help will be heard and you will be released – *if* you walk towards the door. If you continue to be awkward, you will suffer a rather different fate.'

'But people will see Thelnetham's body, and—'

'Not until it is too late to matter.'

'Please do not do this,' begged Bartholomew, appalled by the meticulous planning. 'Our friends will be among those drinking this wine. And how can you leave Horneby to take the blame?'

402

Welfry winced and looked away. He regretted Horneby's fate. 'He will be dead by now. Odelina is nothing if not thorough.'

'She is in Michael's custody, and Horneby has escaped.'

'I do not believe you.' Welfry took a step along the beam. 'I gave you your chance, Matthew, and you refused to take it. I dislike killing, but you leave me no choice.'

Bartholomew had no strength left to repel an attack. 'All right,' he said wearily. 'I am going. But bear in mind that even if your plan succeeds, you will never be safe. Michael will find you.'

'I doubt even his influence extends to the place where I am bound,' said Welfry softly.

Bartholomew frowned. 'What do you mean?'

Welfry held up his gloved hand. 'I tell everyone my hand is marred by a childhood palsy, but it is leprosy. I shall end my days shunned by all, dead before I am in my grave. *That* is why I shall not sell the *signacula* and St Simon Stock's scapular – their collective holiness will release me from Purgatory. I started amassing them after a pilgrimage to Canterbury, some eight years ago.'

'But there has not been a case of leprosy in Cambridge for years!' cried Bartholomew. 'It is almost certain to be something else. Let me examine it.'

'It is too late. Now start walking before—'

At that moment, the door flew open and people began to pour in, yelling and laughing boisterously. Bartholomew did the only thing left to him: he started to bawl a warning. Immediately, Welfry lobbed the knife. It thudded into the wood near Bartholomew's shoulder, and his involuntary flinch caused him to slip. He grabbed the post, and for a moment was suspended only by his hands. With agonising slowness, he struggled to haul himself up again.

As soon as he was safely on the rafter, fingers locked

around the crown-post, he started to shout, but the refectory was now full of people, and his was just one voice among many – he could not make himself heard. And Thelnetham lay in the shadows, so not even the presence of a corpse was going to tell them that something was terribly wrong.

Welfry touched a flame to his fuse.

'No!' screamed Bartholomew, although the racket from below drowned out his anguished howl. Then the Michaelhouse Choir began an impromptu rendering of a popular tavern ballad, and he closed his eyes in despair, knowing he would never be heard once they were in action. Welfry was crouching in the shadows of the doorway, watching his fuse burn towards the pulleys and buckets. He ignored Bartholomew now, seeing his presence as irrelevant.

Then Michael entered the refectory, beadles at his heels, looking everywhere but upwards. The monk began to mingle with the crowd, stepping between groups that would have swung punches and clearly far too busy to think about the Dominican and his plot.

Welfry's flame was burning steadily towards a lever, and Bartholomew knew there were only moments left before something terrible happened. His stomach lurched as he looked at the people below – his sister and her husband, Michael, Gyseburne, Tulyet, most members of his College and others he knew and loved were going to be among the casualties.

But there was one option left open to him: he could jump off the rafter and plummet to his death. *That* would make people look up, and when they saw the ropes and buckets they would run to safety. Unfortunately, he could not leap from where he was, because Edith was almost

404

directly beneath him and he could not risk injuring her. He took a deep breath, ducked around the crown-post and took his first step along the beam, back towards the door.

A wave of dizziness assailed him, and he thought he was going to fall. But the feeling passed, and he took another step, and then another. He was aware of Welfry glaring and making meaningful pushing gestures with his hands, but it did not matter, because there was nothing he could do to Bartholomew that Bartholomew was not already planning to do to himself. The fuse burned closer to the lever.

Welfry's jaw dropped when he understood what the physician intended. He started to shout, but Bartholomew could not hear him, and would not have paid any attention if he had. Only a few more steps now. Bartholomew sensed Welfry starting along the rafter towards him, but took no notice. Two more steps would put him over the middle of a table, and no one would be hurt when he jumped. He glanced at the fuse. The flame was almost there: he was going to be too late!

A flicker of movement caught the corner of his eye, and when he looked up, Welfry was gone. But something was happening below. The laughter and merriment had changed to cries of horror. He risked a glance downwards, and saw Welfry sprawled unmoving on one of the tables. People were beginning to look up, pointing. In his determination to stop Bartholomew, Welfry had lost his own balance.

'Everyone out!' bellowed Michael, when he saw the ropes and the pails. 'Now!'

'So the greedy Colleges can have all this free wine?' demanded Neyll. 'Not likely!'

He grabbed a cup of ale and toasted his cronies, who responded with a rowdy cheer. There was a resentful growl from Bene't and the Hall of Valence Marie.

405

'Out!' hollered Michael. But hostels were bawling insults at Colleges, and those who could hear the monk ignored him. The noise level intensified again, and although Bartholomew yelled until his voice cracked, he knew he was wasting his time. He took another step along the rafter, trying frantically to control the shaking in his legs. Perhaps if he could reach the fuse . . .

He was aware that Edith and Michael were two of those staring at him. Within moments, their upturned faces were going to be showered with some unspeakable substance, and they would die a terrible death. Desperation gave Bartholomew the strength to gain the door.

But there was no time for relief. He forced himself to turn and inspect Welfry's fuse. It had already burned out of reach. He hauled off his tabard and flailed it at the flame, but flapping only made it glow more fiercely. He leaned out as far as he could, and flung the garment across it, but the material merely smouldered and the fuse hissed on. There was nothing he could do to stop it. Defeated, he felt himself slump, then begin to fall.

His downward progress was halted by an intense pressure around his middle, then strong arms were hauling him to the safety of the doorway.

'Christ and all his saints, Matt!' cried Michael. He rarely cursed, and that, coupled with his white face and shaking hands, was testament to his fright. 'We almost lost you!'

'My sister,' gasped Bartholomew, thinking only of Welfry's trick. 'The wildfire . . .'

'No one will leave,' shouted Michael in despair. 'And the place is too crowded for me to force them. There will be carnage, and there is nothing we can do but watch.'

Bartholomew saw the flame reach a bucket, which began to upend. It initiated a chain reaction, and the rafters started to vibrate as pulleys swung into action. The first pail tipped, emptying its contents on to the crowd below. It was followed by a second container, and a third, and then there were more than he could count. Howls followed.

He closed his eyes, not wanting to see. But then it occurred to him that he and his colleagues had not created *that* much of the deadly substance. He pulled away from Michael and sat up. The yells were not of agony, but of shocked indignation. And there was laughter, too.

'Water!' he breathed. 'Welfry's trick was water!'

Michael was inspecting a sheet that had been attached to one pulley. He grimaced. 'Water that was set to culminate in a rather inflammatory banner being hoisted – one that claims this to be the victory of bold hostels over the stupid Colleges. It would have caused a fight for certain.'

But people were beginning to flee the room, unwilling to stand around and be drenched. Outside, Michael's beadles were waiting, to ensure they dispersed.

'Welfry miscalculated,' said Michael, gazing at the spectacle with saucer-like eyes. 'The water was meant to infuriate, and cause a great battle. But instead, it doused the skirmishes already in action, and drove the participants away.'

Bartholomew was too numb to feel elation. 'He failed in a spectacular manner.'

'And he wanted your substance not to spray over hapless victims, but to create a fuse,' said Michael in relief. 'It is over, Matt. My beadles will ensure there is no more fighting.'

'He killed Thelnetham,' said Bartholomew brokenly.

'Thelnetham is not dead. He is not very happy about being knocked over the head, but he will survive. Gyseburne and Meryfeld are tending him.'

'Welfry tried to make me go through that other door,' said Bartholomew tiredly, waving a vague hand towards it. 'He did not want to kill me, either.'

Michael snorted his incredulity. 'The stairs have

collapsed behind that. Had you stepped through it, you would have fallen to your death. You are a fool if you believe Welfry would have let you live after the kind of conversation I imagine you had.'

Bartholomew would not have been able to walk down the stairs had it not been for Michael's helping hand, and when they finally reached the ground, he leaned against a wall and slid down it until he was sitting on the floor. There was a brazier on the wall above his head, and its illumination showed how unsteady his hands were. It had been a terrible experience, and he felt as though he had been to Hell and back.

The refectory had not cleared completely, because those very interested in drink had lingered, prepared to risk a soaking for free ale and wine. Bartholomew saw with relief that his sister was not among them, and nor were his Michaelhouse colleagues. Langelee was, though, his eyes fixed unwaveringly on Kendale and the students of Chestre. Cynric was with him, also glowering, and Bartholomew wondered whether they intended to pick a fight over the stolen gates.

'I feel a little cheated,' said Michael, looking around him uneasily. 'I was expecting something truly diabolical, but . . .'

'It would have been diabolical had it worked,' Bartholomew pointed out. 'A bloodbath as Colleges and hostels clashed in a fairly confined space, and townsmen joined in. Are you sure Welfry is dead? The reason I ask is because he did not use all the substance he stole from Meryfeld for his fuse – there is still a lot missing.'

'Quite dead,' replied Michael. His eyes narrowed. 'Neyll and Ihon are coming towards us. Stand up. You do not want them to think you a weakling.'

'I do not care what they think,' muttered Bartholomew, declining to comply.

Ihon removed his cap as he approached. 'We want to apologise for taking your gates,' he said, loudly enough to attract the attention of a number of people, who came to see what was happening. 'There, I have said it. Are you satisfied?'

'It was only a joke,' said Neyll. He held a camp-ball, and was rolling it from hand to hand. It looked heavy. 'You should have been able to take a joke.'

Casually, he hefted the ball in his right hand and took aim, narrowing his eyes in concentration. Bartholomew twisted around to see what he was looking at. The brazier. He glanced back to Neyll, and noticed a black, sticky substance oozing through the ball's seams.

But there was a sudden thump, and Neyll gripped his chest with a grimace of agony. A blade protruded from it, and Bartholomew recognised the letter-opener he had given Langelee. Neyll pitched forward, but not before the ball had flown from his hand. It landed on the edge of the brazier, and teetered there. Bartholomew surged to his feet, aiming to punch it away from the flame, but Ihon dived forward to stop him, knocking him off balance.

There was a muffled explosion. Bartholomew was already falling, so it was the hapless Ihon who took the brunt of the blast. The student crashed backwards in a billow of smoke. The wall behind him was splattered with gobbets of the substance that burned with a devilish glow, and one or two onlookers began to bat at smouldering clothes.

'I thought the beadles had searched everyone for knives,' said Cynric to Langelee. There was admiration in his voice.

'That is not a knife,' replied Langelee smoothly. 'It is a letter-opener. And thank God they let me keep it. You were right to warn me there was something suspicious about that pair, Cynric. If their plan had succeeded, it would have deprived me of my two favourite Fellows.'

'And many innocent bystanders,' added Cynric, inspecting the sticky substance with a grimace of disapproval. 'I love a weapon as much as the next man, but there is something unspeakable about this one.'

Michael shuddered when he saw what had happened to Ihon. He turned to Neyll, whose eyes were already turning glassy. 'Why in God's name did you do that?'

'We had a letter from Emma de Colvyll,' whispered Neyll. 'She told us to do it, because it would score a great victory for the hostels. She wrote it this morning.'

'Welfry,' said Bartholomew heavily. 'Emma could not have written anything today, because she was too ill. Will the man's tricks never end?'

'You will just have to wait and see,' breathed Neyll with a ghastly grin. And then he died.

EPILOGUE

A week later

It was pleasant in Michaelhouse's conclave. Rain pattered against the window shutters, and the night was bitter, but there was a fire in the hearth and wine mulling over it. Bartholomew sat at the table, reading a book on natural philosophy that Thelnetham had lent him, while his colleagues talked about the remarkable lecture Horneby had delivered that day. Bartholomew had not been there: he had been with Meryfeld and Gyseburne, discussing which of his poverty-stricken patients they were going to take off his hands.

He experienced a twinge of guilt when he thought about them. Both had been on his list of suspects for the killer-thief, but they had been entirely innocent. He was glad, and looked forward to resuming his experiments with them to develop a steadily burning lamp – assuming they only did so when they were sober, of course.

'Our roofs have been restored to their original condition,' reported Langelee, changing the subject to one he considered more interesting. 'Unfortunately, the "original condition" means they still leak, but at least it is only drips, not deluges.'

'We are back where we started,' said Suttone gloomily. 'All that disruption was for nothing. Worse, we owe Blaston *and* the mason we hired to replace Yffi for their labour.'

'Emma gave us enough to pay them, in return for

411

Michael keeping Odelina and Heslarton out of his official report,' said Langelee. His face darkened. 'Although I could not prevail on her to give us more. Still, I suppose you cannot blame her, since he then declined to let them escape.'

'Of course I declined,' said Michael indignantly. 'It would have been very wrong.'

'The family *did* love each other,' said Clippesby with quiet compassion. 'Indeed, it was affection that brought about their downfall: Heslarton's love for his daughter led him to help cover her crimes. And Odelina's love for her grandmother gave Matthew and Cynric a chance to escape – she wanted to kill them immediately, but decided to let them save Emma first.'

'That is one way of looking at it, I suppose,' said Langelee. 'But as far as I am concerned, they were all villains. I wonder whether the *signacula* Welfry accrued will help them on Judgment Day. The holiness may have rubbed off on their fingers when they touched them.'

'They *will* help,' said Suttone, while William nodded agreement. 'Handling such sacred objects will see them skip through Purgatory.'

'They will not,' countered Clippesby. 'The tokens were stolen, so they cannot claim any benefit from them. Besides, a person is judged on his merits, not what he manages to touch during his life.'

'You are right, Clippesby,' said Thelnetham, who was polishing his nails with a piece of oiled cloth. The conclave smelled strongly of perfume, and no one was sitting too close to him. 'And—'

'It is a pity we have lost so much from this unpleasant business, though,' interrupted Langelee, not very interested in another theological discussion. 'A benefactress, a host of prayers to be said . . .'

412

'What do you mean?' asked William suspiciously. 'What prayers?'

'Before Emma agreed to pay Blaston and the new mason, she made me promise that Michaelhouse's priests would say masses for her, Heslarton and Odelina,' explained Langelee. 'And also for Fen, Poynton and the two fat nuns.'

'I am not saying masses for them!' declared William indignantly. 'None are worthy. Did I tell you why Fen was always so wan and pale, by the way? Because he offered to sell Kendale some books!' His lips pursed meaningfully.

'Yes, he told us,' said Bartholomew. 'One by Bradwardine on natural philosophy.'

'That was a lie. What he actually offered were banned books on alchemy.' William hissed the last word, giving it a decidedly sinister timbre. 'It was guilt that made him sheepish. Moreover, those fat nuns are bigamists. They say they were both wives of Hugh Neel, but how is that possible? If he took two wives, one of them should have been dead first. And as for Odelina and Heslarton . . .'

'Perhaps this is why Emma thinks they need our masses,' said Clippesby gently. 'I have said a few prayers for them already, poor lost souls.'

'Have you?' asked Langelee, rather belligerently. 'I wonder if that is why Heslarton and Odelina are not hanged, as they should have been, but ordered to abjure the realm. Perhaps we should withhold our blessings for a while. With luck, someone will murder them on their way to the coast.'

'Really, Master!' exclaimed Clippesby, shocked. 'That is not a kindly thing to say.'

Langelee shrugged, unrepentant. 'I have never made any pretensions to being kindly, and I speak as I find. Incidentally, did you know that Emma has decided to join

413

the Gilbertine Order, and will donate all her worldly goods to the Mother House at Sempringham?'

'Yes,' said Thelnetham smugly. 'Prior Leccheworth is delighted. He is even more delighted that she intends to live there, and not with us. He wants her money, but not her company.'

Ayera regarded Bartholomew disapprovingly. 'When you pulled her tooth, her howls could be heard all along the High Street. You should not dabble in surgery – it is not right.'

'No, it is not,' agreed Thelnetham. 'But a new surgeon should be arriving from York soon, so he will not have to do it much longer, thank God. His reputation as a warlock is doing Michaelhouse no good whatsoever, especially after he invented the substance that killed Ihon.'

'The Archbishop of York is very interested in finding out what went into that,' said Langelee. 'Indeed, he has offered a princely sum for the recipe. We could do the with money . . .'

'No,' said Bartholomew firmly. It was not the first time he had been approached for the formula, and he had a bad feeling it would not be the last, either. 'I cannot remember.'

'Good,' said Thelnetham with a shudder. 'It is best forgotten.' He changed the subject. 'I heard all the pilgrim badges have been returned to their rightful owners, Michael.'

'All except the most important one,' said Michael gloomily. 'Mine. The others were under Welfry's bed at the Dominican friary – he was so confident he would never be caught that he made no effort to hide them. He had St Simon Stock's scapular, too, and Etone was delighted to have it back. Personally, I think it is a fake.'

'I *know* it is,' said William. He shrugged when everyone

414

looked at him. 'A few years ago, a Carmelite novice hacked a bit off one of my habits. I have always wondered why. Yesterday I went to the shrine, and compared my damaged robe to that holy scapular. They matched perfectly.'

'You mean pilgrims have been worshipping something of yours?' asked Thelnetham, regarding the Franciscan's revolting clothes in stunned disbelief. 'That is worse than sacrilege!'

'It is not my fault,' said William stiffly. 'Clearly, the business started as a prank, but took on a life of its own, as these things are apt to do. To make the "relic" appear genuine, the jokers must have wanted something . . .' He waved his hand.

'Old and filthy,' supplied Langelee. 'Well, it worked, because it looked real to me. Perhaps we should fabricate something to attract pilgrims ourselves, because we are desperately short of funds.'

'Again?' sighed Michael wearily. 'I do not think I can take much more terrible food.'

'It is Bartholomew's fault,' said Langelee. 'He told Walter to feed his peacock grain, rather than wine-soaked bread, and the wretched beast has devoured all the seeds we were going to plant for vegetables this spring.'

'Really?' asked Michael, brightening. 'That is good news. I do not care for vegetables.'

There was a silence as the Fellows pondered their lot.

'Tell me again, Brother,' said William, a little while later. 'Who dispatched whom? I did not follow your explanation after the camp-ball game. It was too garbled.'

Michael obliged. 'Odelina killed Alice and Drax, so her father and Celia could marry and live happily ever after. Heslarton stabbed Poynton by accident during the camp-ball game, and then knifed Yffi when he tried to blackmail him over it.'

'Odelina killed Gib, too, with her father's help,' added Thelnetham, who had not found the monk's explanation garbled at all. 'And Welfry suggested they tie a yellow wig on him, to make Michael and the Sheriff think the killer-thief was dead.'

'I see,' said William. 'And Welfry stole the *signacula* and St Simon Stock's relic because he thought he had leprosy and he needed them to see him through Purgatory.'

Michael nodded. 'But before being sentenced to spend his dying days in some remote hospital, he decided to do the University a favour, and rid it of one of its more troublesome elements – Chestre, who were stirring up strife between the hostels and the Colleges.'

'So he needled Kendale with tricks, challenging him to reply in kind,' continued Thelnetham. 'He thought this alone would see Chestre suppressed, but it did not. So he elected to see them accused of more serious offences instead, and ordered Heslarton to plant "evidence" as proof.'

'He was an odd man,' mused Michael. 'He tried hard to calm the rivalry Kendale was inciting, by inventing clever but gentle tricks and encouraging the hostels to respond with their wits, not their fists. And he certainly saved King's Hall with his timely riddle. Yet he would have seen members of Chestre punished for crimes of which they were innocent.'

'*I* cannot find it in my heart to blame him for taking against Chestre,' said William. 'They *are* an obstacle to peace and a burden to our University.'

'Not any more,' said Michael smugly. 'The fact that Neyll and Ihon almost succeeded in killing people with their camp-ball "bomb" was enough for me to close the place – along with the fact that they and Gib pushed young Jolye in the river and refused to let him out again. Kendale probably was ignorant of both incidents, as he claims, but I told him that was no excuse.'

'Where is he now?' asked Bartholomew, not liking the notion of such vitriol at large.

'Oxford,' said Michael with immense satisfaction. 'And his surviving students with him. He claims he will be more appreciated in our sister University, but he will soon learn otherwise.'

'But he will make trouble there,' said Bartholomew, appalled.

'Almost certainly,' agreed Michael smugly. 'And bene-factors will disapprove, and look elsewhere for recipients for their largess. Perhaps we shall not be doomed to poor food for long after all.'

'Never mind Kendale,' said William, cutting across Bartholomew's shocked objections. 'I am more interested in Welfry. *Did* he have leprosy, Matthew? You examined his body, I understand.'

Bartholomew dragged his thoughts away from the hapless scholars of Oxford. 'No – and it is the worst part of this entire business. All his terrors about a lonely death were unfounded. He had a skin condition that I have recently learned how to remedy. Had he let me examine him—'

'You mean a smear of balm might have prevented all this?' asked William.

'I am not so sure,' said Michael, before Bartholomew could reply. 'Odelina still would have dispatched two people so her friend could marry her father.'

'Would she?' asked Clippesby. 'She confesses to killing Alice, but not Drax.'

'She is lying,' said William contemptuously. 'She cannot open her mouth without poison issuing forth, and we should not believe a word she says.'

417

'Isnard has a lot to answer for, though,' said Michael. 'It transpires that he is a smuggler, although Dick Tulyet and I cannot prove it. However, I am dismissing him from my choir.'

'Do not do that, Brother,' begged Bartholomew, recalling the anguish the bargeman had suffered the last time Michael had expelled him. 'It would break his heart. And he is generous to the Blaston family, which is a point in his favour. They would starve without him.'

'Well, in that case, perhaps I shall overlook his crimes,' said Michael. 'Blaston is a good man, and I should never have included him on my lists of suspects for Drax's murder.'

The following afternoon, Bartholomew went to watch Blaston putting the finishing touches to the roof. Langelee had been overly optimistic when he said it had been restored to its original state, because tiles had cracked when they had been removed, and the guttering was now damaged. The roof was likely to be a lot more leaky than it had been, but at least it was not open to the skies.

'Have you heard the news?' asked Blaston. 'The barge carrying Odelina and Heslarton to exile sank in the Fens, and there are no survivors. Word is that Isnard arranged for it to go down, to make amends for dabbling in the smuggling business.'

'It was not Isnard,' said Bartholomew, recalling a remark Welfry had made. 'Welfry said that particular barge was unseaworthy. Obviously, he tampered with it before he died.'

Blaston stared at him. 'You may be right. He had a funny sense of justice, and probably would not have liked the notion of Odelina and Heslarton escaping to France after all they had done.'

418

Bartholomew was sure of it. 'I had a bad feeling that we had not heard the last of him.'

'Celia has confessed all, too,' added Blaston. 'She admitted that she lied when she claimed she was with Heslarton the night Gib was murdered, reading a psalter. And that she claimed to be illiterate, when she can read very well. It was Drax who had no letters.'

'A lot of people lied. It was why the case was so difficult to solve.'

Blaston was silent for a moment, then changed the subject to one that was more cheerful. 'I heard it was you who recommended me for the task of repairing the Gilbertines' refectory. It is good work – well paid – and will keep me indoors for the rest of the winter. And Prior Leccheworth says I can have kitchen scraps for the children. My financial problems are over for a while.'

'It is a pity for Drax that they were not over sooner,' said Bartholomew softly.

Blaston gazed at him, alarm in his eyes. 'What are you saying? Brother Michael told me I am completely exonerated. Odelina and Heslarton are responsible for Drax's death.'

'But you and I both know that it would have been impossible for them to bring Drax's corpse in here without being seen by you – and Heslarton has an alibi for the killing, anyway. You did not speak out about what you saw for a reason: that reason is that *you* killed him.'

'No!' cried Blaston. 'I *would* have told you if I had spotted Heslarton and his daughter—'

'You were afraid that if you admitted to seeing them tote a corpse into our yard, awkward questions would have been asked. Such as how did you know Drax was already dead? You were terrified that a clever man like Michael would catch you out.'

419

Blaston put his hands over his face, and seemed to shrivel before Bartholomew's eyes. 'It was an accident, I *swear*! I confronted Drax about his outrageous prices in Physwick's dairy, and he laughed at me. I had a sick baby, and he laughed! Then he drew his dagger, and told me to get out of his way.'

'What happened then?'

'I was too angry to slink away like a beaten cur, so I tackled him, and we both fell. We landed hard, and I got up, but he did not. Odelina must have stumbled across him later.' When Blaston looked at Bartholomew again, his face was whiter than the physician had ever seen it. 'What will you do? Tell Brother Michael?'

Bartholomew sighed. 'What good would that do? And you say it was an accident.'

'It was,' said Blaston fervently. 'And I know God does not hold it against me.'

'You do? How?'

Blaston pulled at something he was wearing around his neck. It was the pilgrim badge Bartholomew had brought Michael from Santiago de Compostela.

'Because I found this in the High Street. God would not have led me to such a beautiful thing if He thought me wicked. I shall wear it for the rest of my life – or until we have another hard winter and I need to feed my family.'

Bartholomew stared at it for a moment, then smiled reluctantly. 'In that case, you had better keep it safe. And never show it to Michael.'

HISTORICAL NOTE

On 28 December 1349, the Archbishop of Canterbury wrote a letter to the Bishop of London ordering him to ensure that God was suitably thanked for rescuing the country from the 'amazing pestilence which lately attacked these parts and which took from us the best and worthiest men'. The people were urged to 'break forth in praises and devout expressions of gratitude'. It is almost impossible to imagine the impact of the plague on those who survived it, but some would certainly have thought that mere prayers were inadequate to express their relief, and would have undertaken pilgrimages.

Pilgrimage was thus big business in the fourteenth century, and like the tourist honeypots today, places that attracted large numbers of visitors were considered lucrative propositions. Not only was there accommodation and food to be supplied, but shrines also did a roaring trade in souvenirs – from simple scallop shells to elegant creations in gold and precious jewels. Many were in the form of badges, which the pilgrim could wear to let everyone know what he had done. Indulgences and *signacula* were highly prized, and the unscrupulous almost certainly scrambled to profit from them.

Besides the great official pilgrimage sites, such as Canterbury, Santiago de Compostela, Rome and Jerusalem, there were many local ones, such as Hereford and Walsingham. There were also unofficial cults, like the one surrounding John Schorne of North Marston in

421

Buckinghamshire. Schorne was a rector who was said to have conjured the Devil into a boot, and whose spring was thought to cure gout. He died in 1315, but pilgrims continued to visit his shrine right up until the Reformation.

Another popular medieval pastime was camp-ball, a game that was still played well into the twentieth century. It could be extremely violent, and although there were rules, they tended not to be ones that protected the players. Sometimes, the teams comprised a limited number of competitors in a field of a specified size, but at other times an entire settlement might be considered the 'ground', and participants could number in the hundreds. Injuries were commonplace, and deaths not infrequent. Savage-camp was an even rougher version of the game.

Real people in *The Killer of Pilgrims* include John Gyseburne, who was a Cambridge physician in the mid-fourteenth century, and his colleague John Meryfeld, who later went to work in St Bartholomew's Priory in London, and became a famous *medicus* in his own right. Thomas Kendale, from the York Diocese, studied at Cambridge in the late fourteenth century, and so did John Jolye.

Michaelhouse's Master in 1357 was Ralph de Langelee, and Fellows included Michael de Causton, William de Gotham, Thomas Suttone, John Clippesby, William Thelnetham and Simon Hemmysby. Thomas Ayera and John Valence were members much later, and Ayera donated property to the College. Michaelhouse, along with neighbouring King's Hall and several hostels, became Trinity College in 1546. Michaelhouse's name survives in St Michael's Church, which has been lovingly restored, and is now a community centre, art gallery and a popular coffee shop. For more information, visit www.michaelhouse.co.uk.

Michaelhouse, like all early foundations, relied heavily on charitable donations for its survival. In return, its priests